We're Going

Book 3 of The Guardian League

Steven J. Morris

We're Going on an Elf Hunt
Book 3 of The Guardian League
Steven J. Morris
Copyright © 2021 by Steven J. Morris

1st Edition
All Rights Reserved.

This book is a work of fiction. Any references to historical events, real people, or real places, are used fictitiously. Any resemblance to actual events or locales or persons, living or dead, is entirely coincidental.

The scanning, uploading and distribution of this book via the internet or any other means without the permission of the publisher is illegal and punishable by law. Please purchase only authorized electronic editions, and do not participate in or encourage electronic piracy of copyrighted materials. Your support of the author's rights is appreciated.

No part of this publication may be reproduced in whole or in part without the written permission of the publisher. For information regarding permission, please email grundlegatekeeper@gmail.com.

ISBN 978-1-956105-02-5

Book 3, Part 1

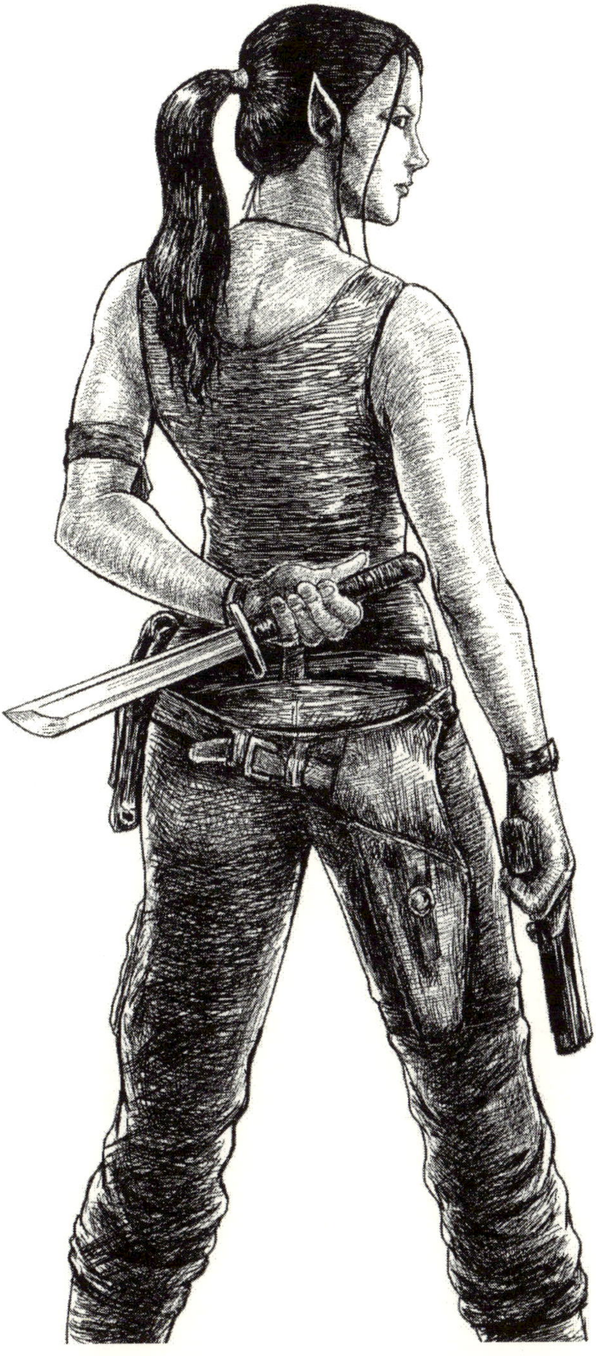

Prologue

High Lord Slooti Falinus Halabrinner, Banishment Ceremony for

Galadrindor Arafaemiel Terebra'an

I took no pleasure in Banishing Galad. His parents had been old-fashioned, but they'd been as close as family once, eons in the wind. And I'd raised Galad like one of my own children. Still, Galad had wrapped himself up in the mess with the trolls, sealing his fate. Things had gotten out of control ever since he'd disappeared a century before. As the most powerful Empath alive, his own pathetic debauchery had cast a pall on generations of elves. He'd made it easy for me to rule. Since he'd disappeared, all the unrest in the outlier worlds had begun to simmer on El'daShar. I needed to rein them all in, for their own good.

No attempt to break Galad out of prison had materialized, despite Paragondriel's report that a dwarf intended to do just that. Said dwarf may have recovered the Amp from the troll's treasury, though more likely the Infected had killed the dwarf back in the AllForest. We would go back after the Banishment and look. *I might have to use Gavriel for that...* Paragondriel claimed the 'Port location to be overrun by the Infected, but Gavriel would chance it. *For me.*

We'd maintained a tight guard on Galad and the troll, thwarting any thought of rescue. And the Banishment Chamber sat ready. We were crossing Avalark's Bridge, and I sighted the end of the problem called Galad. The Banishment Stone, *Hughelas's gift*. I chuckled at my joke, then scowled when Tarandrigal glanced my way. The Stone, a yellow gem—moving specks of darkness would be visible within were I closer—sat atop a small stone dais grown from the cave floor. A ring of rock poked up from the floor, its breadth several strides long, marked the floor where the field would appear that whisked away those who needed to go. Only one elf knew how it worked. Well, one elf that I hadn't Banished. And I'd held that elf under lock and key for centuries. Possibly millennia. *My, how time flies.*

A sudden movement and a blow like thunder rang out in the bore, startling me out of my reverie, unbalancing me when the bridge beneath me shuddered. A squat but hulking form had jumped out of nowhere and pounded the bridge with a war hammer. *The dwarf?* I stood stunned—not by the fact that he struck the bridge, endangering us all, but by the sight of the hammer itself. How could a dwarf wield *that* hammer? I cast a spell of levitation on myself. Tarandrigal, the AirWorker, shoved the dwarf back before he inflicted a second blow and sent us plummeting. Not that I would have fallen, but it would be a chore to regrow the bridge.

"Activate the Stone!" I shouted to Paragondriel. "Get the prisoners inside its field!" Once we caged the prisoners, there would be no getting them out. And then we would focus on the dwarf and whoever he had brought with him.

But no other antagonists joined the fray, and though he fought like a madman, there was only one of him. We had him outnumbered and outmatched. Still, if his antics somehow freed the prisoners, they would be difficult to recapture—I could not use the trick that had captured them in the first place. Not with so many elves around. But while the dwarf engaged my warriors, Paragondriel activated the Stone, and the prisoners, still bound and Compelled through their enchanted shackles, marched inside the translucent field. Done.

The dwarf backed toward the field, hemmed in by my people. *He must know he has lost. Why does he look triumphant?* He secured his weapon and pulled out... *Mother of Trees*, he had the Amp! The dwarf's eyes locked with mine—they held no sign of fear or resignation. Once in the field, the prisoners could not be retrieved. If he didn't know that—if he didn't realize his actions were futile—it made him all the more dangerous. He began a spell, and I dropped to the ground, throwing a magical shield over me for protection, not knowing what to expect.

Nothing happened.

I pulled my eyes up from the dirt—the dwarf's eyes laughed at me. He wasn't a mage. I'd kill him for that bit of trickery.

"You don't know how to use that," I barked, reining in my rage. "Get that jewel from him," I commanded my people.

"Here," the mongrel said. "It's yours." The smirking, muscle-bound oaf threw the Amp high in the air in my direction. The Amp, one of the most powerful artifacts of magic yet encountered—all that I needed to complete my plans—flew to the top of the large cavern and arced back down. I dropped my shield, diving to catch it, but Tarandrigal also attempted to snag it using a cushion of air. The combination resulted in the Amp hitting my head, then colliding with a stalagmite and shattering.

No!

But then it struck me that the Amp wouldn't have shattered. Couldn't have shattered. I needn't even have *tried* to catch it. It had been forged by a world whose natural pressures were too much for an elf to survive for even a minute—it would not break so easily. I'd been duped. Again. I would kill that dwarf twice over.

Burning with anger, I prepared to lance him with a bolt of fire that would separate his cocky head from his troublesome body. But I found he'd joined Galad in the field. He sat upon a trunk that I hadn't even seen... more trickery... holding... *Feathered Demons*, he had the Amp! I shouted for Paragondriel to stop the device, but I knew halting the Stone was impossible. And a moment later, they vanished.

Mother of Trees with the Feathered Rutting Demons!

I took a few breaths.

"Get a StoneWorker to mend the bridge," I said, as the elves around me tried to avoid my attention. Giving orders helped me to focus. "Paragondriel, take me back to my chambers, please."

Elves hustled to follow my commands. Paragondriel 'Ported me back to my chambers, and I sent him away. He left eagerly enough, not wanting to chance my anger. And he chose well. I burned. But I also had something I wanted to do that I didn't want Paragondriel to see.

Once I was alone, I brought out a glass globe that fit in the palm of my hand, filled with a white coruscating liquid we had picked up from troll-mining. The last troll-mining we would be able to do. I couldn't find another Amp... not with the trolls all gone. My plans were coming undone. Were there other creatures who could survive those harsh climates besides the trolls? There had to be. But how would I find them, with the clock ticking? How would I save my people? How would I save *myself*?

The flashes of light from the white liquid drew me out of my mental death-spiral and back to the task at hand. Like the Amp, the fluid was imbued with a Gift, enabling manipulation of the underpinnings of magic. I'd put some in a tiny glass affixed to the clasp of Galad's shackles. It was just a little test. An experiment.

I cast a spell, not my Talent, but one I'd mastered to such an extent that it might as well have been. A Vision spell, one which enabled me to see around corners, through walls—which had been foundational in becoming the High Lord—and I'd practiced it a great deal. I sent it into the liquid. As before, it tried to show me many things... too many things. Lightning storms wreaking hell upon the world where we had found it; a vision of me, peering into a globe of coruscating white liquid; my own bed-chamber, where I'd left another globe after first stumbling upon the liquid's quirky twist on magic. But I pushed that all away, concentrating on the tiniest speck. I latched on to the vision of that horrible dwarf, working the shackles loose from Galad, having already freed the troll. Light shined forth from the hammer—further proof of the hammer's identity.

He snapped the shackles off with a chisel, and they dropped to the ground. My view changed, looking up at everyone. They armed themselves with equipment from the trunk. *Damn that dwarf! That chest...* I'd encountered it before and hadn't realized its enchantment. *Damn him!* I'd been so close! *Damn them all!* Once they had what they wanted, the troll picked up the chest, with the ease of an elf picking up a small end-table, and they left me in the dark.

Other duties demanded my attention, but one thing I'd learned repeatedly: chance favors the attentive. I'd learned to feed the liquid, make it grow, and I'd begun to fashion more. All the while I Watched through it, and the act of peering into the darkness, waiting, kept me afloat in the sea of wretched elvish discord that continued to boil. I lost track of the days, one of our worlds after another declaring their independence, and then worlds disappearing, one after another. *It serves them right!* But my vigilance paid off; at first I thought I dreamed it when the vision shifted from darkness to light. But if I had been asleep, the adrenaline jolt would have shot me out of bed. The light grew, and I twitched with impatience as someone entered the chamber. Chance favors the attentive: *she* came in.

My heart stopped when I saw her. After *so* long. *Hughelas, you naughty, conniving elf, I will have to change your guard.* Elliahspane Baelsbreath... Elliahsaire daShari Fortiza… Elliah… 'Leah. She'd aged, which I had never seen in an elf, but after fifteen millennia on a planet with a dead sun, that price she'd paid was cheap. She took up the discarded shackles, and like the witch she was, looked right at me. With the blink of an eye, the spell died. But I'd seen enough.

If she had survived that long on a planet with a dead sun, then *I* had a chance. A new plan took root in my mind.

Chapter 1

Galad

"So, can we go back now?" I asked. It wasn't a need to get off the planet—if anything, I'd come to like Earth. No, I wanted to get back to what I'd left behind. Yes, it also moved us closer to saving her world, getting the Mana'Thiandriel we needed to protect it. I could use that. No one would question that motive.

Mort chuckled. "In a moment," he answered, ogling the retreating form of the red-haired young woman covered in blood and ichor. She had dropped behind the others when she'd slipped on a bit of goo that had dropped from her rifle. "Hair the color of flames is not something I have seen before."

"We're saving a world, and you're delaying it to look at someone's *hair*?" I said, my disbelief sounding thin in my own ears. *Who was I to say that, given my own motive for leaving?*

"It's not her hair I'm looking at," he answered.

"And *your* big hurry," Hirashi said to me with a mischievous grin, "is all about saving the world?"

Fair enough. I wanted Red to know we had convinced Hirashi to part with Mana'thiandriel. I wanted to see her reaction, wrap my arms around her... okay, he could have his moment to stare.

"Humans don't live very long," Elliah commented, "and yet they so often let opportunities pass. I've always found it a little sad."

Mort's eyes got big, and he disappeared, reappearing down the hall in the path of the red-haired soldier.

"That's better," Elliah smiled, then twitched in that queer fashion of hers. It wasn't as extreme as it used to be—she was getting better. Healthier.

"Indeed," Hirashi echoed, a sad smile playing across her face. I had no difficulty believing that the young leader had let some opportunities pass her by—leadership had a price.

"Why is that *better*?" I asked, irritated at the delay despite my understanding. Hirashi and Elliah shared a look.

"If ever I needed proof that you are an Empath that stays out of people's minds," Hirashi stated, "this is it."

Women. *Who wants in their minds anyway?*

Rocks maneuvered toward us, skirting outside the train of people heading through the tunnels to the stairs. Medics had carted Staci, a mage rendered unconscious in the battle, to the elevator atop a gurney, and the doors had swallowed her up. The medics would find no physical wound—she'd drained herself of mana. She needed rest.

Rocks inched forward, placing his artificial leg with precision, in order to navigate the grime that had dropped from those who had 'Ported back from the fight. His jubilant expression contrasted his cautious movements. "We did it, Galad!" he cheered, as he grew near, holding up his hands in a gesture I recognized from my time spent with Red's psyche stuck in my head. He meant for me to slap hands with him, but I stood, frozen, recognizing the gesture too late.

He corrected and put his hands on my shoulders, patting them.

"You all did it!" he said, turning to include our whole group. Hirashi and Elliah smiled at him, but their enthusiasm burned less brightly than his, and his smile dimmed. "What?"

"I'm burdened by knowledge, and frightful of what has become of the elves," Elliah said. Elliah looked different... younger than I remembered. Her skin was smoother. She caught me looking but said nothing.

"And I am still frightened for my people," Hirashi echoed. "You may be able to fight the Infected, but neither is this world a safe haven. Also, if the Infected adapted to track the elves..."

"They can adapt to this world," Rocks concluded, his enthusiasm dampened. "Damn."

Rocks looked down at his feet—the one real and the other artificial. I stayed out of his head, but I didn't need magic to see how our words wearied him. He closed his eyes, took a breath, then eased them open, plastering on an encouraging smile.

"Well," he said, rallying, "we saved El Paso from getting nuked, so that will play well on the news."

"Harry is going to be so angry that he wasn't there," I thought out loud, buying me several strange looks. I shrugged. Nothing for it.

Mort popped back into our group, smiling mischievously.

"Can we go back now?" I asked again, ready to get back and share the news with Red.

"As I recall," Hirashi said, "you were going to show us around this world some."

I sighed. That had been the plan. "I thought, with that battle, we'd convinced you."

"I am convinced that you can fight the Infected on your world, but I'd still like to see something that convinces me you have the population you mentioned. Are all of the battles like that one?"

"No," Elliah said, "that one was rough. Usually we deal with but a handful. We've only had one other battle like that one, and the results were much less favorable—the entire city and its surroundings were destroyed."

"What stopped them that time?" Hirashi asked.

"I did," Elliah answered. "With a weapon that kills entire cities in one blow. It was... terrible. And necessary."

After a somber moment, I helped Rocks enjoy his victory. "But this time," I said, "we stopped them. And we will get the Mana'thiandriel and stop them again. Let's do a tour of the world we'll be saving."

Chapter 2

Staci

I opened my eyes in a hospital room, confused. I wiggled my fingers and my toes. My blood coursed through me as it should, the liquid kissing my magic. Hospital equipment stood at the ready, but none forced their unwanted attention upon me. Other sources of water called out in greeting—a sink in the room and pipes in the walls, an adjoining bathroom, a bottle of water, and another person.

"You're awake." Phillip peered at me over his laptop, the tip of an AirPod protruding from his ear. He faced me from a short couch set up for visitors. The laptop brightened the dark room, outshining both the dim glow coming from night-lighting over the bed and the New York City glimmers illuminating the window.

He set his laptop to his side and rose, the constrained light from the screen brightening the back of the couch and casting the doorway into shadow.

"Am I okay?" I asked.

"Galad says you are. You just needed rest."

"Then why the hospital?"

Phillip shrugged. "They were just being cautious. They cleaned you up, double checked for wounds…" He shrugged again. "Now, they're keeping an eye on you," he said, pointing up at a tiny red LED.

"And you?" I asked. "Why are you here?"

"The same. Just wanted to make sure you were okay. That was quite a fight."

Fight.

Memories swirled. Blood, darkness, bodies all around me. I couldn't make sense of it, and my panic spiked. My breath wouldn't come.

"Whoa, whoa, it's okay," Phillip said.

But it wasn't okay! I couldn't remember why, but it wasn't okay. Something had me trapped! Pinned down!

Phillip reached out and I swatted him away, not even able to shout "Get off!" over my labored breathing.

"What the hell!" he shouted, but he wasn't looking at me. I followed his eyes to find an Infected stepping out of the shadows of the doorway, stalking toward my bed.

The window shattered, glass flying in and slicing into the Infected. Wind and shrapnel pushed the monster back toward the door, which rattled in its frame from the force of the rushing air. My head throbbed with the increased pressure as the gale circled the outside of the room, moving the couch and bed in a swirl as it searched for an escape.

I used my magic to spike the pressure in the sink, blowing the valve and getting a stream of water I could use.

I leaped off the spinning bed to join Phillip, the bed becoming a fool's barrier between us and the Infected.

Phillip calmed the wind in our corner, but encouraged the mini-cyclone in the room, making it hard for the Infected to regain its balance.

Blood spear, my memory hinted. A spear of water would do. Even better, I made a thin sheet of water and hurled it like a high pressure guillotine blade at the neck of the Infected.

Its nightmarish head flew off, and blood spewed forth, the wind whipping it toward us, but Phillip steered it hard away. I couldn't feel the blood with my senses for a few seconds, the magic of the Infected protecting it. Phillip kept the blood circling as more blood joined the vortex from the headless body. The furniture settled as Phillip focused the wind into tighter circles around the slain monster.

All at once I sensed the blood—the magic that protected it had died out. "Okay, Phillip, I've got this," I told him. I stopped the sink water from spewing forth, and in the same way I kept more blood from escaping the headless carcass.

I formed the blood in the middle of the wind into a bubble, and Phillip set the wind free out the window. He sighed with relief as the wind rattled and screeched its way out.

I deposited the blood into the sink, letting some water from the faucet escape to coax the blood down the drain.

The door flew open and banged against the body of the Infected, springing back on the intruder. "Shit!" came a male voice, then a slower prying open of the door as the carcass slid deeper into the room. "Shit!" he said again, pointing a handgun down at the corpse.

I giggled, with a slight element of uncontrollability, and sat down next to Phillip, who I hadn't realized had plopped to the floor. I leaned against him—safe.

He mumbled, "Shit shit shit…" and I laughed quietly, as the guard flipped on the light and took stock of the room.

"You okay?" he asked, looking over the bed that still blocked the middle of the room.

We looked at each other, assessing our condition. Phillip answered for us. "We're alive, not too damaged, and not Infected, so… " and he gave the guard two thumbs up.

I heard myself giggling, a touch of madness trilling in my head. Still, as a sign of support for the only-slightly-annoying man who had saved my life, I echoed Phillip's gesture.

Chapter 3

Cordoro, First of Emerald Farms

I sipped my wine and chewed on Crooney's words. They stuck in my brain like a seed in my teeth, resisting every attempt to dislodge them.

I'd been quicker than the Empath, getting away before his magic ensnared me. I hadn't had time to get the others. If that old dodderer, Broxton, hadn't been so jealous of my potential, he'd have taught me some of his tricks before he passed on. Same for that arrogant Mort. So the fault lay with those stiff-necked leaders; had they shared their secrets, I would have freed Hirashi from that hole in the ground instead of abandoning her to an Empath. Not that it hadn't worked out in my favor... mostly.

"How am I better off with *you* as Regent?" I asked. With Hirashi gone, shouldn't the Council of Elders choose one of her Firsts, in particular a Teleporter, to become Regent?

"You'd be a great Regent, Cordoro," Crooney, as his name suggested, crooned. "I have no doubt about that. You *will be* a great Regent."

Okay then.

"Here's the problem," Crooney said with a sigh.

Here we go, I thought, taking a long drink of the wine I'd pilfered from El'daShar. I savored the taste on my tongue, the delicate and alien flavor with its silken smoothness. *How could such a despicable race create such a delicious liquid?*

"We depend upon you for our very survival," he began.

I rolled my eyes. I anticipated sitting through Hirashi's litany of demands about the necessity of getting our produce off of Emerald Farms to generate the money we needed to pay the Forsaken, the Savage, the Artifairium...

"When the Twelve meet, they spend hours, sometimes *days*,

negotiating." Okay, Crooney's speech would not mirror Hirashi's. "I'd hate to see you spend your valuable time *bargaining*," and he spat the word out like it was rotten meat, "instead of pursuing issues that only someone with your Talent can pursue. You are our hope and our salvation, and you deserve so much more than you've been given." He looked around at all my beautiful things, the gold and silver wine goblets, my fine sofa of the most supple calfskin from Drover, the grown-wood statue from Vibrant. Yet I knew he had more, his wealth making mine appear paltry.

And he thought I deserved more. If only Allania had inherited Crooney's refined tastes. It was a shame I'd had to leave her to die with the others; she would have made the perfect addition to my *beautiful things*. Crooney knew I'd left her behind, but hadn't once brought it up. They'd been estranged for years, and he'd never been the doting father, his tastes being, like mine, *refined*.

I looked for the trap in his words. Over the years, Crooney had been nothing but good to me, but with others, he'd acted a clever and manipulative entrepreneur. But I saw no ill intent—he had a point about the Conclave. I desired respect, and the power to call the shots. I had no interest in negotiating trade agreements. I sipped my wine, thinking.

"Mort appointed a representative to attend the Conclave of the Twelve," I said.

Crooney nodded, deep in thought. "I hadn't considered that. You're right—*you* don't have to deal with the pompous windbags on the Conclave. You could find some poor bastard to do that for you."

I took another sip of my wine and popped a ball of cheese from our sister colony of Galene into my mouth. Why couldn't *we* make cheese like that? *Because it takes a person who has mastered the craft.* A surge of pride shot through me at the clever idea that formed in my mind.

"I know someone who can do that," I said.

"Perfect. We'll need to let them know gently though. Make the job sound interesting…"

We? He thought to control me by deciding who I would pick. I smiled at my own machinations.

"You," I interrupted.

I enjoyed his stumbling halt.

"You should do it, Crooney." *Chew on that, you entitled ass.*

"But I have responsibilities to the people working my land..." he protested, but I stopped him.

"We all have responsibilities, Crooney." Oh, I enjoyed being on the side of the fence that *gave* the orders for once. Forcing the situation. And I'd seen the conditions of the people working his land; I had difficulty understanding why a high-valued crop such as mageroot left his workers in such squalor. They needed to work harder and stop relying on Crooney's goodwill; I felt no qualms about their plight.

Crooney looked downcast. He stared at his feet as I took a sip of wine.

Finally, he sighed. "As you wish," he said, his voice resigned, "but I wonder..."

"Yes?" I said, indulging him.

"I think... to be effective..."

"Spit it out, man!"

"To be truly effective, I think we should consider seating new blood on the Council of Elders."

I sighed again, sipping, feeling a little sluggish from the wine. "An Elder serves for *life*," I thought out loud. "Or until they step down by choice." Which was generally how it happened, after a few years. "Or the seldom-invoked clause to remove someone mentally unfit." Which was how Crooney ousted Hirashi when I'd called an emergency session upon my return. I didn't mind that we'd lost that son of Broxton's, a constant reminder of the pretensions of my old teacher. I'd hoped to convince Allania to be mine—that I'd left her behind rankled.

"Yes," Crooney said, nodding his head, but with his brows pulled heavy over his eyes as he puzzled through the situation. "But there *is* a mad Empath loose. It may be that their lives *are* in danger."

The Elders? Why would the elf kill the Elders? "Bah," I said. "There's no reason to think that." *What a strange thing to say.*

"I don't know," he corrected me, getting up to leave. He paused at the door. "If a closed Council were attacked, only the survivors could say what happened."

Well, yes, obviously, but what…

The glass slipped from my fingers when my mind grasped his meaning. *Only the survivors could say what happened.* I skirted the thought, knowing it to be *wrong*. I danced around it like the mad Forsaken around one of their burning pits of lava. Sure, I'd used my Talent to procure goods here and there, getting people what they needed. Black market trading, while technically illegal, was the lifeblood of some worlds. My conscience poked holes in my bubble of self-justification. I did it, not for the help it brought others, but for what it brought me. But I'd never killed…

The wooden clunk of the shutting door pulled me out of my dark contemplations. I started toward the entrance, needing to be sure I'd understood Crooney's meaning, but startled when my foot kicked the glass I'd forgotten about, sending it skittering across my rug. A splotch of red pooled in the white fur at my feet, and tiny dots spattered the carpet in the travels of the glass.

I tsked at it, the blood-like stains reminding me of the foul direction my thoughts had taken. *Murder!* I couldn't *kill* people. It was unthinkable. *Leave that to the Forsaken and the Savage.* But…

Leave that to the Savage…

Hmmm…

Chapter 4

Rej

I would've liked to travel to the abandoned world of the elves. The very idea of constructs created by alien minds, with alien perspectives of beauty—it drew me like a moth to a flame. To see some examples of architecture created with the forces of magic... surely that would open up my mind to new possibilities.

But, alas, they'd grounded us. Not grounded like schoolchildren; rather, pinned down by our duty to protect *our* world.

Breathe. My mind ran loose between the past and the future, darting between what could have been and what might still be. I could have gone to another world. I had been *right there* when the others had left—a few slight changes and it would have been me. Perhaps one day I might still go... and see alien architecture.

The past and future were exhausting. I pulled my focus back to the movements of my body from my breathing. *Breathe.*

Tap, tap, tap. "Cyrus, you're needed in medical," a man's voice shouted from outside my room. He'd called me Cyrus, my last name, so not someone who knew me—must have been military. *Tap, tap, tap.* "Cyrus?"

Well, I thought, *at least my mind is back in the present.* "Coming!" I relayed through the door, giving up on my mindfulness exercise. I opened the door, finding what I expected.

"You're needed in medical," said the man at my door. The Guardian League had not settled on a uniform, so we still had people in various lines of military clothing. The particular gentleman who called upon me wore Army fatigues. He had a pin on his uniform—a mask like Zorro with spiked hair?

"It's the official symbol for the Guardian League," he said, following my gaze and answering my unspoken question.

"What is it?" I asked.

"That's *the mask*. The one the woman with the knives used, and elf ears."

"Wow," I said. It was hideous.

"I know, pretty cool, right? Come on, I'll take you to medical. It's not far."

"Okay," I said, still in awe of the horrible pin. I hoped I wouldn't have to wear that.

He led the way, and true to his word, it wasn't far. They had converted rooms from an intended wing of a hospital into housing. Apparently, some of the rooms had not undergone any transformation, as we took neither stairs nor escalators to reach our destination.

Alex joined us, appearing without an escort where three hallways merged. It made sense that he knew where to go. As former head of security, he still kept the pulse of the building's operations.

"Morning, Alex," I said. He looked tired—probably hadn't slept well after the nightmarish battle of the day before.

My own sleep was mixed. Yes, the battle had been a nightmare, but it had also been so very exhilarating. I had controlled rocks on a level I never hit during our practice sessions—for a brief time, I had felt inexhaustibly powerful, unstoppable. And then it had all crashed, leaving me empty and exhausted. Though nightmares nipped at my sleep, some of my dreams inspired me—dreams of creating colossal constructs from my magic! Forming towers and Sphinx-like monuments that would withstand the test of time. And I hated when I woke and the dreams fled like scattering clouds.

"Morning, Rej," he replied, as we joined ranks and followed the former Army gentleman to the correct hall. The right room was obvious by the pair of guards stationed outside of it, and Elliah standing with them, her stern gaze taking us in. The room across the hall also churned with activity, and as we approached, they wheeled out a full body bag, Mr. Penbrook following behind.

"Oh, no," Alex whispered. "Staci?"

"No," Elliah responded, stopping the gurney. She waved us over and unzipped the bag partway. Nice. Infected with its head detached—as though I hadn't seen enough of the damned things torn apart in the battle. The man pushing the gurney sniffed, drawing my attention away from the Infected. With dark hair and blue eyes, his chiseled looks were... unusually attractive.

Then the pieces clicked together in my brain, and thoughts of the medic fled my mind. "Wait, *that* was *here*?" I asked. It had come into *our* building? *My* building? *Again*? The last time the Infected had attacked, my atrium had been destroyed. But they'd been drawn to the magic of the otherworlders. Why had one been in the building while I'd slept?

Elliah was nodding her head yes. "It attacked Staci when she woke up. Appeared right in the room, according to Phillip."

"They're all right then?" Alex asked.

Appeared right in the room?

"They dispatched this one with no serious damage to themselves," Elliah answered. "I've already Healed their bruises. But I wanted you *all* here before digging any deeper into *why* it happened."

She zipped the bag back up, Mr. Penbrook adding, "We need to keep this quiet." He directed his next words to the medic, "You've got my instructions." Elliah waved the gurney on its way.

My eyes lingered on the attractive man pushing the gurney, long enough that he locked eyes with me, raising an eyebrow. I looked away, blushing at my actions, but found my eyes drifting back to him as he retreated down the hall. He looked back over his shoulder as he turned a corner. Was he looking at me? He sniffled again as he disappeared, and I imagined myself arguing with him about taking his allergy meds before he left for work.

"Elliah," Mr. Penbrook spoke again, interrupting my ill-timed fascination. "We can't afford for word to spread that those monsters are Teleporting into our headquarters."

"I understand," she said. "But you should understand that the attack was not random. You need not be any more fearful than you already were. I need some time with my team. Alone. I will keep them safe."

Penbrook didn't like that. But ultimately, Elliah could Teleport us away if she wanted. He had no choice. He nodded and started after the gurney.

Elliah opened the guarded door and entered. Alex let out a huff of air, as one might do before jumping into a pool one knew to be too cold, and followed her in. I nodded my head in agreement and came in last, shutting the door behind me.

The room contained a bed, but no one occupied it. Instead, Staci and Phillip used the bed as a table, the laptop perched atop it while they sat on the couch, worshipping the tiny computer. Staci wore hospital robes, sitting cross-legged on the couch and leaning forward to type into the laptop. Phillip sat with his gangly legs stretched out, pointing at something on the screen.

They looked up as we walked in and paused whatever they were doing. Phillip stood, unlocked the wheels on the bed with his foot, and slid it back, freeing Staci from her penned-in position on the couch.

"Pardon me if I don't get up," Staci said, "but hospital gowns don't leave quite enough to the imagination."

"Here," Elliah said, handing her some clothes. Where had she been hiding *shoes* when we came in?

Staci looked at the clothes Elliah had given her. "These are not…"

"Just put them on," Elliah said. "You can change into your clothes later. Unless you want one of us to go through your room to find something for you…"

"No, no," Staci said. "These are… lovely." She stood and shuffled sideways to the bathroom.

I looked at the laptop screen to give Staci some privacy. Code filled much of the screen, but a frame at the top right played a movie. "Is that… " I began.

"*Game of Thrones*," Phillip said.

"But the sound is off," I said.

Phillip shrugged. "We turned off the sound during the dragon porn section." *Dragon porn?* "We were working through some of the code Scan had created for that off-world Teleport," he said, pointing to the code on the rest of the screen. "Practicing how to string pieces of spells together."

"Elliah," Phillip said, getting her attention, "I couldn't help but notice I ran out of mana very quickly when that Infected came into my room. But during yesterday's battle I had no trouble keeping spells going. My mana felt recharged when the fight began in the hospital room, but drained so soon compared to the bigger battle. I don't understand the difference. Why was I able to fight so much longer in El Paso than here?"

Staci cracked the door of the bathroom and added, "Same for me. I was out of mana from the single Infected we fought here, but had gone on casting much longer in the desert." I heard the shuffling of clothes as she talked. She pushed open the door as she finished. She wore a robe that had patterns I associated with Galad's clothes. It was red and purple, and suited Staci with her purple hair well. Red sandals complemented the outfit. The tattoos on her arms extended the symbols on the outfit. It all fit together.

"Me," the elf said. "*I'm* the difference. I taught you all how to recharge each other's mana. That's my specialty."

"But you told us you didn't have a Talent," I protested.

"Technically, it isn't a Talent. It's a Gift. They're different."

"A Gift?" Phillip asked.

"Talents are specializations in a field of magic, like Healing or any of the Elemental work that you lot do. Gifts work on the foundations of magic. It is what your friend Scan uses to *see* the magical threads that enabled us to Teleport off this world. My Gift is an ability to transform magical energy."

While I puzzled out the distinction, she continued on.

"I lived on Earth for a long time before learning of this Gift. Magical energy was abundant on the elven worlds. There was no need for my Gift. But here on this world…"

"Dead sun," I said.

"Dead sun," she agreed. "Without the energy from a nearby star, I began to sense other forms of magical energy. Very subtle ones. Suffice it to say, when you're working with me, I can keep your mana charged."

She looked at Staci. "I can also cut you off. That's what I did with you in the desert. You might have killed us all with the spell you'd weaved."

Staci blushed, but not deeply enough to match the red in her elvish robes.

"So what's the other source you draw on?" I asked.

"Let's go somewhere more private, shall we?" We gathered up and she magic'd us back to her bubble under the sea.

Chapter 5

Rocks

"Sir," Simmi piped through the phone at my ear.

"I'm on my way back now, Simmi." I'd been working with some tech guys on creating something we could carry to a planet with no sources of electricity to display the video we'd recorded. I wanted to get back to my desk to clear my calendar and take care of a little virtual paperwork I couldn't do from my phone. Especially not on another planet.

"Sir. Hubbard is waiting in your office."

Well, hell. That can't be good.

"Thank you, Simmi. Start clearing my calendar for a couple of days, please."

"Yes, sir." Message delivered, she hung up.

I slowed my pace, having more important things to do than deal with Hubbard.

I dialed.

She answered.

"Urggh," she grumbled.

"Feeling any better?" I asked.

"I'm hungry and nauseous. My head and feet hurt, but only a little more than everything in between."

I grimaced. "The doctor said it's a good thing," I tried to reassure her. "It means the baby is healthy."

"I know what he said." Then she burped. "Oh, Lord," she sighed.

I didn't see how our conversation could go well. "I have to go away for a day or two," I said.

No response.

"You can go with me," I suggested.

"Travel? Me? Now? That sounds horrible." Good. I disliked the idea of her Teleporting with our baby. "I'll be okay, Reggie. Do what you have to do. Save the world."

"I wish there were something I could do to help you." Watching her struggle with her pregnancy disturbed me. If I could have carried some of the physical burden, I would have.

"I know, Reggie."

"Love you, Cynthia."

"Love you too, Reginald Penbrook."

I finished the call in my outer office, Simmi giving me a nod to let me know Hubbard was still inside. The outer office, where Simmi worked, was becoming a mini-Sec Ops. I took a moment to look at the wall monitor with the world map of human population overlaid with the red of possible Infected sightings—the neural nets algorithms searching for the distortive effects we had learned to track. Ever since the El Paso attack, Calloway had piped us the info from the CIA databases for pings on the potential sightings of the Infected.

Satisfied that I spotted no aberrations, as though I would be able to tell before the software, I scanned the other monitors. We still had an influx of new recruits, and Simmi had a color coding set up so that I could judge whether we still had the budget to bring them in. I spotted notifications of updates to several programs, but I would have to get to my laptop to see the details.

I had hoped to spot something that would give me a clue about Hubbard's reasons for intruding. In his last visit, not only had he tried to browbeat me into abusing my power, but Simmi had learned a spy had been present in the outer office—someone masquerading as a technician. She'd found the same man dead in his rooms. She'd had the computers replaced, but had connected no dots on finding the secret agent.

I opened the door and found Hubbard at my desk, flipping through pictures of an electronic photo album Cynthia had populated with pics from before—when I was just a man fresh out of the Army, trying to carve out a new life, under tough circumstances, with my lovely librarian. He set down the gadget—a picture of me, Red, Scan, and Bear at a booth in Tom's Tavern—and it tugged at my heart. Bear had been such a good man. Having to navigate life without him as my moral compass daunted me.

But Hubbard didn't rise from my seat. A power play. It didn't bode well. He thought he held some cards. Was he bluffing?

"Under different circumstances," he began, "you and I would have been friends."

Interesting. At least it was an admission that we were *not* friends. Hopefully, we had finished that particular dance.

"Maybe," I said. Maybe, if I had continued down the dark path I had started on when joining the Army. Maybe, if I hadn't met Bear and Red. Scan and I, unburdened by morals, might have burned some new tunnels to hell.

I closed the door. He still didn't rise.

"I have work to do," I said. "And you're in my chair." *Let's get this done, friend.*

"I won't keep you long. I'm here to help you with your PR problem."

"Which PR problem is that? The one where we fended off an alien attack without nuking our own country?"

Hubbard's smile stretched across his face, the perfect, political smile, but something undefinable in his posture conveyed mockery. "Congratulations on that. Never been to El Paso myself. Comforting to know it's still an option. No," and he stopped smiling. "I mean the problem with Infected appearing in your building."

Shit. I'd kept that information close. I knew, from the dead technician, that at least one operative stalked the halls of the GL. Hubbard had revealed that the spy worked for him. While I'd venture that Calloway had lodged someone inside the GL too, either she hadn't snagged the intel on Infected in the building, or she'd realized using it against me would do more harm than good.

I kept moving to my desk. *How do I want to play this?* I stopped with the desk in between us. *Deny? Admit, but pretend I don't care? Go on the attack?* I wanted to know what he was after. I took too long to decide, and he dug deeper.

"The PR problem that comes when the public knows your hunters are being hunted."

My gut tightened. His knowing that level of detail limited the information leak to a small group I thought I could trust. The hunters themselves, the two guards plus the ones at the cameras, and the medic. Unless there had been a tap on the video feed or its storage.

"So," I responded, looking him in the eyes, "you would make that information public, knowing it would weaken our position, and put the entire world at risk?"

"No, Penbrook, I'm here to help." He smiled. "I want to keep a lid on the information. But I need your cooperation in order to help you."

I bet.

"One of your family's companies makes a drone. I think there's an opportunity to use them in the fight against the alien invaders."

That gave me pause. It aligned with what he had done before—try to use my family's businesses to the advantage of the GL. But it was also way more specific. A drone. To my understanding, we were already looking at drones.

"I can look into it," I said, knowing his request hid *something*, but wanting to keep the fish nibbling at the bait. The same as he was doing with me.

Hubbard rose, signaling the end of our painful repartee. "I'll send you the details."

"And my PR problem?" I asked as he headed for the door.

"I'll help you keep your information bottled. If you ever want help with information security, let me know." And he left.

Yeah, that'll be the day. This round goes to you, Hubbard. The genuine questions I had to grapple with? Had Hubbard pointed toward his endgame, or was the conversation a distraction? And how had he gotten the intel he'd used against me?

Chapter 6

Scan

I sat in an elven clothing shop on El'daShar, laptop in front of me, screen dark. Night had settled in, the temperature dropping enough to drive me indoors. A mage from Mort's crew of warriors had shown me how to trigger the magical lights.

I'd taken down one light and studied it. Elliah had somehow connected a motion sensor in the tunnels under Jerusalem with a magical relay and power source. Could I do something similar to either recharge my laptop's battery or provide direct current to my laptop?

Nothing I'd tried had worked, but neither had I blown up the light or laptop. It was all just energy—but transforming energy required clever constructs. Man had built water wheels, harnessing a river's energy to run mills and grind wheat. Later, we had invented turbines to convert the physical force of water into electricity. Electricity would go into batteries that powered engines, converting electricity back into physical power. There had to be similar processes for electrical and magical energy, but I knew too little.

"Scan?" a voice asked. "You okay?" Smith had walked in and seen me staring at the screen of my blank laptop. Probably thought I was losing it. Or had already lost it.

"Hey, Smith. Yeah, just trying to work out how to power this thing."

"Did you need something from your laptop?"

"Not specifically, no, but I use it to help organize my thoughts. I feel a little, I don't know, half-brained without it."

Grundle had moved in behind Smith. "Like most good wizards without their spellbooks," he said, nodding his head and grinning.

"There's something to be said about simple paper and pen," I said, my smile wry as I thought about all I *couldn't do* with my laptop on a planet with no internet.

"Until you spill your wine on it," Grundle responded.

"This computer wouldn't do any better with wine."

When the pause dragged on, goosebumps crept down my arms.

"Is there something I can help you with?" I asked.

"It's just, well…" Smith looked embarrassed, or… guilty? "Let me ask this way… how hard was it to grow those talons?"

"It wasn't easy. I guess hard. Not really, really hard. Why?"

"How hard would it be to do again?" she asked, turning bright red.

I thought about it a moment, then realized why she was asking. "Pffft," I laughed. Grundle looked displeased. That didn't seem safe at all. I held out my hand to forestall his threats. "I can do it again. Give me a moment, let me think." I wanted to laugh some more. Crazy.

I had an idea… a wonderful, awful idea. I looked more closely at Grundle, opening my eyes to my magical sight. The how-to of converting magical energy to electrical eluded me, but Grundle's construction, magically-speaking, lay open to me as clear as glass. I turned my sights on Smith—in most ways even more of an open book, having more experience with humans. I could try solving the problem before me in one of two ways. It required a bit of extrapolation and guesswork. But I knew which way they'd prefer. At least I thought I knew.

"Now?" I asked them both.

"I don't know that we will get another chance," Smith answered. "This feels to me like a 'calm before the storm' situation."

Okay. I felt good about the chances that my attempt would work. "You okay with the whole 'breaking the Second Law of Magic' thing? I am, but you used to be in law enforcement and all."

Smith sighed in irritation. "Will you do it or not?"

Smiling, I stood up. "Calm your horses." A catch-phrase I'd picked up from Red years ago, which consequently made her stop using it. "Come over here," and I waved them both over. They joined me near my unpowered laptop, and I smiled, trying to reassure them.

I put a hand on Smith's arm. I studied her—trying to see enough to be able to undo anything I changed.

This won't do. I couldn't trust myself to remember *everything*. I needed something else to remember *for* me, like storing a database. Galad had talked about Empaths creating Elder Stones, gems that stored people's memories. I looked at my attempt to connect the magical light source with the laptop, and knew I couldn't literally store Smith's genetic code in a database.

But I could work with live things. I needed a place to store her code, her essence, the magical equivalent of her DNA. There may have been a way to store it within her, but I couldn't see how to protect it from what I planned.

"I need somewhere to store your blueprint," I said aloud. Grundle's rocky brown eyes pieced into mine. He was clever. He held out his rocky arm.

I put my hand on his stony arm. I could carve out a little space almost anywhere, but I wanted it to be somewhere that his own body would accept it, not fight it like a cancer. The romantic in me—and despite what people thought, there *was* one—said I should store her essence in his heart. But my pragmatic side told me that introducing a foreign magical structure in the heart reeked of creating a health risk.

I had a thought. "How much do you care about having children?" I asked Smith.

"Um, that's not really a concern," she said, giving me a queer look.

"Just making sure," I said. I chuckled under my breath at my cleverness in finding a place to store her magical DNA, given their intent. But I did it; I stashed her magical blueprint in his reproductive organs.

"You should take off any jewelry," I said, "and grab a blanket."

Smith worked the bracelet off her wrist, rings off her fingers, and picked up a blanket we had used for bedding. "Why do I need…"

Now, the fun. I took *his* magical blueprint, and I ran it over Smith. I had done the same with a small subset of Smith before; I had grafted the claws from those bird-bats in the cave onto her hands and feet. In that misadventure, the keys to her blueprint remained in the rest of her body, so I'd been able to call her hands and feet back. But for the transformation I intended, I hoped to change… everything.

She grew, taking on the height of a troll, her skin becoming rocky, tearing through her clothes. But she grew too big… bigger than Grundle. *Hmm, something's not right here...* There was an abnormality, but it wasn't Smith—Grundle was the one out of the norm, a recessive gene that made him… small? Wow. *Grundle, at nine feet, is small for a troll.*

Time to improvise. The transformation would be a temporary deal anyway. *I'll just copy that recessive gene from the Y chromosome to the X. There.* Smith shrank back down from crouching in the twelve foot high room to Grundle-sized.

"Wow," Grundle admired.

Done and done.

Chapter 7

Rocks

My head throbbed. Thinking about what I had to get done before I left with Galad daunted me. The thought of going to a whole different world should have been exciting... energizing. Instead, especially with Hubbard's visit and my wife's pregnancy, the excursion had become distant and surreal, a dreaded business trip.

"Simmi, all clear?" I asked through the open door.

She poked her head in as I worked my way around my desk to take the seat Hubbard had vacated. "All clear," she answered.

"Can you try and get me a meeting with Calloway?" I needed an ally, or to know if I couldn't have one.

My phone buzzed. Pulling it out as I sat, I saw it was Calloway.

"How many bugs are in this office?" I mumbled.

"My doing, sir. I had a call in."

I squinted at her. "Are you part Empath?"

"Not that I'm aware, sir. You'd better answer it so you can get moving on your trip."

I shook my head in disbelief. She smiled and closed the door as she left. She persisted in wearing her Army fatigues. I wondered if I had a soft spot for women in fatigues—I seemed to listen to them a lot.

Answering my phone, I pinched the bridge of my nose to relieve some pressure. "Calloway. This is Penbrook. Reginald Penbrook. Thank you for taking the time to speak with me."

"What do you need?" she asked, sounding busy.

"I just had a visit from Hubbard. He knew some GL internal intel that he shouldn't have."

There was a long pause at the other end, followed by a sigh. "Look, Penbrook. Indulge me—let me explain my perspective on your job."

"Please," I said, my tone inviting.

"Okay. Hubbard runs the FBI. His jurisdiction is national. The CIA is broader—worldwide concerns. We have a lot more to cover, and we can't go into national affairs with the same depth as the FBI. The GL... your expanse is broader still than the CIA's. You have multi-planetary responsibilities now. Originally, I didn't think your organization should exist. I thought it should be a part of the CIA. But, as I understand it, you are preparing to leave for another world. Operating as an independent entity makes sense."

"You know I'm leaving," I commented.

"I have people in your org. That's another reason I'm not too worried about your org being independent. You've pulled in many people still willing to report back to me. I get plenty of intel."

Great. I already knew Calloway's statement to be true. But it surprised me when she'd admitted to it.

She chuckled. "If it is any comfort, what I hear is good. You're motivating people, empowering people—building loyalty. You're doing the right things for a startup."

"Lovely."

"My point was about scope and resources. Your scope is larger than mine. My scope is larger than Hubbard's. I can't know the details at the national level that he does. Unless someone tells me where to look."

"I won't tell you what he used against me. The less people who know, the safer we are." *Assuming you don't know already.* "But what he asked for was drones. I don't have the details, but he wanted me to buy drones. And there's another piece to the puzzle." I sighed.

There was a pregnant silence on the other end. Then, "I'll let you know what I find. Unless I think we're safer without your knowing, of course. Precedent."

Ouch.

I sighed. "Let's just say I have a problem with aliens targeting my building."

"How did you find *that* out?" she asked. Was she bluffing?

Just seeing how hard she could push me?

"The hard way. It's taken care of. But that information would be... bad for business."

Another pregnant pause. "Agreed. A moment. I'm checking our records on sightings."

Our internal camera footage shouldn't have been available to the CIA.

"Yeah, I see a hit. We can do better than this. Any place else being targeted?"

She couldn't see—or so I chose to believe—but my eyes got big. *We could do better? Was anyplace else being targeted?* Elliah's hideout, but I didn't know where that was.

"Do you know where Elliah takes the apprentices to train?"

Calloway laughed, a rueful harrumph. "She's been on my radar for a while, but no. And I didn't know she wasn't human until she revealed herself. Or even that she was a *she*. Be careful with her. I can tell you this much—she isn't working alone."

Great.

"Okay," she said. "We will monitor your building more closely. If anything triggers, we will let you know immediately. *We* will keep your base safe. *You* should be careful on your trip. Do Earth proud." And the line went dead.

Chapter 8

Red

"And that's how we arrived on Earth with a trunk full of magical artifacts," Harry finished with a flourish before the small crowd of warriors from Mort's colony and myself. Smith should have heard his story—where had she gone?

The tiger stalking him in the night was irrelevant to the story, but it sure had added some excitement to what otherwise sounded like a dull trek with a heavy trunk.

"So that's an elvish hammer," I stated. The runes did look elvish, but I hadn't paid it much attention.

"She's her own hammer," he declared. "She goes with whom she pleases."

Weird.

Crash! Everyone jumped up at the sound of splintering wood from the direction of the shop where we'd made camp. But only Harry and I ran for the building—Scan had been inside! Magelights from within made it easy to spot amongst the dark buildings that edged the square, and the starry night illuminated our mad dash across the smooth, elven-crafted cobblestones.

I reached the shop first and sprang through the door we'd propped open, to find Scan smirking at a hole in the back of the shop. He heard me and turned.

"Um, you can put those away," he said. My daggers were out. Why was there a Grundle-sized hole at the back of the shop?

Crash! The sound came from behind the shop—another wall being destroyed? I started through the shop toward the hole at the back.

Scan held out an arm to stop me, smirking. "Trust me, you *really* don't want to find out what's making that sound."

"What?" I asked, as Harry joined us. "Is Grundle okay?"

"Oh, he's okay," Scan said, laughing. "Just let him be. I promise he doesn't want more company."

"More company?" Harry asked.

"Just have some faith—leave him be," Scan said, still amused.

The others had approached more cautiously. "Everything all right?" Lani called out, poking her head in the shop but listening to something outside. I'd found an odd connection with her even in the short time we'd been together—like rejoining an old friend.

"I'm told so," I answered, as another sound of distant disaster reached us. Was that a tree falling? Yup, that was a tree falling. Scan started laughing again.

"Mort's back!" came a voice from outside the door, and I paused. If Mort was back, that meant...

"Aww, hell," Scan mumbled. "Back to work." He saluted the hole in the back of the shop and started packing up his laptop.

I walked, slow as I could force myself, to the front of the shop. I looked out, scanning the darkness. Where was he? A light flared and floated above the newcomers, and I spotted him. Robed as usual, with his sword at his hip, pointed ears peeking out of his hair. He saw me and smiled—was it warm outside? I thought I remembered it cooling off.

"That's gruesome," Scan said, having come up behind me, and looking past me out the door.

I hadn't noticed—Mort had a staff, hewn sharp at one end. It was a shish kabob of heads of the Infected, pierced through the ear holes, severed at their necks. He stood there, muscular and commanding, displaying his macabre trophy, as his men approached and cheered. Hirashi was there too, smiling at the effect of the scene, and I saw...

"Hey, Rocks came!" Scan blurted, pushing past me to get out to his friend.

I cast a last look at the hole in the back, noting that Smith had never turned up. Also, Harry stood to the side of the warriors, frowning at the display. I had *such* strange companions.

I walked over amidst the cheering, eyes locked on Galad, whose crooked grin grew as a blush crept down his face. *Okay, it is definitely warm out here.* I slowed as we got close.

"It's good to see you," I said. *Shit. It's good to see you?* I should have waited for him to talk. Geez, it was hot.

Galad brushed his elegant fingers across my cheek, sliding his hand behind my neck as he leaned in for a kiss. I kissed back. We had a moment of blissful silence as I sunk into the kiss, then cheers and hoots erupted around us.

Men! And Lani, which made me smirk.

We pulled apart. "Good to see you," he said under the noise of the hoots.

"What is it with this planet?" Scan mumbled without explaining himself.

Rocks put a hand on my shoulder and one on Galad's, saying nothing, just connecting to us. His satisfaction brought me joy.

"We did it," Galad said to me. "This is a pit stop. From here we go to Hirashi's world, collect the Mana'thiandriel, and bring them back to your world."

"Specifically," Rocks said, "that's what *I'm* doing. Galad has a new mission." He stepped back, giving us some room and looking around.

I raised my eyebrows in interest. "And what, pray tell, is your new mission, Minty?"

"Minty?" Galad questioned.

"That was the name of our Elf on the Shelf when I was a kid, and you do smell kind of minty," I told him, shrugging.

"That clarifies surprisingly little," he responded, amused. "My new mission is to find the elves, while you lot figure out how to take the fight to the Infected."

"My lot?" I asked, faux appalled. "Need I remind you I found an elf on my world, where only two existed on a planet of eight billion!"

"Fair point," Galad conceded. "So you find you have an affinity for elves then?"

"Heavens no! It's the minty smell that gives them away."

Galad winced in mock injury, then smiled. "Your credentials seem adequate," he decided. "You may join me on my quest." I pulled him close and rewarded his decision with a sloppy kiss that Mom would never have approved of.

"Who do I kiss to get in on the elf hunt?" Scan asked.

"We're not hunting the *elves*," Galad said, his tone critical.

"What?" Scan said, full of bemused innocence. "In an Easter egg hunt you search *for* eggs. How's this different?"

"What's an Easter egg hunt?" Galad asked.

I answered for Scan. "It's where a rabbit hides decorated eggs that came from a chicken, for small children to find."

"Because...?" Galad asked, his voice hesitant.

"To celebrate God's resurrection, of course," I finished with a note of triumph.

Galad nodded along. "Of course. Unrelatedly, it's a good thing we kissed *before* I learned about your belief system."

"I want to see children hunt for decorated eggs," Lani said with cheer, while I laughed lightly. *Everything was wonderful in the Universe!*

"And I want to *help find* the elves," Scan said.

"What about figuring out how to stop the Infected?" Rocks said, frowning at Scan.

"You've got people on that," Scan answered reasonably. "I'm willing to bet Galad thinks they're tied together, or he wouldn't have taken on the search."

Galad blushed. "Maybe," he said. "There's a possible connection to the origin of the Infected. But Elliah also thinks there's a fair chance the elves have done something... very stupid. They may be trapped. And despite my excommunication, I don't want to be one of only two remaining elves."

"At least the other elf isn't another man," Scan said without thinking, and received a death stare from me. His eyes grew wide and he shrugged an apology.

"Where's Grundle?" Rocks wondered aloud, saving Scan from his faux pas.

"Don't ask," Scan said. "He's fine. He'll be back before morning."

We heard a tree crashing in the distance. Mort looked our

way, asking with just a raised eyebrow whether we should go investigate. Galad closed his eyes for a moment, then blushed. "It's fine," he said, waving Mort to continue his tale of the battle on Earth to his men.

I caught bits of Mort's story myself, and questioned Rocks, "That sounds like another abnormality, like in Bata?"

"It was," Rocks said, "but between the mages and automatic weapons, this time we *won*!"

I half-smiled. It was great that we won, but... "Do we have any more clue why these aberrations occur?"

"Some clue, yes," Rocks answered. "Both were sites known for human trafficking. We don't know how the pieces fit together yet, but we're going to add such places to the list of sites where we try to draw them out." Rocks grimaced before continuing. "It was El Paso this time, Red."

Shit. My parents lived in Texas. Admittedly, over 500 miles away; even so, that was too close. They'd live through the initial blast, but...

Rocks saw my look, and Galad felt my tension. Galad beat Rocks to the punch. "We won, Red."

"This time," I said, "but what about the next time? We have to *stop* them." I paused, realizing what I'd just said. "After we find the elves."

"With my help," Scan chimed in. "Probably Rocks and Smith as well," he added.

I looked around for Harry, who nodded his head at me. Harry was in.

Almost the old team. I looked at Rocks, expecting I knew the answer.

His eyes held a glimmer of sadness, a subtle no. "Wow," Rocks said, chiding us, "I can't find *anybody* that wants to celebrate!"

"Grundle is celebrating," Scan snickered, drawing a blush from Galad and confused looks from me and Rocks.

Looking around, Rocks barreled on. "Let's take a moment to appreciate the successes. I mean, I can't believe I'm on another *planet*. I can see I am, but... wow. Just wow!"

The stars shone down, showing the outline of a forest behind the shops, with the elfin towers climbing in the other direction, all the roads leading into town.

"What's that?" Rocks asked, pointing at the one object lighting up the elven city, that glowing egg atop a tower.

"I don't know," Galad answered. "They created it after I left."

"There was one on Hirashi's world too. Hirashi!" I called, getting her attention and drawing her away from the warriors and Mort, over to our party. It looked like their story-telling had wrapped up, and Mort followed Hirashi over.

"Hirashi, what is that?" I asked, pointing at the egg. "I saw one on your world as well."

"The elves installed those, around a season before they disappeared. They were communication towers." She reached in her pocket and pulled out one of their gem-phones. "We could make calls across worlds once they were up. I have no idea how they worked, but they stopped working when the elves left."

Scan perked up at this. "Wait, wait, wait," he said, waving his hands. "You're telling me that, between the time that Galad left and now, the elves introduced a series of towers on every planet, and then disappeared? Does no one else see the big, shining *clue* on the horizon?"

"They're communication towers," Mort said, "just for talking." He mimed holding a phone to his mouth, explaining the concept to the Muggles.

"I suppose it explains how they *coordinated* the evacuation," Galad began, "but I don't see…"

But Hirashi's look told me she wasn't so sure. "Can we take a closer look?" I interrupted, looking at Mort.

He shrugged, and *bamf*, we stood high above the ground, on a platform under the glowing egg.

Chapter 9

Red

Whoa! Why would anyone build something so dangerous? The top of the tower was a square ledge, three feet wide and nine inches thick. Small spires at the corners held up the twenty-foot long platforms formed of a grey marble wrought with veins of black and white. The outside rounded outer edge overlooked a hundred-foot drop to the ground. I slammed my eyes closed to fight off vertigo.

The wind whispered past, but even the small breath of it made me uncomfortable. Not looking down, I cracked open my eyes. The rules of the Teleportation spell eluded me; we had arrived in a different formation than we'd left—from a huddled mass we became lines along two of the adjacent ledges.

The egg floated inside the ledges, several feet above me and out of reach. *Not floating,* I amended myself. A clear ring of crystal held it aloft, with the crystal attached to angled posts at the four corners of the ledge. It put me in mind of a giant Easter egg set out to dry.

That close, I could make out the clear shell of the egg. On Earth, I'd have guessed the shell's material to be plastic. On El'daShar, more crystal?

White fluid moved inside the crystal like a lava lamp. Veins of light and dark swirled, the light bright enough to make the whole egg glow from a distance.

I chanced a look at my feet. Okay, the granite platform revealed aesthetic similarities to the veins in the egg, but seriously? Who could tell unless they were standing on the damn ledge, and what idiot would stand on that ridiculously thin ledge?

Other than this idiot, who hadn't realized what she was getting into.

"I'm too far," Scan shouted from the adjacent ledge. "I need to get closer."

"That spell you cast on us in the bore!" I shouted to Galad. *Geez, cast it on me too, please?*

"Already on it!" he shouted. Was it my imagination, or did I feel a little tingle when Galad cast the spell on me?

"Look up and walk toward it!" Galad yelled to Scan.

Scan took a hesitant step forward and up. Not off the ledge, but his foot hovered in the air above it, and he brought the other one up next to it. He made a face—an okay-that's-interesting face—and started up toward the egg.

He put his hand on the egg, staring into it. After a minute, he yelled, "Mort, can you 'Port to a tower on another world? Tell me what you see? I'm going to try something!"

Mort gestured, a movement whose details I missed, but it must have meant yes because he poofed away in a giant flash of light. I felt a ping of worry that one of us might fall and the Teleporter would not be around to save the day. But Galad caught my eye and gave me a nod of reassurance—he had it under control. I took a calming breath and nodded back.

Scan created a ball of light, and pushed it into the egg. He shifted it through some colors—green, red, blue—then white again. Finished, he let it drop, and walked back down to the ledge.

Mort reappeared seconds later in another flash. "Light!" He shouted. "It shifted colors—white, green, red, blue, then white again."

"Okay!" Scan answered. "Let's get back to the others!"

Mort had us back in the square in moments.

As a general rule, heights didn't scare me, but I felt relief at being back on the ground. Mort's men gathered around.

"So, it connects spells over long distances," Galad concluded, his voice no longer a shout.

"Not just connecting up distances," Scan said, "but also connecting up multiple points. It was the strangest thing I've seen... so far. In a Teleport spell, I can see the endpoint of the other location. What I saw in the fluid was a ring with multiple drop-off points along the ring."

I pursed my lips, trying to grasp the importance of a ring of magical threads.

"When I cast that light spell," Scan told me, "it didn't just light up wherever Mort went; I think it lit them *all* up. I'm guessing I saw... I don't know, fifteen times twenty points on the ring."

"That's roughly right," Hirashi said. "Many of the Colonies, the dwarven and elven worlds."

"Galad," Scan asked, "could you Compel strongly enough to convince an entire *world* to leave? Mort, same question about Teleportation."

"No," Mort answered. "I've managed twenty-six people on a raid, but that was pushing my limit. An ancient and practiced elf could get perhaps ten times that. There had to be a million elves."

Galad looked stricken.

"What?" I asked, grasping his hand. Through our touch, I felt his dismay.

"Harry," he squeaked out. "Harry!" His shout rang out in the hub.

"Over here!" Harry called, and the warriors parted to let him through. He rushed up, alarmed by the fear in Galad's voice.

"Harry," Galad said, grabbing Harry's shoulders. "I should ask this in private. I'm sorry, Harry. But given the situation..."

"Out with it, elf," Harry said, concerned.

"When you brought the trunk," Galad said, "there was a stone. You know the one. What did you do with the real one?"

"Why?" Harry asked. "Grundle told me to keep it out of the hands of the elves."

"That stone. It was a treasure unearthed by the troll slave labor on the 4D Planes. It was an artifact imbued with a Gift—it could amplify a spell. You combine those things," he said, waving at the glowing egg, "with the power of the Amp, and you could Compel every elf, group them up, and send them *away*."

Galad looked up at me, his worry palpable, and I put a hand atop his on Harry's shoulder.

"Harry," Galad said, drawing Harry's eyes back to his. "Is it possible the elves found the Amp from wherever you stashed it?"

Harry's eyes narrowed, "We have to get to DwarkenHazen!"

Chapter 10

Alex

"This is the Bubble?" I asked. We were *not* in the coliseum where we had battled fantastic monsters in order to train. Instead, we had Teleported into a room large enough for ten people, lined with racks of pink crystals about the size of a finger. A slim door, reminding me of a submarine hatch, closed off the room.

"This is the control room," Elliah answered.

"So we're part of the *in crowd* now?" I asked. She'd not let us see more of the Bubble than the proving grounds before.

"You earned your big boy pants," Elliah chuckled semi-sweetly. "Render to all what is due them: honor to whom honor."

Oh, Lord.

"As long as I've earned my big boy pants," I said, "what is the story behind all the Bible quotes?"

Elliah picked up a handful of the crystals that lay in a pile on the only table in the room, examining each and then putting it in a slot in the wall-racks of crystals. "Kept me sane when I was older," she answered.

Only one chair occupied the room, and no one took it. We all stood there, wondering what the hell the crazy elf was talking about.

She hadn't yet dented in the pile, but she stopped and sighed. "Perhaps you all can help me with this." It wasn't a question. We shuffled forward and everyone picked up a crystal. Mine was pink, like all the others, about a finger's width and length, like all the others, and otherwise distinguished itself in no discernable way from its neighbors. I stared at it and picked up another, trying to tell it from the first, then I looked at the rack. I had no clue.

Elliah looked up. "It all ties together. I promise."

No one had fared better than I. As a group, we set our jewels back down and waited.

"Let's start at the end," she began. "What I'm about to tell you... the story has to stay in *this* group. Galad knows—he needed to know to understand why he had to find the elves—but *no one else!*"

We all nodded. Finally, some truth.

"The source of magic on this world, where the sun provides none... it is *you*." She looked around. "Not you specifically; you collectively. Humans."

"We're being used as batteries? Like in *The Matrix*?" Phillip asked.

"Good movie," Elliah said. "'Listen to me, Coppertop. We don't have time for 20 Questions.' Very insightful."

"Wait," Staci said, "we're floating in a bubble of Artificial Reality, and you're telling me we *power* it?"

"This?" Elliah said, waving her arms about her. "No, not this. This is from the 4D Planes."

Ah, yes, I thought sarcastically, *good ol' 4D Planes.* But she did not give me the opportunity to inquire where and what that might be.

"Like I said, it's stable. It has gobs of power in it. You just can't power anything *from* it."

"So not like *The Matrix* then," Phillip concluded.

"No, but it was still a good movie," Elliah defended. "What I learned after coming here, after thousands of years, is that humans emit a tiny amount of magic. The amount for any one person is negligible, but now that you have eight billion?"

"It moves the needle," I said.

"It damn well does," she said. "The elves that came here, we all started aging once we arrived. Slowly, but surely. We learned we need magic to survive. For thousands of years, humans struggled to take control of this planet. But the elves that stayed away from humans, those who isolated themselves... they aged faster. They died first. Those of us who stayed around, poked about in human affairs, we fared better. And, in the last 300 years, the balance flipped. Eight billion people create more magic than a live sun, if you can figure out how to use it."

We all waited to hear what that last statement meant—clearly humans had not figured out how to use their self-generated magic.

"My Gift manifested in that time. Perhaps it was always there, unneeded when I was on the other side of the Universe, bathed in a direct source of magic. Here, in its absence, I became more sensitive to other sources. The spells I've taught you to recharge your mana—the ones that work better than what Galad taught you—those are based on skimming magic off of your own kind."

"Are we *hurting* them?" Staci asked, her face pinched and her shoulders tightening.

"No," Elliah answered. "This is magic that humans emit regardless. Most of you are engineers. You know that humans absorb radiation from the sun and emit heat. Think of it like that. Only, unlike heat, you're taking something that most people cannot even sense or use."

"If there's that much magic emitted," Rej asked, "why haven't more people manifested magical powers?"

"I suspect they will, eventually," Elliah said. "Humans don't use the same magic that they emit. It isn't natural for elves either. I've figured it out, and I imagine there are others that could, but it isn't how you're *wired*."

"So we emit trace amounts of unusable magic, only you've figured out how to use it," Phillip stated. "And you're growing younger because elves' bodies use magic to fight aging."

"You've got it. See, my roots are black again," she said, tilting her head down. I looked at the other guys awkwardly, unsure how to respond to this mundane observation that engulfed so much revelation of magic and humans and elves.

"Very nice," Staci answered. "But you'll have to bleach it now if you want to color it." Staci ran a hand over her own purple hair, then jerked it away when she caught Phillip staring.

"It's been thousands of years," Elliah continued on, ignoring the awkwardness. "Three hundred years ago, I was basically a bald skeleton, held together by I-don't-know-what."

"Which brings us back to your Bible quotes," I said.

"Oh, like I said, it was those of us who stayed close to humans that lived the longest. I lived through a lot of the stories, and as I aged, I found myself drawn to the reminders. Fighting off memory loss," she said.

She gave a small shrug and continued.

"I am happy to say that most of what seemed lost just got hard to get to—now that my brain is restored, many of the memories are still there. Not all... I have gaps. The Dark Ages are rather... dark." Her eyes grew distant. "I remember lots of fighting in Jerusalem."

She shook herself, and it wasn't as alarming as it used to be—not as spastic, more healthy. "The fight in El Paso—I let in a lot of magic, which has restored me more quickly. My brain has healed, more or less." She smiled a devilish smile. "Now you're dealing with my normal level of crazy."

We looked at each other nervously.

"Any more questions?" she asked. "Because we have an entirely different topic we need to discuss."

"Why did you come here, to Earth, in the first place?" Rej asked.

"How do you Teleport into a bubble that constantly changes its location?" Staci asked.

"Where do you keep your nukes?" I added.

"Did you ever meet Jesus?" Phillip asked.

That one got looks from the rest of us. He held up his hands. "Well, she was *there*."

"And the question *I* want to discuss," Elliah said, pausing for dramatic effect. "Why are the Infected attracted to *Staci*?"

Chapter 11

Red

Harry's eyes narrowed. "We have to get to DwarkenHazen!" He turned to Mort. "Can you get me there?"

"I cannot. Never been," Mort said. "I'm sorry. The dwarves have little use for hired warriors."

"Cordoro has been there," Hirashi said. "We've delivered food shipments before."

Harry swore. "That ass-wipe wasn't inclined to be helpful."

"I can make him go," Hirashi said. "But it will take a little work." She paused for a moment. "I think we need to plan out all we have to do and figure out the best next steps. We've got a lot in front of us. Get to DwarkenHazen…"

"Get the Mana'thiandriel for Earth," Galad said.

"Find the elves," I said.

"That's one of the goals," Hirashi said. "Getting to DwarkenHazen helps with that—"

"My supposition regarding the elves was pure conjecture," Galad said. His uncertainty sounded hollow to me, like he didn't want to believe it himself. "But it is a logical avenue to follow."

"Have you noticed the similarities between elves and Vulcans?" I asked Scan, trying to lighten the mood, and received an answering grin from Scan. Galad squinted in puzzlement. *Guess you didn't pluck Star Trek from my memories.*

"We need to figure out how to fight the Infected," Rocks added to our growing To Do list.

"I have a next step for that," Galad piped in. "Elliah and I think we will find clues back on FreeWorld, the first planet destroyed by the Infected."

"FreeWorld?" Mort said, his face scrunched in doubt. "I believed that to be a fable."

"It *was* real," Galad assured him. "It was the first world lost to the Infected, *abandoned* long ago. The only ones that would know how to get there would be ancient elves born with the Talent of Teleportation."

"Which leads us back to finding the elves," Hirashi said. "We need more Teleporters. That's the bottom line. Look, I said before that the humans needed to find the elves. They'd taken something we needed. It's the Teleporters themselves that we need. We can't maintain our colonies without trade—each colony is too specialized. We depended on the elves for transportation."

Hirashi looked at Mort, who nodded his agreement. "You are correct. I know every moment I am away makes things harder for my people. And yet I know that, even with exhaustive Teleportation of goods, I cannot keep my colony alive."

"The rings in the vault," Scan said. "The Teleportation Rings."

"They aren't enough," Hirashi said.

"What are they?" Rocks asked.

"Two rings, large enough to walk through, that connect up two points, even across worlds," Scan replied.

"We can connect two worlds then," Rocks said. "I promise you we can cart enough supplies to any *one* world through a ten-foot ring to keep it alive. Colonies of fifty thousand—definitely doable."

"We would put one end on earth," Scan considered out loud, "and move the other end between the colonies. Twelve colonies. That's about six hundred thousand people. That's a tall order."

"It would buy us time," Hirashi said.

"I've used that phrase too much of late," Rocks said. "I owe somebody a *lot* of time at this point."

Hirashi smiled, but the heaviness in her eyes weakened it. "Okay, I propose this. Let me go back with Mort to my world and re-secure my position. You're with me?" she asked Rocks. He patted his backpack and nodded. "I'll return with Cordoro and the Mana'thiandriel. *You*," she said, pointing at Scan, "go down and get the Teleportation Rings and bring them back here. Brox, help them? Lani, can you come help me gather the Council, please?"

The two fighters nodded their willingness.

"We can look for more 'Port Rings too," Scan said. "How long do you think you'll take?"

"Several hours," Hirashi said. "Why don't we plan on meeting back in the morning?"

From the corner of my eye, I witnessed a quick kiss between Brox and Lani, before Lani joined Rocks and Hirashi. I hadn't realized they were a couple.

"Sounds like we have the roots of a plan," Rocks said as he adjusted the straps on his backpack. What did Rocks have in that pack? "Shall we?"

Everyone nodded their readiness. Mort did a last look around and cast his spell. He took Hirashi, Rocks, Lani, and four of his band of warriors with him.

"Do we wait for Grundle?" Harry asked.

"No," Scan and Galad both answered.

I shrugged and started off, leading the way, when Harry asked, "Where's Smith?"

The question made me fumble a step, and I wondered, at the sound of a distant crash, what-exactly-the-hell Scan had done.

Chapter 12

Phillip

"Targeting *Staci*?" I said stupidly. The Infected had converged on her at the battle in Texas. One had popped into her room when she'd awakened. I looked around the small, crowded room like an Infected might step out of the small pink crystals that littered the space.

"I thought those monsters didn't strategize," Rej said. "Mindless beasts attracted to dense populations?"

"Now that I've seen them with Staci," Elliah answered, "I recognize a similarity to another being I've encountered. I talked with Galad about it, and we're not completely sure, but we think we know what those things are, or once were. It begins with a race that became bent upon destroying the elves… the goblins."

Elliah paused, staring through the pink crystals she held into some distant memory.

"Anybody else craving popcorn right now?" Staci asked.

"Popcorn?" I asked, startled by the intrusion into Elliah's dramatic pause. *Goblins?*

Staci explained to an amused Elliah. "We're about to hear the epic backstory, right? So… popcorn."

She had a point.

Elliah nodded toward the door. "First door on the left, there's a kitchenette. You'll find microwaveable popcorn in the cabinet." She started back in on the pile of crystals. "Bring some beer too, please."

"What?" Staci said. "I was kidding. I mean, I wasn't kidding—popcorn would be great, but I assumed… there's really *popcorn*? And *beer*?"

"It's a kitchenette. Smaller than you're used to, and you're from New York, so don't get too excited. But you can bring the whole six-pack. I'll share if someone else buys next time."

"Um, maybe you should stay here," I suggested to Staci. "You know, just in case." *Just in case the Infected show up.* "I'll go."

"Very noble," Elliah said. "Shoo now. Bring beer."

I moved past people to the door. Alex joined me. "I'll go with you," he offered.

"Don't go poking around," Elliah said without turning.

"Why? What will we find?" Alex asked, pausing as he turned the handle for the door latch.

"It's what will find *you*," Elliah answered, chuckling mysteriously. "Oh, I'm just kidding. Look around if you want."

Crazy damned elf.

Alex opened the door, the metal swinging outward with a heavy groan.

The hall, like the room, put me in mind of a submarine. The red-black metal walls and ceiling pinched me in. Six doors stood closed along the short hall, three on each side, with a seventh at the far end, some twenty feet away. A low light came from nowhere—magical.

"Close the door, would you?" Elliah urged politely. "Safety first."

"Why do I feel like we're being set up?" I asked Alex as he closed the door, leaving us trapped in the metal tomb.

"Because we are. You ready?" he asked.

"I suppose," I said, as Alex pulled open the door on the left.

It swung open, silent despite being the same type of heavy metal door as the one behind us, and a light flicked on.

Kitchenette.

Small fridge under a counter; microwave mounted above. Coffee-maker, electrical stovetop, sink, wooden cabinets and drawers. The ten feet of outdated and uncoordinated appliances, woodwork, and tiles would have earned two out of five stars on Yelp. The whole counter sat low—like something from an episode of *Tiny Houses*.

"Well, I'll be," I said, moving in, stunned that a monster hadn't lurked behind the door.

Alex moved past me as I started opening cabinets. He looked in the fridge at the far end of the room. "Beer," he announced, confirming the validity of our mission.

"And here's popcorn," I said, pulling out a bag. I picked the Movie Butter flavor from a small assortment.

"Better do two," Alex said. "Pass 'em this way." Alex had the beer on the counter. I handed him a couple of bags. "See if you can find a bowl."

He ripped the plastic off one and popped it into the microwave. He fumbled with the controls for a short time, but got it going.

"I was expecting a monster behind the door," I confided, as I treasure-hunted through cabinets. "Oh, bowls!" I pulled a stack out, got a good-sized one, and put the rest back. "I guess she lives here? Can you imagine? *Living* down here *alone*?"

We heard a door bang against a wall. We hadn't closed the kitchen door, and the door to the control room remained closed.

"Hey, Leah, did you bring any more toilet paper?" came a gravelly voice, "we're on the last… Aaargh!"

A *creature* had jumped back from the doorway. I'd only caught a glimpse, but it was a creature, not elf, human, troll, or dwarf.

"Mother of friggin' Trees, Leah!" it shouted. "You said you'd warn me!" Then, more softly, "Greetings, humans. Allow me to introduce myself."

It inched into the doorway, first revealing its long, pointed mouth at about the height of my stomach. It held its arms up to show it meant no harm. "I'm Dobby, the house elf," it said. The sharp teeth in its mouth made it look like an alligator with a vampire complex.

What??

"Heh, just kidding. Wonderful book though, right?" I wanted to look at Alex, but I couldn't take my eyes off the thing. Was it trying to put us at ease?

"I'm Matt," it continued. "I'm a goblin." It made a wide-eyed face and said, "I mean you no harm." Then it barked a startling laugh. "I hoped to meet you at my best, not just out of the shower with but a towel as my attire."

"Um," I stammered. "The towel fell when you came in the doorway."

The goblin—*Matt*—looked down, yelped, and jumped out of sight. A hand with sharp two-inch nails reached into the doorway and grabbed the towel, pulling it out of my vision.

I felt It would be okay to look behind me at Alex, that the self-proclaimed goblin would not suddenly attack me. Alex's eyes were wide, but he suppressed a smile.

"It is a pleasure to meet you, Matt. I'm Alex, and this is Phillip. We are here to help Elliah."

"Yes, yes, I know all about you." He reappeared, towel reapplied. "I was hoping you would gain Leah's confidence. I've so wanted to meet some humans."

The microwave dinged.

"Oh, popcorn!" Matt said, closing his eyes and sniffing the air. "Are we watching a movie?"

"Um," I said, still off balance, but recovering. I heard Alex start the second bag of popcorn. "Elliah was going to tell us a story about, well, *goblins*, I believe."

"Oh, good. How about the time goblins dug under the wall of that city, Jericho, and made it all collapse at once? I love that story. Horns blaring. Angelic visits. Splendid stuff."

I poured the first bag of popcorn into the bowl. Matt, the goblin, picked a piece out and popped it in his mouth. Matt... the goblin.

"Is Matt a nickname?" I asked, just trying to keep the ball rolling.

"It's short for Matthew," the goblin answered. "But I prefer Matt."

Ding. Alex retrieved the second bag from the microwave. Matthew... the goblin. No, that was no better.

Matt pulled another piece of popcorn from the bowl. It surprised me that he could use his long nails to pluck a single piece—they looked better suited for rending flesh from bone.

Alex opened the popcorn and handed it to me over Matt, who had worked himself between us. I poured the popcorn in the bowl.

"Trash goes under there," Matt informed me, snagging another buttery kernel. I threw our wrappers away, and turned to find

Matt walking out with the bowl.

Alex followed and I trailed. Matt balanced the bowl on one hand and opened the door to the control room with the other.

"Popcorn's ready," Matt announced as he shuffled in, then paused in the doorway. "Friggin' bark munchers!" he exclaimed, looking back at Alex. "Why didn't you say there were more of you here? Now I just look foolish." I reached past Alex, trying to hand Matt the towel that had snagged on the door of the kitchenette.

Matt took the towel in his free hand, turned and set the bowl on the table, and wrapped the towel back around himself.

"Allow me to introduce myself," the goblin said after taking a calming breath.

When he told his Dobby joke, Staci laughed. Matt turned to me, saying, "*She* got it."

"Matt's the name," he said, turning back to the rest and grabbing a piece of popcorn. "I keep this thing," he waved around the room, "going when Leah is away."

"Going, but not clean," Elliah commented as she continued to file away crystals.

"That's unfair," Matt replied with a pout, "These things all look the same to me, and you know it. I can't see how you're filing them."

"Yes, Matt, I know. I can't help but tease you sometimes." She smiled at him with fondness. "Well, we have our popcorn." Alex set the six-pack on the pile of crystals by the bowl. "And we have beer. It's story time."

"Oh, goody," Matt said. "Which story?"

"I doubt you've heard this one," Elliah began. "It's a story of great sadness for goblinkind—it is the story of the beginning of the end of goblins."

"Oooooooo," Matt responded in fascination.

"Beer, please," Elliah said. Alex popped one out of the plastic holder and handed it to her. She took it and sat in the room's solitary chair. It put her at an awkward height, looking up at those of us standing, but I began to suspect we four humans were not her target audience—she was eye level with the goblin.

Opening her beer, she took a sip and briefly closed her eyes.

"Goblins, like humans, were not natives of AllForest, the elven homeworld. They were one of the races we discovered in our explorations."

"This sounds like the story you tell for the goblin mating ceremony," Matt commented, still plucking single pieces of popcorn. I took a piece from the bowl, and Staci did the same. When in Rome.

"Different story," Elliah said. "You aren't going to like this one."

"I dislike the other too," he replied. "So sad."

"This one is sadder," she said, and to his credit, he just nodded his head and continued consuming popcorn.

"The goblins were natives of a planet that the elves called El'daShar." She locked eyes with Matt. "It was a planet bathed in intense magic, and the elves, who were first welcomed by your people, proceeded to destroy your ecosystem. You see, goblins are cave dwellers by nature…"

Chapter 13

Elliahsaire daShari Fortiza, about 15 Earth millennia in the past

"Goblins are cave dwellers by nature," I told Jeb, who stood no taller than the goblin before him. Jeb stared, transfixed by the fearsome-looking creature. I'd cast a Translation spell so that we could all communicate, but I knew no spell to reduce awkwardness. Still, Jeb had an innate curiosity, and I knew he would not pass up the opportunity to explore past his usual boundaries.

Jeb reached out a finger and poked the goblin. The goblin's own skin, or hide, was a mix of greens, and it wore a darker, leathery hide over its midsection, though its arms and legs remained exposed. Its bulbous eyes of a light brown color blinked once. I feared how close Jeb's hand lingered near that long snout with lots of pointy teeth, but the goblin made no move to use them. It did reach up a hand, imitating Jeb's poke, and I got a good look at its sharp talons—fully capable of sliding through elven flesh.

"Jehokim daShari!" I admonished. "You don't go poking people you've just met!" I placed my hands on my hips while rebuking my son. I knew it to be a suitable form for scolding, but more importantly, it positioned my hands next to my daggers—the one I was ready to draw, and the other that I would never draw, not even to save Jeb.

The goblin halted at my admonition.

"I'm sorry, Mother," Jeb said.

"Don't apologize to me. Apologize to Nogural." I had not determined how to tell the males from the females, so I failed to use a proper title. Nogural would have to do.

"Would I apologize to a *troll*?" Jeb asked, trying to antagonize me. I'd scheduled the outing to address that bad attitude—he had begun to imitate his father's belligerent arrogance.

I frowned—parenting the heart was the hardest part of the job.

Those species that raised multiple children at once... insanity. "Jeb," I said, my voice gentle, "if we've done someone wrong, whether it is a troll or your father, we should apologize." *Okay, maybe not a troll.*

"Or this thing?" he asked.

I closed my eyes in frustration. The problem was one of my own creation—I'd noticed Jeb's poor attitude growing, and had sought an opportunity to show lives harder lived. I thought a little perspective might do him some good. I'd found one of the indigenous creatures of El'daShar, the goblin standing before us, and asked it to bring us into its home.

"Apologize, Jeb," I commanded.

"I am sorry, *thing*," Jeb said.

Gah! All those studies that said pinching their ears was bad for them—five hundred years ago we pinched their ears, and they turned out fine. *Kids today are spoiled!*

Nogural was inscrutable—it simply watched, still as a statue, save for its eyes, which shifted languidly between Jed and me.

We crouched on a grassy knoll near one of the flat stone outcroppings that marked an entrance to a goblin cave. The circular outcropping stood the height of an adult elf above the ground, flat but not smooth across the top, and as wide as fifty to sixty elves with their arms outstretched. I'd examined one of the grey stone outcroppings before—finger-sized holes adorned the top. I'd wondered what purpose they served. Rain collection? Ventilation? Multiple doors adorned the perimeter, stone slabs that pivoted outward. None of them locked, but each had a simple latch and handle to hold the door tightly closed, usable from either side. I'd opened one just to see. The inhabitants had worked out basic mechanics; that had been part of what convinced me they might provide a pleasant distraction for Jeb.

"I apologize for the rudeness of my son," I said to Nogural. "I hope you will still show us your home."

Nogural looked from Jeb to me and nodded, then turned and walked to one of the doors. "Follow me," it said, opening the door and disappearing into the darkness inside.

The door swung smoothly shut behind us, wrapping us in

darkness, and I invoked a spell to illuminate our passage—so easily cast on El'daShar—testing the door to be sure that I could open it from the inside. I started after Nogural, urging Jeb along. He gave me a skeptical twist of the face, and I had to use *the look* to get him moving.

The hall turned to the right, then followed the edge of the circle I'd seen from the surface, or so I pictured it. We veered to the left, circling down gradually, the ceilings tall enough for me to stand, but close enough to make me uncomfortable—some elves would hit their heads. We must have gone a couple hundred paces when the hallway branched.

I split my magelight, keeping one with me, and sending the other down the branch that the goblin didn't take.

"Those are just storage rooms," Nogural explained. "There's nothing particularly interesting to see. But we can look if you'd like. I suspect they're empty right now."

"I'd rather see what we've talked about—your living spaces," I told the goblin. *Him? Her?* The creature nodded and continued down the slope.

I followed, and Jeb, already bored, started creating some multicolored lights and dancing them around. Jeb was a prodigy with magic—at a young age he could do more than he should have been capable of doing. We hadn't observed a specific Talent yet, nor did he have a greater rate of learning than the other children. But the size of the spells he could cast were too big for his age. Instead of a single ball of light, he was twirling three, then five, then… ten? Twelve? Mother of Trees, *I* couldn't come close to that!

Trying not to let Jeb know that he'd impressed me, I continued into the cave. We passed another level of storerooms and then an area the next level down where the ceilings were higher and more side passages appeared.

"These are the oldest houses," Nogural narrated. "They're crude but usable. A hundred years ago, they were full."

A hundred years ago. "You've moved to newer homes?" I asked.

"The acoustics are better below," Nogural answered.

The acoustics?

We passed another level of empty homes, my magelight revealing small, drab caves, but the next level showed a little activity. Nogural had us walk across the flat avenue that plowed straight through the center of the circular area. Some doors were closed, but eyes peered out from the darkness of a few open doorways, reflecting the light of our spells.

The goblins did not shy from the light, though they dwelled in caves that showed no evidence of torches or magelight. At the center of the round cavern was a ten-foot wide circular basin filled with water, a small trickle of water coming from above and filling it. The water must have been running out somewhere, but its exit point wasn't visible to me. A wrinkled goblin sat on the stone basin.

"Nogural," it said in neither a friendly nor unfriendly greeting.

"Himiney," replied Nogural.

The aged goblin rose and inspected me. It looked at Jeb. "This is your child?" it asked.

"I am Elliah," I said. "This is my son, Jeb."

"So you already know the gender!" Himiney said, its lower jaw shifting forward.

Jeb and I looked at each other, his eyes bigger than mine. "Um... yes," I said.

"Very nice, very nice. And you're what, then, the mother or the father?"

"Himiney," Nogural hinted, "they consider it rude to ask their gender."

Himiney's lower jaw jutted out farther, and it blinked rapidly. "That must make mating season interesting. Well, I hope you get to see the nursery." The older goblin tottered off down the passage we had just left.

Just as with Nogural, I had no idea what gender Himiney was. They all looked similar. Long mouth with sharp teeth. Reptilian skin that varied from grey to grey-green. Crazy sharp nails similar to many other species on El'daShar. They wore nothing distinctive that indicated their sex.

"Well, let's carry on," Nogural said. "I took you across this level so that you might have a glimpse of our history, and what we fear." *What they fear?* I wondered if my Translation spell worked properly—I'd seen nothing to fear.

We continued on in the same direction until we hit the far side of the chamber. A curved ramp led deeper. At a guess, we followed the edge of the outcropping at the surface.

We started down the ramp. "Nogural, if I may ask... is it not considered rude to inquire about someone's gender in your society?"

"Indeed not."

So they must struggle to tell even with one another—it isn't just my blindness.

"May I ask..."

"I am a male," Nogural interrupted. "Himiney is a female."

"I see. I am..."

"A female," he said. "I know. I have spent enough time with elves to see how you look slightly different and decorate yourselves differently."

Decorate?

"I still struggle with children, but I heard you say 'son.'"

Jeb looked perturbed.

We spiraled down another collection of increasingly active streets, where we drew more attention. But Nogural continued onward, and the goblin eyes just stared. They seemed rather dull, but they were, after all, cave-dwelling creatures.

A dim light glowed at the next opening in the tunnel, and a hum grew louder as we approached. The path opened up into a high-ceilinged chamber that spanned a distance as vast as the stone outcropping that sat on the surface. A river carved its meandering path through the vast space, snaking its way through with enough force to generate a gentle vibration in the floor. There were small goblins running around, playing games and even splashing in the water.

Adult-sized goblins stood around, talking, sometimes playing with little ones, guarding some of the more dangerous points, like where the water swept back into the rock wall.

Ambient light allowed me to see the far side of the room,

though I could not discern the light's source. A small group of children huddled on the ground nearby, laughing, as some older children put on a show.

"This is the river Klona," Nogural lectured. "It was the first river found in this bore, and we weaved it back in here and there." If I wasn't mistaken, Nogural was more animated, excited about our surroundings. He didn't comment on the light—his eyes darted around, taking in the activity.

"How old are those children over there?" I asked, pointing at the children laughing at the story.

"The ones listening are about three or four years old. The ones telling are about ten." They aged quickly compared to elves. "How old is Jehokim?"

"Jeb is thirty-seven. I would guess that's about the equivalent of your eight-year-olds."

"Moooom!" Jeb protested.

"Maybe seven," I mumbled to myself. But I thought Nogural heard. Was that jutting of their jaw how they smiled?

"I am twenty-three," our guide said. "And the woman you saw upstairs was probably sixty. That's about the end of the climb for us."

Sixty years. That sounded so short—Jeb wouldn't even be fully grown at sixty. How could you accomplish anything in that time?

"May I ask, what is your age, Mistress Elliah?"

"Oh! My apologies. I don't really know anymore. Your years are longer than ours. Maybe ten thousand years."

The goblin twitched like I'd startled him. "I'm sorry, did you say ten thousand *years*?"

"Yes, once we hit maturity, we don't continue to grow older."

"That's... incredible," Nogural said, eyes wide. Then his eyes darted to some children chasing each other gleefully.

"Do you have children, Nogural?" I asked.

He frowned. "No," he said, his eyes still watching the darting movements around him. "Not yet."

His mood had turned somber. He walked us across a bridge over the river and to the exit.

The next level down revealed more homes, and then a level

that grew crops of a fungus, with goblins tending and harvesting the plants. "One of our food sources," Nogural explained, dismissing the effort with disinterest.

We finally entered a section with shops, and it contained a building that begged for attention while suggesting formality—an entrance lined with columns carved with faces of goblins. The walls had geometric patterns tracing them, casting fantastic shadows as Jeb's lights danced among the columns. The goblins stopped to stare, making sounds of interest, and then began tapping their sharp claws against nearby stone walls and columns. Their reaction proved as fascinating to Jeb as the lights seemed to be to the goblins.

"What are they doing?" he whispered.

"It's how we show appreciation for a good performance," Nogural replied.

Jeb smiled.

"What is this building used for?" I asked.

"Shows. It is an old theatre, rather small. But that makes it better suited for some performances. *This* use, your dancing lights, is novel—it will inspire similar performances."

Jeb's interest waned, and I put a hand on his soft, dark hair, letting him know it was time to stop. Jeb waved to the goblins as he calmed his light sources down, letting them be, once again, just lights floating nearby and illuminating his path.

***

"They'd built these massive cities," I summarized for my audience of humans and one goblin, "straight down into the ground. They were... amazing. Cities carved in perfect cylinders for thousands of feet. Homes, shops, theatres—they loved the theatre."

Matt smiled, showing vicious teeth meant for tougher material than popcorn. "You've never told us this story," he said. "Why not?"

"As I've said, it is a tale of great sorrow."

"Hope springs from the ashes of sorrow," the goblin told me, laying a razor-clawed hand gently atop my soft flesh, then nodding at me to continue.

Chapter 14

Hirashi

Mort had brought us into the colony council chamber, outside the chamber proper. The morning sun peeked above the horizon, sending dim light through an open window—a stark contrast to the early night on El'daShar, and a reminder that I'd already been up a full day. I hadn't been on El'daShar long enough for my body to adjust its sleep cycle, but Teleportation-lag would still wear me down as the day proceeded.

I'd calmly caused a mad tizzy of activity with my return.

"Bring the Elders to the council chamber, please," I requested of Allania, "and get Cordoro here as well."

She promptly left to gather students who would, in turn, gather the Elders. I had a little time to wait and think.

I brought Rocks and Mort into the council chamber with me, leaving Mort's warriors in the waiting room. "Be ready for foul play." he cautioned them.

"When aren't we?" a massive, heavily-muscled man replied with a grin.

Mort nodded, but I scolded him. "This is Emerald Farms. You think our farmers will storm the council chamber?"

Mort shrugged. I knew vigilance to be integral to the Forsaken's culture. I'd seen hints of it in his uncle, who had taken his newborn son, Brox, and come to live on Emerald Farms some twenty years prior. And the same vigilance had been carved into Brox, despite his growing up in our more… nurturing… culture.

Once inside, we quickly verified that, as expected, we could not converse with Rocks. The chamber was a dead zone for magic, so the Translation necklace failed. We had anticipated that; Rocks would deliver a message without talking—he set the backpack he'd carted from Earth on the table and leaned against the wall. He winked at me once, then closed his eyes—he looked even more tired than I felt.

The alien devices he unpacked reminded me of his world. A planet so full of people as to leave me dumbfounded, the size of its cities rendering me minuscule. Earth, they'd called it. *We should have called our world Earth, being farmers and all.* Instead we'd called it Emerald Farms—of course that name predated me, so I needn't have felt bad about it. Still...

His world filled me with wonder and terror, all at once. Galad had only taken us to a handful of places, every one of them in an isolated part of a population center—riverfront lowlands too wet for construction, abandoned work yards, man-made parks—but Mort had then whisked us to the buildings visible from those locations. That many people in one city—how did they manage the logistics? How could they feed them all?

My thoughts drifted to the upcoming confrontation. Power-hungry Teleporters were dangerous. Enemies of an ambitious Teleporter disappeared. Cordoro wanted to lead Emerald Farms, like Mort with the Forsaken. What Cordoro failed to understand was that true leadership required sacrifice, and not the sacrifice of others.

Mort hadn't achieved his leadership by knocking out competitors. He'd done it by giving to his people—his time, his energy, risking his life on campaigns. The warrior colony paid for their food and goods by contracting out. Every colony needed fighters on occasion, but the work could be sporadic. Mort, unlike his predecessor, had not been shy about helping colonies with non-fighting tasks. He'd spent a summer at Emerald Farms as a child, with his uncle, and he'd learned to raise crops. I think he learned much of his values that summer.

Cordoro, on the other hand, was a pampered brat. Had been even before his Talent had manifested. He squirmed his way into the world a few years after me, and in a colony of just fifty thousand, we could not avoid one another. As a child in school, he'd refused to get his hands dirty… on a farming colony! His mother had come from Artifairium during the same exchange that brought us the Elder Broxton—not all trees bear fruit. The manifestation of Cordoro's

Talent had validated his right to privilege, at least in his own mind. While almost nobody liked him, the colony needed him, *especially* once the elves disappeared. From his mansion of self-delusion, he failed to notice the signs that the colony struggled—broken equipment not being replaced, food sitting in the granaries because we could not reach buyers. His pantry remained full, his wardrobe new, his land cared for by others. He spent his time eating delicacies and drinking fine wines, trying to bed women from other colonies—no one from Emerald Farms would have him.

Only an Empath could capture a Teleporter who went rogue—hence Cordoro's utter distaste for Galad. That, and Cordoro's xenophobia—he hated anything non-human. Though his cellars didn't lack for elvish wine. Hypocritical moron.

The silver lining? Cordoro was lazy, and not that bright. He had obtained his small fortune by trading with people who had need for his Talent. He had ambitions of power, but lacked the wherewithal to act. Unfortunately, scum floated to the top. Cordoro found people—or they found him—willing to pay handsomely for more power for themselves. And they would best achieve their own ambitions by elevating their Teleporter ally.

Elder Greenly arrived first—he saw me, and his weathered face broke into a friendly grin. He nodded and hobbled past on his cane, bottling his curiosity about the alien devices and the stranger in our midst, moving to his chair, the first seat on the right of the long table. The other six Elders came in one by one, most of them long-awake from pre-dawn work on their land. The exception being Crooney, who was twice as clever as Cordoro, and ten times more dangerous. From the looks of him, he hadn't yet slept. That pretty profligate, though only a few years my elder, had wreaked havoc on our colony with his charm and ambition.

He stopped dead in his tracks when he spotted me. "Has no one told her that her authority has been suspended?" he blurted, not taking his eyes off of me. His lips pinched in what could have been a smile. More quietly, almost sweetly, he continued. "Your authority has been suspended. You cannot summon the council."

God, what a slimy ass. He'd had me suspended in the span of

two days.

"I call the council of Elders," Greenly told the room. What a dear man.

Allania stood at the chamber door, and I gave her a questioning look.

"Cordoro said he would be along shortly," she informed me, a queasy look on her face, like she had swallowed something distasteful. Cordoro had that effect on people.

"Thank you, Allania," I responded. "Please close the doors." She followed my orders, to Crooney's frown.

Crooney turned to Greenly, all indulgent smiles, "To what purpose do you call the council, Elder Greenly?"

"Hadn't you urged us to elect an interim leader?" Greenly responded with civility. "I merely accepted your proposal to do so." *Oh, I could kiss the man.* "But now I find before me Hirashi, free of the mad elf Empath who enslaved her, and I wonder if perhaps we were misled." Not mistaken, *misled*. Nicely done.

"She could be possessed even now," Crooney pointed out.

I rolled my eyes. "We're in the council chamber. Magic doesn't work here. As interested as I am in the fascinating story of my own enslavement, I have more urgent matters."

"You all know," Crooney said, directing his speech to everyone else, "that an Empath can leave a mind brainwashed without leaving it enchanted."

"You can no more prove that my mind is brainwashed than I can prove that your mind is *not* brainwashed by an Empath," I rebutted.

"I haven't run afoul of an Empath!"

"That's exactly what an Empath would program you to say."

I was getting under Crooney's skin. Still, that fight could wait—I would choose my own ground. Crooney moved to the seat at the far end of the table, on the same side as Greenly. The Calynx twins navigated slowly to the two seats farthest from the door on the other side of the table. As the oldest of the Elders, almost eighty, the process took some time.

"We needn't decide which of us is brainwashed just yet," I

said, the twins finally seated. "The information I bring stands on its own legs." That drew every eye to the one-legged man in the room. "This is Rocks Penbrook." To my people, that name suggested working the land, but they knew from looking at him that he was not from our colony.

Rocks noticed the sudden attention and smiled like he had a joke to tell.

"Unfortunately, he doesn't speak our language," I informed them.

"He doesn't speak Human?" Crooney asked, dripping skepticism.

"His world has many different languages," I answered. "None of them ours."

"A delightful tale." This came from Elder Sprouti, a stern woman in her sixties, who sat next to Greenly. I'd positioned myself standing between Greenly's and Sprouti's seats. "First, prove it. Second, so what?"

I loved Elder Sprouti—one could always rely on her to call people out. In fact, I had counted on it.

I nodded to Rocks. He pulled a contraption out of the backpack he'd set on the council table. He had to reach between Crooney and Sprouti to set it down, and he positioned it to point at the wall opposite the doors. Then he connected it to what he called a battery, and a phone.

"You know magic won't work in here," Sprouti said, lecturing me like I might have forgotten.

"I believe I just said as much myself," I answered her, as Rocks switched it on, creating a beam of light leading to an image of The Palace, a building the likes of which no one in the room had ever seen.

Gasps and startled movement filled the room. Two mages, not including myself, occupied the room—Sprouti and Elder Hearth, who sat opposite Greenly. They proved to themselves that they still could not cast magic, that the field preventing it was still intact, and acknowledged this fact to the others in the room. Elder Hearth arose and inspected the device, its wires and connections, without touching. He unabashedly looked at Rocks's artificial leg, and Rocks obliged him by lifting it up and placing the end on the table. While it looked stylistically different from anything we'd seen, that lightweight metal with clean lines could also have been forged by magic—no proof there of other worlds.

Then, Rocks removed his leg from the table and fiddled with his phone—Times Square, he'd called it, at rush hour. The image panned around, relaying the noise of the city—honking, yelling, construction—and finally, it showed Mort and myself. We stood, waving, and in the video, I shouted, "Welcome to Earth! Population...," then a brief pause as I got pushed aside by a large man talking on his phone as he walked by, and I had to get back on camera, "Population eight *billion*!"

He then changed the video to another site. I couldn't remember the name. I didn't appear in that nighttime scene where the lights from the buildings outshined the stars. He next showed the one where the top of the building looked like a boat—Nautica would love that one! I enjoyed watching the pictures and videos, refreshing my memories of those incredible locations.

Finally, he displayed the site of the battle with the Infected. People in uniforms carefully cleaned up the carnage. Mort had ported us in, and while Rocks filmed, Mort summoned a pole arm. Mort walked around in the video, his sword in one hand, severing heads of the Infected, and in the other, he collected their heads on the sharpened end of the pole.

A few of the more observant Elders eyed the blanket draped over something leaning in the back corner. They took note of its particular lumpiness. Mort stood on the opposite side of the table from Rocks and myself. As Mort moved to the blanket-covered object, all eyes followed him. He brought the object back to the table, waiting for the video to end. In the silence, he pulled the blanket free, then lifted the macabre collection high, and set it on the table before Crooney.

"It's a trick," Crooney whispered emphatically. "I don't know how you did it," he said more loudly, gaining confidence, "but it's a trick!"

"It's no trick," I said calmly, gently. "They're from a distant world. The Infected are weaker there. We fought them. We won."

I looked around the room. "But they need help," I told the dumbstruck chamber. "They need the Mana'thiandriel we collected in order to continue fighting."

"Ha!" Crooney barked. "You seek to steal that prize from us." As though we'd had it forever, and not merely a week or two from raiding the elves.

"Our problem is not a lack of magic," I informed them. "Theirs *is*. Would you have them die? Eight billion people?" I knew Crooney's answer—better them than us—but before he spoke, the chamber doors burst open.

Four armed brigands entered, dressed in the attire of the Savage—mercenaries! Two held crossbows, and the other two waved swords. Mort's guards had vanished, though I *did* see Allania lying in a pool of blood, and striding over her prone form came Cordoro.

Well, hell. I'd misjudged—I'd believed Cordoro incapable of outright action, much less betrayal. While alarmed by the immediate danger, my mind also registered the longer term problem—how would my colony survive with one less Teleporter? We would have *none*.

Cordoro stood outside the chamber—giving himself full access to magic while we mages inside remained replete with emptiness. Rocks had pulled out one of those weapons they'd used to fight the Infected, but a smaller, single-hand version. The crossbows were both aimed at Mort. They failed to recognize the threat Rocks posed.

"Put your wand down, fool!" Cordoro barked at Rocks. "You're in a Dead Zone."

"He doesn't understand you," I said calmly. "He's not from the colonies. Don't do anything stupid, Cordoro. Or at least nothing *more* stupid."

"Rubbish," Cordoro barked. Sneering at Rocks, he began to cast a spell. Rocks hadn't missed the interchange, and he turned his weapon toward the caster and fired.

Mort had jumped to the side, which was fortunate, because the crossbowmen had itchy trigger fingers, and the sound of the gunshot had startled them. One bolt missed entirely while the other bit into Mort's arm, but not anywhere that would ultimately matter once we got him out of the room for a Healing.

Rocks turned his gun to the crossbowmen next. It was the wrong move, as those bolts took time to reload—he should have aimed at the swordsmen. I heard two more explosive sounds from the weapon while I moved to intercept the swordsman on my side, my daggers drawn. I hoped Mort was in good enough shape to defend his side of the table.

The swordsman ignored Elder Greenly, instead moving quickly to me, the youngest armed person in the room. But that proved a mistake—Greenly stuck out his cane and tripped up the swordsman, making my job easy, as I drove a dagger into his gut and let his falling weight push it home.

But Greenly's eyes grew wide, and I felt an intense pain in my own midsection. I looked down in surprise to see a sword being pulled back through my body from behind. How had the other swordsman gotten around the table so quickly?

I fell forward, turning to see the fight. *Shit!* I'd forgotten about Crooney. That back-stabbing bastard had been my undoing. Rocks was down alongside me. That left only aged Elders on our side of the table. Crooney had already danced around the still-seated form of Sprouti.

Looking to the other side of the table, I saw Elder Hearth down. Mort had taken out his swordsman, but bled profusely. Mort hobbled toward the doors. *Yes, Mort! Get out, Heal, and go for help. That's the right move. Don't let your pride make you stay and fight!*

But Crooney didn't waste time. He slid across the table, dropping down by the seat that Elder Hearth had fallen from, cutting off Mort's slow escape.

Shit.

I tried to rise, but a sharp pain told me that wasn't going to happen.

In a fair fight, Crooney would lose to Mort. But it wasn't a fair fight. Mort had two crossbow bolts protruding from his torso, one in his chest and the other in his shoulder, and a slice bled on his sword arm. He stood hunched, bleeding, breathing hard, blood running from his mouth, but knowing he had to get out that door.

Looking around with desperation, I spotted Rocks's weapon on the floor. I couldn't get up, but I dragged myself toward it. I looked back and saw that Greenly, aged and wobbly, had flanked Crooney, and held his cane before him like a sword. If it had been just himself, Crooney would have eviscerated Greenly, but Greenly was providing just enough of a distraction to give Mort a better chance.

The other Elders had arisen and were moving around the table to Greenly's side. Good, they wouldn't hamper Mort. I knew my Elders were smart, and I knew they were tough, but their gumption impressed me. Being betrayed by one of their own had inflamed their determination.

I continued to pull myself in some kind of worm crawl toward the weapon.

"Crooney, what do you possibly hope to accomplish now?" Greenly asked. "If you manage to kill us all and get away, what then?"

Yes, keep him busy. Keep him distracted. *Crawl, Hirashi, crawl!*

Crooney remained silent, making a jab at Greenly that caused Greenly to expose his bad leg. Crooney hooked Greenly's bad leg with his own and sent Greenly sprawling into the Elders that had come to help.

Shit.

That left Mort, who looked like he'd rather be leaning on his sword than swinging it. Crooney shifted back to better block the exit, and Mort moved in. He knew time was not his ally.

I had reached Rocks's weapon. I wrapped my hand around it. The mechanism to activate it looked much like the trigger on a crossbow.

But I had Mort between myself and Crooney. I couldn't use the weapon. Unfortunately, I got my chance—Crooney got in under Mort's guard and sliced the muscles in the forearm of his sword hand. Mort lost his sword, then Crooney kicked Mort farther into the room.

But I had my opening, and I pulled the trigger. The force of the hand-sized weapon shocked me, and I dropped it, but it accomplished its job. Crooney lay bleeding on the floor.

"Get Mort out of the Dead Zone!" I shouted to the Elders. "Mort, you have to get help! Get the elf and the Healer!"

The Calyx twins started to drag Mort out, each grabbing a foot, but even together, they still progressed with dreadful sloth.

Elder Greenly hobbled over to me, and held out his staff. "Grab it as best you can," he said, "and I'll drag you out."

"Get Mort out!" I screamed in pain and frustration.

"There's not much I can do to help them, and I sense your Healing will be needed. Mort has lost a lot of blood."

Damn, damn, damn. I reached out and grabbed his walking stick. He pulled, and it hurt like hell. "Wait!" I screamed.

I pulled myself closer, so my arms were not outstretched. "Okay, go," I told him through gritted teeth.

He began pulling, and I moaned.

"No one will think less of you for screaming," Greenly said, never stopping his slow movement, syncopated due to his bad leg.

I obliged. It was probably only a minute or two, but it felt like hours before my connection to magic returned. I let go of the staff.

Mort lay beside me, unconscious.

"What does he need?" I asked, panting.

"This one, I think," said one of the twins, pointing at the bolt in his chest. "It pierced an organ. If you have one shot, make it this one." She shoved the shaft of the bolt deeper, then grabbed the head from out his back and yanked it through. "Do it now."

Oh my. One shot, and I wasn't brilliant at Healing. Blood poured out. I took a breath, put a hand on Mort's chest, and did my best.

My spell activated, and Mort jerked in a cough. Though awake, blood streamed from multiple wounds. "Mort, you have to go! Go get Galad and Scan. El'daShar. Go to the transport square in El'daShar!"

He coughed. I couldn't tell if he heard me. "Mort, you have to…"

Bamf

Chapter 15

Elliahsaire daShari Fortiza, about 15 Earth millennia in the past

From there downward, the city became more... dynamic. Buildings occupied multiple stories, taking up only part of the circular space, stone pathways wrapping the constructs in increasing elegance. The bases of the buildings perched at different heights, clinging to the outer walls like fanciful torches held by artistic sconces. By effect, the buildings appeared to spiral as you gazed downward, becoming more elaborate as the eye descended.

Jeb and I let our magelights fade—more than enough light emanated from the depths below us, revealing the increasing splendor of the architectural marvels the deeper one's eye traveled.

"Whoa..." murmured Jeb.

I understood his sentiment. The stone caverns we'd hiked through had been chiseled, carved from the rock. What lay beneath us had no marks, no scars—rails as smooth as glass. Further down, stone that didn't belong together intertwined in strands that formed beams. Stairs and ramps glistened and sparkled with bespeckled jewels. Buildings curved and swooped, frozen in polite nods to their brethren, decorated with their own variegated textures and colors and shine. Though not the style of elves, it rivaled any elven towers. I knew what that meant. "Nogural," I asked through a gut-plummeting nausea that had nothing to do with the chasm beneath us. "Do your most important goblins live at the bottom of your cities?"

"Yes," he said simply.

Their cavern reflected our elven towers—in our towers, the most important elves, key leaders, lived at the top; theirs at the bottom. I hungered to see the base, the fanciest of the goblin constructs.

We continued down, bathed in stares and chatter from increasingly populated buildings and walkways. Little hands with short talons pointed with excitement in our direction. I towered over even the adults, but I noticed the little goblins egging each other ever closer to Jeb as we descended.

We continued down the walkways, which no longer clung to the outside of the circular bore. They weaved in and out of the center, arcing around buildings, often appearing to be held up by nothing.

"Is this all carved out of the stone that was here originally?" I asked, amazed by how complex that would be. We built up from nothing; they carved out from the same nothing. It would be like sculpting—needing to see the image within the stone.

"Mostly," Nogural answered. "We do have some stone weavers, else we would not be able to repair damage, but stone singers wrought our home from the solid stone of the bore."

Stone singers. They must be like our elves that had natural Talents with the earth.

As we trekked through the increasingly well lit city, the amount of artwork continued to increase. Stone statues of geometric patterns, friezes that told unfamiliar stories—those particularly drew me in, and more than once Jeb had to drag me onward before we lost sight of Nogural. Meanwhile, the children had overcome their fears, and moved on from touching Jeb and running off, to creeping closer to me.

There came a point when I realized I'd grown mentally intoxicated, the sights and sounds having put me in as drug-addled of a state as too much wine. We'd seen bore wurms, domesticated creatures that slithered between bores, providing transport at alarming speeds, crops of fantasy plants and fungi that were alien and bizarre, and an ever-increasing amount of exotic architecture and light. The light confused me most of all, for it lacked any explanation.

At long last, Nogural halted. We had walked a very great distance, and my legs had grown weary. Jeb looked exhausted, but also as lost in the goblin's dream-world as I.

"We're at the end of the tour," Nogural informed us, the lie clear by the obvious paths leading further down. "Below us is off limits."

"The elite don't allow others in?" I asked.

Nogural looked puzzled. "*I* don't want you in. It would be unnecessarily risky."

Tired, I became cranky quickly. "I come all the way down here, and on the threshold of the doorway to your leaders, you stop me? For fear of what, some kind of disease we might carry?"

Nogural looked even more confused. "Leaders? Some day, I suppose. I... I thought you'd understand. You have a son."

"What?" He'd totally lost me.

Nogural stared at me, his jaw sliding back and forth. "I assumed... because you have a child..." He trailed off, looking at me, then Jeb, then down the ramp.

"I asked earlier," I said slowly, my irritation cooled, "if you housed your leaders at the bottom of this bore." Light danced on the walls around the next curve, its brightness somehow penetrating the very stone and creating the ambient light that had continued to increase in intensity as we had descended. I wanted to see what magic their leaders kept hidden at the base of their city.

"You asked if our *most important* people were at the base," he drawled.

"He's right, mother. That's what you asked," Jeb chimed in.

I looked at the light from below, then back at Nogural. If not their leaders...

"Below here is our hatchery," Nogural said. "It is not what it once was, but it is still our most important..."

I waved him to silence, feeling stupid. With a tug at my heart, I pulled Jeb closer. "I understand now," was all I mustered. Hatchery—their young were born from eggs.

"So, *your* towers?" Nogural began.

"Children are born in their homes, and raised in their homes." How could I explain it? "Those homes... they're not in our tower. That tower is a building for running our government. There are no families there, just the leaders. All the families live in other buildings—the children are in homes with their parents.

Nogural looked thoughtful. "How do you decide with whom the

children go?"

How do we decide with whom the children go? What was behind that question? Better get back to basics. "Elves don't have eggs. Well, I suppose we do, but they're inside of us... and stay inside until..." I trailed off. I considered myself quite knowledgeable, but explaining this—particularly with my son right there, even though he knew the basics—stymied me.

"May we talk about this on a later visit?" I asked. "I find myself quite exhausted."

Nogural nodded acceptance. "Of course, though if you're tired now, the climb back out will require some rests."

"Oh!" I said. "I was going to 'Port out. Is that acceptable?"

Nogural looked confused again. "I'm sorry, I don't know what that means."

They lacked the magic to Teleport. I'd thought of goblins as scarcely above animals when the day began, but the structures, elegant carvings, and domesticated transport told a story of a level of sophistication I hadn't realized. At some point my brain had snapped over to thinking of them as something more, and I had forgotten that they knew nothing of wielding magic in the manner of elves. Though I'd seen many hints that they used magic during the day's outing. "You see," I began, and I cast a spell that created some symbols before me in the air. Nogural's eyes got wide, but not frightful. "These show a representation of our location. These," and I pointed at three, "tell me where we are, and these three, where we are going." I cast another spell that pushed the symbols onto the wall, imprinting them there. In seconds they faded, but I had a simple cantrip to draw them forth again when I needed to see them. "With that information, I can go up and back again. Would you care to come with us?"

"I would. Just for the sake of trying it, yes."

"All right, gather close." Jeb and Nogural came closer, Nogural stopping at the same distance he saw Jeb stopping. "Here we go." I cast the spell and...

Bamf

"Whoaaa..." Nogural breathed, echoing our own sentiment

from discoveries in the goblin city.

Jeb tittered, and I shot him a scolding look. But Jeb looked genuinely joyous, not mean-spirited.

"Sir Nogural?" Jeb asked. *Sir?*

Nogural still looked wondrously about him, but steadied his gaze on Jeb.

"Might I return some time to your city? I very much enjoyed seeing it."

Wow! I'd set out to improve his attitude by showing him how privileged a life he led. Instead, we had both been schooled in our own biases. And yet I could not ask for a better end result. A humble curiosity had replaced Jeb's petulant pouting and aristocratic superiority.

"Oh, most certainly," Nogural answered. "Can you go back the way you came out?"

"I can," I told him. "But I have no way to tell you I'm coming. May we return at the same time tomorrow?"

"Yes, that would be acceptable," Nogural responded. "I will be waiting for you at that spot."

I nodded back, and cast my spell that marked the location, placing the marking by the goblin cave entrance. "Shall I 'Port you back?" I queried.

"No," Nogural answered, smiling. "I think I'd like to walk. You've given me much to think on. Thank you though. Until tomorrow then," and he waved and disappeared down into the cave.

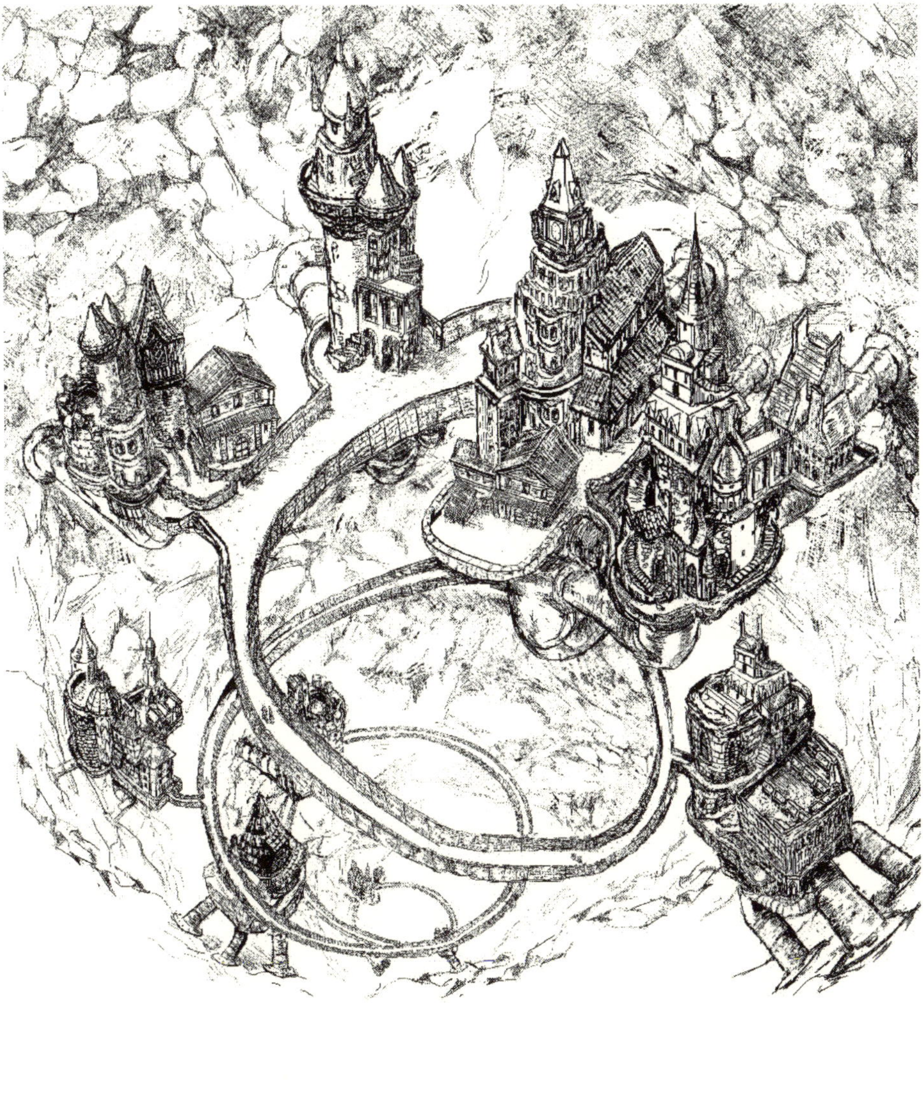

Chapter 16

Scan

We were going to be spending some time in the Vaults, so Galad took the time to work out the 'Ports, choosing a location just outside the Vaults, and a location close to where we had been meeting in the transport hub. With that, he could 'Port back and forth between the two.

I would have liked to practice working on the 'Port myself, but my special skills were needed—I had to open the vaults. Each lock was a little different, and the settings on the master key had to be adjusted.

"The settings are undoubtedly marked in their system somewhere," Galad had commented, "but it would take luck to find where." Fair enough. If it had been computers, I felt good about my chances of finding my way to the information. Elven gem interfaces to a magical net? Not so confident.

Red and Harry, along with Brox, stood guard in case one of those bore wurms came back, and Galad watched over my shoulder, in case there were any traps in the boxes. Once bitten, twice shy.

I started with the big boxes. We found some beautiful but unuseful items—a musical instrument, a collection of large paintings, a statue. The musical instrument looked like a distant relative of a pipe organ. Paintings in exquisite wooden frames filled the second container, illustrating breathtaking forest views. The statue portrayed a female elf carved in wood as solid as stone, where, upon close examination, I discovered plants constituted the elf's details. We found magical items as well in the big boxes—a suit of armor that glowed with a faint light, a boulder with slowly swirling brown and black patterns that Galad warned me not to touch, a sarcophagus that Galad said would make me really, really unhappy if I opened it.

But we did also find another pair of Teleportation rings

amongst the boxes. So, two pairs of rings in total. Galad 'Ported them out of the box, one at a time. It looked like a great strain for him just to move them those twenty feet, so too much for me... possibly one day I would be practiced enough and would store sufficient mana. I assumed moving those Rings would have been easy for Mort.

With the largest boxes emptied, I should have been opening smaller ones, just to see if they held anything useful—more Mana'thiandriel, One Ring to bring them all and in the darkness bind them, maybe some Flubber—but my mind spun on another problem.

Galad returned for the last ring, and I stopped him. "Hold up."

Galad paused, looking like he needed a breather anyway. Harry, Red, and Brox huddled up close enough to hear.

"You said we needed to find the elves, so that we could find this FreeWorld—we hope there are answers *there* about the origin of the Infected."

"That's right," Galad said. "The Infected destroyed FreeWorld when I was just a child. No human would know the way—only an elf, a Teleporter that had been alive back then, would know the way."

"Okay," I said, "I have two questions. One, how was FreeWorld found in the first place?" Surely we could re-discover it. "Second, you said once that people banned these Rings because they believed the Infected were coming through them."

"That's not a question," Red pointed out.

"You're usually more helpful than that," I said. "I don't like what having a boyfriend has done to you."

She twitched when I said *boyfriend*. Ha! Good times.

"Okay," I barreled on, "so question—do we need to find FreeWorld directly, or can we just find a *Ring* that's on another world that connects to FreeWorld?"

That gave Galad pause. "I'm not sure that helps. Most of the attacks happened when I was very young. We locked down quickly on Teleportation across worlds. We would still need someone with a very long lifetime to find any of those worlds."

"Harry," Red interjected, "didn't you say you raided Galad and Grundle's world for treasures, after the Infected had invaded? It's how you got your hammer."

"Aye, that's right," he said. "Dragged a trunk right through a field of them. It isn't for the faint of heart, but it can be done."

Red nodded. "I'm sure there's few as brave as you," she said, keeping a straight face the entire time, "but it's possible others have tried. Perhaps we short-lived races still know some of those worlds?"

"Easy enough to ask Mort," I said.

"The Savage may know more than Mort," Brox commented. *Savage?* "But they won't talk."

"Or my cousin, if you can ever find the time in your busy schedule to get me to DwarkenHazen," Harry added.

"Perhaps after our tea break," Galad commented, then put his hand to his head. "Oh, wait, I don't know how to get there," he finished snarkily.

"Having a girlfriend hasn't done wonders for your personality either," Harry responded.

I held out my hand for a high-five, and he tapped it with his hammer. Good enough.

"What kind of puzzle piece are you hoping to find on FreeWorld anyway?" I asked.

"That's a bit of a long story as well as a long shot," Galad admitted. "Elliah helped put together some pieces for me. Unfortunately, it might be a red herring." *What phrase did Galad use that translated as that?* "The bottom line is that we hope to find some records."

"What kind of records?" I asked. "Like the crystals upstairs? Would those have lasted the fifteen millennia since the first attack?"

"Possibly," Galad answered. "Written documents would be gone. You've heard me mention Elder Stones?"

"Those are the things *you* can make," I said. "Empaths I mean. You brought it up ages ago, but you didn't explain them."

"Okay. In the simplest terms, an Elder Stone is a gem imbued with the mind of a living being."

"A thinking rock?" Red asked. "Like Grundle?"

"Nice one," Galad said. "Thinking rock isn't quite right though. More of a bundle of memories and knowledge that can be called upon. They don't have any sensory input unless connected to a living being, so we don't believe they *think*; rather, they replay what the original owner was thinking. Yes, we had talked about using them as a method to get a message off of Earth."

"And you think we might find some that are helpful on the world that was first attacked?" I asked.

"Like I said," he replied, "a longshot. Even if we find one, only the race that created it can communicate with it, and we might not have the right race amongst us."

"Bessie says you're wrong," Harry piped in.

Galad squinted at him. "What?"

"Bessie says… I dunno—a sympatric?—connection is required. No, that's not right. She says a *mental sympatry*. That mean anything to you?"

Galad stood there with his mouth hanging open. After a few seconds, Red reached out and closed his mouth.

"Are you telling me," Galad said, "that *your hammer* actually talks to you? Has been talking to you *all this time*?"

Harry looked at Galad like the elf had made a poor joke. "What did you think I was doing when she and I were talking?"

"I… I just thought you were rowing your boat with one oar."

"Me too," I said.

"Me three," Red echoed.

Harry looked at us all, shrugged, and walked back to his defensive position at the bore.

"So when can we hear the long story about why you think there might be records on FreeWorld? And how elves got there in the first place?" I asked.

"Once we finish this work?" Galad suggested, shrugging.

"Well, how about the big, strong elf finishes his chores so that we can hear a story?" Red said, tapping his cheek, sliding a finger along his ear, then stepping back toward the bore to stand guard.

Aaaand she's back in the game.

Galad watched her go and… growled? Purred? *What the hell kind of noise was that? Either way, score one for Red.*

Galad got his head back on straight, and I gave him space to

85

'Port. "This really is quite tiring. I might just have to leave you all here a few hours and rest up. Or you could walk back…"

"You make me walk back around that circle," Red replied over her shoulder, "and I will find you and use your boots as my personal vomitorium."

"Vomitorium? Ah, I see." Had he read her mind? He continued in a sing-song voice, "It will but remind me of the first time I tried to kiss you." *First time?* Red chuckled.

Bamf

Seconds later I felt a whisper in my head, and Red jerked like a puppet on a string. She waved the rest over, hurrying to me. "Be ready!" she demanded, all seriousness.

Be ready for what?

Bamf

Galad was back, looking even more drained from lugging that Ring. He wasted no time, but began the spell to 'Port us back. Red had her daggers drawn, and I was armed with my rapier wit and my near endless bullets of movie quotes. Oh, and a handgun.

Bamf

Back in the Transport square, Mort's troops huddled around… *aw, shit.*

I rushed over to Mort, beginning the mental adjustment to use my special vision even before I'd reached him. When I got to him, I sealed off the outer wounds so there would be no more blood loss. A lung had filled with blood, which I wasn't sure how to fix. I repaired the muscles that were cut and torn, but I couldn't see how to empty the lung.

Geez, I'd turned Smith into a freakin' troll. My magic enabled me to grow things, repair damage, but I couldn't empty a lung. *He will drown!*

Oh. The solution struck me—this was going to be dicey.

"Gimme a dagger, Red." She handed one to me. "Now keep those guys back for a minute." I angled Mort's body and plunged the dagger in from behind. I sealed what I could to keep the hole open, and the blood flowed out, joining the mess around us. I kept his lung from collapsing while I encouraged increased blood production as an afterthought—he'd had a lot of blood loss.

I thought a little fluid left in the lungs would be okay—didn't resuscitation for a drowning victim force water out of the lungs? *Sheesh, I should actually read a medical book.* When I guessed enough blood had drained, I fixed the hole I had made, sealing him back up.

Well, that was it, more or less. I gave his body an overall Heal, willing all of the connections that his body already knew how to make to speed up their efforts. His head jerked up, coughing blood away from me.

I looked up to see Mort's men coming out of a hypnotic stasis. Guess Red hadn't had to put on her mean face.

"We have to get back!" Mort sputtered out, between coughs. "They're dying!"

Oh, duh. Of course his wounds hadn't been self-inflicted. *Rocks had been there with Mort!* Even as he coughed out more blood, he 'Ported us away.

Bamf

Chapter 17

Elliahsaire daShari Fortiza, about 15 Earth millennia in the past

"Goblins were much more than I had bargained for. They had tunnels connecting their cities, and they'd domesticated things like your snakes that were large enough to use as transport between their cities. It was truly fantastic to see. Unfortunately, the way they had built their cities, they somehow *collected* the magic from their sun. While that helped the goblins to breed and multiply, it also drew the elves to the same locations. But elves are surface dwellers—originally creatures of the forest—and they built above the goblin bores."

***

Jeb and I traveled to the goblin kingdom many times after our initial visit. Nogural invited us to watch a show—a comedy—and the writing proved so clever, even through magical translations, that we laughed in ways I couldn't remember having done since my childhood. Jeb had laughed himself to tears by the end. Days later we watched a tragedy, and I cried in frustration as a misunderstanding that I didn't quite follow caused a rift between groups of goblins that resulted in both sides dying. Despite not understanding the details, the hurt and pain sufficed to pull me along—it struck too close to home.

I'd known elven storytellers, as well as actors and actresses, but even with all of their decades of practice, they could not compete with the goblins. More elves needed to see the goblin creations.

We also joined Nogural on a bore wurm ride between goblin cities. Goblins attached a harness to the wurm that fit cleverly between the flat teeth of the beast and stretched over its top in thin strips of a hard leathery material, running the length of the wurm and pulling a wheeled wagon behind it. The wurm moved almost noiselessly, but with incredible speed, carrying us to another city as we whooped and cheered. The destination was not as grand as the bore we had left, but unique and interesting in its own ways.

Dhura was the bore we had started from; Ghara, the destination. Where Dhura had crops of fungi and stalky plants that grew in magical light, Ghara farmed flying creatures half the size of the goblins themselves—dusk flyers. I suspected, but didn't want to *know*, that they ate the meat, and that the tough skin became the leather of their clothes and tack. The birds sported sharp talons, the stone-like material characteristic of many of the creatures on El'daShar.

Our visits tapered off because of other duties, but we still showed up at least once a ten-day and spent time with the goblins. Nogural and I learned more about each other: I told him something of how we elves had come to El'daShar, where magic poured down so strongly. He appeared both surprised to learn of my involvement and, I thought, a little sad—my ability to read the emotions of goblins had improved after watching their dramas. *Why sad?*

Nogural built things, created new things—an inventor. He'd excitedly described a new kind of waterwheel he'd crafted, where the water pushed through the inside of the wheel, what I thought of as where the spokes would go, causing an axle attached to the wheel to spin rapidly. It wasn't exactly my cup of tea. Still, he offered to show me, and one day, when I'd needed a distraction, I took him up on the offer.

I'd argued with Jeb's father, and wanted some time away; the fight had taken a nasty turn. Nogural expressed his disappointment that Jeb had not come, and then he'd walked with me in silence, caught up in his own thoughts, just as I dwelled on mine. We weaved up through the city from the location we had established toward the bottom as my Teleportation point. I had been there enough that I no longer attracted the same attention as with my initial visits—goblins went about their day around us. Though I'd become more accustomed to all the climbing, we traveled a long way, heading up to the river I had seen on my first visit, and I eventually had to pause.

Nogural stopped alongside me, and I looked down at the brilliant light from below, wondering again about its source. "What is your wheel to be used for?" I asked.

"Ironically," he answered, "I've been working on a way to move goblins up and down the bore more efficiently. It is absolutely required if we are to keep expanding," he finished excitedly. Then he immediately became somber.

"What's wrong?" I asked him.

He bobbed his head, goblin for "don't want to talk." I pried anyway.

"Sir Nogural," I began. "I can see that something troubles you. Please share it with me."

"It will only cause problems, Mistress Elliah," he responded.

"Call me Elliah. We are friends, are we not?" His eyes grew wide. "And it seems to me the problem is already there. However, we can do nothing about it, as I don't even know what the problem is!"

His mouth worked, no words issuing forth. Then he said, reluctantly, "Nobody will need my inventions, because we are no longer growing."

"What?"

"Our eggs just hatched. Or *should* have—not enough did. Our population is declining." He put his head in his hands and cried. "None of mine, Elliah, not one."

Ahhhh. Goblins prized their children; I'd seen enough of their culture to absorb that. And Nogural wanted to be a father. Jeb's staying behind had worked out—it would have been difficult for a child to understand.

I put a hand on his back, and he startled, but I'd seen in their plays that they touched for comfort. "I am sorry, Nogural. Truly I am. Will there be more opportunities?"

Nogural snuffed. "Yes, we have already prepared the next round of eggs. But the rate of successful fertilization is dropping. The population is declining. Is it even right to bring a child into such a world?"

I thought back to my first visit. The empty housing at the top. What had he said? Oh, yes. "A hundred years ago," I said, "this bore was full and growing." He stiffened. A hundred years ago, the elves had moved from tentatively exploring El'daShar to making it our home. A hundred years ago, we took over.

Sweet Mother of friggin' Trees.

***

"The elves interfered with the goblin magic," I told my audience in the control chamber of the Bubble. "I don't know if it was living above the goblin cities, or magic being depleted by the elves, but in the places where elves built cities, the goblins' birth rates had decreased. Their population had begun to decline. We were killing them—not directly or intentionally, but nevertheless, we were."

I took a swig of my beer. Alex picked up a can and opened it, and Staci tapped him to get one.

"The elves had ignored the goblins. Ignored their plight—ignored *them*," I said.

"Yourself included?" Matt asked.

"Myself included, dear one," I said. "At least for a long time. The magic on the surface of El'daShar was as amazing as the cities you had built underneath. It was intoxicating. We didn't want to notice the harm we had caused."

Chapter 18

Staci

"Okay," Elliah said, standing, "we still have work to do."

"But epic story fun time?" I whined.

"I've been alive a very, very long time," Elliah said, stretching. "You're getting a few hundred years, which is more of a short story. Even so, it's going to take a while."

"The good stories do," Matt agreed.

"Matt, can you check where we're supposed to be next, please?" Elliah asked him.

He nodded and scurried out.

"Can we get the CliffsNotes?" I asked.

"CliffsNotes?" she asked.

"A summary," Alex explained.

"You may not," she answered. "There are important lessons that will be lost."

"Like never stick your hand in a popcorn bowl that a goblin is reaching into?" Phillip said, his hand dripping blood.

"Sort of." Elliah cast a spell and the wound closed up. "Never let something you want cloud your view about who you're hurting."

"Hmmph. Thanks, Yoda," Phillip quipped.

"Most welcome, you are," Elliah responded.

"Shanghai!" Matt called from down the hall.

"Gather up," Elliah said. "Work now. More story later. Everyone… keep an eye on Staci. Until we understand why the Infected targeted her, we must remain vigilant."

I blushed. "Maybe I should stay here."

"And get Matt killed?" Elliah asked. "What did he do to you?"

Blushing more deeply, I said, "I thought this was a safe zone."

"Might be," she said, "but I don't *know* that it is."

Was her gaze lingering on me?

There really wasn't anywhere to gather. The room was not large. So we all just inched a little closer.

She cast her spell and took us to work. Presumably Shanghai, but it could have been anywhere—we'd arrived in an open field. *That had to be hard to find near Shanghai, right?* Elliah set up the canned magic and activated it, drawing the Infected. The ensuing fight still scared me, but the Infected didn't single me out. It was a normal fight, like the videos we'd seen of Ms. Hernandez—Red—with just a few handfuls of Infected. Still hard, but not end-of-the-world crazy, like El Paso had been.

When we finished, she took us to the Palace. Exhausted, we rode the elevator up to our dorm floor, but oddly, Elliah rode along with us. We didn't chat, didn't banter, unable to relax with her there.

When we split for our rooms, Elliah followed me.

Stopping, I looked at her.

"We need to talk," she said.

In my room? Eep.

"And," she said, "you shouldn't be alone."

Sighing, all I could think was that I didn't want her to see my paintings. What a stupid reason to keep someone away, when my life was in danger from teleporting monsters. I nodded my head and continued to my room.

She followed me in and, as soon as I turned on my lights, her eyes lingered on the area with items covered in blankets. My paintings. The edges of the canvases peeked out in places, enticing attention.

"Would you like some coffee or tea? Some cheese?" I wasn't much of a hostess. The number of times I'd entertained in my home, I could count without using *any* fingers.

"Beer?" she asked.

"I have wine. Pinot Noir or Chardonnay?"

"Pinot, please." She'd scanned the rest of the room, but her eyes drifted back to the covered paintings.

"Phillip has grown on me," Elliah said from nowhere, and I splashed some Pinot onto the countertop.

Grabbing a napkin and swabbing it up, I tried to ask

innocently, "Oh?"

I rounded the counter that separated the mini-kitchen from the living area, handed her a glass, and took a drink of my own—I needed to calm my nerves.

She smiled wryly. "Cowardly at first. But, in combat, he grew a pair."

"Pfffffffft!" Wine spewed over the counter, out of my mouth and nose. *Ouch! Wine burns the ol' nostrils!*

Wiping my nose, and the counter for a second time, I looked up to see her laughing lightly, her glass already empty and standing before me for a refill.

I poured again, more generously, as she continued on. "People learn a lot about themselves in a fight," she postulated. "Or when being hunted. Most of all, when they choose to stop being hunted."

I raised my eyebrows and waited for her to explain.
She didn't.

"Anyway," she said, "I like the man Phillip has become."

"Do you... " I began, and stumbled to a halt. I looked down at my wine, suddenly nervous about my words. When I raised my eyes, she nodded her head for me to go on. I took a drink and barged ahead, "Do you sleep with humans?"

"Human *men*, you mean?" she asked, which left me feeling like the conversation might be heading somewhere entirely different than I'd expected.

"Guh," I said, taking another drink.

She laughed again. "Yes, I have slept with human men. I'd guess my age right now to look approximately mid- to late thirties for a human. Correct?"

I nodded my head. That looked about right.

"Young thirties would be about the age I've been most of my life. On this world, I aged, and my sex drive dropped, eventually to zero... but I looked like a mummy at that point anyway, so you would have needed to find someone pretty odd if he, or she, wanted sex with me." She looked up in thought. "Maybe a necrophiliac."

I choked again—tough night on the wine... and the counters.

"But now that I'm young again, I'm feeling… interested. More interested than I remember being in a long time, in fact."

"And Phillip is your Person of Interest?" My stomach fluttered at the thought of Elliah pursuing Phillip. *Wait, why do I care if she's interested in Phillip?*

"Oh, heavens no!" The sense of relief that flooded me was my wake-up call. *I have a thing for Phillip. Wait, what's wrong with him that she doesn't want him?*

"I find, after all this time, that I want an elf!" She said it decisively, smacking her empty glass on the counter and pushing it my way. Okay, Phillip could never be that. Poor Red. I hoped she found the elves soon.

I refilled our glasses, emptying the bottle. The wine had disappeared quickly.

"I've never painted," she said, taking the conversation in a new direction, with no signal whatsoever. *Blinkers, woman!*

"I mean, I've been alive forever, so I *have* painted. But I've never tried to become good at it. I do appreciate it though. I used to have a picture, someone's idea of the Mother of Trees, something of a legend for elves. It looked nothing like her, but I appreciated its workmanship and beauty. May I see yours?"

She had already risen and begun walking to my paintings.

"Well…" I said, then realized my mistake too late. She wasn't waiting for an answer.

"Wait!" I said, setting my glass down and rushing over. But she didn't. She'd pulled off the sheet off of the nearest set. The one at the front of the dominoes of canvases was my painting from right after we had Teleported Galad and friends to the other world.

"Wow!" she said. "That's remarkable. You've captured the Elements in paint!" She turned her head to one side, then the other way, then back. "It's strange to think how few people on Earth would know what that was, but how many off-worlders would recognize it. But it is pretty. Even a Muggle would see that."

She waved around the room. "Are all of these from after you became a mage?" she asked.

I shook my head no. I still couldn't speak. She was poking

around in my Sanctus Sanctorum, my Fortress of Solitude. She had crossed the forbidden zone. And, yet... nothing bad had happened.

"Which ones are older?" she asked, and I waved my hand. Every other group of paintings pre-dated my transformation into a mage.

I wandered back to the kitchen, retrieving my glass. Opening another bottle, I poured generously. Why had I kept my secret for so long? She would be furious.

"Wait, you're telling me you painted these *before* you were in the explosion?" The alarm in her voice frightened me.

I nodded my head yes. She couldn't see me, but speech eluded me. I heard her fumble with the pictures, then stalk back in behind me.

"Even *this* one?" she asked, her voice still loud and squeaky-high with emotion.

I looked and nodded my head. It was a picture of a dark humanoid form, skin like night, taloned hands and feet, eyeless, mouthless, with two holes where the nose should have been.

She'd find more when she looked through all the paintings. She'd see I'd been painting Infected since my childhood. I knew I had some explaining to do... but I had no explanation.

Chapter 19

Hirashi

We all did what we could to help. I'd sent Sprouti to fetch others. She was younger than the twins and walked without a cane, but she wasn't fast.

I'd asked the twins to pull Cordoro into the Dead Zone. They busied themselves tying his hands and feet with sections they sliced out of his robes. Greenly was doing his best to pull Elder Hearth *out* of the Dead Zone, for when Mort came back with the Healer. *If* Mort came back with the Healer.

Mort would come back. *Please let him have gone to the right place.* It struck me that Mort had Healers back on his planet. Either of those destinations should have been okay. Just please let him have gotten somewhere he would be Healed. If the only 'Porter we had left was Cordoro... I shuddered at the thought.

Sprouti would have headed to the school, one of the few occupied buildings that lined the courtyard. Before the elves had disappeared, the open area outside the council hall would have been bustling with merchants, but Sprouti would find only the green lawn before reaching the school. I didn't want any children to see the carnage of our council chamber, but one of the teachers could Heal. Allania's wounds looked bad, but she lived. If a Healer reached her in time, she would make it. I pulled myself nearer to her.

"Cut that out!" one of the Calyx twins barked at me, as they finished tying up Cordoro. "You're in no state to be crawling around, opening your wounds further."

I ignored the admonition and finished my short but slow journey, to the tsk'ing of the twins. I did my best to stanch her bleeding, wondering what had happened to Mort's men. Cordoro must have 'Ported them away somewhere. Why hadn't he done the same with Allania? I attempted to reach for my magic to Heal her, but none came forth.

Crooney I left alone—if he bled out, the world would be better for it. *Harsh, Hirashi,* I chided myself. But not worth crawling to, even if I could manage it.

Time to take the twins' advice and lay still. Turning my head toward the council chamber, I asked, "What happened to Rocks? The visitor I brought from the far-off world?"

The twins shuffled over to the body of the man from Earth, and Greenly hobbled his way there. Once they'd moved, I saw the four attackers that had fallen—clearly from Savage. They wore colorful hides, sloppily sewn together. Bone and gruesome jewelry decorated necks and piercings, and they'd filed their front teeth to points.

"Just a bump on the head," one twin called. *Guess the twins won the snail race.* I giggled slightly at the thought. Bad sign. The world grew dark around the edges.

A sudden and familiar noise startled me, pushing back the darkness. But I couldn't think why the noise was important.

"Not that one," I heard Mort say, coughing. *Mort!*

Mort had returned. I could hold on a little bit longer. Well, possibly.

All at once, I felt better. Not great, but better. I opened my eyes to find the elf crouching over me. Galad. "Be still. Wait for the Healer." He'd done minor Healing only while triaging. Smart.

I got up on my elbow to see more, but otherwise remained still. The one they called Red had taken over from the Elders and pulled Rocks out of the council chamber. Broxus crouched over Lani; the dwarf, Harry, used his hammer to do minor Healing as well.

The Healer, Scan, worked to stabilize everyone that needed to be breathing. Mort skewered Crooney on the swine's own sword, while the couple of Forsaken he'd 'Ported in examined the bodies of the Savage. And I thought *I* was harsh. Yet, I couldn't muster any sympathy.

"Does Cordoro live?" I asked the twins. They'd tied him up in the council chamber and left him there, where he could not use his magic to get away. But no one could Heal him in there either.

"He lives," one of them answered. I pinched my eyes shut for a moment. A part of me wished they had decided what to do with Cordoro, relieving me of that burden.

"Drag him out, please," I said with regret. "Galad, I need you to keep him from 'Porting."

"On it," Galad answered, and moved from helping Scan with minor Heals to pulling Cordoro out of the room. His action embodied trust—I'd explained the Dead Zone to him, before I'd left El'daShar, as a place where his magic would not work, and he'd walked in anyway.

A group of older students came racing in just in time to see Scan working on Allania. Not all of them had seen a life-saving Heal before, and they paused in astonishment. Others had, including Bloom, the Healer who also acted as a teacher, and their eyes leaped to the remaining occupants of the room—to me and others still wounded. I imagined the scene from their eyes: Crooney lying dead, his own sword protruding from his chest; an elf pulling the tied-up form of Cordoro out of the Dead Zone; Forsaken looking for something to kill while Savage littered the floor in the council chamber. It would have been a lot for a teenager to take in.

I changed my mind—the children needed a glimpse of the harsh realities of life, but I wanted them ignorant of what would happen next. "Students, out! Go get more Healers." Though, in truth, Bloom and Scan would be enough.

"Ewin is already running for a Healer," one of them informed me. They continued to protest, wanting to help.

"Mort," I said. "Can you have your men go with the students? We need some privacy."

Mort nodded to his men, who left without question. Broxus followed after them, dragging the students along like magnets. I trusted Broxus enough to have him stay, but I couldn't think of a way to keep him without insulting Mort's men. Allania rose shakily to join them, Healed, but her tunic still dark red with her own blood. "You, stay," I told her. "We need to hear your story." She nodded, tired but willing. She closed the door to the building, Mort's men standing ready outside.

Scan kneeled beside me. "Take care of the others first," I told him.

"No," he replied. "We've triaged. You're next."

So much for my authority. But I would be glad for a Healing. Whatever Galad had done was superficial, stitching up my skin without fixing anything in my gut. I could tell by my distended stomach. Oh, and the massive pain was another clue.

He put his hands on my belly, and seconds later, the pain eased. He started to speak and I interrupted, "I know the routine. Expect blood in my bowels and urine for a few days—Healing doesn't clear it out."

"Hmm, not your first time to be stabbed then," Scan replied. "And, sadly, I'm learning from you—I've only been a Healer for a couple of months now. I bet there *is* a way to clear that blood out; I just haven't figured it out yet. Besides, what I was going to say was 'cool tattoo.'"

I looked down at the tattoo normally covered by my clothing—magical ink just under my left breast, creating a stalk that pushed up out of the ground and grew to produce a pale flower that contrasted nicely with my dark skin. Not proper in Emerald Farms, to be sure. The flower had meaning to me—simply called The Royal, it had the unique magical ability of making plant-eating animals and devouring insects uncomfortable, keeping them away. They produced beautiful natural sanctuaries for other flowers, but they also always grew in isolation—one stalk, one flower, protecting others for their brief time.

I shot Scan a malevolent glare, but truthfully, his quick wit on El'daShar had impressed me, and his quirky sense of humor meshed well with mine. So I glared, but I didn't rush to pull my shirt back over the skin, and he didn't pull his hands away from my stomach, though he'd finished the job.

Well then.

I filed that away for later and rolled onto my side to push myself up, forcing Scan away. I looked around the room and it looked like everyone was up that we wanted up. Red talked with Rocks, who gathered his Earthly devices. Bloom still busied herself checking on people. No more major Healings needed, except for

Cordoro.

"Can you Heal him and keep him under control so he doesn't 'Port?" I asked Galad regarding Cordoro.

Nodding, Galad cast the Heal. The weapon from Earth had torn a hole in Cordoro's shoulder, but the amount of blood loss paled in comparison to Allania's wound. I wasn't entirely sure why he'd even passed out—probably from seeing his own blood.

Cordoro jerked up, sputtered, and froze like he watched a beautiful sunset, or whatever was the equivalent for Cordoro... a woman who actually showed interest in him?

"First thing—what did he do with Mort's men?" I asked Galad.

"They're in a forest," Galad answered. *Aw, hell.* He'd dumped them out in hostile territory—he'd left them to the forest. "I... I can't make any sense of it. Can I loop someone in that knows the area?"

"Do it," I said. And, again, *aw, hell*, because despite my bravado, I disliked the idea of someone messing around in my brain.

"Include me, too," Mort said, "I need to get them."

Aren't we all just a big bundle of trust today?

I sat down as the world faded around me.

***

I stabbed that heartless tease twice in the back, drawing the four warriors to come at me—just as I'd predicted they'd stupidly do. Old Man Broxton had kept the secret of Teleporting distant objects to himself, the selfish bastard. He'd kept so much from me... taken my birthright by keeping secrets, taken my future, and even his son had taken from me. I had to draw those warriors in close to Teleport them—stabbing the woman who'd chosen Brox over me was a bonus.

I 'Ported them with me to my secret place in the forest, where a rocky crag kept the trees at bay. Then I Blinked away, and the four angry warriors swung their swords uselessly into thin air.

I gave them time to realize their mistake and look me in the eyes, before I left them there to die.

The world faded again.

***

I stood on the crag, the four warriors in front of me, frozen in time.

Galad and Mort stood at my sides. My first thought? How would I ever work with such a horrible man, no matter how much we needed his Talent?

Then I focused on why we were there. Mort and Galad looked about, but nothing else moved. Far beyond the time-locked warriors, the colony wall jutted above the treeline. But which wall? I tried to move closer to the warriors to get a better look, but it didn't work.

"You can't see anything beyond what Cordoro could see," Galad explained. I looked behind me—beige nothingness filled the tableau.

"However," Galad said, thinking, "he's been here before. His mind will connect up pieces for us." He closed his eyes, and the beige nothingness behind him filled out with sketchy, translucent images. Some trees were bare as in the throes of winter, while others sprouted the new leaves of spring. Beyond and above the trees towered a hazy and shifting range of mountains.

Mountains. The south wall. And, as I thought of the mountains, they solidified. I tried to create a mental map as though looking down from above, placing the wall and mountains, guessing at where the rocky craig must lie.

"Good enough," Mort said. "Take us out."

The world around me faded.

***

I opened my eyes.

"To find my men," Mort said, "I need to establish line of sight." As he explained, he headed for the door by foot.

"I'll go," Red chimed in.

"Me too," Harry added, but he pointed his hammer at Galad as he followed Mort to the door. "Don't you let him die before you get the 'Port to DwarkenHazen out of him."

Scan looked around and then joined them as well. "They may need me, and it looks like you're in good shape," he said as he left.

I pointed at Allania to get her attention and waved my finger for her to stay. When Mort and the others had filed out, she paused at the door while she waited for Sprouti, who had lagged far behind the much younger children on the return trip, then she closed the

door with an ominous click of metal sliding home.
We still had Cordoro to deal with.

Chapter 20

Elliahsaire daShari Fortiza, about 15 Earth millennia in the past

"You believe the elves prevent your eggs from hatching." I wasn't asking a question; I had puzzled it out. I spoke it only to make it more tangible. But it was impossible... unthinkable—we hadn't blocked their cities. We had merely created our cities near the bores, because the magic seemed to... pool... there. *Oh.*

We used *their* magic. We took magic from their unborn children and consumed it to weave our spells. Even as the thought came forth, I fought it. It was ridiculous. We hadn't *stolen* anything. We hadn't *harmed* anyone. We were *elves!*

But... magic didn't *pool*. I knew the puzzle pieces fit; I just didn't want to believe the picture it formed. After all, I had been involved in finding El'daShar. It had been my effort, my drive, though I lacked the Talent to get us there. Ultimately, any harm done to the indigenous species of El'daShar rested at *my* feet.

"We have to talk to Slooti," I whispered.

"We've tried," Nogural whispered back. "He won't listen. He doesn't want to hear. Perhaps your next leader will."

That Slooti would ignore the goblins came as no surprise. He'd self-importantly created an entire set of laws about the governance of hereditary belongings. He'd done it just to get his hands on a damn rock of which some distant relative had possession. It would take decades to undo the damage done to elven law. I had overheard a proposal for construction of a hideous structure that he was naming The House of Contested Gifts. Idiot.

Still...

"Elves don't age," I reminded him. "If you're hoping that you can wait out his reign..."

Wait. He knew elves didn't age. Yet there was something in Nogural's statement that hinted at a new beginning. "Nogural?"

"I do not think you will see me as a friend after today, Mistress Elliah, though I do wish it could be so." He looked very sad.

"Nogural," I began, my body tensing, "what have you done?"

"I? All I've done is fail to stop the Tribunal," he said, his eyes conveying a chasm of sadness. "I did try, but I failed. I made things worse, in fact. They used the information from my arguments to formulate an attack."

My heart raced, blood already strumming through my veins from the realization that elves sucked the magic from unborn goblins. "Nogural! What attack?"

The floor shook beneath me, then stilled.

"It is done," Nogural whispered.

My chest tightened and I shot Nogural a look overflowing with fear, but I wasted no time asking more questions. I cast my return spell and *bamf*, I 'Ported back to the surface.

I spun, scanning the horizon, and spotted a cloud of smoke. *Oh, Mother of Trees. Please, no. Not today. Not today of all days.* I cast my spell to return to the Tower, but it failed. Of course it failed. I saw with my own eyes... the Tower was gone.

We were once creatures of the forest, and I ran with the abandon of my youth, tearing through sections of untamed ground. Later, it would occur to me I could have used Blink to speed up my journey, but it wouldn't have mattered.

The cloud of dust grew closer, and I broke through a final copse of trees into a clearing, to find a group of elves already at work clearing the rubble, a magical wind keeping the dust at bay. One elf worked more madly than any other, using shields to lift large chunks of broken rock that had once composed elegant archways, and pitching them away.

"Slooti!" I yelled. He couldn't hear me. I magnified my voice with a spell. "Slooti!" I bellowed again.

He turned to me with madness in his eyes. I already knew the answer, but feeling the gnawing emptiness already growing within me, I cried out, "Where is our son?"

***

"The goblins fought back." The weight of those words, spoken thousands of years out of context, still tore me apart. Thousands of years had made it digestible, but only through shared pain and hardship. "Fighting was very hard for them—few goblins actually wielded magic, and nothing like an elf could do, but goblins had numbers, and they could dig tunnels like you wouldn't believe. In a direct battle, elves would have massacred the goblins. So the goblins chose a different gambit. One fateful day, the goblins, in a bold move, took out an elven tower. It was cleverly done," I told Matt, able to admit the truth and encourage one of my surrogate children, even over the loss of my own flesh and blood. "Tiers of tunnels so that, when they triggered the collapse, the entire tower dropped ten feet, then collapsed in on itself."

I paused, my memory of the rubble clear, even millennia after the fact. A fleeting thought dashed across my mind of the unfairness of what I'd forgotten, and what I had not. "There were many deaths," I breathed out.

I took another abeyance and drank. Beer planted me firmly in my skin, a beverage unique to Earth. It didn't hold a candle to elven wine, but it didn't care either.

"The goblins had attempted to kill our leader. Had the elven deaths been constrained to those normally in the Tower, there might have been a lesser reprisal. The goblins might have stood a chance." Fifteen thousand years, and I still wondered what I could have done differently. If Slooti and I hadn't argued about Jeb spending too much time with the goblins, Jeb would have been with me. If I'd fought harder and taken Jeb despite Slooti's protests, Jeb would have been with me. I'd spun countless scenarios that ended so differently. But I'd let his father take him to work that day.

"But that day, we lost the treasured son of the High Lord Slooti Falinus Halabrinner, and the fate of the goblins was sealed."

Chapter 21

Venki

When I'd needed to blend into the crowded streets of New York City, pulling on my hoodie had allowed me to hide in plain sight. Given my newfound abilities, I stayed off the radar with comparative ease. Or rather, getting the hell *off* the radar if and when I stumbled onto it—fairly easy. In a suburban neighborhood in Texas, wearing the same hoodie made me stick out like a sore thumb. But so did not wearing the hoodie.

I'd awoken a few weeks prior in New Jersey. Specifically, in an abandoned building that took me some time to recognize. I'd eventually realized it to be the Gingerbread House, a place my friends and I had dared each other to enter as kids—historically part of an amusement park, but abandoned sometime in the seventies.

I retained a fuzzy memory of having been in a dangerous situation with my own government. All of my memories since the night of the explosion in the Palace jumbled and fragmented and left me confused. I had bits of memories involving Yelton and fleeing The Palace, but flashes of memory, which I could not quite reassemble, told me he was dead.

On my first visit to the decrepit amusement park as an adult, I awoke in daylight, thankful that I didn't have to piece together my location in the dark. Also thankful because I knew the place to be pretty creepy at night. I had looked out a window to confirm my location, and my ill luck re-emerged—someone in uniform spotted me, yelled officiously, then picked up a radio and barked into it. Police. What were the chances? Well, I'd gotten into the building somehow—someone had seen or heard something and reported it.

I ducked back out of sight. *Great.* Why did I wear a hospital gown? Why was I in an abandoned park? I had a gut-wrenching belief that being caught by any kind of authority would adversely influence my lifespan. When had I become the bad guy?

I looked out the window, my angle keeping me out of sight of those below. Across the way sat an abandoned factory, and beyond that lay some woods. Nothing had changed significantly since my childhood.

I looked longingly at the woods across the way, knowing the spot where I wanted to be like the back of my hand. I felt it calling to me, drawing me. I let it.

Bamf

The cop with the radio still watched the house. But I stood behind him, at the edge of the woods, baffled but... also not. Taking a last look around, I disappeared into the woods before someone spotted me.

I found, over the day, that the thing I could do—move between two spaces within visual range—became easy. I couldn't do it frequently—like a battery, I needed a recharge. But once I had the energy, it became as simple as walking the same distance.

Because I'd awakened in the Gingerbread House, I suspected I had the ability to do the same with locations I couldn't see. But I didn't know the trick to it.

As a former FBI agent, some things I had to do to get going again disturbed me. I needed clothes and money, in that order. Getting them hadn't been hard. Given that I could see into shop windows, even after the shop had closed, I had access to what I needed. The first move had been the hardest—I raided a Salvation Army for clothes. Then I went on a burglary spree as I moved toward Manhattan.

I had a few hundred dollars in cash by the time I reached NYC. I hadn't taken so much from any one place that it set off a manhunt. But even with money, I didn't have much of a plan.

I'd caught up on news in small towns, watching TV at sports bars. The world had changed. That fateful night that the Tower had come down had begun a new era. Aliens walked among us—not many, but a damn sight more than zero—and more importantly, they used magic.

So that's what I was doing. I used magic, and the explosion

had somehow triggered it. At least that was my operating theory. Disjointed memories troubled me—hadn't I seen others in the building as Yelton and I fled? Yelton had died, I felt pretty sure. Had I really seen others? Had they survived?

So what was my role in the new world? I wasn't going back to the FBI. My heart sank a bit at that—it was all I'd wanted to do for so long. I felt so utterly betrayed by a group I would have called my family.

The new organization, the Guardian League, was my logical next step. I wasn't by nature a rogue ready to live my life in isolation. I'd been heading to Manhattan anyway, drawn like a bee to honey.

But when I arrived, I'd had no idea what to do. I couldn't just walk in and identify myself. Neither did I think it wise to magic myself past security and casually wander—cameras would betray me.

I wanted to talk with one of the humans that had been in the videos. The big guy had died, transformed by those attacking aliens, then cut down by his own friend—horrible. That left the woman.

I walked into the Apple store and pretended to be interested in laptops while I did a little web research. A bio of Ms. Hernandez appeared easily enough, and I quickly decided my path. I couldn't fly—they would ID me—and I didn't know how to magic myself all the way to Texas. The most low-key way to travel that far was a two-day bus ride.

In the quiet of the bus, I'd been able to make some plans, but I hadn't been able to truly relax. The first attempt to simply ride hadn't gone well at all. I'd nodded off and had nightmares of being torn apart by doctors in a lab. I'd woken with a start... back in the damned Gingerbread House. My backpack stayed on the bus, but my clothes came along—I learned the hard way I'd have to be more careful to hold on to my possessions as I nodded off.

My go-to place when scared shitless turned out to be the very place that had frightened me most in my childhood. Realistically, I appreciated knowing that I could Teleport long distances, though I wished to control it.

Regardless, I'd had to try again, collecting more money along a different route, boarding from a different start point. I feared using drugs to stay awake for 48 hours, so I instead focused on remaining calm. After all, so what if I ended up back in the Gingerbread House again—just a setback.

A setback I avoided on the second try—I completed the bus ride! *Strange thing to be proud of, completing a bus ride.* Still, small victories. From there, I took city buses to get close to the right neighborhood, then made my way on foot. There were woods with hike and bike trails running through that part of Austin, and I used that to my advantage.

But I couldn't wear the hoodie without drawing attention, and I didn't want to show my face. If it would just cool off, it would look natural, but October in Texas withheld the promise of cold weather. So I was close, but bode my time and waited for an opportunity.

Chapter 22

Elliahsaire daShari Fortiza, about 15 Earth millennia in the past

I'd lost offspring before. I'd lived *thousands* of years, and I'd had many children over the ages. They'd died mostly as grown men and women, and it hurt less, knowing they'd truly lived for some time. I'd lost two as children. That had hurt more. Times had been tougher then—we expected to lose young children. Somehow that kept you moving forward.

The hollowness was agonizingly familiar. Experience taught me it would pass, someday far down the road. There would be a day when I would wake and smile at the sunlight. But the emptiness would be my companion for many years.

I did nothing. I hid away in a room and allowed time to swallow my days. I basked in my grief—the antithesis of warming myself in the sun. Some visitors came and went, passing on their condolences. I should have done more, been more to the people I had led to that world, but I could not find my way out of the pit of despair.

My return to reality arrived with an unexpected visitor. "High Lady Elliah, there is a Gavrial Norrengate here to see you," announced my lady-in-waiting. Gavrial Norrengate? The name rattled in my head, but produced nothing.

"He is in the service of the High Lord," she explained upon seeing my confusion. Someone who served Slooti, whose name I did not recognize, who had no title, and who wanted to speak to me.

"I will see him," I said, curious despite myself.

She led in an elf—a blond-haired stranger, looking unsure but resigned. He approached me as I sat, my assistant closing the door for our privacy.

"My Lady Elliahsaire," he said in somber greeting.

I stared at him, not helping. He fumbled with his clothing and fidgeted. It told me he was young—always hard to know from a face. And that he had struggled to drag himself in front of me.

"My Lady Elliahsaire," he began again. "I came here to apologize."

Not condolences? An apology? I still said nothing. I couldn't muster the energy. Though I felt a touch of curiosity.

"I…" he began.

I remained silent.

"I was the Teleporter tasked with saving High Lord Slooti."

My stomach knotted. He had gotten Slooti out. Not Jeb. Not my Jeb. A fire burned just under my skin.

"I am so sorry," he continued. "I… I should have saved your son. It isn't…"

"It wasn't the job you were tasked with, or trained for," I said, trying to justify his decision to myself.

"Even so, it was the wrong choice. I… I am so sorry." He looked me in the eyes, no longer fidgeting. "I pledge that I will forever be in your service."

That was a big pledge. Elves could live a long time. Still, he had not made the pledge lightly. But he was young—he didn't know. Nothing lasted forever.

"I thank you," I told him, the heat under my skin not abating. I felt trapped by the conversation—trapped in the room—trapped with my thoughts. I needed to get out. "I won't be taking that pledge. You were doing your job. Jeb… he wasn't supposed to be there."

He stood silently a moment. "Nevertheless, I pledge my services to you. I just wish there were more goblins to destroy for you."

Yes, I burned with anger! I wanted to…

"Wait. What was that?" I croaked out.

"I wish there were more goblins to destroy, but I've just dropped the High Lord and his Fire Masters at the last nest of those monsters. There will be no more to kill after today…"

He trailed off as I shot up. "What!?"

"He's burning their homes," Gavial hesitantly proclaimed, uncertain as to my mood or sanity. "The fact that they build straight down makes it simple for our Fire Masters to incinerate..."

He trailed off at the look on my face.

"Where are they? Where are they *now*? Ghara? Dhura? Where?!"

Gavrial stood frozen, bafflement and panic etched across his face. I think, with my last words, I had spat upon him.

"What?" he babbled out. He didn't know the goblin cities by name. No elf did, save for me and my dead son. And Gavriel's answer would make no difference—I knew how to Teleport to only one of the bores. I wouldn't in my right mind have Teleported from my rooms—never good to create a direct connection to your room, but it was not the time for right minds.

Bamf

I appeared outside the entrance to Dhura. The stone covering Dhura still stood. Looking up, I spotted Slooti floating there, above the stone, with a cadre of mages surrounding him. Fire Masters, Gavial had said. A plume of smoke rose in the distance behind Slooti. Ghara—the only other bore nearby.

Gavrial appeared next to me. He was a very Talented Teleporter if he had followed me, but it may have been a lucky guess, or he may have known Slooti's location.

I Blinked my way atop the stone, standing between Slooti's Fire Masters and the defenseless Dhura.

"Stop!" I shouted, getting Slooti's attention. "You can't do this! We're elves! We *respect* life!"

Slooti practically growled. "We cannot respect life that does not respect *us*! They killed my son!"

My son. My precious Jeb.

"He was special!" Slooti shouted down.

Special. Yes, he was.

"He had a Gift!" Slooti shouted.

A gift. Wild and petulant, but also kind and generous.

"He could amplify magic!" the High Lord continued to shout.

He could make goblins laugh.

"With him, we could have done *anything*!" yelled our leader.

We could have made El'daShar a better place.

"I can't let you do this," I said, no longer shouting, but he heard me.

"Cast your spells!" he shouted to his cadre.

One of them actually spoke up. "But the High Lady..."

"She will move! Cast your spells!" he bellowed.

And they began to create their fire. I would have to move, or die. I made my choice.

Bamf

I had not been there since Jeb's death. And yet, Nogural waited, as if we'd planned a meeting.

He jumped up at my arrival. "Mistress..."

Ignoring him, I bolted past to the glowing lights below.

"Stop!" he bellowed. "I can't let you down there!" he yelled, but I dared not stop. There was no time.

A rock jumped out of the wall, knocking me aside. Looking behind me revealed Nogural running toward me. Other stones moved to impede my journey—*he's a Stone Singer!* Another thing we hadn't shared. But I had no time to dwell on that thought.

I Blinked, bringing myself past the magically-grown stone. Then I Blinked again. The stone walls tried to crush me, but I stayed ahead of them, and I finally rounded a corner where I looked into the room. Ignoring what my eyes beheld, I Blinked deep into the room.

Fist-sized spheres floated everywhere, creating such a cavalcade of light that I could scarcely process it. Their colors ranged from a deep pink to purple, and each glowed, pulsed, hummed.

I felt the room growing hotter. I needed to go, but I brought nothing in which to carry eggs. I gathered what would fit in my arms.

Nogural ran into the room and spotted me standing amidst the eggs, gathering them. He charged at me, flesh-rending talons extended. The temperature rose rapidly—the heat those Fire Masters poured down was incredible.

I panicked, and clear thought eluded me. I couldn't just 'Port them back out to the entrance. If Slooti spotted me with the eggs, he'd destroy them.

The room was becoming an oven. I had to go. But where?

There was a place I traveled with Jeb sometimes. A place in

the forest, by a river. I hoped the hatchery was close enough to my normal 'Port location, because I didn't have time to calculate a new one.

All those eggs. My tears evaporated before they fell.

I cast my spell.

Bamf

***

"Slooti became insane with hate." I had the team back in the control room of the Bubble. I suspected, but didn't know, that the Infected would find it hard to enter the Bubble. But I also brought them back because I wanted Matt to hear the story. "He did the unthinkable. He ordered the destruction of every one of the goblin cities. He incinerated them—had them blasted with fire as hot as the sun, until there was nothing left but giant holes in the ground. It was... horrible."

As horrible as growing up with dreams haunted by the Infected? A different brand of horrible. I'd backed off after discovering Staci's paintings. I would be around to keep her safe, and be available when she chose to share, but I didn't need to push her. While understanding that connection would undoubtedly provide value, it didn't remove the danger from the Earth. The Infected would keep attacking. Like the trolls attacked the elves. Like the elves attacked the goblins.

My eyes could not meet Matt's. "I'm sorry," I said, feeling the tendrils of my past pulling me down even millennia after the fact. "I have not talked of this in a very long time." Avoiding the small, crowded room, I took another long drink. "I lost a child in the Tower, just like the High Lord, but I could not sanction that perversion of justice."

"How many of us were there?" Matt asked.

"Before? There were millions. It was like Earth 300 years ago. You were on the threshold of greatness. After the blasts, hundreds. Goblins that had been traveling between their cities survived. Soon after, less than a hundred."

"That *was* a sorrowful tale," Matt said, reaching into the bowl and finding it empty. "I've never heard you tell that story. Why do you refrain from telling us?"

"Oh, I have before. I stopped at some point. It seemed so pointless for so long. And then I grew old, and I had trouble remembering. It's been many, many generations of goblins since I've shared this."

"I know. Are you going to tell the rest of the story?" Matt asked.

I choked on the last of my beer. "What?" I sputtered out.

"FreeWorld, the Infected, coming here? Are you going to tell that part?" he persisted.

"How do you know about that?" I heard the astonishment in my voice.

"Goblins like the theatre," he said, the answer obvious. "Robert tells the story better than you, but you're just an elf after all." He shrugged, showing his sympathy for my dilemma by birth. "Still, there's always something special about hearing the stories from someone who lived through them."

"Oh, you dear people," I said. "You kept hope when I had lost it."

"We lose hope all the time," he said, placing his razor-sharp talons gently on the soft-skinned back of my hands. "Sometimes it turns up in the strangest places." He looked thoughtful, like he'd remembered something, but then decided to keep it to himself. "Other times it's right where we left it. Go on then," he urged.

Chapter 23

Galad

I brimmed with self-loathing. After all my promises, I found myself doing exactly what I had never wanted to do again—prying in someone else's mind. And Cordoro's mind was so exceedingly depraved. I felt like I swam in sewage.

At that moment, I merely locked him into a mesmerized state, not dipping in any deeper—staying as far away from his psyche as I could. The brief glimpse I'd had earlier kept me at bay.

"Can he hear us right now?" Hirashi asked.

"No, but I can allow him to listen if you want," I replied.

"No, not yet," Hirashi began. "Allania, was there some history between you and Cordoro?" Hirashi had seen what I'd seen—Cordoro had used Lani's stabbing as a distraction, but he'd done it with pleasure.

"When I showed up at his residence," Lani answered, "he acted very excited to see me. He carried on about being worried I'd been lost, and eventually propositioned me. I told him I was already seeing someone. He got kind of weird about it, accusing me of making it up. It ticked me off—he'd left us in a bore to save himself, and then he expected me to swoon? I tore into him a little. When I told him I was seeing Broxus… he went a little nuts. Started swearing. Said he'd be in the council chamber shortly, and slammed the door in my face."

Hirashi growled quietly, deep in her throat, eyes fixed on Cordoro.

Lani saw the look in Hirashi's eyes, and continued. "The stabbing I received here was more enjoyable than the one he intended in his room." After a moment, she added. "Probably lasted longer too."

Hirashi barked a sudden laugh and covered her mouth

quickly. Lani looked at her with a sad smile, and Hirashi uncovered her mouth, saying, "I'm so sorry."

"Don't worry. I said it to relieve the tension," Lani offered.

"No, I'm sorry I let him have free rein for so long," she said.

Hirashi closed her eyes. "Push him into the Dead Zone please, Galad."

"You understand I won't be able to keep him under control in there?" I reminded her.

"I know," she said, resigned.

WIth Cordoro's hands and feet tied, I dragged him backward into the Dead Zone. I could have made him walk, at least until he entered the space where my magic would not work on him. The particular form of magic, or anti-magic, in that room I had never encountered. Another human invention, I supposed. I could have made Cordoro walk, but I didn't want to call out my Talent any more than I already had, in front of the humans who remained. Truthfully, I didn't want to force my will on anyone. But I especially didn't want to dig into the vile Teleporter's mind. So I prepared myself—when we crossed the line, his thrashing didn't stop me. I deposited him in a chair, and Lani pulled out a dagger and held it to his neck, walking behind the chair and shooing me out of the room.

I gladly left the Dead Zone, where I had a haunting reminder of what it had felt like after I had blocked myself off from everyone when the Infected had destroyed my world. For a time, I'd treasured that feeling, but I had changed again—I wanted to feel that my friends were okay. And Red—she was close enough that I felt her steely determination. That, I treasured.

I missed whatever calmed Cordoro's thrashing—either the knife to his neck or his seeing the body of Crooney with the sword protruding from it like a pincushion.

"Enough," Cordoro spat. "If you thought you could afford to kill me, you would already have done it."

I knew too little of the situation to know whether or not he spoke the truth.

"Can we really not afford to trade without him?" an elderly man asked. *Greenly*, popped the name into my head. I'd been staying out of people's minds, but someone had pushed that to me, causing me to startle.

Hirashi sighed, while I cast about discreetly for the source of my information. "We can barely afford to trade *with* him. It isn't like he goes out of his way to enable us. Equipment is breaking and we cannot get more. We cannot get our production crops off-planet to sell. We will soon have granaries, storehouses, and depots filled with rotting goods, of no benefit to anyone."

She became more animated, pacing as she waved her arms. "I fear to think of us with our only recourse being 'Porters from other colonies. We will be the only colony without a 'Porter, and they will rob us blind!"

Cordoro smirked.

"But we also cannot let this monster be our only recourse!" Sprouti interjected. *Who was telling me their names?* "He leaves us no better off than the other colonies—we're just choosing between our rapists."

"*You* have no worries from me on that account," Cordoro commented snidely, and a trickle of blood ran down his neck from where Lani tensed. He wisely shut up.

"If I may," I offered, and all eyes turned to me.

Calyx twins. Bloom—Healer. Someone in the room had Empathic abilities, possibly so low-level that they didn't even know. Or perhaps they knew and kept it secret; life as an Empath could be difficult.

"We found two pairs of Teleportation Rings in the House of Contested…" I stopped myself. Scan's name for them would translate better. "In the Elven Vaults." I let them chew on that thought for a minute. From the lack of reaction on Hirashi's face, Lani had already informed Hirashi of the Rings. Why would she string out the information instead of jumping to the point?

"We should set one up from Earth to El'daShar," Rocks inserted. "We need to communicate, and we can get you equipment. And remember, Earth doesn't have a Teleporter either."

"And we set the other one up between Emerald Farms and El'daShar," one of the Calyx twins suggested.

Her sister chimed in, "That sounds reasonable. If we did that, why, *we wouldn't need a Teleporter.*"

Everyone got quiet and let that sink in for Cordoro. Knife at his throat, dawning realization that his services were no longer needed, the smug smile slipped from his face.

I realized why Hirashi took the circuitous path she'd chosen, when clearly she knew the information. It wasn't for Cordoro—she'd already written him off. It wasn't for her own people—the best thing for them would be to have me alter Cordoro's mind to be more receptive to their desires.

Hirashi wasn't putting on that show for any of them. She was doing it for *me*. She had believed me when I said I deplored manipulating people's minds. And so *she* was doing the manipulation. *She* was sparing *me*.

"Please don't kill me," Cordoro finally squeaked out. "I can move so many more goods than any artifact. You know I can move more goods than that Ring."

"The Rings never have to sleep," Hirashi pointed out, which was an interesting point. The Rings were only limited by how fast you could move goods through. With the technologies I had witnessed on Earth, I imagined we could transport loads of items quickly. *We?* The mental shift where I considered Earth as part of my *we* astounded me.

Sweat dripped from Cordoro's brow. "I can do more," he sputtered. "I know where some things are tucked away. Things you'll find useful."

"What kind of things?" Hirashi said, bored.

"Elvish wine," he said, and Hirashi shook her head no.

"Elvish weapons," he suggested, moving on.

Hirashi appeared to ponder this. Not saying yes or no.

"Dwarvish weapons," Cordoro added hopefully.

"Now that's interesting," Hirashi commented. "Where did you stash those?"

"They're on DwarkenHazen." he answered eagerly. "I can take you there."

"You have a stash of weapons on DwarkenHazen? What

kinds of weapons? How do you have any space of your own there?" Hirashi asked these questions analytically, without heat, but Cordoro saw danger within them.

Cordoro's mouth worked soundlessly as he tried to think of how to best present his ill-gotten goods. "Just items I've found on my journeys. I was waiting for a time of need..."

Lani rolled her eyes and the knife shifted, halting Cordoro's effulgent deceit.

"Okay, Cordoro," Hirashi said, "When Mort gets back, we will look at your weapons stash."

Emboldened by desperation, Cordoro ventured, "You'll get nothing without a guarantee of my freedom."

That got a chorus of scoffing from the room, and Cordoro had to freeze again lest he decapitate himself on Lani's blade.

"Guarantee?" Hirashi drawled, quieting the room with the metal in her voice. "You just attempted to kill the entire council of Elders. It will take more than *dwarven black-market goods* to rebuild trust."

"But I didn't even want to do this!" Cordoro exclaimed. "*He* forced me!" he exclaimed, nodding his head toward the impaled Crooney, which was tricky to do without getting his neck sliced.

I hadn't done enough digging in his head to know whether the plan to attack the Elders was Crooney's or Cordoro's, but I had been able to tell that no one had forced Cordoro. I shook my head no, which caused Cordoro to seethe with anger.

"You would believe this *elf,*" he spat out the last, "over *me*? He's lying. He's an *elf!*"

"Enough!" Hirashi barked. "He fought against the Infected. *He* and his friends saved my life on El'daShar after *you* abandoned us. Galad, would you be so kind as to drag this scum back out and mez' him until Mort returns with the men that he *left to die* in the forest?"

"No!" Cordoro wailed. I ignored his voice, rising with panic and chanting a litany of "You can't do this to me!" and "Get your hands off me!" and did Hirashi's bidding. If nothing else, when I pulled him out of the Dead Zone, I was glad for the quiet.

Chapter 24

Hirashi

"Allania," I said, "would you please bring in some guards?" I didn't want Galad to have to hold Cordoro in a mesmerized state for long. It wasn't fair to Galad.

Allania nodded, sheathing her dagger.

"I'll go with her," Elder Greenly said, "if you can tolerate my pace."

Allania smiled and lent Greenly a helping arm to lean on.

"On the matter of the Mana'thiandriel, you have my vote," Greenly said.

I'd forgotten, in all the mayhem, why we had met in the first place. How could I have lost track of the need for Mana'Thiandriel? I gave him a nod of thanks. For the thousandth time, I mentally thanked my former mentor.

"We have matters to attend to on our land," one twin said.

"We *also* agree that you can use the Mana'thiandriel as you see fit," said the other, the same voice issuing forth from another body. They started their own conversation about some matter on their land, and left together.

"I'll go back to my farm as well," Elder Hearth said. "I believe my vote makes the issue unanimous." He looked over at Crooney's corpse meaningfully, then back at me. "Get them the Mana'thiandriel. I'll be ready when you want to talk about next steps."

"Bloom," I called out, halting her from also departing. "I find there's an opening on the Elder Board."

Her eyes shifted to Crooney. "Yes," he said, "and as dearly as I love the Calyx sisters, you should consider who will replace them as well. I think you'll find transitions go more smoothly when all parties are still breathing." She frowned a moment. "Not always."

She turned to go and I stopped her a second time. "Please

recommend some people," I said.

She nodded, smiled, and started out.

"Make sure your name is among the recommendations," I said to her back.

She paused at the door, sighed softly, and left, closing the door behind her. That left me alone with Galad.

We sat there in the quiet for a moment, but I broke our individual contemplations. "He was further gone than I'd realized."

Galad knew whom I meant, and he grimaced.

"I knew he was power hungry, but I never thought he would harm people directly," I said. "My underestimation nearly cost a lot of good people their lives."

"He's had some influencers pushing him," Galad said. "That was one," he said, pointing at Crooney.

"Yes, I knew *that one* was a nasty piece of work. I'm glad to see him gone, though there will be a price to pay."

"How so?"

I couldn't tell if he was genuinely interested, but I wanted to talk.

"I pulled the trigger that harmed him, but Mort was the one who ensured no Healing would ever be performed," I said, waving at the sword. "Crooney—that's *his* name—had attacked Mort, nearly killed him, and Mort is from one of the Warrior Colonies. In situations like this, I prefer their justice system, but on our colony, we require a trial."

"So now," Galad began, "instead of Crooney being tried for whatever law he broke…"

"Attempting murder," I inserted.

"…it will be Mort being tried for…?"

"Murder," I answered. "It may be that I am also tried for attempted murder, but that shouldn't be a problem." The Elders would back me on my role—my attack being necessary to preserve myself and the other Elders.

"Because Mort is from a different colony, this has to be judged by the Twelve," I said. "That's a whole different nest of snakes."

I sighed. I didn't know how I would navigate that.

"We need that Teleportation Ring," I explained. "But I don't know how to justify a claim on it. The Twelve will maneuver to get it taken away, most vehemently the other Warrior Colony, and I'm afraid they'll use *this,*" and I waved my hand to indicate the entire room, "as a means to that end."

"Hmmf..." Galad muttered.

"What?" I asked. That sounded like a chuckle.

"It's ironic," he said. "Before I traveled back to the AllForest and, eventually, threw in my lot with that walking pile of rocks, I spent centuries working legal cases on matters of possession for elves." He shook his head ruefully. "Looking back, that was such a total waste of time."

I narrowed my eyes. Did he not see the relevance of those skills in our predicament? I wanted to ask more, but Allania returned with a pair of guards, interrupting our discussion.

Sighing, I got up from my chair, then jumped, startled by a flash of light as the room filled with people—Mort had 'Ported back in.

Judging by the cheers, they'd recovered Mort's men, but I did a quick survey of the room and found them for myself. All of them.

I let them celebrate, recalling Rocks's words about needing to rejoice in what victories we could.

Harry ran out of patience first. "Can we get on with it? There was a certain matter we needed to check in DwarkenHazen." Harry gave Galad a not-subtle look of impatience.

"If I may," Galad said, "I would recommend setting up the Teleportation Rings first. It will ease the burden on Mort, and establish some precedence on possession."

Harry threw his hands up in exasperation, but I needed the thinking that Galad brought. I understood Harry's concern—he hadn't spelled it all out, but Harry had secreted away something powerful, something that might explain how the elves had vanished.

I nodded my head in agreement. "Mort, would you mind? I think getting those 'Port Rings established first will get you out of the bottleneck."

Harry growled with frustration. Mort put a hand on Harry's

shoulder, saying, "I thought that giant ball of rock was something to watch, but you put him to shame out there."

Really? I wished I had seen *that*.

Harry relaxed a hair, and Mort continued. "It is not my desire to disappoint such a great warrior." Harry stood straighter. "However, Hirashi is right. If anything happens to me, two colonies are dead. We need to get those Rings in place."

"If you're worried about your own incapacitation, why not fight to have the Rings in your colony?" Harry asked shrewdly.

"One, I'm not dead yet. Two," and Mort locked eyes with me, "I plan to move my colony to El'daShar."

His words didn't surprise me, and he saw it on my face. "It makes more sense than us moving there," I said. "Everyone still needs food, which requires the land. From your colony, the export is the people. I have to admit I'm jealous of the treasures you'll find."

"Ironically," Mort said, "my concern is that life there will not be challenging enough and we will grow soft."

"I wouldn't worry about that too much," I said with false cheer. "The Universe hasn't been known for coddling. You'll have the Infected and inter-colony war, not to mention that Warlord we left running loose."

Mort cheered a bit. "You're right, and we have those bore wurms if it isn't enough."

I rolled my eyes—he'd cheered himself with the thought of bore wurm attacks. The differences in our cultures never failed to astound me.

"So we agree?" I asked. "We take some time to solidify our position before moving to find the elves?"

"Agreed," answered Mort immediately.

"Agreed," echoed Rocks.

I looked at Galad. "If you think there's something I can do to help," he said, "let me know. Otherwise, I will focus on finding the elves."

Fair enough. I nodded in agreement. Finally, I looked at Harry.

"Fine," he said, letting his shoulders drop. "Just hurry up about it. I don't give a damn about finding the elves, but I want to know why we haven't seen any dwarves."

Chapter 25

Scan

I felt a rising sense of urgency to return Smith to her human form. Mort returning to El'daShar on death's door; an attempted coup on a world I'd never heard of; a beautiful woman who I *thought* might be interested in me; and the other idea I'd had while Healing Mort—I needed things to be... well, *normal* probably wasn't the right word... *settled*. I headed to the clothing store we'd made into a camp, and Grundle and Smith joined me cautiously through the hole they'd made with their hasty departure. They must have been watching for my return.

"Ready to be human again?" I asked when they entered.

"Where have *you* been?" Smith-troll rumbled angrily.

"Conversion first, explanation later. We have little time. Do you want to be human again?" I asked. Had life as a pile of rocks grown on her?

They exchanged a look that told me they'd thought about it.

"We think the breaking of the Thaumaturgical Laws will cause you too much trouble... it might result in your death," Smith said. So she did want to remain a troll. She just didn't want to get me in trouble.

I bobbed my head around indecisively. "Okay, let's change you back for now, and see if we can find another opportunity down the road. I'm sure we can find a quiet planet where you two can retire. If anyone stumbles upon you, no reason for them to know you weren't always a troll."

"Just do the change," Grundle said quietly. "Others are coming."

"Stall," I said. "No, wait! I need the blueprint from you to do this." He looked at me oddly, as I put my hand on his bare arm. I'd left a blueprint of Smith in her human form tucked away inside

Grundle. I pulled it from him quickly, shooing him away as I held the light like a floating tattoo in my hands.

Smith and I approached one another, and I took her hands. I began the conversion, not visibly watching, but I saw the magical transformation even with my eyes closed. She shrank, her skin softened, and her hair regrew. It took a little time, but we managed without interruption.

"There," I said, letting her go. She snatched up a blanket and covered herself, moving to the clothes to choose an outfit.

"Warlords are always men," Grundle said.

I gave him a puzzled look.

"Anyone *stumbling upon us* would know something was up when they saw a female troll my size. It doesn't happen. Ever."

Oh. That was the chromosomal change I'd made. Well, crap.

Our time had run out. Red and Harry strode in, not that *they* would have had a problem with what we had done, but Lani accompanied them.

"Grundle," Red said, her tone suspicious, and worked her way around the hulk that leaned against the door, slowing her entry.

"Red," he answered, finding something on his fingernail very interesting.

"So, Scan brought you up to speed?" she asked.

"Scan was too busy ogling Ambassador Smith," Grundle said with a sad shake of his head, "and then there was a lot of yelling…"

I froze. All eyes turned to me, except for the noted absence of Smith, who was rustling around in the racks of clothing.

"I'm changing!" she shouted from amidst the clothes. "Damn men!"

"What?" I said, raising my hands in defense. "I said she looked like Leia in the Jabba scene. That's a compliment!" *See, I can keep secrets.*

Red shook her head, looking at me and then Grundle, her eyebrows scrunched. Maybe I wasn't as convincing as I thought. But she didn't push the issue.

"We intend to get the Teleport Rings in place and secure this area," she said, voice raised. "We don't have specific trouble we are expecting, but enough has already gone wrong that we need to be smart about it."

Smith came out of the clothes racks, wearing a dress of elven style, and she *did* look pretty good. "What happened?" she asked, slipping her jewelry back on.

"There was an attempted coup," Lani answered. "It got a little bloody."

Red piped in, "We nearly lost Mort, Hirashi, and Lani—and Rocks wasn't mortally wounded, but I can't imagine they would have let him live."

Grundle raised his rocky eyebrows. "I missed all the fun."

"*All* the fun?" Smith asked crossly. Red didn't miss the rebuke in her tone.

"*Someone*," Red interrupted, "at *some* point, is going to tell me what the hell you've been doing. Are we clear?"

Grundle chuckled, the noise sounding much like rocks had broken off from the smashed hole in the wall.

I shook my head, trying to clear it of a sudden concern that the roof might collapse on us all. "So, " I said, attempting to hijack the conversation, "here's the plan. We're getting a pair of Rings between Emerald Farms and here, and another between Earth and here."

"You found another set?" Smith asked.

I nodded yes. "Mort is going to bring some of his people here, to hold the area, while Hirashi gets the Mana'thiandriel so that Rocks can take them back to Earth."

"Wouldn't it make more sense," Grundle said, "to use one of the Rings to move the troops first? Mort is going to have some heavy lifting to do with the Rings already."

"Shit, you're right," Red said. "Lani, can you go tell Mort?"

"And miss *this*?" she said, waving her hand at Grundle and Smith. She looked around expectantly, waiting… waiting. "Aww, man…" she said as she dejectedly shuffled out the door.

"Well?" Red asked.

"Now isn't the time, Red," Grundle said.

"Okay," she answered. "I'll let it go." She turned to me. "But you know me, Scan. If you tell me about a problem, I'll do my best to fix it. If I have to stumble on it on my own, you'll have hell to pay."

Grundle laughed his deep, rocky laugh, and I couldn't help but glance at the hole in the wall to be sure it held.

"Um," I said, "if we're done with that, *for now*, I have something I'd like to try. Now that all the people are in the right place."

Red nodded her go-ahead, and I let them know what I was thinking.

Chapter 26

Rocks

I stood in the transport hub on El'daShar, enjoying my alone time. Red had pulled Galad aside—I smiled as I considered how much she'd had to overcome to let herself love again. And whether she'd admitted it to herself yet or not, I knew she headed toward love. She still had plenty of opportunity to choose a self-destructive path, but I hoped she would give it a chance—though Galad was a tough cookie to read, I put him in the "good" bucket.

It irked me that the dandy on Emerald Farms had gotten the better of me. I'd even seen it coming and couldn't move in time. Yes, I'd found my new place, running the GL, but it *irked* that I couldn't do what once came easily. A small, glowing thing floated lazily by, as I mulled my failure, not seething, but troubled by my loss. When would my inability to fight cost me someone I held dear?

It hadn't even been a day yet, but I missed Cynthia and her not-yet-obviously pregnant belly. I wished she could have been there. I took videos on my phone to show her when I got back. The elven towers, the occasional alien animal that walked or flew, or *glided* close enough.

Nobody needed me until Mort was ready to take the Teleport Ring to Earth. He'd brought a Ring to his world and had some Forsaken leaders he trusted come to El'daShar. As head of his colony, he had some work to do organizing the movement. He led well, spending his time explaining why they were migrating, and letting others organize the how. His people, being a colony that traded via warfare, were a mobile lot, and they busied themselves establishing a foothold.

"Rocks!" Red called. "Galad!" She stood outside the shop they'd set up as their base, waving us over. I'd noticed Galad staring at the glowing egg atop a distant tower, but had left him to his own thoughts.

Guess my moment of peace is over.

The shop was breezier than I expected, and the alien patterns were a sight. Ah, the hole in the back explained the breeze. My spidey sense went off—everyone stared at me.

"You sure you can do this?" Red asked.

"Yeah, I'm sure," Scan butted in, "if they can do their part."

"Do what?" I asked, my guard going up.

"How would you like to have two legs again?" Red asked, shifting restlessly with a half-smile.

Oh. Oh, wow. I'd gotten a lot better with the artificial leg. Almost normal. But that pretty boy in the council chamber had gotten the better of me because of the leg. I couldn't do missions with Red with a prosthetic leg.

Then again, I had other responsibilities. I couldn't run off and join our old group. Responsibilities to the world, responsibilities at home. I couldn't run off, but I also couldn't *run*, at least not like I used to.

"That... would be amazing," I drawled, my thoughts and emotions tripping over each other. "What has to happen?"

"Do you trust me?" Scan asked.

That was easy. "I do."

Scan nodded to Galad, who sighed and frowned. Red shot him a complex look, filled with sympathy and need.

At once, I found I wanted to walk to the cleared out section of the floor and lie down. A part of my mind wondered about the oddness of that decision, but that part of my mind wasn't very loud about it. Just intrigued.

Scan kneeled, removed my prosthetic, and put a finger on the stump of my leg. "Right here," he said. That seemed odd, but not alarming.

Grundle nodded and readied his big war axe. Man, that thing was big and sharp. He touched the tip of the axe to the point Scan had indicated. *What a curious thing to do.*

He reared back, and the little curious voice in my head had a moment of *oh, shit*, but couldn't force the rest of my brain to wake up from its stupor. Then came the pain, and blood, and Scan's hand on my leg. But I couldn't scream, couldn't pull away, couldn't move.

I watched as the leg began to grow, first a little festering nodule where the bone sat in the leg. Then it extended to form a baby's leg that tapered from my thicker thigh. The leg grew like a fast forwarded film, extending and thickening. It hurt like hell, but I didn't react to the pain, frozen by magic.

Unable to move, I watched tiny toes growing and moving away as my leg extended. I felt the absurd sensation that shifted from pain to something more like a bump growing after a good hit on the skull.

The leg stopped growing. The length matched the other leg. My nerves were atingle, but not with pain, rather like a sleeping leg after having sat on it strangely for too long.

Scan removed his hand and nodded.

"Aaaaaaaaaaaaaaaaaaaaah!"

Who the hell was screaming? Oh. Oh, yeah.

Everyone waited, leaning in as I panted. All the emotions that I hadn't been able to express when frozen whizzed through—fear, pain, even some wonder.

Scan held out a hand to help me up and I took it. I leaned on my known good leg, but the other one was there. Still atingle, it wouldn't do what I wanted. I fumbled several times, trying to put weight on it, then pounded the sleeping foot on the ground.

"Asleep," I said, explaining to at least the humans what I was doing.

"It's good you can even do that," Scan said. "At least you're controlling it."

He was right of course. The nerve jangles receded, and I balanced myself on *my* two feet, in the awkward way one does when one foot sleeps. I took a step, and the leg gave way, Scan and Red catching and righting me.

I sighed and tried again. Better. Each step produced improved results, with occasional setbacks where something moved wrong— the knee buckled, the ankle turned. Red and Scan held me up as I stumbled along.

"Just so you're aware, Scan," Galad said calmly, quietly, "that was *not* Healing magic."

"What do you mean? I Healed him."

"I've seen some of the better Healers, watched them return a limb. They don't *regrow* them like that. I'm sorry, I don't know what's different—it isn't my Talent. I'm just warning you—don't let others see you do that."

Scan exchanged a look with Grundle, who nodded. There was a secret hidden in that exchange. But I had other concerns.

Within minutes, I was able to let go of Scan's arm. I smiled at the crew, choking out the words, "Thank you."

Cheers and whoops erupted all around me. Tears rolled down my cheeks—too much emotion overwhelming me as I laughed and cried all at once, wishing I'd brought Cynthia. I loved my friends, but in that moment, I sorely missed my wife.

"It feels okay then?" Scan asked, as the cheers died down, and I pulled myself together.

"It doesn't feel quite right, but I think it will, with time," I told him.

"You'll be rejoining us then?" Scan asked.

I realized I was shattering Scan's hope when I explained that, grateful as I was, it didn't change where I needed to be.

Chapter 27

Red

Once Mort enabled the flow of people from his planet to El'daShar, his direct involvement in planning and organization diminished. He spent his time speaking to groups of his people, explaining why they took that particular beachhead. Mort continued to impress me with his leadership.

I heard murmuring as I passed through, walking freely among them like I was one of their own. The Translation necklace allowed me to grasp the pieces of conversations as I passed.

"She's the one from the 13th colony." Female voice—Mort's scouting party has been all men, but the foothold troops on El'daShar were a mix of genders. *Thirteenth colony—interesting.*

"I can see that, troll-bait. Those aren't exactly local fashions." Male counterpart, pausing in the work they were doing to establish temporary camps. The camps were expanding into lines that connected town and forest across the transport hub square.

"I hear she bested Mort..." Who had spread that bit of info? One of Mort's scouting party or Mort himself?

"Are you serious? That little thing? Then I have some farmland you can buy back on Forsaken." *Ass.* I hoped I'd get a chance to practice with some of those warriors. I experienced a strange sense of being among *my people*, even though they were literally from another world.

"It doesn't make it farmland just because you spilled your seed all over it, orc-meat." Yup, my people.

As I continued on, looking for Mort but appreciating the efficiency of his people as they streamed in, I heard other bits of conversation.

"Mort says we'll have to hold this land against the rest of the Twelve."

"You worried about Savage?"

"Of course not. I'm worried about how we get paid."

"New trans-world order. Emerald Farms will hold their grain here."

"So we're only fighting ten of the Twelve. What about the 13th colony?"

I kept moving, realizing how hard it would be to locate a man who could Teleport as easily as walking.

Other groups focused on billeting, both short- and long-term, and I picked up pieces of conversations where folks speculated about which colonies were likely to cause problems and which would not get involved. Others talked about fighting that had nothing to do with colonies.

"I hear the bore wurms are the toughest natives on this planet. Have you seen one?"

"No, but did you see Mort's spike with the heads of the Infected?"

"No! Are you serious?"

"You should go look. He left it by the latrine." Clever, everyone would need to pass it there.

"Great, now I'm afraid to empty my bladder."

"But it'll help evacuate your bowels."

"There is that. So we're fighting Infected now?"

"Not yet. Finding the elves first."

"The elves whose homes we're taking over right now? We want them back?"

"Well, fighting other humans isn't much of a challenge now, is it?"

"There is that."

Cocky, but looking around, I had to agree that they had muscle and scar to back up their words. Ironically, their smiles and grins suggested a companionship and closeness that counterposed their might. They talked with distaste, but a healthy respect for, the skills of the Savage—the other warrior tribe. I'd seen corpses of the Savage after the Emerald Farms attack, but I didn't understand enough to grasp what made them different.

I finally spotted the familiar form of Mort, but before I drew near, he poofed away, not having seen me at all. Dammit. My height did not play to my favor.

I couldn't see over everyone, but my eye easily found one of the largest men I'd ever seen. He rivaled even Bear. My heart constricted at the thought that I would never see Bear again, never get to hear his simple but guileless words. If Bear had been there, he would have been able to see over everyone... I walked up to the Goliath, who carted around massive stones like they were grocery bags, using them to create a makeshift wall.

"I need your help," I said. "I'm Red."

"You're brown," he said, smiling indulgently. "Did that help?"

Ho boy.

"I'm looking for Mort," I said, not giving up.

He was as big as Bear, but not as slow-witted. I missed Bear. The warrior stood taller and looked around, but shook his head—he didn't see Mort. He set his stones down, nodding me over. He crouched down. "Stand on my shoulders."

"Stand?"

"You'll be fine," he said. I wasn't worried about *being fine*. I didn't think anyone had ever invited me to stand on their shoulders as an adult. Still, I needed the height.

I put one foot on a shoulder and did a herculean one-legged squat to get the other one up, aided by his massive fingers stabilizing my calf. He rose as he grabbed the other calf. "They call me Bellows." Bellows, like the forges for making weapons. Cool.

I didn't know how they exchanged pleasantries, so I just went for it. "It's a pleasure to meet you, Bellows," I said as I looked around for Mort. A few heads turned our way, but no one stopped working. They knew what they needed to do, and how quickly they needed to do it.

"I've got a *thing* for calves, so I'm pleased as well." I looked down, and couldn't tell if he was serious or not. Probably not.

Oh, there he was! "Mort!" I yelled out. No response. I got louder, "*Mort*!" Still nothing. He was too far away.

"*MORT!*" came a roar from between my feet. Oh, *Bellows*.

Okay.

Mort turned, saw me, and held up a hand.

"Okay, you can put me down now," I said.

"Or you could climb down," he suggested.

I pulled my daggers and squatted, setting one blade on his left hand and the other I slid carefully between my boot and his neck. "How about we do this the easy way?" I asked.

The big man rumbled with suppressed laughter as he squatted back down, bending low enough that I jumped off, spinning, facing him when I landed.

He picked up his stones. "Never has a woman invited me to do anything the easy way before," he said, laughing and moving on with his stones.

A light flashed and Mort appeared before me.

"Bellows give you any trouble?" he asked as the giant retreated.

"No," I said, "he seemed nice enough."

"He is. But people have misunderstood his sense of humor often enough, and he doesn't have a lot of reason to rein it in."

"Bellows!" he yelled, and the behemoth turned with his stones, and looked at Mort. "This is the one I told you about, who beat me in a fight."

Bellows started laughing and continued laughing as he walked away with the stones that probably weighed as much as I did.

"You needed something?" Mort asked, smiling.

"Just getting a schedule," I said. "When do you want to get the Ring to Earth? When do you move the Ring from your world to Emerald Farms? When do we go to Dwarkenhazen?"

Mort sighed. "Let's get the Ring to Earth now. Defending this ground will not be easy. Supplementing with some of your forces is the wise move. We need a day to move more people through the Ring from Forsaken. Dwarkenhazen immediately after."

"Okay," I nodded, and *bamf*, we were back at the shop where we had made camp for the people from Earth.

Everyone turned our way; meals stopped; conversations paused.

"Time to get the Ring to Earth," I said, and Mort nodded his greeting to everyone.

Rocks walked over, slowly, to Mort, whose eyes found the metal leg on the ground, no longer needed. Mort nodded appreciatively. "We have some warriors who could use similar help," he said to the room.

"How true is your moral compass?" Scan asked. *Geez, Scan, way to be subtle.*

"My moral compass points true north," Mort said. "I've found it is the rules created by people that impede the needle."

Grundle laughed.

"You can send some folks this way," Scan said.

Mort nodded. "Let's walk back to the Rings," he said. "That will get more attention than my saying anything. Plenty of people have already admired the crafted leg—they will notice you have both legs."

Rocks smiled his wicked, good-natured smile. I grinned, still reveling in his returned leg myself, even if he couldn't rejoin us. He pulled an elven robe off the rack, slinging it over his arm without explanation. A gift for Cynthia? "Okay, troops," he said. "This might be it for a while. For the foreseeable future, I'll be coordinating from the other side of the Universe."

I gave him a big hug. Not something we used to do, but I had grown head space to accommodate both my disciplinary militant side and my emotional side.

"Rocks," I told him, "you've got to be careful bringing troops in. If you bring too many, it will draw the Infected. Fifty-k max, and that includes the Forsaken. Give Cynthia my love, and take care of her and baby Pebbles."

"Pebbles?" he said, then groaned. "Oh, bad one, Red. Keep each other alive. I don't have time to come save your sorry asses every time you mess up."

We exchanged stupid, sad little grins with each other, recognizing the parting of our ways.

"Here," he said, handing me his backpack. "It's a projector and some video from Earth. You'll need it to convince others. It's got a few hours of batteries as well."

Scan gave Rocks a bro-hug. "Hey, I had an idea."

"Of course you did," Rocks said. "What do you need?"

"I need my laptop to work. More batteries, generator... all good things."

"Those were on my list already. What's the weird ass thing you're about to ask for?"

"A tank."

"A tank," Rocks deadpanned. "That won't fit through the Rings, and from what I understand, it's too heavy to Teleport. How about tank *parts*?"

"A lot less useful. In the 1920s, there were small tanks, tankettes—shoot for something that would fit through a Ring intact."

Rocks shrugged. "Anything for the guy that gave me a leg up in the world."

"Holy crap, man, that was worse than Red!"

Rocks bowed with a flourish of his arms and walked out of the shop.

Mort nodded and followed him, but my mind latched onto the visual of the door closing behind Rocks—not just a chapter closing, but a book ending. The Healing, or *regrowth* or whatever, had taken out the bookmark that kept returning me to that page in the story of my life. Rocks was no longer being forced out; he was choosing to leave. He was walking away, literally and figuratively, and not out of loss or pain, but to be helpful in the best way he knew how.

I sidled up to Galad and slipped an arm around his waist, and he put an arm around my shoulder, pulling me close. He already knew it was what I needed.

Chapter 28

Rocks

I had my cell out even as Mort brought us back to Earth. How had that tiny maintenance room become a focal point for not just international travel, but interworld travel?

"Follow me," I told Mort. "I'll show you where to put the Ring." He hadn't brought it, though we'd walked to it before leaving El'daShar, and he'd stared at it like one might examine a refrigerator before trying to get it through one's door. Then he informed me he wanted to see the destination. Before we left, I'd slipped on the elven robe, and quickly practiced a limping walk. It wasn't quite right, but good enough. Mort had raised an eyebrow but didn't ask.

In the tunnels—where we'd fixed the wireless reception problems Red had encountered early on—I texted Cynthia to let her know I'd returned. It pleased me when I found Gil in the tunnels, in position and ready. I left Gil and Mort to work.

I texted Elliah to ask her to come to my office to collect the Mana'thiandriel, and at that point, entered my outer office myself.

"Welcome back, Mr. Penbrook," Simmi greeted me without a smile, still wearing her Army fatigues to work.

"Can you get Calloway on the line? No hurry." I had other work to do while I waited. Simmi stared at me suspiciously as I hobbled by.

"Yes, sir. Did you get what you hoped for?"

"I did. And a lot more to boot." The Mana'thiandriel. A bump on the head. A new leg. Somehow, sharing with the world the fact that Scan had gifted me a second leg and a second chance—before I had shared the same with Cynthia—just felt wrong.

"Nice robes," she called out, not able to see me through the doorway, though I'd left the door open. She was fishing, I thought, but she would have to be content without a catch that day. I just needed to wait for Elliah, get the Mana'thiandriel transferred, and then I would go see my wife and share my news. After that, the rest of the world could know.

Well, maybe. We couldn't, logistically, run to El'daShar and Scan for every person in the world who needed a limb replacement. My experience with Grundle's Illusion amulet had given me an idea, *one that might keep my secret a little longer.*

The buzzing of my phone jarred me out of my planning. Calloway. 7:06 am on the East Coast and she was at work, and Simmi had found her.

"Morning, Calloway," I chirped.

"Penbrook. Sounds like things went well."

"It was touch and go for a bit." We'd nearly lost the Teleporter willing to help us, and my only known way to get back to Earth. "But in the end, we got the Mana'thiandriel."

"I'm glad to hear it. I'm afraid I haven't been as successful. The drones request, the specific ones Hubbard wanted you to invest in, built by one of your family businesses—"

"Yes?" I was bracing to hear about some dark secret. *Please, don't let my father be involved.* But even if he'd had no part in my brother's schemes, the public would implicate him.

"We haven't found anything," she said, surprising me with her non-answer after that build-up. "No financial trail back to Hubbard. The investment is largely military, mostly Army. They're basically SeekBots, built to find things. I have to admit, I'm considering how we might use them in your infamous Where's Waldo effort."

No, that couldn't be right. "You don't blackmail someone," I explained, "to get them to do something they would have wanted to do anyway." Hubbard was up to something. I just knew it.

"You might if you'd already burned a bridge and thought it was the only way," Calloway replied. "Or it could be a distraction. Something to keep your attention—"

"Inflatable tanks," I interrupted.

"Pardon?"

"Sorry, a friend put a worm in my brain. In World War II, we used inflatable tanks to convince the enemy to look for us in the wrong place."

"Also good for children's parties," she deadpanned. "You'll need one in a few years."

Ha! If we all lived that long.

"Anyway, we will keep looking, but my advice would be to play along. If it's not a trick, you get some new tech."

"And if it *is* a trick?"

"Everything I've read about you suggests there's no one better at springing a trap from the inside and having it snag the one who set it."

Aw, hell. I hadn't done so well on the last couple of traps. I hadn't walked away from either of them. But the Universe had given me another chance. My stomach tightened at the thought of one more gamble.

Chapter 29

Staci

To my shock, Elliah had dropped the topic of my paintings—or rather, the *Infected* being in my childhood paintings—shortly after seeing them. She'd cycled through the rest, and I hadn't tried to stop her, but the more she looked, the more she changed the topic. I knew the paintings of my youth were not so good, but my skill had improved, my paintings had improved, as I'd grown older.

Viewing my paintings over someone's shoulder was a novel experience. Elliah had paused on one which brought to mind a childhood home. Another triggered memories of a trip to an aquarium. Looking at my collection, I imagined it would be hard to conceive of how I had landed on a path that led me to software. But there had been a point when painting had begun to drive me mad. And later, when I'd hidden it all away, buried it for years inside me, there had come a point when I would have gone mad without it.

That night, she'd tucked me into bed, like I believed a mother would have done. She'd gone to the other room and had sung, softly, beautifully. It was all very… different. It wasn't my usual calming mechanism, and yet, it worked. No painting, no wailing Pandora while I'd consumed a little too much wine. And yet it had worked. I'd slept.

In the morning, she had breakfast waiting for me. I didn't know where she got it—the food she provided was not in my pantry, and there were no pots and pans out, but I'd appreciated the meal. She didn't push; she didn't pry.

"Come on," she said when we'd finished eating. "We need to sync up with the efforts going on in the Palace."

"That's it?" I asked. "No 'When did you first paint those monsters?' or 'Why didn't you tell me?'"

"Nope," she said. "I got a rough idea of the dates from the

paintings, and I don't think you *know* why you've had visions of the Infected, and I can understand why you wouldn't bring that up without knowing."

I had risen, and she put her arms on my shoulders, looked me in my eyes, and smiled. "We'll figure this out."

She didn't give me a chance to bawl, which I would have done. "Let's go," she said. I'm glad she didn't—that's not me. But I would have, for nothing had conditioned me to that kind of care from another. Phillip danced around it, but… I let that thought drift away untethered.

Elliah had notified the others, and we met the head of the GL in his office. I couldn't believe I was so close to someone who ran a whole agency, one devoted to protecting the world from alien invaders. Or that *I* was a key player in said defense, because I could move water with my freakin' mind. It still seemed exciting and scary and insane.

Elliah and I entered last. Phillip's smile when he saw me was genuine and easy, and… somehow *more* than it had been the day before.

"Bring us up to speed," Elliah said.

Mr. Penbrook, seated behind his desk in an elven robe loosely covering a tattered dress shirt, smiled his cute, mischievous smile. "We've involved the CIA and military in locating and cracking down on human trafficking. That's a common element in Bata and El Paso. It isn't going well everywhere, but in places, I'm happy to report that it is."

"Seems like something you should have done even without the threat of alien invasion," I said, my snark-factor through the roof.

His smile dropped. "I'll be blunt. There's money in selling people, and money buys blind eyes. It had been hard to justify the expense to the public. Now it is not—the attacks from the Infected have at least made *this* social injustice easier to fight."

"For how long?" Alex asked the air. *That's right, he's a veteran. He knows how fickle the public can be.*

"At a guess," Penbrook continued, "public sentiment will remain behind this for a while… but public sentiment does not withstand the test of time, particularly for protracted wars."

"That is the kind of battle your friend, Red, waged well," Elliah contributed.

"Yeah, and do you know why she was so effective?" Mr Penbrook asked.

"Because she genuinely cares," Elliah answered. "She doesn't have to be asked or told to do it as part of her job."

Mr. Penbrook's mouth worked soundlessly, his answer stolen from him.

"So, why don't you call her back?" Elliah asked.

"A part of me wants to," he said, sighing, "but we have people who can do it almost as well, even if their motive is that I told them to do it. And people I can set loose on another world to solve the ultimate problem of the Infected?" He shook his head side to side. "She's my best bet."

Elliah nodded. "What do you need from us?"

"Continue doing what you're doing. The attacks on dense populations don't seem linked to human trafficking. We need your ability to get that Mana'thiandriel to the right places quickly. Keep the Infected hobbled."

She nodded and looked around at us. Was she asking? I nodded my agreement, unsure whether I truly had a choice. The others nodded as well. We were *in*.

Mr. Penbrook pulled a Mana'thiandriel out of a pack atop his desk and handed it to Elliah.

"Thank you," she said politely, almost hesitantly. "Let me know if you have need of it. I can make do for periods without it."

Mr. Penbrook squinted at her. "You... didn't actually *need* this, did you?"

"I needed you to get it," she said, not blushing. "And we will do better with it than without."

"You needed us to figure out how to get back," his look of suspicion sustaining its hold.

"If you didn't, you would have ultimately lost," she replied. "I thought, with your short-term thinking, you would find that argument unmotivating. Your brains aren't wired for long-term prioritization. I made the problem more immediate."

He continued to stare suspiciously, thinking through what he'd been told.

"You're welcome," Elliah said, stashing the Mana'thiandriel in her bag.

Mr. Penbrook nodded in begrudging acknowledgment. "Okay then. We'll keep sending you locations, and I have your hotline in case we have another El Paso."

"Okay team," Elliah said, "let's do a little work, and then back to my place for more ancient history lessons." And those history lessons had continued, alongside a popcorn-crazy goblin.

"That reminds me," Penbrook added. "We've got extra security watching for manifestations of the Infected in The Palace. Until we figure out why they're drawn to Staci, should we do the same at your headquarters?"

"That won't be necessary," Elliah said. "They won't go to my… headquarters."

Plus, I thought to myself, *deep down, I think I already know what draws the Infected.*

Chapter 30

Elliahsaire daShari Fortiza, about 15 Earth millennia in the past

A moment after the 'Port finished, I felt Nogural's claws tear into my gut. Stupid of him, considering I had been standing amidst precious eggs that his people held so dear. He would understand how precious, if I could refrain from killing him while trying to make him listen.

I'd spent hundreds, perhaps thousands, of years fighting hostile forces on AllForest. Even though the last age had been relatively peaceful, I'd had *a lot* of fighting skills trained—sometimes beaten—into me over time. I turned and kicked, sending Nogural flying.

I released my cargo with haste, my back exposed but the eggs protected, then spun back to deflect the next attack. With no time for unsheathing my dagger, I took a defensive stance, but found Nogural standing back and watching. Blood dropped from his talons—my blood. But he withheld his attack as he angrily barked, "What are you *doing*?"

"Saving your damned eggs!" I shouted back.

"You're stealing them!" he shouted back. I cast a short Heal spell, while he shouted, to close the wounds he'd inflicted.

"Dammit, Nogural! The elves were incinerating your home! Couldn't you feel it? There's nothing left of your Hatchery but *these* eggs."

He shook his head in denial.

"Look!" I said, pointing through the trees to two plumes of smoke. They rose from Ghara and Dhura. Once majestic cities, they had become melted slags of molten rock pooled at the bottom of each bore.

"No," he whispered, then came charging me. "Noooooo!" he screamed, wild with rage.

I used his momentum to send him sprawling off to the side, away from the eggs and me. While in my right mind, on a better day, I would not have faulted his reaction—that day, I was still full of vitriol myself. "You destroyed our Tower, Nogural! Jeb was in the Tower that day. You killed my Jeb!"

That cooled Nogural's temper. "You told me elves raised their children at their homes," he whispered, stricken. "You said the Tower was just for the leaders."

"Jeb was the son of the High Lord," I cried out, flopping onto the dirt, seeing that the fight had gone out of Nogural. "He was in the Tower that day because his father thought I had him spending too much time with the goblins."

"Jeb would have been the next leader?" Jeb, who made the goblins laugh. Nogural plopped down in the dirt beside me.

"I am so sorry for your loss, Mistress Elliah." Then, after a moment, without looking at me, "The goblin cities are truly gone?"

"I am sorry for your loss as well, Nogural. These eggs are all that I know remain."

We sat looking at the eggs. They were round, each about the size of my fist. They were soft, almost gelatinous, and emitted light, nearly unnoticeable in the daylight. There must have been hundreds in the Hatchery—the light down there had shined brighter than daylight. They looked like they would be sticky and fragile, but they must have been stronger than they appeared, as they'd all survived the trip. I counted them, not knowing how many made the Teleport.

Thirteen eggs. Thirteen eggs—and Nogural—were all that was left of thousands, maybe millions, of goblins.

"Have these been fertilized?" I asked.

"No."

"What need be done to protect them?" I asked.

"The normal things," he answered. "Keep predators away, keep them from getting too cold or too hot," and he closed his eyes in anguish. I imagined his pain, losing *all* of the hatcheries… *all* of the goblins… burned.

"There must be other survivors," he said, slow and determined. "Goblins who were traveling between bores."

"They would be trapped," I said reasonably. "At least for a time. Until the fires stop. Nogural, where can you go? Where can we take the eggs?"

"There are caves," he said, his voice hollow again. "Places our ancestors used."

I cast a spell, enveloping the eggs in a protective red bubble that I floated to my side as I rose, feeling as hollow inside as Nogural sounded. "Let's go."

He nodded, not questioning that I would accompany him. He cast a longing look at the plumes of smoke, then turned and started down into a valley that housed a river separating us from the rocky crags in the distance.

***

We slowly descended into the forest, moving in a heavy silence not born of necessity. Neither of us cared to speak. I could only imagine that his depression rivaled my own, but the Jeb-sized hole in my heart left little capacity for empathy. If anything, I wallowed in my numbness.

We crossed the river in the evening, finding a section that was wide and shallow. We climbed the other side, continuing even after the sun had gone down. I cast a spell that aided my night vision, and Nogural could see in the dark. We reached rockier ground shortly after climbing from the river.

Nogural rejected a few caves before settling on one he deemed acceptable. The cave he chose was deep, had several alcoves, and a cavern where water dropped from above to pool in a tiny pond. Thinking back, I'd lived in worse.

I moved the eggs into a defendable alcove, and removed the magical bubble that had protected them on the journey.

"Oh, my," Nogural said in concern.

"What? Are they harmed?"

"Nothing too bad, but I think all the activity has moved up their timetable. They need to be fertilized."

"Right now?" *Ho boy.* "I'll just go stand guard at the cave entrance."

"No," he said, "I need you to see this."

"Nogural, that's... a little weird."

"Elliah, if I die, and any of these live, who will tell them how this works?"

"I'm pretty sure they'd work things out," I commented drily.

"How?" He looked genuinely perplexed. "I mean, *I* wouldn't have figured it out."

Okay, I'd been around a long time, and I'd never encountered a race that thought their own mating routines were difficult to understand.

"How do you think the first two goblins had children?" I asked him.

"The Singer instructed them," he responded, confused by my confusion.

I squinted, dumbfounded, waiting for the punchline, but none was forthcoming. After long seconds had passed, I said, "Okay, what do you need me to do?"

"Just watch and listen. I only wish you'd gotten to see the eggs created. Is there some kind of magic you can use to guard the entrance, so that you can focus without having to keep an eye open for attack?"

"Yes," I said, "just give me a moment," and I Warded and shielded the door. It would stop most things, and warn me of anything it couldn't stop. "Okay, it is done."

Nogural sat down on the floor and placed the eggs on his left side. I knew nothing of what was important here. Did the left side matter? Was it the right time to ask?

Nogural picked up the first egg and hummed. In all of the performances I'd watched in the goblin cities—the comedies and tragedies, the light shows and dancing to rhythmic music tapped out on drums—one thing I'd never heard was singing.

Nogural began a haunting, deep song. The light in the eggs, not just the one he was holding, but all of them, pulsated in rhythm with his song. With great care, he freed the one he held, and it continued to float there, spinning as the light pulsed with the music. The song exuded sadness, though I had no idea what it meant, despite my translation spell.

Light pulled from Nogural's fingers, slowing the spinning of the egg as the lights from his fingers reached to connect with the pulsating lights from within the egg. After a final crescendo of the song, the egg stopped spinning with a burst of light. Nogural reached out to catch it, and then nestled it amongst its brethren. The egg gradually returned to something like its old pattern, but if I looked at it compared to the others, I thought I observed a difference.

Nogural repeated the pattern twelve more times, moving the eggs from left to right, fertilizing them with his magic, transferred through song.

Truly, how had the first two goblins figured this out?

Chapter 31

Elliahsaire daShari Fortiza, about 15 Earth millennia in the past

"I have to go back and see for myself," Nogural stated… pleaded.

"That's stupid," I told him. Again. "You're likely to get caught, and your eggs need you."

Nogural cringed. He'd already fought the internal battle with himself and lost. I doubted I would change his mind.

"I won't get caught. And I just have to see it."

The conversation irritated me; I switched tactics. "How long until the eggs hatch? Is there anything I should do to help them? Sit on them perhaps?" His eyes got big—the answer was clearly no. "Once they've hatched, what do I feed them? Bore wurms? Songs? Stories perhaps?"

Nogural's mouth hung open, then he blurted, "Twenty-eight days—just make sure they don't get eaten. Yes, they can eat bore wurms, songs, and stories. How did you know so much already?"

It was my turn to be taken aback. "They eat *songs*?"

Nogural's face twisted in a dull memory of a smile. "No, I just see through your ploy. I'll be back well before they hatch. And if I'm not, you've got the right of it. Bore wurms, dusk flyers, pretty much anything that moves and any plants that would grow in a cave, except the glowing violets of course—they're poisonous." Glowing violets? I didn't think I'd seen those.

"And they'd love songs and stories, as any creature would, whether or not they understand the words. Now stop acting like you can't sort this out. The only thing complicated about goblins is procreation." I found that to be patently untrue—as evidenced by the goblin arguing with me at that very moment.

"I *would* like to hear the story about the Singer providing instructions…" I began.

"My heart is too heavy for more sad stories just now," he said, his face falling. "Another day."

How could the gift of life from a Creator be a sad story? Regardless, I was losing. One more tactic. "If you're not back in three days, then I will assume you are dead and make my own plans."

Nogural struggled, but did not voice his conflict. I imagined the trade-off between leaving the eggs versus rescuing any other adult goblins tore him apart. In the end, even that tactic failed me.

"That sounds fair," he said sadly, "but I *will* be back in three days."

***

Three days came and went both more slowly and more quickly than I would have expected. Alone, I wallowed in despair and found hours had drifted by, punctuated by moments of unbridled worry about the eggs and Nogural. During those moments, time refused to inch forward.

The first day I could not muster the energy to eat. I sat, alternating between despondence and worry, but either choice immobilized me. The second day, I realized I had eaten little even before I'd fled my home. A tiny dusk flyer glided out just as the sun set, and my growling stomach mocked my previous condescension regarding goblins eating those avian creatures. Long ago, elves ate meat. Long ago, *I* ate meat. And with my mouth watering, I felt foolish for my previous criticism of goblin eating habits. I had misjudged the goblins in so many ways… and elves as well.

The next morning I sealed the eggs up in magic and foraged near the cave. If a woodland creature had ventured near enough, I would have added it to the menu. I forgot about my hunger when I discovered I'd lost my dagger. Not my usable one—the one that was never to be used. The one I kept on my person to ensure no one ever used it. The rising panic at that realization overwhelmed my dull lethargy, eradicated my hunger. I could not remember when I had felt it last at my side. Had I left it in my rooms? Lost it in the bore? Had it fallen when I'd fought with Nogural and I had not noticed? I knew I needed to look for it, but I could not leave the eggs.

Unbidden, like a thought from another's mind, came the words, *What makes the elves worth saving?* But I detected no

Empath in my head; I could not blame the thought on someone else. Leaving the dagger unsheathed... it could have been the appropriate response to what we had done. My panic died like a fire in a downpour, and the dull lethargy that had been my boon companion returned.

That day, I ate weeds—not, perhaps, filling my stomach, but satisfying my basic need for sustenance.

Nogural did not return, and I had tried not to think about it, but the time had come to make my own plans. Oddly, I slept well that night, for the first time since I'd last seen Jeb.

***

When the sun rose, I spent some time learning the mystic coordinates of the cave and then tagging them on a wall. I felt the magic coming from the eggs and did what I imagined I could to leave the power of the eggs alone, pulling energy only from the sun. I even envisioned letting a little of the magic I collected from the sun drift over toward the eggs—silly, but I did anyway. If we could draw on their magic, we could resupply it. Right?

I cast a protective bubble around the eggs, and a second shield tucked inside the entrance, not visible from the outside. Afraid a normal Ward might draw attention from an elf, I crafted something special, a foreboding danger that made one's skin crawl and instilled a longing to be away. My past offered a cornucopia of situations that scared me shitless—I drew upon those, and I laid it on heavy, locking it onto the cave with another spell that used radiant energy to refuel, in case I was away longer than I intended.

Having done what I could for temporary protection, I 'Ported—*bamf*—not to my home, but to the bore outside of Dhara. Smoke and the smell of death still emanated from the bore.

I scanned the horizon and spotted no prying eyes. Kneeling down, I touched the ground, and then the inside wall of the bore—both were cool to the touch. The heat must have burned very far below.

Had Nogural gone into the bore? Or maybe Ghara? Had elves caught him?

My 'Port destination below would not work, just like the one in the Tower that the goblins destroyed. I would only be able to descend with difficulty.

Deciding against any plunge into the bore, I moved to a familiar point, double-checked that I wasn't being watched, and 'Ported—*bamf*—back to my private room at home.

I knew the risk—I didn't want to be seen, and if anyone were in my room...

"High Lady Elliahsaire," said a voice from my recent past.

Of the four voices most likely to have greeted me, it was the one I had been hoping for. I scanned the room to be sure it held no other listeners.

"Gavrial Norrengate," I said.

Gavrial, slow and careful, rose from his seat, either stiff from a long wait, or not wanting to startle me. We stood in silence. Finally, Gavrial broke the quiet. "What now, my Lady?"

"Why me?" I asked. "Jeb was Slooti's son as well. Why make a pledge to me and not Slooti?"

"I..." he paused, whether needing time to make up an answer, or out of concern for his answer, I could not tell. I waited, watching him. He appeared young for an elf—his face revealed an internal struggle, one harder to notice as elves aged.

"I dislike Slooti," he spat. "He does things... inconveniences others for his own convenience, grips tightly to power when he already has so much, dismisses people easily... he is not the elf I imagined he would be." Gavrial blushed at his own words. "You treat people like equals. You loved your son for who he was and not what he would one day be."

Slooti and I had been together a long time. Five centuries? Through my effort, working with other elves, and his clever tongue, we had discovered El'daShar. But a root had grown between us since arriving on that world. We likely would have ended the relationship after Jeb came of age—the timetable had simply moved up.

"Are you certain?" I asked. "This won't be easy for you. I promise you that. Life is—"

"I am," he said, cutting me off.

His tone left no doubt as to his understanding of the gravity of his statement. I nodded my head, accepting his offer.

"You know how to block an Empath?" I asked him.

His eyes got wide. "No," he said. "I didn't know that was possible."

"It's not widely advertised, especially to Telepaths. An Empath is the only way to stop a Teleporter that has gone mad."

"What stops an *Empath* that has gone mad?" he asked.

"Very little," I answered.

"That explains why Slooti couldn't find you," he said thoughtfully. "But he knows you're alive."

I grimaced, resigned. The dagger did not rest in the spot I had left it when I slept—I had not forgotten it in the room. If I had dropped it in the goblin Hatchery and it had incinerated, then all hell had already been loosed. If lost in the forest, then I had little chance of finding it again.

"I'll teach you," I told Gavrial. "But not here." I 'Ported us back to the spot near the river in the woods—*bamf*.

We spent an hour there, Gavrial learning the spell that wrapped his own thoughts in protection. It wasn't foolproof, and an hour wasn't enough time. The more experience the Empath had, the better chance the protection would fail. Similarly, practicing the spell of protection gave you a better chance to resist an Empath. I spent that time surreptitiously kicking the earth, hoping to find the dagger. In that I failed.

Satisfied that he had the gist of it, at least as well as I could judge without an Empath testing him, I said, "Okay. Let me show you what you've promised," and I cast the spell that took us back to the cave.

Bamf

I'd taken us outside the cave, the spellcast shield not visible from our angle. He was a Teleporter. He would be able to return to the cave easily. I'd trusted out of desperation. I hated to think of what I would have to do if I'd misjudged.

Nodding for him to follow, I led him to the cave. Dismissing the shield, I brought him to the alcove that held the eggs, still safely tucked away from harm and prying eyes.

I put the shield back up behind us at the cave entrance. If Gavrial were not a Teleporter, that would have sealed him in. I'd already created a weapon in providing him the means to block Empathic control. It was time to see if the weapon would truly be mine to wield, or if it would be used against me.

I removed the spell that protected and concealed the eggs. Round, about the size of my fist, glowing, and—I could add to the list—emitting a quiet hum. That was new.

"What... am I looking at?" Gavrial asked, curious.

I put my hand on my dagger—my usable dagger—in case of any sudden moves on his part, and answered, "Goblin eggs."

Gavrial closed his eyes hard. He spoke, his voice slow and soft. "You're protecting them." Then he reasoned it out. "You didn't want them dead, despite the harm they caused. I'm missing something."

He didn't sound angry, or frightened. He sounded resigned. Resigned was good—it meant he was already considering why I would have a gaggle of goblin globes. Globlins?

"You are correct. You don't know the entire story. The three key points are these. First, we, the elves, were harming the goblins, so they had reason for their attack. Second, Jeb had a fondness for them. Third, they thought to attack Slooti, not Jeb. I truly believe they would never have destroyed that tower if they thought there were children inside."

"Why didn't they approach us in a less aggressive manner?" Gavrial asked, his speech slow with thought.

"They did. Slooti wouldn't take their complaints seriously."

Gavrial was still staring at the eggs.

"So," he said, "we destroyed an entire species of intelligent beings, because of a misunderstanding?"

"Not quite all of them," I said, gesturing at the eggs he hadn't turned away from.

Haunted and weary, he asked, "What do you want me to do?"

Chapter 32

Staci

Elliah continued to tell us her story, train us in the damned bubble, and take us out on fights. I spent my nights with Elliah nearby—I didn't know when *she* slept, but I didn't ask, and she didn't seem worse for wear. The overall formula became something of a routine, constantly with my team and yet... so very alone. *Secrets keep me apart... they always have.*

The stupid thing was I finally didn't *want* to be apart.

"Do we ever get a weekend?" Rej asked after a gruelling training session where horrible little bugs stung us to death, repeatedly, thanks to the powers of the bubble. She forced each of us to learn how to protect ourselves separately—super-useful but not super-fun.

"A welcome artifact of your seven-day week," Elliah answered. "I think it's only on the seventh day that you are granted rest."

"More religion," Phillip said. "You never did answer my question about meeting Jesus."

"No, I don't believe I did."

"Wait," Phillip looked at her with amusement, "you never met Jesus or you never answered my question."

Elliah teased, "I never answered your question."

"So, you met Jesus?" Alex drew himself into the conversation.

"I did, in fact."

"Hold the phone!" Alex said. "You met *Jesus*? All those *miracles*?"

"Oh, he used magic."

"So that's it then?" Rej said. "He was real, but he was just a mage, like us?"

She laughed lightly. "He walked on water, Healed, even raised the dead. He summoned food. No, he was not *like us*. I've met no one who had more than one Talent. And there was one miracle that convinced me more than the others—the wine."

We all looked at each other, confused. *The wine was the clincher?*

She sighed, thinking back. "I'd been on this planet for what, thirteen eons or so at that point. Thirteen thousand years. Imagine that for a moment. Then one day, at a wedding where I was literally little more than skin and bones, I was served not just wine, but *elven* wine... that was a sign for me that kept me going."

"So you believe he really was God?" Alex asked.

She smiled wistfully. "It's only been two thousand years. These things take time to decide."

As a team, we continued to share looks. Was she teasing us?

"Come along," she said. "You'll have your seventh day. New York City?"

"Yes, please," I said, still trying to process that she met Jesus and might think he was truly the Creator.

Before I knew it, she had deposited us in the tunnels under The Palace. "The morning after tomorrow, I'll be back to pick you up. Enjoy your seventh day."

"Well, I'm going to get in touch with my daughter, take care of a few things," Alex said, nodding at us and taking his leave.

"I have a book waiting for me," Rej informed us.

That left me with Phillip. Ever since Elliah had brought it up, I'd been noticing him more. Wondering.

"Want to get some food? Catch a movie?" Phillip asked. But he asked as a friend. He wasn't asking me out on a date. Was he? If he was, did I want that?

"Uggggh!" Oh, crap. Had I said that out loud?

"Um, okay..." he said, confused and... a little hurt? He turned and started to leave.

"No!" I shouted, stopping him. "I mean yes! I mean... *ugggh*, that wasn't a response to the question." He walked back to me. "Well, it *was*, but it was a response to my internal monologue, not the que..."

He surprised me with a kiss, short but sweet, right on the ol' lips.

I couldn't move, couldn't speak. I didn't even know my own thoughts.

"Would you like to get dinner," he asked again. "Watch a movie?" He'd left no doubt about it being a date.

Still speechless, I nodded my head yes.

He took my hand. *He took my hand!* And he led me out of the room and into the tunnels, up the stairs, and out into the night.

It was only much later, after a heady evening of surprisingly fun conversation, that I remembered to feel alone, and *why* I was alone, and how very alone I needed to be.

Chapter 33

Elliahsaire daShari Fortiza, about 15 Earth millennia in the past

"We need to get them off-planet," I told Gavrial. "Our people will hunt them here."

Gavrial rubbed his head. "Did you have something in mind?"

"I haven't kept up," I explained. "I was busy getting us *here*, to this world, then establishing our colony. Then slowly suffocating the natives," I reminded myself.

"You've not heard of FreeWorld then?" he asked, ignoring my dive into the deep waters of guilt.

"I have not. Tell me of it."

"It is a harsh world. On the whole, elves have stayed away. The fauna is poisonous; the flora is poisonous. Every new creature they find is worse than the last. The colonists settled on lands consisting partly of impenetrable bedrock and partly of sands that flood and sink. Forests surround it, producing fresh surprises weekly, even after a hundred years."

"People stayed there for a hundred years? Why?"

"These are people who don't want to bend a knee to rulers."

"Criminals then," I said, doubting his judgment.

"Some. At this point, mostly the children of criminals. Many are multi-generational now, and they've never been off FreeWorld or committed any crimes. They're a tough group, out of necessity, and there are very few rules, hence the name."

"And that's where you propose they go? This harsh world founded by criminals?"

"Criminals did not found it," he said, his voice raising with a bite. At least he showed some backbone. "But it provided refuge for many trying to get away, and it still does."

Ah. Trying to get away, to a place they will be left alone.

"You've been there?" I asked.

"Yes. I searched there for someone—Slooti wanted him brought in. Before you cast aspersions, consider whether Slooti will ask for you to be brought in. I found the elf. He was hiding from Slooti, helping the people of that world as best he could."

"Why did Slooti want him?"

"Do you believe in Gifts?

"Don't be silly," I said, but my bravado was a cover. The elf that had helped us first get off the AllForest, Hughelas Do'wood, had a Gift. He dreamed of other places. It wasn't a Talent; he couldn't *go* to those places. But he envisioned them, including their elemental composition, and we worked out how to get to the places in his visions—with an Empath, we connected his dreamscapes to a Teleporter, and made our first venture off-world.

Rumors of Gifts, special ways of seeing and interacting with magic, had existed for thousands of years. Once such a power became known to be real, we feared its abuse. I'd even considered whether Jeb's unusual ability was a Gift—the power to amplify magic, creating tens of magical lights where a normal elf could only produce one or two.

"I didn't before I met this guy either," Gavrial said. "But he showed me things I couldn't explain with Talents. I left him there… told Slooti I couldn't find him. Doesn't matter anyway. He's not the point. Though he might help."

"So other elves live there?" I asked.

"A few. None that would be welcome here. None that would welcome *you*. You were part of the royalty from which they fled."

"I don't need to be welcomed," I said.

"They're a tough bunch, as I've said. If you're thinking of going there yourself…"

I closed my eyes. *Elves today.* He had no idea what tough was. The world was tame by the time he was born. *Somebody* had tamed it for him.

"Okay, let's go…" I began, but a tapping on the stone interrupted me. I looked down at the eggs, but it wasn't them. They continued to hum gently.

When the tapping came a second time, I realized it was from

outside, the wall on the other side of my shield.

"I swear I didn't bring them here," Gavrial claimed, lifting his hands palms-up.

But I knew that already. If it had been the elves, they wouldn't have knocked. Smiling, I moved to the entrance and dropped my shield. I moved my magelight behind and above me, so I would have lighting without blinding myself.

To my pleasure, Nogural bounded in, towing two other goblins behind him. Their eyes darted around in fear—the effect of the Ward—but they'd overcome the spell to get there. Nogural cast a suspicious gaze upon Gavrial, but Gavrial just moved back to make room. Nogural's eyes jumped to the eggs, and he relaxed, scooting farther in, allowing the two others to come in as well.

"Lady Elliah," he said, "I apologize for my tardiness. I encountered some goblins that needed help. May I introduce Lodi and Fendal? Ladies, this is Lady Elliah."

They stared in fear. I didn't want that.

"Please," I told them, "call me Leah."

Chapter 34

Elliahsaire daShari Fortiza, about 15 Earth millennia in the past

FreeWorld proved as harsh as Gavrial had described, and then some. He'd failed to mention that primarily humans and orcs inhabited the colony, with a smattering of dwarves, and only the very rare elf or troll.

Even the transport hub we 'Ported into was damp and dismal, too hot and humid by far, and ripe with bugs ready to poke you and suck your blood, or nestle under your skin for a comfortable place to lay eggs.

Our glowing goblin eggs drew unwanted attention. I encased them in a bubble shield, but we had offers to buy them, from both humans and orcs, even before leaving the brackish hub. One day, El'daShar would need such a transport hub—it surprised me that FreeWorld already housed one. I imagined the home I left behind, the home I had worked to create, expanding into a bustling elven city. Yet, I could not shake the sense of it being built atop a massive graveyard.

The three goblins and two elves drew attention as well, though not as much. At a guess, FreeWorlders gauged our general threat assessment as *low*.

Gavrial had picked up silver and gold—the currency on FreeWorld—from my treasury before we left, and we used it to secure a modest room to stay in while he sought his elven contact. He'd brought me some of my weapons and books as well, along with some packs to carry them. I sighed in resignation, thinking of my lost dagger and the danger it posed. I may have doomed the elves with my carelessness in my grief. But that would have to wait. *And maybe we deserved it.*

I was not overly anxious in my surroundings. I'd been in worse conditions. Gavrial's contact might give us a leg up, but I knew I could navigate the river solo if I had to. Looking at the goblins and their eggs, my confidence lowered—could I steer a boat laden with such strange and precious passengers?

In the tiny housing he found us, we had no space away from the humming eggs, and the goblins singing to them. Not that I wanted to. The way the eggs responded to the goblin song fascinated me. The magic on FreeWorld did not flow as strongly as that on El'daShar, but it flowed. Its magic reminded me of the AllForest, though it had a unique flavor, a distinction I couldn't recall noticing before. I listened to the slow melodies and mentally encouraged the magic to make the embryos strong, though I knew it to be silly hope.

"Will they be okay?" I asked Nogural. The other two were still too timid to speak with me.

"It's remarkable," he breathed happily. "They're all okay. *All* of them! That would have been remarkable even at *home*." His voice cracked on the last word, the joy of the healthy eggs fractured by the memory of being an orphaned race.

Looking back, I believe I helped with the safety of the eggs—the infancy of my Gift. I didn't know it then, but I believe I provided the eggs with what they needed.

Several hours later, a soft knock on the door drew my attention, and a quiet voice from outside spoke, "It's Gavrial."

I released my magical shield and opened the door, choosing my dagger over my sword in the close quarters.

Gavrial came in, followed by an old colleague.

"Hughelas!" I said in pleasant surprise.

He greeted me with a scowl on his usually cheerful face. "High Lady Elliahsaire."

My guard shot up. Something had changed between us. It hadn't been that long, not in terms of elf lifespans—a hundred years?

I backed up toward the goblins and the bubble protecting their eggs, giving Hughelas some room, keeping my dagger ready.

"You have always called me Elliah," I said carefully.

"You are the High Lady," he replied, just as carefully.

"She *was* the High Lady," Gavrial interjected. "Elliahspane."

Deposing me that quickly—Slooti had moved with alarming speed. The name shook me.

"Elliahspane?" I asked. Worse than I thought—I couldn't count on help from any elf.

Hughelas studied us, weighing our words and expressions.

"Hughelas," I said. "These are Nogural, Lodi, and Fendal, goblins of El'daShar."

Nogural bowed his head in greeting. The women remained too cowed to speak. Even Nogural remained quiet, unsure.

Time for next steps. Hughelas would have to make a choice.

"Are there any caves?" I asked. "Defendable places underground?"

"No," Hughelas answered. "We've got impenetrable bedrock and quicksand. They build all structures atop the ground here."

"Forest I can hide in?"

"Someday perhaps. The ecosystem on this planet is insane." His eyes drifted to a window. "The Whorlfangs are bad. They're the most immediate threat this season, but the cornucopia of deadly species on this planet is astounding!" In his distraction, he'd smiled. I'd hit a point of interest. Not surprising with Hughelas. "There's these acidic slimes—I haven't decided yet whether or not they're sentient. Then the giant spiders, the enormous flying… well, they're not birds as we know them. And practically everything is poisonous…"

I waved him down. His smile faded as I distracted him from his interest, but the scowl didn't creep back in.

"That sounds lovely," I said. "Any other ideas?"

"Just rent a room somewhere," Hughelas said. "I can recommend some places. If you need money, there's plenty of work."

"And if I need to be home, to raise children?" I asked. "If I have many mouths to feed?"

His tone did not mock, but his answer had teeth. "Around here, if you don't work, you don't eat. Welcome to FreeWorld, my lady *Elliahspane*."

Chapter 35

Red

"Well," Galad said, as we walked back toward the little shop, his arm around my shoulder.

I wasn't really listening. My mind was replaying the reels of my life with Rocks... our time in the military trying to create change in the war-torn desert communities, his marriage to Cynthia. I blushed as I remembered the time he hid us away in a brothel. That invariably led to thoughts of Murphy and the gut-wrenching days of learning about his betrayal and then his redemptive sacrifice that took him out of our lives.

"I wonder what we could do to kill the time," Galad said, sliding his hand down my arm and onto my hip.

"Tch," I mouthed, taking a step to the side to regain my freedom. "Maybe, once in a while, you *should* use your Empathic abilities."

We walked on, and after a moment, he put his hand back on my shoulder. He pulled me closer and kissed me on the side of my head.

"Sorry," he apologized. "You're thinking about Rocks."

At that point, I didn't know if he had used his powers to read me or not. Sometimes it seemed like we were almost speaking in our minds. Other times, we had massive misreads. Truthfully, elves and humans had a thousand tiny cues that were different, and while I'd seen a lot of them when stuck in Galad's mind, they weren't part of my DNA. It was like watching a movie with subtitles—you knew you weren't quite capturing everything that someone who understood the native language would get.

"He and I have been through a lot together," I said with a sigh. "We've *grown* a lot together. Now, we've gone our separate ways, but we'll each keep growing. Differently. It won't be the same." I paused, trying to articulate my thoughts.

"You're afraid you won't be the same people when you meet again," he said, his tone thoughtful. "That you're done."

I bit my lower lip and nodded my head.

He pulled me in close again.

"No words of wisdom?" I asked.

"No. I'm sorry... again. I've closed a lot of chapters... even a lot of books... in my lifetime. Many, I didn't realize were closed until much later, looking back. Some I thought were closed and it turned out I was wrong. No, no wisdom. Mourn your losses... enjoy the sweet times. I suppose, if there's one thing I've learned, at least a little, it's not to let my losses blind me to the good things." He pulled me close and kissed the side of my head again.

My heart lurched at his stupid, dumbass, Hallmark movie actions. Before he could pull his head away, I turned and pulled him in for a long kiss, almost crying with joy or sadness or... hell, I didn't know.

Lips still locked, I laughed.

God, stupid Hallmark! Ruined any chance of my actually enjoying a heart-wrenching kiss.

Galad pulled away, a small smile on his lips.

I sniffed and shook my head. I couldn't explain myself.

"C'mon," I said, taking his hand and drawing him to the store. Remembering what Scan was using the store to do—restore limbs of those who had lost them in Mort's colony—I pulled Galad around the shop to the back.

"You're not trying to relive the memories of our respective first kisses, are you?" Galad said playfully. "Because I don't remember that going well for either of us."

"Shut up," I told him, locking my hands around his face and pulling him in for a kiss.

And it wasn't just a peck on the cheek. I slid my tongue across his teeth, noting the sharp canines, and wondering very briefly how bad my breath was before letting the thought go, and letting myself go.

We pulled apart, panting, and looked in one another's eyes.

He leaned back in for more, sliding a hand under my fatigue shirt, touching the skin on my waist, while the other hand held the back of my head. The hand on my waist inflamed my senses, but also awoke a slew of memories.

I had been stuck in Galad's head after he recovered his Empathic abilities. While trying to untangle our psyches, I'd seen countless trysts between Galad and elven women. The face-sucking, caress commencement was a shamefully familiar move that I'd seen from *his* perspective, in *his* memories, more than a handful of times.

I pushed him away. "Whoa, Minty! That ain't gonna work."

He cocked his head at me.

"Galad, what *am* I to you? Just another blip?"

"No, Garnet Hernandez. You are not *just another blip*." He barked, a hint of anger peeking through.

"Ultimately, what else could I be? My whole life is a blip compared to yours."

His narrowed eyes burned with an inner fire. "You believe I want that? You think I take advantage of your short lifespan? That loving you, choosing you, knowing that if we survive *this*," he said, waving his arms at our surroundings, "I will still *lose you* in tens of years... you think that's *easy*?"

"I... " I didn't know where to go from there. "You're not getting it! It's all the women, Galad. I was in your head. I've seen all your..." I pinched the bridge of my nose, embarrassed by the awkwardness of my own words. "... amorous rendezvous," I finished lamely.

"I..." he began, then shook his head, confused.

"What makes me different? What makes me *special*?" I asked, needing... I wasn't sure what.

"You don't get it," he whispered. "Those weren't... I wasn't..."

He trailed off, face red. But he'd left the anger behind—his face burned from embarrassment.

"What?" I said, my shoulders slumping. Why did everything have to be so difficult with men? Why did I always screw up so badly? Echoes of my mother's indictments rattled through my mind.

"It's embarrassing," he said. "I let myself believe you'd worked it out already and were okay with it."

He couldn't meet my eyes as he explained. "Empaths can be very good, or very, very bad, lovers. Think about it for a moment."

What? Empaths saw inside others' heads. Oh. "You know what the other person wants," I realized.

"And we can emphasize the positive feelings."

"Why very, very bad?" I asked.

"Some Empaths can never get past their own desires and, instead of fulfilling the other person's wishes, they use their powers to get their own fulfillment."

I squinted at Galad. "So are you good? Or very, very bad?" I asked, suddenly very, very uneasy.

He looked at me like I was an idiot.

"Well, what, then?! You're good at pleasing women and so you did it a lot. Lucky you. Yay for Galad. But that doesn't make me feel very special. I suppose I'm being ridiculous. You've been alive freakin' forever; it's not like I should have expected you to wait."

"It was my *job*!" he blurted out.

The otherworldly equivalent of crickets chirped in the silence. Wisps wisping?

"Your *what*?" I finally asked, voice deadpanned, but eyes wide.

"My job," he mumbled, hanging his head.

"You were a male *prostitute*?" I asked. "A *gigolo*?" I teased him, certain I had misunderstood.

But his cheeks glowed bright red, and I got quiet. He said nothing and I thought through what I knew.

"You said you worked in something like law," I said. "Arguing for the House of Contested Gifts?"

He nodded his head, his answer quiet but containing some heat. "It took me a very… very long time to figure out I was being used. I argued law, and seduced women, in order to acquire items for the state."

"The state?"

"The High Lord. Slooti. He used me to get items from people—collect them to be put in the Vaults. He misled me with rhetoric about *truth* and *rules*—about playing my role in making sure we preserved our heritage through the proper system of inheritance."

"So you didn't do it for money." Maybe not a prostitute then. I dunno. Sleeping with people to get things—why not call a spade a spade?

His revelation changed things. My understanding of his memories shifted as I recalled clues. The blond-haired elf sentencing him, and Galad's jumble of emotions around it. That elf had raised him, and betrayed him, had tricked and used him... and discarded him.

But did it change the way I felt about him? If anything, I felt closer, more protective of him. He'd been hurt too. He'd lost too.

"And *me*?" My question was important. "What am *I* to you?"

"You're not the first woman I've loved," Galad said. "Nor the first woman I've tried not to manipulate to get something. But you are the first I've loved *and* with whom I've tried to establish a romantic relationship. I just want... *you*."

He finally lifted his head and looked me in the eyes again.

"I just thought," he said, his golden eyes beaming his earnestness, "I might have a little bit of joy, even knowing the pain of losing you was inevitable."

It struck so close to the message I used to deliver in the desert, the message an owner of a brothel had repeated back to me. *Do what you can, with what you have, where you are.* I remembered thinking I hadn't meant it the way she had interpreted it. But she was keeping children from working in the brothel. I later decided I *had* meant it the way she'd interpreted.

"Oh, Galad," I said, opening my arms for a hug. His mouth twitched and he moved into my arms.

"But we gotta figure this out, because the things in my head, your memories—they're a real mood killer."

We held each other, just being together and letting our new reality sink in.

I started moving, steering him back around the building. "You know, what you did... you were something like a spy. An evil one, of course, but a spy."

"Oh?" he said, not really listening.

"Spies are sexy," I informed him, sliding my hand down his back, then realizing I couldn't really get to his skin because of his wizardly robes.

"Oh!"

I stopped, and waited for him to come back around to me. I kissed him, sliding my hands from his face, slowly down his chest. All the while, I explored his mouth with my tongue while he made that elven purring noise. I pushed myself away with my hands on his flat stomach.

Hot damn, I thought, catching my breath.

I turned and started back to the front of the building. "Aren't you coming?" I asked, not looking back.

"Umm... I'll just wait here a minute," he choked out.

Then, I looked back, raising an eyebrow at the contours of his robe around his waist. "I'd assumed you'd exaggerated things somewhat in your own memories." I pursed my lips. "Good to know I was wrong."

And I turned and left him there.

"Hot damn," I heard him swear softly, and I laughed. We'd figure it out.

Chapter 36

Elliahspane, about 15 Earth millennia in the past

Gavrial stayed with the goblins while Hughelas showed me a handful of reputable places we might inhabit. I had no sense of what I could afford, because I didn't know what work I could do.

Wooden buildings piled atop one another wherever rock protruded from the goopy sand, with rope bridges connecting the ramshackle islands. The town smelled in the sweltering heat, reeking of foul waste and mold.

"Why is nothing larger than two stories?" I asked.

"Several reasons," he answered. "We get fierce storms, sometimes whirlwinds. Tall buildings don't make it. They also fall prey to the Lycos… which are just normal, giant birds, not the Yargle… Never mind, you'll see in time."

I decided the smell combined swamp stink from the sands with orc and human sweat and excrement. Garbage flew from a window to splat into the sludge, where the heavier bits began their slow descent, and similar piles dotted the sands.

I chose a place on the edge of town. Its floor was bedrock, and it had a nice groove that I thought the eggs might sit in, providing them a hint of extra safety. A farm stood nearby, the only one I had seen.

"Farming was and *is* an expensive venture," Hughelas explained. "They carved into the forest, claiming a chunk of the arable land. It was a constant battle to secure, costing many lives. And now the forest wants it back, sending constant attacks. Signing on there might be a fit match for you."

I agreed. Not as a farmer, but I could be a guard. We made arrangements and traveled back to the transport hub for Gavrial.

"Would you mind," I asked Hughelas, "staying with my friends? I trust you with them, and I think you might like to see them tend to their eggs."

He looked at me skeptically, and I removed the protective bubble from around the eggs. They sat on the stone floor, glowing and humming, rolling slightly after being released from the shield, and Hughelas's eyes lit up. I knew I could count on his curious nature.

I took Gavrial from the room, closing the door as the goblins began to hum to their eggs.

"Come," I bade him. "Let me take you to where I'll be staying, so you can 'Port the goblins. That should make our trail harder to follow." I led the way, having made a point of memorizing the route. "What will you do now? Stay or go back?"

"Where am I more useful?" he asked.

"I don't know," I said as we walked, my focus on navigation. "It would be good to know what Slooti was up to, and having you bring that information would be valuable. It also puts you in danger of being caught. Having you here would be useful for getting started, but this world is inherently dangerous, and your disappearance would make your culpability obvious, also placing you in danger."

A large orc started down the other end of the wood-plank rope bridge, coming toward me. I looked back and saw a similar sized orc behind us—I couldn't back up and let the orc pass. *So that's how it's gonna be?*

"You could," I suggested, "go back and actually *do* your old job." I drew my sword, and the orc opposite me did the same. I charged the orc, in order to take them on one at a time. "That would be the safest move," I said, as the shockingly slow beast swung his sword. I surprised the orc by jumping over the rope rail. I hooked my arm in his and used his weight to carry myself up behind him. Hamstringing the beast, who was off-balance from my maneuver, I kicked him off the edge.

Gavrial stood, sword at the ready, facing the orc that had been coming behind us. As I walked up to join Gavrial, the orc tipped his head to me, did an about face, and walked away. I didn't know if he promised vengeance in the future, or acknowledged a job well done.

The orc I'd kicked off the bridge descended into the sands, blood pooling and attracting insects before getting slurped down into the sandy muck. The smell overpowered the town's normal stink.

"That's what I think you should do," I continued as we set back on our way. "Go back, lay low, forget you ever helped me. Can you do that?"

Gavrial frowned. "I don't think I can. I've seen too much. I cannot go back to serving Slooti. And I wear my emotions like clothing—I couldn't spy worth a damn."

"It's a skill worth learning," I told him, without judgment, steering us onward.

"I thank you for considering my safety first, but I've already chosen sides."

I stopped, causing him to jerk to a halt.

"Listen to me closely," I said. "There are no sides here. I'm not fighting elves. Do you have any idea how many elves have *my* blood running through them? I'm helping the goblins. That's it."

"Something has to be done about Slooti," he said calmly, but with the steel of anger running beneath his words. "He's taking us down a dangerous path. Elven lives above others, his at the top."

I narrowed my eyes. "You think me so different. You aren't old enough to know what it was like—it was elves against everything our world had to throw at us. Ask Hughelas. I'm not some idealist. Yes, elf lives first! It's why I won't fight Slooti. He will meet an end from his own ill-formed plans. It will not be from my actions. I will *not... fight... Slooti!*"

I started walking again.

"Then why are you helping them?" Gavrial yelled after me. "If it's all about elves, why help the goblins?"

"Mother of Trees!" I shouted, spinning back around. He backed up a step.

"How old are you?" I asked him, my question genuine.

"Five-hundred thirty-one."

He still counted the individual years.

"You've got fire in your veins," I said. "You see a wrong and you want to right it. I get it. I do."

I let my own fire dim and carried on with less heat in my voice. "You think the Mother of Trees is a story, a fable. I assure you, she was real. Had she not interceded on our behalf, the trolls would have eradicated elves millennia ago."

I watched as his brain churned through the stories he'd heard. I spun on my heel and walked away.

"Wait!" he called out, jogging to catch up. "You're serious? There was really a Mother of Trees?"

"She was as real as you or me."

"But the stories... she guarded us from the trolls, taught us to protect the trees from needless destruction, that we didn't need meat..."

He stopped when I laughed at the last one. "Sorry," I said, "it's funny. The meat thing was not her. Doesn't matter." Once again, I softened my voice. "I'm not starting a revolution. I'm not attacking Slooti."

We walked on in silence for some time before he interrupted my peace yet again. "So if the Mother of Trees actually existed..."

"She did."

"...and saved the elves, does that make you, as savior of the goblins, the Mother of Elves?"

"Mother, Grandmother, Great-Grandmother, GreatGreat-..."

"Okay," he said, laughing quietly. "I'm going to pretend you said something wise that kept me here."

"And you said you couldn't be a spy."

He laughed again, as I unlocked the weather-beaten wooden door that opened to our new lives.

Chapter 37

Elliahspane, about 15 Earth millennia in the past

Disappearing in the backwaters of FreeWorld proved simpler than I'd feared. Staying alive turned out to be harder.

Gavrial 'Ported to our old location and returned with the goblins and Hughelas. We arrived to find Nogural explaining to Hughelas the circumstances that led to our arrival, and the goblin continued the tale as we settled in. The groove in the floor proved too small to hold all of the eggs, and the females moved the eggs aside and began carving into the ground with their taloned fingers.

Hughelas interrupted Nogural's monologue. "You have no idea how much that's worth here," he said to me, gesturing toward the eggs.

I scowled. "The eggs are not for sale."

He waved dismissively. "Of course not! Don't be daft. What they're doing—cutting into the rock here is damned near impossible. People will pay for their services."

"The stone is very tough," one of the females agreed—the first words I had heard from either of them. "This goes slowly."

"Agreed," Hughelas said. "But you're far more effective than anything I've seen so far, and that includes a troll and some dwarves."

"So what's next?" Gavrial asked.

"My general plan," I said, "was to offer my services to protect the nearby farm. It's why I chose this location… plus the floor being on the bedrock—I thought the goblins would like that."

Gavrial nodded. "Any objections to my doing the same?"

"None. We will go in the morning."

I didn't elaborate because I wanted Nogural to continue his tale. From our time together, I knew he considered himself an engineer, but he told the story with passion. The females finished enlarging the groove and nestled the eggs inside it. They settled in to listen to Nogural as well, and even the eggs hummed less loudly, as if attentive to his tale. *What do I feed them? Stories?* I shook my head in wonder.

When Nogural finished, Hughelas sighed. "Welcome to FreeWorld, Elliahspane. I'm sorry I assumed you were with Slooti."

"I *was* with Slooti," I said. "And I still don't understand why you were running from him *or* me."

"Another day, Eliah. Another day. Get some sleep. FreeWorld awaits you in the morning."

***

"I don't remember all the details of that time," I told my audience. "The many years on that farm are a blur. *Lots* of fighting. If planets had personalities, that one was angry as hell and wanted to make sure everyone knew it."

Alex chuckled. "Sorry," he said, "I've been to places like that on Earth."

Smiling, I continued. "I do remember enjoying the irony of going from erstwhile Queen of the Elves to Harvest Queen—a title I earned for keeping the crops from getting destroyed for multiple years. The goblins fared well. Hughelas was correct about their ability to carve into that stone being of value. I credit the goblins with the growth of FreeWorld. Several generations in, they carved a passage that connected the city to a nearby rocky outcrop that none had ever held for long, because of the deadly forest that stood in between."

"The Kooshga Crag," Matt interrupted. "They called the route through the forest the Blood Trails. The longest anyone held the crag prior to goblins creating the underground passage was twenty-two days."

"Being able to safely resupply guards on that outcrop," I continued on, "enabled a warning system. Farming expanded, and people targeted greater distances. They found a river, and the world changed again with a fresh water source. This world was becoming ours."

"You changed tense," Matt said.

I raised an eyebrow at him.

"You said '*this* world'. That makes it present tense. You meant '*that* world.' It's poor form to switch tenses in the middle of the story."

I growled softly, but laughed inside. Damned goblins.

"You have to understand," I continued, treading more carefully, "there was something truly adventurous in the collective spirit of *that* world. They were defiant and troublesome, yes, but as a people, they held their swords in the maw of death and muttered, 'Just try to take me.'"

"What of Hughelas?" Matt asked.

"Yes, Hughelas. Thank you, Matt, for reminding me."
Reminding me I cannot tell a story properly, I thought.

***

That the men were quiet spoke worlds to me. I had heard shouting from outside, and made a fair amount of noise as I came in to warn them of my arrival.

The three of them sat in silence at the table, accompanied by a bottle of the swill that passed for alcohol on that planet. I silently removed my jacket, checked on the eggs in the next room—a goblin sang to them—then sat at the table and took Gavrial's glass from him.

After taking a long quaff, I clanked it on the table. "Okay, boys. What aren't we telling Elliah?"

"Things you were very clear you didn't want to be involved in," Gavrial said, his guard down from the drink.

"*I* don't want to be involved either!" Hughelas protested. "Why can't you do me the same honor of leaving me out?"

"You're already involved," said Nogural, the newest member inculcated into their treasonous group. "If Slooti knew where you were, he would hunt you down and destroy you."

"We're not going after Slooti," I said, to a sigh from Gavrial, but that didn't cut it for Nogural.

"Maybe *you're* not," he whispered. I gave him a look, which he returned, defiant.

"You go after Slooti," I explained, "and he will know you still exist. He will find you and kill you, and destroy what remains of your eggs." I knew my words echoed Nogural's own. "Announcing your presence is a death sentence. So keep your mouth *shut!*"

"*You*," I said to Hughelas. "Time to explain. I don't care if I've earned your trust or not. Tell me what you're worried about, or there will be no more of this obnoxious brew for you," I said, topping off my glass.

Hughelas sighed, paused, then spat out, "Slooti is after me because I've found some new Planes."

I sipped my beer. New Planes. What did that mean? His visions had played the pivotal role in how we had traveled to other worlds in the first place. *Technically,* I reminded myself, *we thought he was mildly insane until the day of the meteor shower that blasted the hell out of AllForest, and gave us a century of darkness.* He saw other worlds, but not as pictures one sees with one's eyes, but by the elements that defined them. We could reach anywhere on the AllForest by Teleportation using the elements of water, earth, and electricity. The meteor added the element of fire.

Poor Hughelas had been seeing fire for years—fire, water, and earth—dreaming of a dead world. A large chunk of that world had collided with the AllForest. He'd painted pictures, describing it to any who would listen. While he didn't know what his visions meant, he claimed they had something to do with planets.

Then the meteor came, creating a crater the size of a fairground. The weird thing was that nobody could teleport to the meteor, not until we learned how to weave Teleportation spells with fire. That single spot on our world needed fire, water, and earth, in order to teleport into.

"New Planes?" I asked.

Hughelas blushed. "I don't know what to call them. They're not planets exactly. At least not by my description of a planet." He was getting excited. "You know how we can describe every location on a planet using three elements. Well, I've done some more of the math, and I can show how the elements map in three dimensions!" He slapped his hand on the table in triumph.

I opened my eyes in alarm. "You can figure out how to get *anywhere*?" I understood why Slooti wanted to get Hughelas. The ability to calculate a Teleport to any place you'd never been would change espionage and warfare forever.

Hughelas squinted at me, the haze in his eyes betraying copious amounts of drink before my arrival. "No." Pause. "No, no, no... I said that poorly. Of course you can map physical coordinates using three coordinate axes, hence... maps... and globes."

He stared into his glass, as though willing the words to spring forth from the same liquid that had stolen them away. "I've figured out the math for creating globes of worlds where the elements are axes, so that you can map out a world by its elements." He spoke like he actually believed his words had meaning instead of being gobbledygook. "I only did it for the AllForest, but it would apply for the other worlds as well." He was picking up steam again. "So we can map out any world!"

"So you *can* find your way anywhere," I concluded, puzzled still.

"Noooo," he whined. "You can't map *between* the physical and elemental planes. I *think* the math even shows it is impossible... that's how I got caught by the way—I wanted to talk to Jimeah about the math."

"I remember Jimeah," I said. Brilliant with math... terrible judge of people. He would never have survived the world of my youth. "So you're telling me you've worked out the math to map a world in its elemental axes."

"Right!" he said, raising his glass and having a drink.

"And it doesn't connect to calculating Teleportation locations," I continued.

"Right again!" he said cheerfully and drank.

"So what is it useful for?" I asked.

He slammed down his empty glass. "It's math!" he said in exasperation. "It helps us understand the Universe."

"If you can't apply it to *anything*, you can't even see if the math is correct." Are you kidding me? He was being hunted by Slooti for some *math*?

"Bah!" he said, waving me off, "you're as bad as Nogural. Perhaps you should discard all we've learned and go back to believing the world is being carried around on the back of a giant turtle, like when you were young."

I laughed lightly. "It was a giant space manta ray. How would the world stay on a round shell? Sometimes I wonder about you kids."

They all looked at me like I was crazy.

"Does Slooti understand that there's no way to figure out how to Teleport to any place you choose?" I asked.

Hughelas shrugged. "Who knows. Possibly. Surely Jimeah explained that."

"Then why would Slooti be after you?" I closed my eyes briefly, trying to ignore the impulse to skewer the whole lot of *useless men who couldn't get to the point.*

"Oh," Hughelas said, blushing. "Because after I did the math, I had an idea, and then I had a vision."

I growled; everyone froze. The conversation should have started with the vision. I refilled my glass, and Hughelas's glass for good measure, and to test my own patience. I calmly had a drink.

"Well, I can't think of how to do four dimensions in physical space… but in elemental space, it isn't really a problem. It's just math after all. You can have four, or even all five. I mean, in reality, all five are in play all the time; it's just that only three apply to any given planet. So they really are orthogonal…"

I must have been growling again because everyone froze.

"Anyway, I was thinking about that as I fell asleep, and I had one of my visions. It was a place, but I can't say it was a planet. You see, there were *four elements* at play." He sat back triumphantly, nodding his head at the Astounding News he had just presented.

The Astounding News sauntered its way around my brain, but didn't find any comfortable seats to plop down in. "You have had visions of many worlds. Why would Slooti care about another, no matter the number of elements *at play* on the world, whatever that means?"

"I guess he wouldn't necessarily care. He'd probably look at me like I was insane, like you're looking at me *right now*."

I rolled my eyes. "Maybe I'd be more inclined to treat you as part of the world of the sane if you'd get to the damned point and tell me why Slooti cares!"

"You're really not telling the story well," Nogural told Hughelas.

"You're not the first to tell me that," Hughelas said. "It all makes sense in my head. I struggle when I try to think of what someone else knows or doesn't."

"We call that the curse of knowledge," Nogural explained. "Not being able to remember how you thought about something *before* you knew what you now know."

"Do you mean," I asked, "like how you lot will not remember how to endlessly ramble in your conversations once you *know* that you're at the table with someone who can stab you, Heal you, and stab you again for good measure?"

"Just so," Nogural gulped.

"I convinced an elf, a Teleporter, to take me to the place in my vision," Hughelas said directly. "Yurlynia Gaelstrommer, if you know her."

The name sounded familiar, but I couldn't place her. I shook my head no.

"The land was brutal—scorched, insanely windy, the ground constantly shaking, cracking apart and crashing together. There were no plants, no animals—I didn't see any water or any sign that there had ever been any."

He took a long drink.

"We couldn't stay long. It was quite literally killing us. But I brought something back. A gem, yellow and glassy in color, but stronger than any crystal has a right to be. It's magical—the specks of darkness dancing inside give that much away—but not in any traditional way." He paused, hesitant.

I was, admittedly, finally on the edge of my seat. I nodded at him to continue.

"It doesn't enable some basic spell, like our translation necklaces, nor is it imbued with the essence of a Talent, like the Transportation Rings." He paused again. "It exhibits a *Gift*."

I arched my eyebrows. "You found a magical crystal that lets you tinker with magic itself?"

"It has *my* Gift, Elliahspane. It connects to other worlds. I think that is why I found it—we were like two magnets pulling to one another."

"So Slooti wants the crystal…" I said.

"I fear he not only wants the crystal;" Hughelas said, "he wants to find more like it."

Chapter 38

Rocks

"It has an FPGA paired with an AI core," continued the engineer, "so we can program code in to get blazing speed on our test algorithms, and feed any of that info to the AI. And the FPGA is replaceable—if we work out algorithms we want, we can plug in Hardware Accelerators without changing the board. The swap is EPROM controlled."

I hoped that gibberish meant something to my tech guys.

"SER?" One of my guys asked. Good. Maybe they *were* following.

"Depends on the chip," the engineer from SmartGuard answered. "FPGA is the weak point, for obvious reasons," he said with a chuckle.

The room chuckled along with him. For obvious reasons, I supposed.

I sat at the table, listening to the sales pitch, to sniff out the trap. But Hubbard had camouflaged the trap under a blanket of engineers. SmartGuard had sent five people—four engineers and one bloke from finance. They'd gone over hardware, were currently discussing the chips involved, and I eagerly anticipated the brilliant software section yet to come. I'd made a little game, creating word puzzles out of all the acronyms I didn't recognize, and I had high hopes that the description of software would add some vowels. Unfortunately, I couldn't use AI, because I knew that one to mean Artificial Intelligence and I didn't allow known acronyms—every game must have rules, after all.

They had introduced the fourth engineer as a field tech, and he looked a little checked-out, with his box of Kleenex and bright red nose. They'd brought him in to talk about existing deployments, but they should have let the poor bastard stay home and rest. He had seated himself right next to the head of the table, before he knew who would take said seat.

"But the real magic is their ability to learn," the current speaker continued. *Real magic?* Real magic was Teleporting between worlds. "We modeled the system after the learning cycles of the Tesla. When the drones are recharging, they can send updated data they've collected back to our base, where we use it to improve the weights on the neural nets. Then, after exhaustive software simulations, we send the updates back out to the drones." Real magic was regrowing a leg. I spun my pen, irritated that the speaker had supplied no new ammo for my word puzzle.

"So, basically," one of my guys said, throwing me a lifeline, "you've got mobile cameras that you train to look for whatever you tell them to look for."

"Not just look for, but *act* upon," the SmartGuard engineer/salesperson reported with excitement. "That's why we have the FPGA—we can add hardware and have responses trained. If you're looking to fund your project, attach an arm that picks up coins. If you want to record a conversation, attach a microphone. If you want to eliminate a monster from another world…"

I squinted at the presenter. "You're not suggesting I arm a drone and send it into the city."

"Not on day one! Of course not. But after their accuracy has been proven—"

"I am NOT arming robots and sending them into populated areas!"

I almost stood, my revulsion at the idea prompting me to *do something*. But even in anger, I realized that might blow my cover. I'd crafted my story—the elven robe's magic created an illusionary leg. But I still had to be careful to conceal my lie, and jumping up might overdo it.

Was Hubbard's plan to get armed robots out in the world? And blame it on the GL? Not on my watch!

"Well…" the off-put speaker tried to salvage his spiel. "You could just track them. Find one, follow it, report the location…"

"How would the drone recharge in the middle of following

something?" one of my guys asked. And the technical conversation picked up again. It was just as well; I needed to think.

As the engineers carried on about mass to kiloWatt ratios and how to choose the best battery, I mulled over my past conversations with Hubbard. He had tried to coerce me more than once, and then I'd let him twist my arm into meeting with SmartGuard.

The fellow next to me sneezed, derailing my thoughts, but not slowing the debating engineers one bit. He looked to have tuned out the debate as much as I.

I leaned over to him. "What do you call it when you sneeze loudly at church?"

He shook his head and wrinkled his forehead in puzzlement.

"Blashplemy," I told him with a wink. At least, in the arena of jokes, I knew myself prepared for fatherhood.

He chuckled quietly, then blew his nose and sniffled again.

Where was I...

Hubbard dangled a carrot. And, judging by the response of my guys, a very appealing one. A carrot cake? I could already tell my troops were going to hit me up to buy in. But could I embrace the technology and not follow it to its logical conclusion? I wasn't arming damn robots! The vibrations of the trap rattled in my mind, springs taut and ready to snap. I had to stop them from catching the world in those teeth.

Chapter 39

Elliah

"So Hughelas had gone on a first trek to the 4D Planes, and come back with the stone that I eventually used to bring us all to Earth… but that's jumping waaaay ahead in the story."

"Nice foreshadowing though," Matt said appreciatively. "You're learning."

I smirked at his commentary. "Hughelas had taken a second trek with Gavrial, before they'd pulled me into their story—it was how Hughelas had convinced Gavrial not to reveal his location to Slooti. That adventure resulted in *this* bubble of unstable reality, but it's a story for another day."

"Oh, good," Matt said. "You're planting seeds for other stories."

His compliments oozed enthusiasm, pulling a light-hearted laugh from me. *Planting seeds… how apropos.*

"The next part of our story moves hundreds of years forward," I said. "The goblins have done all right for themselves, but did not thrive the way they had on their home world. Compared to the growth rate of the humans and orcs, even the dwarves, the goblins were becoming a smaller and smaller part of FreeWorld."

"The elven population also grew," Matt inserted, "almost entirely from more elves fleeing Slooti's rule."

"Wait," Staci said, "*almost* entirely? Did you have another kid, Elliah?"

"I had another child," I answered.

"With whom?" she asked, on the edge of her seat, "the Teleporter or the *vision* guy?"

"They did have *names,* you know," Matt grumbled.

"Hugh and Gav—I *listen,*" she replied.

I interrupted their spat. "I put that righteous fire to good use on cold winter nights," I said with a wicked smile.

"Gav!" she shouted, "I *knew* it!"

"Yes, we had an adorable little girl, Ara'andiel. Can I get back to my story?"

Nods all around.

"I didn't realize it, but the goblins' animosity toward Slooti had been festering that entire time, passed on through stories repeated from generation to generation. They'd kept me in the dark—they knew I didn't want to have an outright confrontation with Slooti. I'm amazed," I told Matt, "none of the children ever spilled the beans."

"The best stories are the secret ones," he said.

"The problem began when FreeWorld, largely settled at that point, and *always* challenging conventions, started research that made them a hub of interplanetary interest. They introduced an invention, one born of the problems spat out by that planet. Sandy muck, impenetrable stone, and dense, hostile forests limited the sizes of towns, crowding people in. Traveling between them proved difficult and, too often, deadly. Civilization existed only as a warren, with a few bigger cities, lots of tunnels, and lots of communication bottlenecks."

"On the bright side, they had very little war amongst themselves. Trying to capture a city, besieging it while hunkering down in the surrounding forests, usually resulted in the loss of the aggressors. I won't say there was no war, but having the world as a common enemy forged them as a people more than the lack of resources drove them to fight each other."

"Their solution to their communication problem came in the form of a clever piece of imbued magic—spells weaved into a gem that allowed them to talk over short distances."

"Like a radio?" Phillip asked, and received a shushing noise from Matt for his question.

"Not as you think of them," I said. "A closer idea would be the walkie-talkies from fifty years ago."

Phillip nodded, though I knew he'd been but a twinkle in his father or grandfather's eye fifty years prior.

"They used paired gems, like the Teleportation Rings."

They all nodded, having just seen one activated in The Palace.

"But on a tiny scale, sending only the vibrations of the airwaves. It was a much weaker magic than the Imbuing of the Teleportation Talent onto Rings—magic that worked only on a single planet, using the known three elements of FreeWorld. But while Imbuing Rings required masterful expertise and very high cost, anyone could cast the communication spell. Well, not *anyone*—it was complex—but it did not require the Talent of a Teleporter to conjure. Because many mages could work the spells, they became common."

Images of human children playing excitedly, garbed in their colorful communication-gemstone necklaces, flitted across my memory, jumbled incongruently with young elves decorated in necklaces of teeth. I shook my head, clearing out the memory that didn't belong.

"They found problems with their system—two major ones. One—the connections seemed to break down over distances, and two—the signals between multiple devices would interfere with one another. Neither of those problems happened with pure Teleportation Rings, but those were also *very hard* to create." I dared not tell them how many of the elves' greatest creations grew from seeds of bone, watered with blood, bathed in the light of magic. Though humans had fared little better, if any.

"The dawning of their new age began as innocently as any newborn babe—amidst screaming and pain and sleep deprivation."

Alex chuckled, the only one in my crew to have had a child.

"Farming towns near their equator found themselves in a multi-year drought." Looking Staci in the eye, I explained. "There's only so much a water or plant mage can do once the water is gone." She nodded—I knew she understood from our battle in the desert.

"It wasn't the first drought, and folks knew what was coming. They cobbled together an early warning system—they tied a ruby to a garnet, a garnet to a citrine, a citrine to a sapphire, the vibrations from one stone feeding the next. Using the connected stones, they reached miles into the dry woods in all directions, and so they knew when and where the Fire Elementals attacked."

"Though they had no water, they Teleported in all the fire and air mages they could find." I nodded to Alex and Phillip. "They deprived the Elementals of air, and snuffed out the fire magic that remained."

"With that success, their use of magical communication advanced rapidly. Repeater station farms cropped up between the cities. Although their original purposes were utilitarian, businesses formed around the quick exchange of information."

"Money makes the world go 'round," Phillip said pithily. I grinned when Matt shushed him.

"A clever human proposed how you might carry two signatures on one crystal, and the race was on. Soon, the people of FreeWorld made that idea real. Did the repeater farms get cut in half once a Crystal could carry two signatures? No. They doubled the amount of signals they crammed into one space. Then they doubled it again. And again."

"Sounds familiar," Rej piped in.

I nodded. "It should. Living on Earth the last several hundred years reminded me very much of FreeWorld's glory days."

"Within the span of a hundred years, the people of FreeWorld went from having to send letters or pay for an expensive Teleport, to being able to communicate with most anyone, at any distance, using a device they could fit in a pocket."

I pulled out my phone, still amazed Earth had managed the same with no magic.

"Other planets wanted the same capability, and they were willing to pay for it. FreeWorld became a hub of learning and experimentation. Meanwhile, FreeWorld had turned its attention to finding other success stories. The question they were asking themselves: what other Imbued Talents could they mimic and take advantage of?"

"*My* problem was that interworld attention made it difficult for me to hide. With other worlds watching, and most everyone on the planet able to talk with almost any other, it was only a matter of time before word reached Slooti of my existence and location."

Chapter 40

Elliah, about 15 Earth millennia in the past

"We cannot lay low here much longer," Gavrial said. "We should leave."

A wave of relief washed over me once I learned I wasn't the only one thinking we needed to go. Ironically, had I not brought the goblins there, they would not have created the tunnels that connected the towns; advancement would have been much slower; and we could have hid longer.

How many late night talks had taken place over tables like the one before us since we'd arrived? A thousand? The table had changed; Nogural was long deceased; and we'd moved to the outskirts of one of the major cities—but the discussions carried on.

"I'll miss this world," I said. "The creatures it threw at us, the way the people came together… their drinks." I raised my glass. The alcohol *had* improved. It was still a strong liquor, reflecting the people who made it, but it was more refined and predictable. Ha! Like the people.

I chuckled and drank. Dreglo, the latest in a line of goblins that had stayed close to us, looked down thoughtfully.

"Do you think there are any goblins that would want to join us as we start over on another world?" I asked Dreglo, careful to keep my voice neutral.

She smiled, but the smile held a hint of sadness. "I do."

"And what of the other elves?" Gavrial asked. "There must be a hundred or more here now."

"Most of them are not *banished*," I said. Not like me. Elliahspane. "I think they'll be fine here." Any elf that had made FreeWorld his or her home displayed the fierce independence of FreeWorld's growing population. After a moment's thought, I decided. "I wouldn't stop anyone who wanted to go." *Dangerous move*, I thought. *Secrecy would be better.* I kept a low profile, even among elves, always worried that Slooti had planted a spy. But possibly others saw the same future on FreeWorld as I, and thought to move on.

"More than a hundred elves," Gavrial repeated. "That's a lot of people Slooti has driven away. Maybe it's time to do something about his rulership?"

I rolled my eyes. I'd lost the energy to have that debate decades ago. He hadn't broached it in a long time.

"What about Ara'andiel?" he asked. "Would you have her hide forever?" Ara'andiel was her daddy's girl—his blond hair, his righteous fire, his inability to conceal his feelings. The only things she got from me were the lack of a Talent and a fierce determination. That's hard when you're young. Over time, it strengthens you.

"Nothing is forever, Gav," I said, leaning over and giving him a peck on the cheek.

"Find us a new world to civilize," I told Hughelas, declaring the conversation closed.

"Me?" Hughelas whined. "Why me? Nothing is forever, Elliahspane." He playfully threw my words in my face. "What if I fall in a sandpit? You should learn how to use the 4D Crystal."

"Stop calling it that," I said. "Viewing Crystal? Peering Gem?"

"Sounds perverted," Gavrial said.

"Scrying Stone," Dreglo said.

"Ooooh, nice," I said. "Scrying Stone."

"And you have a point," I continued. "I'm willing to learn to use it. How does it work?"

"I typically just go to sleep thinking about other worlds, and *bam*, I get a dream." A look flashed between us—a shared past, still scabbed over, never to be healed. "Holding onto the details of the dream is the skill I had to learn. I keep a dream journal, and the process of writing out what I saw—well, it strengthened my ability to remember dreams. The dream repeats, and I eventually get all the elements fixed in my mind. Then I have to get that communicated to a Teleporter—I've come up with some spells that help, though if you recall the first time…"

"We used an Empath to connect you up," I said. "I remember. So I should do what, sleep with the Scrying Stone for a pillow?"

"Wonderful," Gavrial said mischievously. "She already snores."

"I do not!"

Hughelas chuckled. "I don't know. That might work, I suppose. Since I already had the visions, I'm not sure what conditions trigger it. For me, having it in the room clarifies my visions. But the 4D Crystal does more than that. Unlike my Gift, which is limited to visions, the Crystal can *take you to the destination*."

"What?" I said, surprised. "You're kidding me. It Teleports?"

"Not kidding. But it isn't a Teleport." Hughelas puckered his face like he'd just gotten off a spinning carnival ride. "I'm not sure what it is, but it gets you there. It creates a field, a dome, that you can walk into, and then it takes you to the other world. Only thing is, you can't take the crystal into the field. So if you don't have a Teleporter with you…"

"One-way trip," Gavrial concluded.

"You've done this with him." I accused Gavrial. "Without me?"

"That was back before I *knew* you," Gav explained. "Things were different."

"Uh huh," I said.

"*Anyway*," Hughelas interrupted. "Yes, try sleeping with it nearby. Picture what you're looking for as you go to sleep. I'll show you how to activate it when you're ready, but it is much like the spell you use to tag walls with your Teleport."

"How did you possibly figure that…" But I stopped myself. "You dreamed it."

Hughelas waggled his eyebrows, smiling guiltily.

"Okay, go get the Scrying Stone," I said. "I'll give it a try."

"Already here," Hughelas said. He nodded toward a sack in the corner.

"Hmm, I think perhaps I was steered into this conversation." I hated that.

"Not really," Hughelas answered. "I figured you were getting close to wanting to leave. So, I've been carting that thing around to our visits for weeks."

I looked at him skeptically, then turned to Gav. "You're sleeping elsewhere, Gav. If you influence that thing, we'll end up on a planet filled entirely with horny elven women."

"Wow," Hughelas said, "you really think I'd still be here if it worked like that? All these wasted years…" he said sadly into his drink.

"But they'd all look like you and have your sweet temperament," Gav said to me straight-faced.

I growled, "I *am* sweet."

"You're kind," Dreglo said. "Sweet is something different." She earned another growl.

Nevertheless, I followed Hughelas's suggestion, and spent many nights with the Scrying Stone nearby. *4D Crystal… what a stupid name.* Though Scrying Stone wasn't much better, given it could Teleport people… or whatever it did.

Choosing what kind of planet I wanted that first night had proved to be its own dilemma. But the dreams came, vivid and clear—fire, water, earth, air, and electricity—and I sketched out what I remembered from my dreams. Some parts were easier than others; I understood many of the images from my dreams. Those I did not recognize, I attempted to paint on my walls with the spell I used to mark Teleportation endpoints. Soon, my efforts to recreate the images from my dreams littered my walls.

The magical images would fade, but I could call forth my magical graffiti with a simple spell. When I did that, the room would alight with color. I hadn't tried to figure out how to erase a tag before, and I whittled away a few days trying to do so.

I knew I dragged my feet, but I did it anyway. A part of me didn't want to go, didn't want to start over again. Again. *Again*. But when I ran out of excuses, I sent Gavrial to Hughelas with the message of my readiness.

Hughelas walked me through it. Activating the Stone involved two steps. Step one was telling it where to go—as Hughelas said, the spells were similar to my own spells for marking locations. The second step activated the magic, which was oddly difficult. You had to bring magical light—composed of all of the five elements—to bear on the crystal.

The activation spell reminded me of Jeb, who would have had no problem with five lights that each represented one of the elements. Easy for him, but I struggled, even though the lights needed only to be faint as stars on a cloudy night.

A translucent yellow field appeared, a half-sphere, maybe twice as tall as I. When I reached for it, Hughelas stopped me.

"Wait for Gavrial," he said. Gavrial had gone to take care of some other business while we worked on the Scrying Stone. Crossing Crystal?

A couple of minutes later, the field faded. We waited for Gavrial and made small talk, but I had a question that nagged at me.

"I know why *I* don't want to fight Slooti," I said. "May I ask why *you* don't?"

"Me? Are you serious? With what am I to fight Slooti? I don't have a Talent. I'm not a warrior. I read, and I learn, and I solve the mysteries of the Universe… and drink and occasionally fornicate, though much less than I'd like."

"Drinking? Or fornicating?" I asked.

Ha!" He paused in thought. "I drink enough, on the whole of it."

"But you do have a Gift. That makes you pretty special."

"Not in a fight it doesn't. Should I distract him with visions? Conjure up a world of horny elven women?"

"Don't think that would be enough for Slooti," I commented. "But I know that's not how your visions work anyway. I don't know, Hughelas. I suppose I just don't like the idea that you're running because you're afraid."

"You're afraid, too, you know," Hughelas replied.

Of Slooti? No, not really. But afraid of starting a civil war that would devastate the elves? Yes, I acted out of fear. I didn't mind acting out of fear for *others,* though. I'd seen a lot of loss in my lifetime. Big losses. I'd seen elves fight. We'd performed more cruelties on one another, devastated ourselves, better than any troll attack ever had. No, I couldn't bear to be the cause of another war like that.

Gavrial's reappearance broke up our sad discussion.

"Got it working?" he asked.

"I did," I said with pride. "Let's go check out my new home."

"Okay," Gavrial answered. "We really ready?"

"I think so," I said. "You'll come back and bring the others that want to join us?"

"Depends on how scantily-clad the women on your planet are," he said with a wink.

I rolled my eyes and cast the spells to imprint the location, but Hughelas interrupted me. "You don't have to set the location again. It will remain fixed until someone changes it." He looked torn.

"Second thoughts?" I asked him.

"FreeWorld has been interesting for you—tons of new and deadly creatures found around every corner. But they have finally tamed the planet, or begun to anyway. They're exploring novel forms of magic that even the elves haven't tried. To leave it now is torture."

"What would you do?" Gavrial asked.

"Change my name. Hide out in the open. It's new magic, Elliah. It's not enough to just watch it. I want to be *involved*."

I mulled that over. Staying was dangerous, Hiding in the open, even if you changed the way you looked—invited risk. Someone would eventually recognize something about him; that was a problem with living so long. I could never get away with hiding out in the open, but Hughelas... maybe. But someone finding Hughelas would be very dangerous not just for him—his Gift made him a very powerful resource for anyone with more ambition than sense.

Still, it was *his* life. I nodded my head and gave him a hug.

I activated the... um... what had I dubbed it? Something Crystal... *Crossing* Crystal. I activated the Crossing Crystal.

Looking around quickly, I stepped through the field. I poked on the field from the inside. It felt like hitting a metal plate, though the yellow, semi-transparent barrier looked as frail as a soap bubble. Wow, without a Teleporter, you'd be committed once you set foot inside. Gavrial had his chance to get rid of me, if he chose to do so. I would go on a one-way trip to a place only I knew.

But he joined me.

Hughelas hadn't lied—it was nothing like a Teleport. And yet, just like a Teleport, it took me to a new world. A new chapter. A new life. A reset. Again.

Chapter 41

Elliah

"The world I found was pretty much what I had asked for," I told my little cavalcade of protégés. "Beaches, warm water, no monsters to speak of. A lazy wind stirred big fronds on tall, thin trees."

"You found a vacation world?" Phillip asked.

"I did indeed. I thought I'd earned one. Unfortunately, it was exactly what I wanted, but not at all what I needed." I sighed, sipped my beer, and looked at Matt. "This is the sad part of your story. The story of goblinkind, I mean. Not because of what was done to you..." I said.

"But because of what we did," Matt said, in rapt attention.

***

We had probably been there a month, gotten supplied and set up. Gav had carried the Crossing Crystal with him, but not Hughelas. About ten goblins had joined us, and as many elves. But Gavrial had not yet brought Ara'andiel, and I pushed him on the topic.

"She's not coming," he told me finally, his face solemn.

"Not coming? Why?" She had been an adult for some time, and though we hadn't grown apart, she was her own person. She could do as she willed, but the thought of living on entirely different worlds saddened me.

"She doesn't want to run from Slooti," he said.

I narrowed my eyes at him. "You've been putting ideas in her head."

"I don't want to run anymore either, Leah."

Closing my eyes, walling off my emotions, I gave the only answer I had. "I'm not going to cause a war among elves, Gav. I won't fight Slooti."

He said nothing until I opened my eyes. "I know," he said, his eyes compassionate. "But I can't do *this*," he continued, waving at the trees and ocean, "while I know the damage he is doing."

"Oh, Gav," I sighed. I wanted to add, "Please don't go." But I couldn't say it. He needed to go. But it would have killed me to cause elves to fight one another. Again.

We kissed, and I recognized it for a goodbye kiss.

"I'll check on you when I can," he said, and then he cast his spell, and disappeared in a flash of light.

And he did come back a few times, but each time the gulf between us grew wider. He was absent, his head on whatever problems he refused to share. After a few months, he did not return.

We didn't have another Teleporter.

And that world grew dull. Had always been dull, though I'd believed that to be what I'd wanted. I could only watch the fish jump and sparkle in the setting sun, colorful birds dancing amongst them... after enough time it lost its luster. Some of the others felt the same.

"We came from FreeWorld," Dreglo said. "'The toughest planet since the AllForest,' I'm told." Goblins didn't smirk, but the dance in her eyes conveyed the same message. "Those who followed you expected more of an adventure."

"Monstrous sea creatures crawled from the ocean this morning," I pointed out.

One of Dreglo's eyes spun. "Whereupon they sang to us and provided fish for dinner!"

"Goblins like songs," I quipped.

Her other eye spun. "The fish wasn't bad either. But it wasn't exactly an *adventure*."

I harrumphed. The fish could have been poisoned.

But it wasn't.

"Why can't we appreciate a little peace?" I asked. "Haven't we earned it?"

My friend's eyes stopped dancing. Slowly, she answered me. "*You* have earned it, Leah." And she left me to stare upon the sparkling fish which the colorful birds swooped through in the setting sun. *Stupid sunset.*

And they gave me room. The goblins did well enough, one

generation growing old, passing down their stories and songs to the next. The planet had magic enough for them, and few enough predators that their population didn't get picked off as readily as on FreeWorld. I could not tell, in just a single generation, but I thought they would grow in numbers on that planet. And that pleased me, brought a modicum of joy in my otherwise troubled heart.

The elves scattered, searching for hardship when none presented itself. It wasn't that all elves had to have challenge; I'd known plenty of elves who would frittered away eternity. But the ones who came to FreeWorld did not comprise that bunch. And I'd dragged them off to a world that offered little resistance, and so they each went searching for the corners of the world where it showed some teeth. We kept in touch. Though no natural Teleporters had come, many of us could Teleport—just not well enough to leave the planet. And though I hadn't brought us to Hughelas's dream world of horny elven women, I'd brought a few such men and women to that world—so they found opportunities to gather. One day their festivities would result in the birth of a natural Teleporter, and with the Crossing Crystal, we would be able to find our way back to other elves.

The Crossing Crystal taunted me. We could go somewhere else—somewhere more challenging. Or we could take our chances on one crossing to rejoin the elves. But, if we did either, we would have to leave the crystal behind, and we would lose our last connection to anything we knew.

Time and boredom pushed me close to using the crystal. *A hundred years*, I decided. At one hundred years, I would leave. I need not take anyone—the Crossing Crystal would remain behind, and they could make their own choices. A hundred years was nothing. Right?

***

"At ninety-seven years," I said, "reality intruded. While impatiently awaiting those final years, news of the loss of FreeWorld reached me via the return of Gavrial. It took some time for my brain to catch up with the other message—about the goblin assassins."

Chapter 42

Galad

"I was very young when this all happened," I explained. Red and I had found a quiet space in the bustling transport hub, and she'd asked to hear about my revelation regarding the origin of the Infected. I'd talked with Elliah about it—a part of me considered it elf business. But Red had a right to know, and anything that shed light on a species that eradicated worlds was every species' business. "Twenty to twenty-five? That's equivalent to being a five-year-old human."

"Wait, elf children grow more slowly than humans?" Red asked. Her response puzzled me; my story had gotten off track quickly.

"That's right. Elves reach adulthood at one hundred years."

"Whoa!" Red exclaimed. "Does that translate to ten years of diapers and breastfeeding?"

I gave her a look.

"What? It's a legit question," she insisted.

I stayed out of her head, but some of her thoughts tickled my own, and I figured out the nature of her questions. "You know *we*—you and I—can't have children, right?"

She shrugged and shook her head no.

"Don't know why, but we can't. Humans and elves have coexisted for thousands of years—no half-breed children. So you need not worry about breastfeeding."

She gave me a look, and without any magic at all, I knew what she thought—that our relationship was stupid.

I pulled her close and kissed her before she could dwell on that thought for too long.

"You worry too much," I told her, smiling. "Most likely we will all be dead soon and none of these concerns will matter."

"Comforting," she said, rolling her eyes in that way she did, with a slight flutter of her eyelids. The extra flutter was a nice touch, breaking my train of thought.

"So," she said, "you were a wee little elfling of twenty to twenty-five…"

"That's right. My parents ruled the AllForest after most of the elves had left. You could think of it like a Dukedom or something. The High Lord ruled from El'daShar, and my family showed allegiance to the High Lord, but he left my parents alone to rule AllForest. I'd known only the AllForest up to that point, a small community, since most elves had left for the greater magic on El'daShar."

Galad's eyes drifted away as he followed his thoughts to the past.

"It was my trip to El'daShar as a child where I first encountered the elven assassins and the Guardians."

***

"Are you certain he is not too young?" Mother asked. Arafaela Karammiel, Duchess of the AllForest, and overprotective mother, fretted over me like I had yet to take my first steps.

My father, Montragon Tereba'on, Duke of the AllForest, winked at me when Mother looked my way. "One can never be certain about such things," he said. "He might fall in love and marry a princess."

"Ewwwww!" I said, wrinkling my nose.

"Oh? Would it be so bad then?" Mother asked. "*I* was a princess, you know."

I cocked my head and stuck out my tongue, unable to picture my beautiful and elegant mother as one of those icky, obnoxious girls.

"He will be *fine*, Ara."

"You don't know that. Those horrible goblin assassins only strike on El'daShar."

"The High Lord commissioned the Guardians. The assassins aren't a problem anymore. Besides, Kelivine will watch over him. The boy would go for a season. Just a season. It will be good for him."

"Why will it be good for him, Monty? This world has everything we need. Does he need more magic coursing through his veins? Does he need the scheming and politicking?"

"He's a child, Ara. He won't be seeing any politicking. Now let it go. You're being overprotective."

"Monty," she said, thoughtfully, "I know it's uncouth, but I want another."

"We've talked about this. Raising two children at once… it's too much. Is a century so long?"

"It seems to me we both want something here…" Mother suggested playfully.

"And you're worried about the politics on El'daShar?" he laughed, shaking his head.

"Go outside and play," Mother told me. "Your father and I have things to discuss." She shooed me out of the room.

"I do hope I can go," I whispered to her on my way out.

"I do, too," she whispered back, kissing me on the head and sending me on my way.

As the door closed behind me, I showed myself down the stairs, through the courtyard where stood the statue of Elvonduil wielding his hammer, and went out to play, practicing minor cantrips in the forest, dreaming of the day I might have a Talent. Healer extraordinaire, or Master of the Winds or Stone, Teleporter… I hoped I would not be an elf who spent their whole lives knowing only normal magic. I shivered at the thought of being one of the Lacking, living life devoid of any ability to cast spells.

Lost in my imaginings, I skipped through the forest, picturing elves still living in the trees, marching to war alongside the trees themselves, burning those horrible rocky monsters to slag, while avoiding the trees of course, and enjoying the cheers of my admirers.

Using a stick, I fended off troll attacks. "Take that," I said, "and that," as I slammed my makeshift sword into a log-turned-troll.

"Heh, heh, heh," rumbled a low and gravelly voice in the clearing. "Fighting trolls, are we?" I looked up, then froze, as not ten feet away sat a troll, leaning against a massive tree.

"Well, finish him off," urged the deep voice, setting something down.

Panicked, I turned and ran, a scream caught in my throat, dashing through the woods as fast as my legs would take me back to the palace.

The voice behind me laughed, but I heard no sound of pursuit. I ducked behind a tree and waited. No footsteps, no roars, no more laughter… nothing. I discarded my boots and climbed the tree, carefully leaping from limb to sturdy limb.

Well above the ground, I crept back through overlapping limbs to the tiny clearing where I'd seen the troll. He still sat there. He'd picked back up what he'd sat down. To my astonishment, he held a book.

Trolls didn't read. They were too big and stupid. They just smashed things and stank and caused trouble. I watched as he flipped a page. He was *reading*. Something else was wrong too—he wasn't as big as he should have been. I mean, he was huge, half again as tall as Father, but only half the size of a normal troll.

I wanted to climb down and ask him why he was so small for a troll, why he was reading, *what* he was reading. But Father would have killed me. I watched a little longer, but he simply kept turning pages. It became… dull, and I didn't want to get in trouble.

As I leapt away, I heard something like rocks grinding together. If I hadn't known better, that trolls were brutal killers, I would have guessed the sound to be laughter.

Chapter 43

Galad, about 15 Earth millennia in the past

Kelivine 'Ported me into an area bustling with people. Mostly elves, but I saw many races for the first time.

"What are those?" I asked Kelivine.

"Don't point, Little Prince." She always called me that. "It's rude."

I put my finger down.

"That is an orc. Brutish, smelly, temperamental, and warlike. Best stay away from them."

Keeping my hands locked at my sides, I asked, "And those?" I nodded my head toward some short, squat beings with long beards. I thought they were dwarves, but I'd never seen one.

Kelivine laughed, and it reminded me, as it always did, of wind chimes. "That nod is no better than pointing, Little Prince. Those are dwarves. Very good with stone—their architecture is amazing."

Marching straight ahead, neither pointing nor nodding, I asked, "And the ones over by that table? They look like us, but their ears are rounded."

"Humans," she said. "Oh, Little Prince," she said, wind chimes ringing, "don't hurt yourself trying not to be rude. You can look a little."

I turned my head for a quick look.

"Humans are smelly and brutish, too. Most elves will tell you they're trouble, but I find them a little… yummy."

"You eat them?" I thought we only ate plants.

"I've had a nibble or two," she said, and I heard a hint of that growly sound in her voice that Father sometimes had with Mother when they smooched. Icky. Adults were so weird.

Apparently it was okay to point at animals and ask what they were, and at the Tower and other buildings. Just not people. The

Tower on El'daShar reached up to the skies, taller by far than the largest trees I'd ever seen, and made the Barrakrea, my parents' palace, look like a summer cottage. I wouldn't be able to look at my home the same way once I returned.

We headed toward the Tower, walking through a park as I babbled and pointed and asked about everything before me. "Whoa! What's that giant hole in the ground?" I cast a light and sent it as far as I could, and it disappeared out of sight. It had to be a million trees deep!

"No one knows," Kelivine answered. "They were here on the planet when we arrived." Something in her voice sounded odd, so I looked back at her. She blushed. I wrangled my brain, trying to figure out why she would lie about a hole in the ground, but I came up empty, and added it to my long list of weird adult behaviors.

She pulled me away from the edge and around to the other side. She dragged me on to the Tower with an invisible rope wrought of the fear of becoming lost in that strange world, though I cast a few glances back at the enormous hole in the ground, wondering...

I knew I was obliged to introduce myself to the princess, about my age, before we settled in. But as we entered the Tower, amazing as it was, I got cold feet.

"Why didn't we just 'Port in here?" I asked irritably.

"I thought you'd enjoy seeing everything," Kelivine explained, wearing a patient smile.

She was right, but I'd grown tired, and, though I wouldn't have admitted it, a little overwhelmed. "How much farther?" I asked.

"Not far, Little Prince."

"Maybe we should wait a day? Rest up?" I squirmed and made myself look pathetic. "Come back fresh tomorrow?"

Wind chimes tinkled. "I've seen you walk ten times that distance just to play. You might as well get this part over with. Meeting Juliaire won't be that bad."

I said nothing, merely trudging along in Kelivine's footsteps. A pair of officious guards stopped us in the hallway shortly after we entered.

Kelivine explained our presence to the guards. One guard

checked her story against a book and escorted us inward.

We encountered only elves from there onward, though not a great many of them. We climbed stairs until I became sick of them, and arrived at an ostentatious set of double doors, with yet another guard positioned outside them.

"Announce us, please," our escort commanded, holding the book out to the door guard to read.

"I can try," the door guard said, his tone dry. He tapped lightly on the door, cracked it open, cleared his throat noisily, and began. "Announcing Baron Galadrindor Arafaemiel Terebra'an, heir to the…"

"Oh, bother," came the sound of a petulant little girl from within the room. "Just bring him in, would you?"

The room guard pushed the door wide, revealing a sumptuous sitting room. The floor, couch, sitting chairs, table, walls—practically everything—was constructed of white wood or stone, decorated with sparkling glass and lace, giving the impression of a winter wonderland.

Rising from the couch as she set down a book amidst a company of its brethren, breaking the snowbound imagery like a puddle of mud, a blond-haired girl about my age stared down her imperious nose at me.

"Well, come in. Let's have a look at you," she commanded.

I was not some prize animal. I scowled and stood my ground, to the quiet tinkling of wind chimes.

"Go on," Kelivine urged. "Do this and I can show you around some more."

Okay, for Kelivine I would do it. I walked toward the haughty young girl, keeping the low table for books between us.

"You don't *look* any different," she pronounced.

"Why would I? Look different than what?"

"Mother said you were from an old, backward world. I thought your bottom might be in front or something."

My bottom in front? How rude! Balling my fists I crouched to jump across the table and punch that snooty…

Was that convincing? Was I superior enough? Is he going to hit me? The voice inside my head was clear, only… it wasn't *my* voice.

I stumbled and banged my legs on the table, but put my hands on my pounding *head*—it hurt!

"Little Prince," said a voice from far away. "Are you okay?" That sounded nearer. The pounding in my head receded, but didn't go away.

I didn't remember sitting on the table, my head held between Kelivine's hands. I stared into her sky blue eyes, my breath slowing to normal as I calmed.

The last of my headache receded, and I blushed. I nodded that I was okay, but I felt ridiculous.

"Maybe you were more tired than I realized," Kelivine said comfortingly. "We should get you to your rooms."

I let Kelivine lead me toward the door.

"Yes, I'm sure he's found a *real* world quite overwhelming," said the horrible little beast.

I turned back in a rage and…

I'll bet they have him in the Dawn Room. Too bad, the Sunset Room is so much easier to get into. My head throbbed again.

Kelivine had picked me up, and she carried me out with my head on her shoulder.

"Kelivine?" I said, my head returning to normal. "Will I be in the Dawn Room?"

"No, Little Prince, you'll be in the Sunset Room." Chimes tinkled, though I heard the tinge of worry in her laughter. "How did you hear about the rooms in the Tower?"

I didn't answer. As she carried me out, my eyes landed on Juliaire, and the brief and genuine smile on her face.

Chapter 44

Staci

Our day off whizzed by in a blur. When Phillip dropped me at my rooms after our date, I'd found Elliah waiting inside. She'd been reading a book, but had put it down to be social… yet I had no idea, even shortly afterward, what we'd talked about. I lost myself in the idea that I'd fallen for Phillip.

That night the dreams hit me hard. They'd started so peacefully, rainbows and friggin' unicorns, figuratively speaking. The details didn't matter so much as the repeat of the magical kiss from Phillip—only the kiss was deeper and longer. But then something twisted inside me, and when I'd pulled away, it had been a damned Infected I'd lip-locked, its lack of a mouth not deterring it.

I'd thrashed my way to wakefulness in a sweat, to find Elliah stood hesitantly in the doorway, caught in indecision regarding the appropriateness of approaching me. I shot her a look that kept her away. *Don't touch me!* I couldn't get the Infected out of my head. My panic rose instead of settling, but then the most incongruous noise distracted me from myself. Elliah had started humming. After a few notes, I recognized the melody of the song she'd sung to me that first night she'd come in my rooms.

Little by little, I got my breathing under control, and when the wildness had fled my eyes, Elliah made her way gracefully over.

She sat on the bed and put her hand on mine, halting her tune. "There's a flower on the AllForest. Its stalks will grow almost anywhere with good soil and rain. It is only in the deep thickets of the Briars, where you can easily lose a finger just for being curious, that you will see the blooms of the MoonPetal burst with their telltale light. A light purple color, like your hair. We *will* figure this out, MoonPetal." Her words resonated with encouragement.

The problem was, I had already figured it out.

When Phillip came by the next day, I pretended I didn't feel well. Then I realized it wasn't a lie—I felt sick to my stomach. I didn't want my secret, but I'd also waited too long to share it, and... and I still didn't want to share it.

But I knew I couldn't avoid Phillip at work, and I spent my day fretting in silence under the casually watchful eye of Elliah.

Elliah and I waited at the elevator Monday morning when Phillip walked up.

"Feeling better?" he asked, smiling his caring smile and making me feel about an inch tall for having avoided him the day before. The jerk.

"Hmph," I mumbled noncommittally, wishing the others would hurry up so we could get some group dynamics going. Luckily, Elliah had come from my rooms with me, so it wasn't just me and Phillip, mano a mano... mano a *womano*.

I moved to put Elliah between us, but she chose that moment to get aggravated with the elevator, pounding angrily on the buttons.

"I enjoyed our evening together," he said, moving closer.

Dammit.

"It had been a long time since I'd seen a movie at a theatre. I'd forgotten how much better sci-fi is on the big screen."

He still smiled, the bright, sappy smile of someone in ...

My anger sparked, because I knew that wasn't my future. That *we* didn't *have* a *future*.

"If you like sci-fi, I suppose," I said snottily, jarring his smile away.

I did like sci-fi, dammit-all.

"But, I thought you wanted to see..."

I did, but that wasn't the point. "I just went along so you wouldn't feel bad."

Phillip blushed and Elliah looked at me strangely, like I was a particularly tricky crossword question.

Alex and Rej showed up, not from the same direction, but at roughly the same time. I thought that would give me a chance to distance myself, but Phillip had never been big on social norms, or we'd just become close enough as a team that he didn't mind speaking his mind in front of them.

"You could have just told me," he said. "I would have been happy to do something else. You should've just said what *you* like."

"Fine!" I said. Double damn, he was trying to make it better. "You want to know what I like?" I blurted angrily. I walked over to Rej and put my hands on his cheeks, pulling myself up on my tippy toes to plant a big ol' kiss on his lips.

Boy, his clothes really hid how strong he was. With all we did, when did he find time to work out? Up close he smelled like… pine and cloves?

The elevator doors opened, and I let go and stormed in.

The others followed, Elliah puzzling out 'eleven-down: crazy Asian Infected-candy, begins with S". Alex examined the ceiling for possible escape routes from the conversation, while Rej stumbled in, dazed and confused. Finally Phillip, red-cheeked and fuming, stepped in and spun, turning his back to me to face the closing doors.

Alex pushed the button for sublevel 2, swiping his badge across the electronic lock. Switching his attention from the ceiling to the floor, he said to no one in particular, "You do know Rej is gay, right?"

I saw Phillip and Rej nod their heads yes, and Elliah shook her head no, then shrugging. No one could see, but I shook my head no. It would almost be comical if…

"If you didn't want to go out with me, you could have just told me," Phillip insisted, walking out the doors as they opened.

Lonely, almost in tears, I stayed in the metal box as the others left. Elliah held the door, waiting. When I didn't move, she held out her hand, beckoning me. "Come on. It'll be alright." When I still didn't move, she said, "I'm not leaving you alone, my MoonPetal."

The way she said it… she didn't just mean protecting me from the physical danger of suddenly-appearing Infected. I walked out of the elevator, and she wrapped an arm around me as we trudged through the tunnels.

Chapter 45

Elliahspane, about 15 Earth millennia in the past

"Yes, I played with *fire*," growled Gavrial. "Someone had to."

Did they? I closed my eyes and shook my head.

"You can't hide under the covers," Gav barked, "while judging those of us that face danger for you!"

"You're not facing it for me," I snarled quietly. And even more quietly, I continued. "And I'm neither hiding nor judging. I've been through too much to judge." My whispered words took the wind out of Gav's sails. I stared at the spot where the Crossing Crystal should have been, its dais in the small open-sky temple empty. Someone had taken it, which meant I had to find it, or use Gav to get off that planet. "Just tell me the situation."

"FreeWorld is lost. A magic-based species of monsters. I've looked around in some quick Teleports—there's no one left alive." *No one left? On the entire planet?*

"Directed by someone?"

"I don't think so. Maybe at its start, but if so, I'd say they lost control."

"So FreeWorld—elves, humans, goblins, orcs..." I couldn't wrap my mind around an entire world, full of people, being destroyed.

"These creatures," he said, ignoring me, "they don't eat or drink. They hardly seem to move at all unless others are around. I've gone to FreeWorld by myself several times now, and they are all frozen in place. If you disturb one, they come alive around you. Other races—humans, orcs, goblins—if one of them is with me, the creatures swarm. I tell you, Leah, they are horrible even when frozen. They twitch, like you've seen something dangerous from the corner of your eye." Gav shuddered, and I knew his discomfort was real.

"So the only goblins alive are the ones that came with me?" I asked.

"I have a handful on El'daShar. There was a cave in the side of a bore. It sits surprisingly close to the High Tower."

"You operate that close to the High Lord?"

"Oh, I operate much closer than that," Gav said, looking disgusted. "I'm back in his court!" He shook his head like he couldn't believe it himself. "You taught me the importance of being a good spy."

I half-smiled. Gav, a spy.

"How did you get back in his good graces, after disappearing with me for so long?"

"That wasn't hard," he said, looking irritated. "I just had to give him something he wanted."

I didn't like the sound of that.

"What did you give him, Gav?"

"Hughelas."

That answer made me fear for my own life. My dagger appeared in my hand, ready to swing or throw if Gavriel 'Ported me into a trap.

"Sheath your dagger, woman. He was in on it. It was the only thing we could think of to get back inside Slooti's guard."

"Hughelas is okay?"

"Yes, as much as any of us are." Gav looked up, pondering something.

"What is it you need?" I asked.

"You haven't changed your mind about overthrowing Slooti?"

"I have not. " I answered.

"Then my ask is that you come take the goblins to safety."

"Come take them? Why did you not just bring them? I can't 'Port them anywhere helpful."

"This place, your little fantasy dreamland—it isn't safe. Besides FreeWorld, other worlds have fallen. You need to get them all farther away."

Puzzled, I asked, "Where?"

"Hughelas has a plan." The way he said it... "You're not going to like it."

Exactly.

"Hughelas thinks we need to go to a world with no magic."

"A *what*? Is that even possible? How would anything *live*?" Life needed magic.

"Hughelas says it's possible," he said, shrugging. "He's dreamed it. There's life."

He had dreamed it. Wonderful.

"What if he just ate some bad roots?" I said, pondering the possibility of a world without magic. Not being able to do... anything.

Don't be daft, I berated myself. *You grew up without magic. You survived.* But I had become accustomed to using magic. I wasn't born to it, but I'd *earned* the use of magic. Hughelas wanted me to give that up?

I looked around, at the relaxing world I had already decided to leave. I had my small cadre of goblins that I kept alive.

"How would the goblins survive? You know they need magic to breed."

"You can keep them alive with your magic."

My withering stare spoke for me.

Gav looked weary and frustrated. "As you will, Elliah. You won't do the sensible thing and come with me to fight Slooti. So stay here and perish at the hands of these infected monsters, or follow Hughelas's hunch and hide your goblins somewhere they won't be followed." He waved a dismissive hand at me.

The sensible thing. Idiot.

"You're hiding something," I said. "You didn't insinuate yourself into Slooti's good graces on the off chance there would be a cataclysm. What else have you done?"

He narrowed his eyes, silent. I returned the facade.

"I trained the goblins to fight back," he finally said. Sighing, he continued on. "Slooti's response was... not good. He created these beings that fight the goblins. Clothed in light, with incredible speed and strength, they proved an effective countermeasure." He shrugged. "My ploy didn't work. The goblins never acted in unison, just individual attacks—it wasn't the revolution I'd envisioned."

"He created beings of light?" He couldn't create *beings*. That was nonsense, or Gav attributing every evil to Slooti.

"He claims to have done so," Gav said. "Realistically, if he had any involvement, it was funding. He could be claiming credit for some cosmic coincidence."

Okay, *that* I would believe. Still, I'd never heard of magic that created a sentient life form. Had someone been born with a new Gift?

So many questions. It didn't sound like I would be bored again any time in the near future.

"Show me these *infected monsters*," I said with some excitement in my voice.

He nodded. "Don't let them touch you."

With a wave of his hand, a blinding light, and a *bamf*, we appeared in a swampy glade where a solitary building watched in the distance. The architectural style had changed in a hundred years. Much more elegant—it looked to be a storage building made of a sleek corrugated metal. We had arrived at dusk, and the setting sun ducked behind the small building as I looked around. Near the building squatted two dark figures, gaunt and lanky.

"What are they waiting for?" I asked.

"I don't know," Gav answered. "That's where they were when I left them. I don't think they've moved. I suspect they're waiting for a signal or sign."

With my dagger out, I moved closer.

"Don't engage them," Gav warned. "If you do, there will be more here so fast that getting away will be risky."

I looked around. There were no more in view.

"They Teleport," he said.

Mother of Trees. That was bad. A race of Teleporting monsters?

"Empaths?" I asked.

"Don't know. Haven't brought one here. But I suspect from the decimated worlds that Empaths can't stop them."

I circled behind them and moved in closer, not making a sound, and when we were several body lengths away, I saw what

Gav meant about the twitching. Every few of my breaths, one would move, but not like a muscle twitch. It was rather like seeing through a curved glass for just a moment, like the image shifted, then shifted back. It was quite... unnerving.

I backed up again. "Okay, so what now?" I asked.

"That," he said, nodding his head at the building, "was a warehouse that Hughelas used as a lab. The Bubble is in there. He said we should get it if we can."

"He found a use for it?"

"So he says," Gav said, clearly unconvinced himself.

But if Hughelas wanted it, I would get it. We crept around behind the creatures, looking carefully through windows until Gav convinced himself no monsters waited inside, and then he Blinked us in.

Trace amounts of light filtered in from the windows, providing hints of workbenches and shelves, gadgets and constructs and books.

"Can I cast a magelight?" I asked.

He nodded. "Keep it small."

I created a small light and better illuminated the room. It revealed, as I would expect from a warehouse for Hughelas, an assortment of projects. There were crystals of varying sizes, vats and vials, some filled with floating eyes or ears or... other unrecognizable bits. Shelves of semi-organized books blocked my view of some sections. Charts lined the walls, and along one wall—

"What is *that*?" I asked.

"They call them—*called* them—conjutors. Creations used to help with spellcasting."

"How do they work?"

But he just shrugged in answer, not caring.

I moved my magelight around until I found the incriminating crystal we knew as the Bubble atop a workbench. I made my way over to it.

"He told me there would be a box of crystals with it," Gav said. "We need that too."

We'd spoiled the Bubble because it sat in one of the rare, tidy areas of a workbench. On each side sat a box. Moving my light over each, I saw one had slivers of pink crystals. The other had necklaces, with crystals on the ends of the chains.

I reached in the box of necklaces and pulled one out. The sky-blue crystal dangled from a gold chain made to drop over one's head and hang low, rather than using a clasp. At my questioning look, Gav shrugged.

"I don't know which box Hugh meant," he said.

I slipped the necklace over my head and waited. Nothing happened.

I picked up the Bubble and put it in the box with the pink crystals. "I'll take this set," I said.

He picked up the other.

"Okay, let's go talk to Hughelas," I told him.

He Teleported us, but the minor flash of light told me we hadn't left FreeWorld. We looked up at a cliff with a decaying stairway connecting us to the top, and with a Blink, we appeared at the top. Traveling with a Teleporter could be a dizzying experience. A decaying city greeted us, one that had been falling apart for some time. Gav had turned around, and I followed suit. Down below nestled a city—wow, how FreeWorld had changed!

It surpassed anything done on El'daShar. The buildings were tremendously tall, scraping the sky. But many had fallen. Recently. A river ran below, and near it stood a tower, pristine, with windmills spinning atop it, and a black mass at the bottom.

"Is that—" I began.

"More of the creatures," he said. "A sea of them."

"Infected," I said, meaning the city.

"It's a good name for them. The Infected. I'll take you to El'daShar. The secret cave. But I don't know if I can get you an audience with Hughelas. He's rather heavily guarded."

"So you'll…" But before I could finish, he whisked us off-world.

Book 3, Part 2

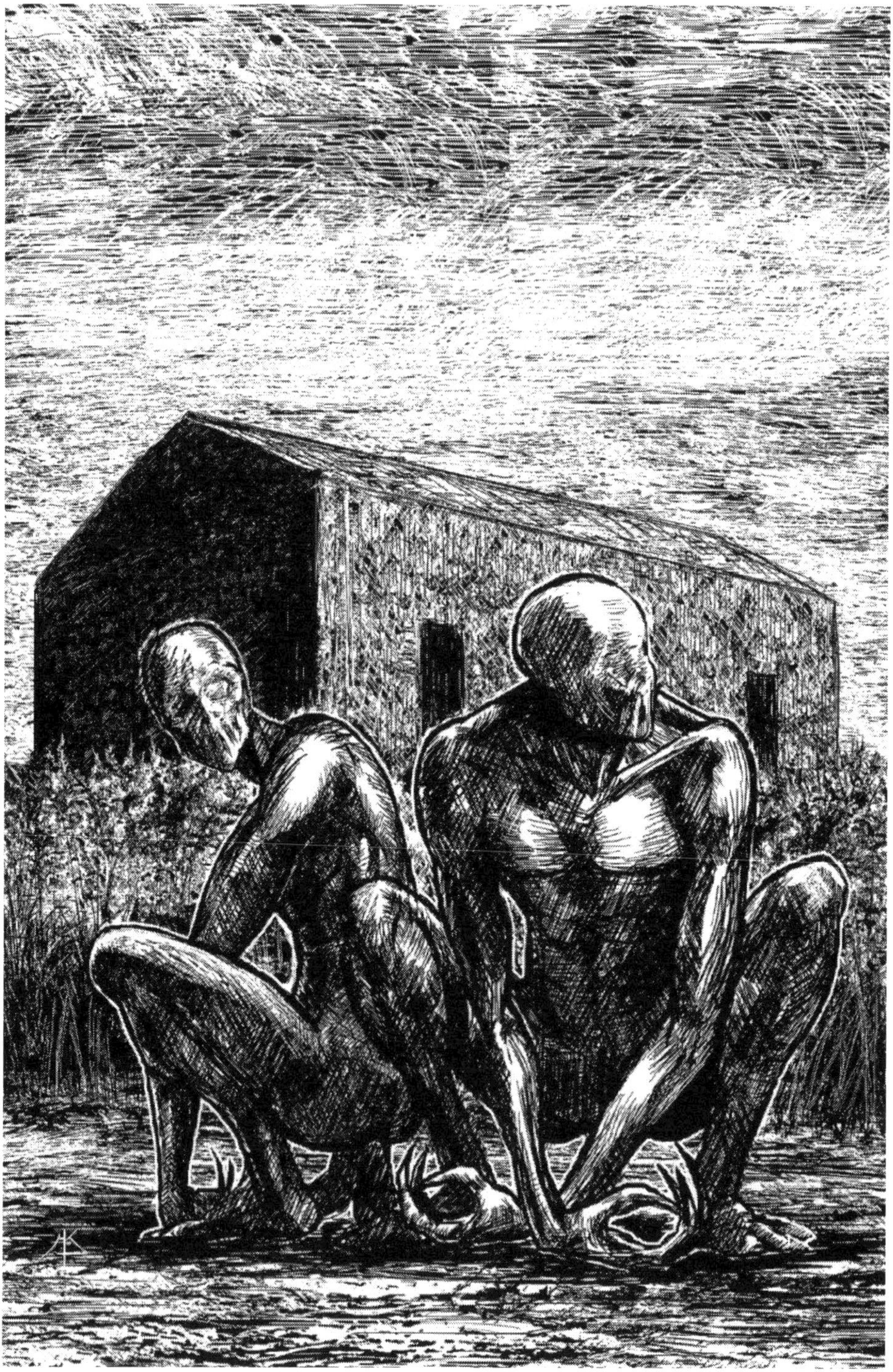

Chapter 46

Galad, about 15 Earth millennia in the past

The harder I sought sleep, the more I woke up. Kelivine had insisted I rest, but by the time we reached the rooms, I had already recovered. The evening had skulked past, the night had settled in, and I stared at my ceiling, wide awake.

Was I to be a prisoner then? Locked in a dungeon of the Tower?

Oh, I knew my bed did not lie in the dungeon. And no one had literally locked the door. But overprotective adults guarded the door, imprisoning me all the same.

I groaned again, flipping over to restart my hunt for sleep.

"Psst," came a sound from somewhere, freezing me in my battle with my covers.

"Over here. Bookcase." The whisper drew my eyes to a wall covered in bookcases, but I didn't see anyone.

"Who's there?"

"The Muuuuuther of Treeees. It's Juliaire, you dolt. Come, let me in."

I summoned a light and fumbled my way to the bookcase from where I thought Juliaire's voice emanated.

"Second shelf from the top, look for *Journey into the Unknown*. Pull it out. The shelf will open."

I had to drag a chair over to see the books that high up. Scanning the titles took some time.

"Do you know how to *read*?" Juliaire asked impatiently, sparking my anger.

I don't like being trapped in this passage.

I closed my eyes hard, trying not to fall over while standing on the chair, my head pounding with my heartbeat.

The moment passed; the pain in my head faded; and I

resumed my search for the book.

Finding it, I pulled *Journey into the Unknown*, and heard a click. I jumped back, off the chair, as the bookcase swung slightly outward. I needn't have worried—it didn't move far.

Juliaire's head popped out and swiveled toward my magelight. "Well, are you coming?" she asked.

"Coming?" I repeated dumbly. Was she inviting me on an adventure?

"Tchuh," she spat, withdrawing back into the darkness.

I hesitated only a moment before the idea of an adventure got the better of me.

The narrow passage housed two small elves with space to spare. She pulled the bookcase closed, whispering, "Don't worry; it won't latch until you push the book back in."

It wasn't a hallway, just a small alcove. Juliaire pulled something, and another door opened opposite where mine had been. She grabbed my arm and pulled me to follow. My magelight revealed a sitting room, but not mine. I wondered briefly if we had secret passages in our palace back home.

"Quietly," she whispered.

"Where are we going?" I asked.

"Out. You'll see," she said, with an air of her earlier snottiness.

It was harder to get angry, knowing her arrogance was for show. I paused, wondering how I knew she pretended, and not coming up with an answer. But I knew. Still, I had other reasons for asking—I didn't want to get in trouble.

"Kelivine will be angry," I whispered, narrowing my eyes at her.

"Adults are always angry," she whispered back.

"Maybe at *you*," I said, dishing back a little arrogance.

"Okay, golden boy." Was she talking about my hair? "Stay here if you want. I was *going* to take you to the spredix races. But if you'd rather sit in your stuffy old rooms..." and she sauntered back toward the secret door.

I didn't know what a spredix was, but I wasn't going to admit that. I stayed put.

"So we're going then?" she asked innocently.

I nodded my head yes.

She grinned triumphantly. "Kill your light."

When I did, she tiptoed to the door leading from the sitting room to the hallway, and I followed suit.

She snuck me down the hallways and stairs, ducking into alcoves and behind vases to let people pass. At one point she jerked me behind a statue that guarded the top of a stairway. Shortly after, I heard Kelivine's voice.

"He was having sudden headaches," she explained to someone. "I thought it best to summon you."

A man's voice answered. "But you didn't tell his parents?"

"I didn't want to worry them. It's probably nothing, but since he's under my charge…"

I peeked around after they'd passed. When I did, the man stopped. He laughed softly.

"What?" asked Kelivine, stopping a little ahead and looking back. I ducked behind the statue again.

"Nothing," he said. "I just had a sudden thought. Carry on." He continued down the hall, Kelivine by his side.

"That was close," Juliaire whispered, then raced on tiptoes down to the next statue.

We neared the main guard station, and she pulled me behind a display case to the side of the large foyer.

I nodded my head toward the guards, raising my eyebrows in question, too afraid to speak.

She pointed at the guards and shook her head, then pointed toward a doorway behind us, an uninviting door that spoke of gardening tools and cleaning supplies.

We tiptoed through the shadows to the door, and Juliaire produced a key. She quietly unlocked the door, and we crept in. When she closed it behind us, I summoned my light, very dimly. She locked the door and led me to some basins of water with floor drains between them.

"Now what?" I whispered.

She pointed down at the drains.

"We're going down *there*?" I hissed in alarm.

She didn't even answer. She moved to the other side of the drain and grabbed it, then nodded toward it. I grabbed my side and we lifted.

We got the heavy grate a finger-length off the ground and moved it to the side by the same amount. Then we slid it, with some effort, to the side.

She put her hands on the edge, turned her body, and dropped in. Her head was still visible above ground, her mouth smiling at me mischievously. She cast her own magelight and ducked down, sending it in front of her as she disappeared.

Not wanting to be left behind, I dropped down and saw the drain and her retreating form. *I guess we leave it open?*

I hurried after her as best I could, ducked down to fit in the small drain. An adult would not be able to follow us without getting on their hands and knees.

I caught up with her as she dropped into a larger drain. I plugged my nose from the smell, moldy and old and dirty. She waited for me to descend, a dry patch on the side keeping us out of the smelly wastewater.

"Okay," she said, no longer whispering. "We follow this a little ways, then go back up to an intersection. There's a way out of a storm drain near the races."

I brightened my light and sent it streaming up the drain.

"Did you see that?" I asked. Something had moved upstream along the side. I sent another light, but saw nothing.

"Just a shadow," Juliaire said. "Or... a gooooooblinnnnn," she said with haunting glee.

Mother had mentioned goblins. Goblin *assassins*.

"What's a goblin?" I asked.

She started walking downstream, staying to the side to keep her feet dry, her magelight floating ahead of her.

"Horrible little beasts from FreeWorld. They came here attempting to kill us. Sneaky assassins."

I hurried to catch up.

"Should we be doing this then?" Every shadow seemed to

conceal a monster.

"Don't worry. Father put a stop to it. He created some beings that protect us from the horrible things."

"Oh, so it's safe?"

She shrugged.

My fear continued to build. We joined another drain tunnel, and Juliaire turned and started up it. When she disappeared around the corner, I felt a moment of panic.

How can he not know about goblins and Guardians?

Ow! I leaned against the wall, head pounding, but the pain receded in a few heartbeats. Juliaire had paused when I dropped behind. I moved to catch up with her.

"Guardians?" I asked.

"So you've heard of them? Yes, our protectors. Guardians. Ah, here's the storm drain we want."

We crawled out onto a back street lit only by the moonlight. Juliaire skittered down the road, and I followed. "We're close," she called back.

She brought us through a building, where we got a nod from an elf resting in an open courtyard, reading a book. She moved on through to a large section of open ground packed with people. Mostly adult elves, but a scattering of other races, and even other kids.

A whistle blew, and Juliaire grabbed my hand. "Hurry!" she directed me.

She pulled me downhill through the crowd to a rope fence and pointed. "Go, Laras, go!" she shouted, and I caught my first look at a spredix. Maybe a flightless bird big enough to hold a rider? A feathered reptile? I wasn't sure, but there were four or five charging around a bend and coming our way.

Magelight illuminated an oval track with a fence in the middle, surrounded by a sloping hill that provided a natural view of the track below. The thundering steps of the spredix shook the ground.

Atop each spredix sat an elven rider, urging their beasts onward, hands grasping reins, legs straddling the splendid creatures. One elf rode with just one hand carrying the reins, the other reaching out to throw off an adjacent rider.

"Laras, watch out! Treachery!"

Watching the spredix charging made my heart leap. I pictured myself atop one, and my blood surged.

Go, Laras! ... Come on Dellineia, knock him off! ... I've got ten copper riding on this... Why do I keep going with him to these races? He never comes with me to look at clothes ... I wonder where I can train to ride a spredix ...

A hundred thoughts echoed through my mind. I felt dizzy and fell.

Then, just as quickly, the voices in my mind stopped, and I heard just the shouts of those watching the race. Just normal shouting.

A familiar voice spoke in my ear, "You need to be careful." A hand—adult-sized—grasped mine and lifted me. I held onto the rope fence and looked around. Who had just helped me? Tired and confused, I couldn't place the voice.

The mystifying events had doused my interest in the race with cold water. What was going on? Every time I was around Juliaire, I caught sudden glimpses into thoughts not my own. Was she an Empath? Should I warn her? Warn the people around her?

The race finished and, though my eyes were on it, I hadn't seen it.

"Come on," Juliaire cried, grabbing my arm and ducking between ropes in the fence. Obedient, I followed and let her drag me to the middle where the racers huddled, laughing and enjoying themselves, any misconduct forgotten.

"Laras! Laras!" Juliaire shouted.

"Hello, Juli," he said with a smile, coming our way. "Who is this then?"

"This is Galad. He's visiting from the AllForest. Oh, Laras, you won! That was so... exciting!"

Laras started to work on the saddle on his spredix, the great beast munching on a bucket of seeds.

"So, do you still want to learn to ride?" he asked. "Even after seeing them race? After seeing how dangerous it can be?"

"Oh, more than ever!" she said.

"Okay, come back tomorrow. There's no races, and we can use the arena."

I watched the crowd file out, hoping to glimpse whoever had helped me. With only one exit, people bunched up as they attempted to get out, giving me at least a chance of—there! I'd seen Kelivine's hair. I felt sure of it.

To get a better look, I dashed to the side, but the crowd swallowed her. Still... Kelivine hadn't helped me up. It had been a man's voice and a man's hand.

"Who are we looking for?" Juliaire asked.

"I don't know," I admitted. I'd been warned to be careful. Did someone else know that Juliaire showed signs of being an Empath?

"You're weird," she answered. "I think we'll get along."

She didn't see me narrow my eyes. We wouldn't get along. I wouldn't let my guard down around a potential Empath.

Chapter 47

Galad, about 15 Earth millennia in the past

"What do you want to do now?" Juliaire asked. "There's music down at the Poem's End, and it's always fun to walk around the bazaar, even at night."

"I think we should head back," I said, expecting some abuse of my character for bailing early, but not feeling up for any more adventure.

Juliaire didn't disappoint.

"Go back? Are you *kidding*?!? What are you thinking? You have so much to see. There's the…"

But she trailed off at the look on my face. Maybe I was better off on my own anyway. I wouldn't feel safe around an *adult* Empath who had mastered her powers. One that was just manifesting her power? Not safe at all. I needed to leave.

I started toward the exit, and to my surprise, Juliaire followed. When I marched back to the storm drain where we exited the sewers, she continued to tag along.

"I thought you wanted to stay out," I accused, as she jumped down into the larger storm drain beside me.

"I did," she said.

"Then why are you following me?"

She shrugged. "I don't know." She looked genuinely puzzled, and a little put out.

Were her motives sinister? Did she need to be near to influence me? What if I ran from her? Then I'd be alone in the sewer… What if I got lost, or missed the drain back into the castle?

I could take to the roads and walk to the main gate, but then the guards would catch me for certain. The idea of explaining that I'd snuck out made me cringe.

I started down the drain, startled by every shadow and drip.

Juliaire followed behind, catching my fear and getting jumpy herself.

The tunnel stretched on, the trip taking much longer than I remembered. Finally, I turned the corner where the two drains connected to a larger one. Trying to distract Juliaire, or perhaps myself, I asked, "Where does that go?"

"It empties into the bore. I've walked down there a few times. It's crazy big and deep. I think we could let this flow forever and never fill it."

The bore? That giant hole I'd seen when Kelivine had walked me through the town? "Did we *make* the bores?" I asked.

"I don't think so. My dad says they were here already. Part of the planet."

Giant holes cut into the planet? Crazy.

I stopped and watched the water flow down the tunnel, in wonder of the giant bore into which it drained. The gentle hum of the running water calmed me. I hadn't noticed or heard the water when we'd passed the bore from above, but the large tunnels suggested substantial amounts came through at times, collecting water during storms perhaps.

When I turned back to continue on, my heart froze. A *creature* stood before me: a vicious, reptilian monster, its eyes even with mine, its long mouth slivered open, revealing its serrated teeth. It just stood there, somehow having snuck up or Blinking between me and Juliaire. Everything about the monster was green save for the dagger it clutched. Dark green, scaly skin covered its back, while its bare, lighter green stomach moved with quick breath. Even its large, staring eyes shone green. But in one hand it wielded a dagger, glowing red, promising pain. I couldn't move—it was going to kill me, and I couldn't move.

Then it turned and looked at Juliaire.

Unlike me, Juliare didn't freeze. She touched something hanging around her neck, and an egg-shaped shield, red but translucent, popped up around her. Her father's Talent was shields—he'd given her something, some trinket imbued with his power. *She was safe*.

The reptile reached out with its free hand, touching the shield, and the shield held, preventing those sharp claws from reaching her skin. I still stood frozen with fear, able only to watch, as it reached out with the dagger, and the red dagger touched the red shield. The shield should have held. But instead, it vanished.

The monster pushed the dagger forward, plunging it into her chest. There must have been sounds—a small gasp or scream, a gurgle—but my ears rang, a sound *inside* my head screaming. A light flashed, as from someone 'Porting, and I expected to see Kelivine somehow there, despite her not knowing I'd escaped my rooms. Instead, I found something I'd never before encountered. Its entire body, larger than an adult elf, shined, illuminating the sewage drain like a blazing fire. The reptile waved its dagger at the newcomer, trying to scare it away.

The being didn't scare; it stood, implacable, between me and my attacker, its light an indictment to the evil intent of the assassin.

The attacker moved in, swiping impossibly fast, but the being of light moved with equal speed. It pivoted to dodge the blow, then caught the attacker's arm and used both their momentum to pull the attacker off-balance. The glowing red dagger clattered to the floor, painting the stones in small drops of red.

The glowing fighter picked up the disarmed creature and threw it hard against the floor, where it lay in a crumpled heap.

And then Kelivine *was* there, appearing out of thin air. She had her sword drawn, and moved to guard me. Seeing the reptile down, and the glowing creature just standing there, she moved to Juliare's prone form. Kelivine ministered to her, casting desperate spells of Healing, but sounding increasingly panicked, with the glowing creature standing over them, doing no more than providing light.

More elves arrived from the direction of the races. We must have been more noisy than I realized. Guards, but also the man we had seen climbing the stairs with Kelivine earlier when escaping the Tower.

One elf, a blond man with a stern face, prodded the crumpled creature with a foot. It did not stir. Most of the guards converged on Juliaire, amid comments about a Guardian having come to her rescue. The blond man hurried to Juliaire, and though Kelivine blocked my view, the other elf disappeared in a flash of light. Another 'Porter. Kelivine moved to the dead creature and rolled him over. I wanted Kelivine to come to me. I wanted to feel safe. But she remained crouched by the body of my attacker. Instead, the man from the stairs approached me. "You and I are going to spend some time together," he said, and pieces clicked in my tired mind—I recognized his voice as my helper at the races.

"Who *are* you?"

"I'm Weylshior," he said, his voice calm and pleasant. "I'm a friend of your father's, and an Empath, and I'll be training you."

The Guardian disappeared in a flash of light, just as it had arrived.

Chapter 48

Elliahspane, about 15 Earth millennia in the past

Stalactites and stalagmites clung to the ceilings and floors of the large cave. Yet no water pooled on the floor, the cause of the rock formations having departed long before my arrival.

Multiple magelights floated near the top, illuminating and casting shadows around the room. Whispers of "Elliahspane" floated around the chamber. I counted roughly ten goblins and as many elves. Worn and ragged, the inhabitants perked up at my arrival.

"I'm sorry, Leah." Gav looked genuinely repentant. "I can't stay. I hope you will find peace with your choices," he finished, setting down his box and disappearing in a small flash of light.

Other elves ended intimate relationships and still remained friends. It was an important skill if you lived for hundreds and even thousands of years. Yet, I hadn't managed it even once. The words of a wise goblin echoed in my mind. *You're kind. Sweet is something different.* Gav and I needed to talk. Still, it was not my first time to be dumped in unfamiliar territory—at least no one attacked me.

"I'm Shiei'el," said a dark-haired elf, approaching me with her hands open, showing me she carried no weapons.

"Call me Elliah," I said, taking a closer count as everyone approached. Nine elves, eight goblins. The elves all looked like they'd been living life hard—a look familiar to me. Bedding lay scattered around the edge of the cave, interspersed with stacks of wood and barrels hinting at water. They'd grown a mushroom patch for sustenance—they'd been there a long time. And since my arrival, everyone had kicked into high gear, filling up backpacks, strapping on weapons, putting equipment into boxes, like they'd been waiting for a signal.

The cave opened into darkness in one direction, and in the other, deep in the cave, a podium cradled a large jewel that I immediately recognized. I moved to the podium first. The Crossing Crystal. So Gav had taken it. Why?

"Hughelas says it is ready," Shiei'el informed me as she cinched the straps on her pack.

Ahh, the world without magic which Gav had mentioned. He'd stolen the Crystal, and Hughelas had set it up. Did he mean to send us to a dead world? How was that even possible? Or did Gav toy with me, trying to force me into a fight?

I set down my box, replete with crystals and the Bubble, in the circle of raised stone next to the podium. It would be inside where the field formed.

Then I walked to the opposite site of the cave, where it opened into darkness. The floor ended abruptly. I looked up, and far above, I thought I saw light. "This is a bore?" I asked, but I knew already that it was.

"Yes, Mistress Elliah," said a goblin that had come near.

"Call me Leah," I said, supplying the name I'd become used to with the goblins.

"Yes, Mistress Leah."

"Just Leah."

"Yes, Mistress Leah."

I rolled my eyes, though no one could see.

"Is this Dhura or Ghara?" I asked.

Over the din of people packing and talking, I barely heard the whispered response. "Does it matter, Mistress Leah?" The goblin looked sad beyond repair.

"What is *your* name?" I asked.

"Noguri," it reported, offering no more.

"You are male or female, or you don't know yet?"

The goblin showed a wisp of a smile. "Female, Leah."

That was better. I put an arm on her shoulder, still staring out into the darkness of the bore.

"There," I heard a voice speak from the distance. "I see light."

"Take a guard. Investigate."

That voice.

I pushed Noguri away from the edge, waving everyone to

move back and drawing my dagger. With a small flash of light, two elves appeared between me and the retreating crowd.

One was a warrior, clad in shining silver armor and brandishing a sword; the other I knew well. I whistled to get their attention. The warrior came at me slowly—no chance I could use his momentum to send him tumbling into the bore.

I didn't have to. Gavrial pushed him unceremoniously off the ledge. Gav looked me in the eyes, all kinds of anger and disappointment roiling behind his, then disappeared in a flash of light.

Seconds later, an enormous magelight bloomed in the bore, illuminating both sides. Across the bore, a hole widened from the size of a single person to something that would allow five elves to pass at once. The distance was too far for me to see clearly, but I knew the voice I'd heard—Slooti led them.

As I watched, stone protruded from beneath the opposite opening.

"Are any of you StoneWorkers?" I shouted back to the cave.

No answer. Damn. No stopping the bridge.

"Any Talents?"

"Water!" shouted one elf, blond-haired with a rough look. One of the more deadly powers in combat. I motioned him forward with my head. But I couldn't use him to get us out of the trap.

Curses! Gav had set me up. Provided me with a deadly weapon, a way to fight… and Hughelas had left me a way out. I pictured their conversation, over a pint of something-or-other. Gav, with his self-righteous anger, architecting my involvement in his fight. Hughelas, who had no combat ability, arguing for me to have a choice. A compromise reached. I hated that I had been played so well, so easily. My desperation from sitting on that lazy planet had made it simple for them.

The stone continued to grow, protruding a third of the way across the gap. The elves walked out upon it. If I had a WindWorker, I could swipe them all off. Or with a StoneWorker I could shatter the bridge. Would I?

Gav would have done better to bring me up to speed.

Throwing me into this situation... I refused to be used by him to usurp the kingdom.

"Gather your things and get near the crystal," I shouted behind me. I turned and marched back. They scrambled, but I had nothing to gather, no role in that place. Dammit, Gav!

Several were ready and gathered near me. It would take two trips.

"When you get to the other side, clear out of the way," I told them, and activated the Crossing Crystal. A globe of translucent light appeared beside me. "Get in," I told them.

A goblin was the first to walk through. It might have been Noguri—I wasn't sure. Once the first entered, elves and more goblins followed. A goblin tapped on the field from the inside. I recalled doing the same my first time. I didn't envy them the trip, but knew my own turn would follow.

The bridge of stone continued to grow—Slooti had recruited a powerful StoneWorker. The damn magic of the Crossing Crystal took too long. Its field held, waiting for more to enter. The bridge would reach our cave before we could activate the crystal a second time.

"Hold them off as best you can without killing them," I told the WaterWorker. I needed to stay near the crystal to activate it a second time. "Everyone who isn't fighting, get near the crystal and get ready to leave!"

Another elf joined the WaterWorker near the edge, as did a couple of goblins. As the bridge neared our end, about ten elves prepared to assault us. Slooti and Gav were among them. Several elves wore armor and wielded swords, and the others dressed as mages.

Something rumbled in the stone above, and a torrent of rock and water came shooting at the elven attackers. The WaterWorker hadn't used the barrels; he'd pulled the water from some underground passage. A shield popped up between the elves and the cascade, and the water and rock fell around them. Slooti's Talent protected them.

A desperate part of me hoped the falling debris would shatter the bridge, but even as I thought that, the bridge reached the other end, solidifying the structure.

The elves rushed forward, the shield morphing to deflect the falling debris out into the bore. Almost too late, the field of the crossing crystal disappeared, taking the first round of evacuees with it.

With no time to lose, I activated the crystal, creating a second field, as the goblin-elf rebellion engaged Slooti's troops.

"Everyone in!" I shouted, moving to help in the fight so others could escape.

One of our elves fell under the attack. A goblin held its own against an elfin warrior. The WaterWorker was doing no serious damage, but he kept the mages busy. I moved in and protected the other goblin, who meant well but didn't have the fighting skill of its brethren. Engaging the warrior, a female with a sword, I fought to merely slow them down, not hurt them.

Most of the second round of evacuees quickly entered the field. There was no going back for them. The goblin that was winning knocked his elven opponent to the ground and stood over him. A tall being, emitting light, appeared out of thin air and attacked the goblin. I locked eyes with Gav, who had held back in the assault, positioned to pull Slooti out should things go bad. His eyes said, "I told you."

I shoved the goblin I was helping toward the field of the crystal.

"Time to go!" I shouted.

I had thousands of years of fighting under my belt—the warriors I fought did not. Slooti used inexperienced troops. Was that his choice? Did he have the more experienced fighters elsewhere? Or had the older elves distanced themselves from him?

I moved to place myself between the mysterious glowing attacker and the goblin. The WaterWorker crept backward toward the crystal, fending off stone and flame as he went. I didn't see the other elf that had defended the goblins. Had he lost or retreated?

The tall being of light moved with speed, and struck with strength, but I'd fought trolls—I'd dealt with worse. And it only tried to get past me—it didn't attack me directly. And then it stopped. A quick glance showed me that no defenders remained save for me. The glowing creature had stopped when its quarry had gone through the field. I looked at Gav one last time, and he looked... irritated. He'd thought I would fight.

I wouldn't.

I stepped into the field. No one followed us in. Slooti walked over to the field, shaking his head. Behind him, the being of light bent down and put a hand on the chest of the fallen elf. The light grew brighter, and then, in a flash of light, it disappeared. The wounded elf was gone. What had I just seen?

Scanning the room through the magical field, I spotted a box. I'd left the damned box of necklaces behind, the one Gav had carried. Looking down, the box I had brought was no longer there, already transported by the first crossing. I hoped I'd grabbed the right box.

In the end, I locked eyes with Slooti, who smiled and waved goodbye.

Chapter 49

Galad

"That last bit is mostly what I dreamed," Red commented. "Though it wasn't in a sewer, and it was just you and the girl… and sometimes the Guardian saved you or the girl, but sometimes not." She shivered, clearly disturbed by the dreams. Scan and Harry had wandered up while I told the story. They'd missed the beginning, but caught the attack in the sewer. Scan looked thoughtful.

"Where did the attack take place in your dream?" I asked, genuinely curious, but also wanting to take the sting out of her memory by focusing on the mundane.

"Up on the streets—not any I've recognized, but it was above ground, with elven architecture. It looked generally like this," she said, gesturing around her. "I had the dream more than once… different places." She shrugged, looking around. "I didn't recognize any of them."

"Dreams are our minds' way of digesting memories and emotions," I said. "The attack was in the sewers. But your mind must have combined memories from—"

"So you think the Infected are related to these Guardians?" Scan interrupted.

"That's my running theory," I answered, looking at Red to see if she needed to talk about her dreams more—she smirked and rolled her eyes, nodding for me to talk to Scan.

"But why?" Scan asked. "I've heard nothing particularly connecting. They were polar opposites. Light/dark. Protector/attacker. Comforting/scary-as-hell…" he trailed off in thought. "Okay," he concluded. "That *is* a good start."

I smiled. The same thought had occurred to me. "That wasn't the connection I made though." I had Scan's attention. "To make a long story short…"

"Oh, please do," Red said sweetly.

"...there was a ceremony not too long after the attack. A group of elves were selected for their valorous deeds, and in a recognition ceremony, the Guardians were summoned via some magic that the High Lord initiated. The Guardians then selected two of the heroes, and those heroes *became* Guardians. The literal movements—reaching down and touching the elves, transferring their magical nature—looked very much like the way the Infected convert people."

We all sat in silence for a moment.

"That's what I saw," Red said. "In the... library. Or in the vortex."

"What library? What vortex?" Scan asked.

Red and I exchanged a look. "Hard to explain," she said. "I hijacked some of his memories."

Scan nodded, taking that in with his usual nonchalance.

"The elf whom my parents assigned to protect me," I said, "Kelivine, was one of the two selected. I never saw her again. The High Lord had made it seem like an honor, but I always wondered if she was happy to have been chosen."

Unable to completely shut out Red's emotions, I felt my story weigh on her, heavy with loss. Bear... Kelivine... countless individuals given over to... to *what*?

"So," Scan asked in the deafening silence, "you've hinted that the Guardians were *created*. What is *their* story?"

"I don't know," I told them. "Elliah doesn't either. She was... not around... when the Guardians were, um, founded," I finished feebly. "We believe the High Lord Slooti commissioned them, in response to the attacks on elves by goblin assassins. And Elliah suspects the work was done on FreeWorld. It's another reason to find the elves, and get to FreeWorld."

"I get how finding the elves might get us more information," Scan said, "but getting to FreeWorld?"

"If the research to create them was done there, then there might be records. It was a little before my time."

Red shot me a look. "Before *your* time?"

I smiled. "But not before Elliah's. She told me that FreeWorld had once been a hub of learning." I shrugged. I found it hard to believe.

"You told us that was fifteen millennia ago," Scan said. "Is there really any chance of finding *anything*?"

"Elder Stones would last that long," I answered. "Elliah said that FreeWorld had the most advanced technology of the time, before it was overrun. There's a chance."

Red stood and stalked away, saying, "I would disembowel every Infected from here to hell for Bear to have had that chance."

Chapter 50

Harry

"You know where else might be helpful to go?" I said, jogging after Red. "And we can go there any time we damn well please?"

I'd had enough waiting.

"Tom's Tavern for a beer?" Red smart-mouthed. Okay, in other circumstances that would have been funny, but it was insane that we hadn't yet popped into DwarkenHazen.

"Harry, we need a *day*," Red said with a hint of exasperation she couldn't keep out of her voice. Galad joined us, putting an arm around her, which didn't reduce her irritation at all. "If we move the Rings too soon, and something goes wrong in DwarkenHazen..."

"I know!" I barked. "But I'm tired of waiting. That's *my* people, *my* family, and I need to know that they're okay."

Red cocked her head at me, and after I sat through her scrutiny like a newfound tunnel under the eye of a miner, she nodded. "Let's go talk to Mort."

"He's near the Rings," Galad informed us, "coordinating some of the initial meetings between the people of Forsaken and the people of Earth."

"C'mon," Red said to me, and I gladly followed her.

You like following her? Bessie asked.

Don't be daft. I told her. She laughed.

I didn't even have to be holding Bessie to talk to her anymore. She just had to be near. And I knew she bantered to distract me from my worry.

We marched through the transport hub. It was looking as busy as when elves had occupied the planet—full of life and activity. Only, humans filled the space instead of elves, with camps instead of small shops to feed and supply travelers.

It didn't take long to reach the Rings. Two of them crouched side by side, one emitting a steady cadence of humans from the Forsaken, the other spewing forth people and equipment from Earth. Though the Rings sat next to each other, like two openings on a pair of brass knuckles, the traffic flowed in opposing directions, so the emerging streams did not collide.

A forklift passed through the Ring from Earth, carting boxes of equipment, its gas-powered engine adding to the din.

"Probably heavy weapons," Red said, answering my unspoken question. "See the way they're moving them to the perimeter? They're securing the area from outside attack."

"That won't do a lot of good against mages," I said. "They can Blink inside the perimeter and get behind your line of fire."

Red nodded agreement. "They're going to mix the Forsaken in with the Earth military. The Forsaken will be a lot better in close combat, and in fighting mages and magic."

We found Mort, talking with some of his leaders and a General from Earth. They looked at paper maps weighed down with rocks on a portable table. Magical overlays floated atop the paper. At a glance, I would have guessed it revealed intended positions of different troops and weapons, and their current positions. They already had a plan; they were working out logistics.

Mort saw us coming and excused himself. He was not creating the magical overlays then—one of his men crafted those spells. Mort looked at Red questioningly.

"We wanted to talk about moving up the schedule," Red told him.

Mort looked back toward the map and overlays. "There's some complicated logistics involved in securing an area this large with the limited transport we have," he said. "I'm open to suggestions, but I don't see how to move a Ring to Emerald Farms until tomorrow."

I grunted in frustration, and Red waved me quiet.

"How about if you drop a handful of us off in DwarkenHazen ASAP, and pick us back up tomorrow?" Red said. "There would be no jeopardy to your plans."

Mort nodded. "I'd rather be there with you, but we can do that.

We will need to have Galad force Cordoro to take us there." He turned to me. "Give me a few minutes to finish here, and we can do this thing."

I nodded. *Finally.*

"So," Red said, looking anywhere but at me, "your hammer. Bessie?"

I squinted one eye at her.

What's she want to know? Bessie asked.

How should I know? Why don't you ask her yourself? I answered.

Don't get your beard in a knot! I was just trying to be helpful.

"Awkward," Red said. "You're talking to her now?"

"I am. She asked what you want to know."

"Umm, why *Bessie*?" Red threw out.

"It's short for Baessendra. Baessendra Montingale was her most well-known name. She was a pioneer in… Imbuing."

"Ah," Red said.

"Why *Red*?" I asked.

"Just a nickname I picked up after a particularly bloody fight. My real name is Garnet, ironically enough. My parents named me and my sisters after rocks."

"I thought Grundle was kidding when he said that," I told her. Naming people after rocks was a very dwarven thing to do, though I was not so be-monikered.

"Nope. My sisters are Citrine and Jade." Galad watched the Earthen vehicle speed back toward the Rings, a slim smile revealing his appreciation of our attempt to converse.

"Nice," I said, smiling indulgently.

Mort interrupted our painfully awkward conversation by returning. "Okay. Ready?" he asked.

We all nodded, and Mort 'Ported us back to the store we'd used for sleep those first nights on El'daShar. The others waited there—Grundle and Smith. Red brought them up to speed as they geared up.

We 'Ported to Emerald Farms and talked through the same updates with Hirashi, who in turn provided Mort with updates on grain silos and food supplies for El'daShar and... blah, blah, blah. Meanwhile, Lani and Red shot the breeze like two childhood cave-sisters hitting the same vein of crystal as adults.

Patience, Bessie encouraged.

"I think we're ready," Mort said. *Finally!* "We will take a quick trip to DwarkenHazen," Mort explained. "Go there, then I come back with Galad and Cordoro and we drop Cordoro off here. Or," he said, thinking through the details, "I knock Cordoro out so that I can leave Galad there—that's safer." Galad nodded. "I go back after we get the Ring to Emerald Farms, and pick them up. So sometime tomorrow."

"Agreed," Hirashi said. Sighing, she looked at the door to the council chamber. "Bring Cordoro out."

Hirashi opened the door to the council chamber. They'd cleared the conference table out and replaced it with a cot. Cordoro was free to roam the chamber, but two Forsaken guards kept him from exiting. When the doors opened, Cordoro stopped pacing the back of the room.

"Bring him out," Hirashi told the guards. They moved in, and Cordoro scanned those waiting outside. When he spotted Galad, he did his best to prevent his capture. But Mort's men, experienced warriors, subdued and dragged their prisoner out of the room. As soon as they pulled him through the door, his thrashing ceased. He stood, calm, eyes glazed over.

"Okay," Galad said, "here we go." He concentrated, and I assumed did his mind trick with Cordoro and Mort to extract the Teleport location from Cordoro. Or possibly he just forced—Compelled—Cordoro to do the Teleport... I wasn't sure and didn't know how to tell. And didn't care greatly about the distinction.

Then, at long last, the room lit with the bright light associated with interplanetary travel and... *bamf*.

Chapter 51

Red

DwarkenHazen, assuming we'd arrived in the right place, put me in mind of every cheesy movie that had taken place on an asteroid. Black, pitted rock jutted from the ground—the debris of missile blasts or meteorites. Night reigned, and the stars camped close and bright. No sign of life greeted me—neither past nor present—no buildings, no plants, no skittering or flying creatures. I had a sinking feeling in my stomach.

"This is it," Harry said excitedly, his positive attitude unclenching the knot in my gut. His face scrunched up. "Strange place to 'Port though. The main entrance to DwarkenHazen is over that ridge." He pointed in a direction that looked impassable. "Why would his 'Port location be way over…"

Thunk, came a noise from behind me, then a flash of light with a familiar *bamf*.

I spun, drawing my daggers, alarmed to find Galad down with a bolt protruding from his chest.

Harry yelled, "Stop!" and moved to protect Galad, hammer drawn. Grundle leaped to cover Galad, and Scan knelt down beside the wounded elf. I looked in the direction Harry faced but spotted nothing. I covered Scan and scrutinized the rest of the rock-blasted horizon, trying not to let my worry for Galad distract me from protecting him.

"Harry?" came a distant voice.

"Yes, it's Harry! Who the hell are you?"

"Don't you recognize your own cousin? It's Bluff Blackvein."

"The notorious thief?" Harry shouted back.

"A thief named Bluff?" I whispered. "That's a bit on the nose."

"I don't think I've got quite your level of notoriety!" Bluff shouted back. "Weren't you Banished to a far-off world without magic?"

"I was, but I forgot my toothbrush, so I had to come back!"

"With an *elf*? I don't care how good your story is; you won't darken the hallways of DwarkenHazen with *him* for company."

Scan had Healed Galad, but Galad chose not to rise and provide another dwarf with an opportunity for target practice. I kept searching other rocks for potential attack.

"Mort, any chance you can follow Cordoro?" Galad asked.

Oh, shit! Cordoro had fled when the bolt or arrow had taken Galad out.

Mort shook his head no. "Under better circumstances, perhaps. That requires a skill level I have not yet reached."

"Then take me back with you," Galad said. "I think I will be more valuable searching for Cordoro than aggravating the dwarves."

Galad looked at me. His blood-stained robe gave me pause, but he pulled the neckline to the side to show me his mended skin. I nodded at him to go, telling him, "Finding Cordoro sounds like a job for an Empath and a Teleporter."

Mort looked at the remaining crew. "I'll be back sometime tomorrow. Everyone else staying?"

We all nodded. Mort cast his spell, and with a flash of light and a *bamf*, they left us.

"The elf is gone!" Harry shouted. "Can we talk now?"

A grey flag rose from over a cratered escarpment not too far from us. "I'm sure I can't wait to hear your story!" Bluff shouted back. Harry started toward the flag and we followed close behind.

The gravity felt stronger on that world than either Earth or El'daShar, the trek requiring more effort than a similar distance on Earth. The rough terrain forced us to climb. Scan brought up a magelight, which cast as many shadows as it revealed because of all the rocky protrusions.

"I like your world," Grundle told Harry. "Cozy." I couldn't tell if he was joking or serious.

Harry grunted. "It's pretty and all," he said, "but there aren't a lot of job opportunities here. Bluff," he said, waving his hand in the direction we were going, "has control of the black market. If you want to do mining, there's still some work here, but going off-world is more profitable. You can't throw a rock without hitting a sculptor."

A sculptor? Why bring up sculpting? The carving in Jerusalem... did Harry want to sculpt?

"Jordi, my Teleporter nephew that helped me get the trunk to Grundle, works for Bluff." I heard worry in his voice as he said the last.

We crested a rise and spotted a group of dwarves, three with hammers and three peering over boulders with crossbows aimed at us. Two more stood without weapons drawn, one garbed in robes that screamed "mage" and the other had a hammer strapped to his back but not drawn.

"What brings you to my home of all places?" the one with his hammer on his back asked unceremoniously.

"Not *what*, Bluff," Harry said. "*Who*. We got a ride from a human named Cordoro."

Bluff scowled. "He's a real piece of work." He sighed. "But a sculpture can't choose its sculptor... he's a Teleporter willing to do business."

"Let me rephrase," Bluff said. "*Why* did you come?"

"Personally," Harry said, "I wanted to be sure Jordi was okay. But, bigger picture, I sent something with Jordi to get it away from the elves."

"The elves got it," Bluff said. "Destroyed half of DwarkenHazen to get it."

So the elves had needed the Amp, and they took it.

"Jordi?" Harry asked.

Bluff shook his head no. "In the end, he took the crystal and ran with it. They had Teleporters experienced enough to follow him. The elves departed from DwarkenHazen shortly after..."

"They got what they wanted," Harry concluded. "How did they know to look here?" he asked himself quietly.

Bluff didn't answer, but I saw more than one guard shift uncomfortably. They'd done something... drawn attention somehow.

Bluff redirected the conversation, "I take it this is the Warlord you threw in with."

"Grundle," the troll said.

"Grundle," Bluff repeated. "And the elf we shot?"

"He was part of the elf resistance that fought for the rights of the trolls," Harry said.

Bluff nodded. "I won't have him shot if I see him again, but I wouldn't take him into DwarkenHazen proper if I were you. Like me, they'll shoot first and ask questions later."

"Any clue where the elves went, or how they all disappeared?" Harry asked.

"None," Bluff said. "The elven attack severely hampered our ability to Teleport. We don't even know *exactly* when they left. From some planets with both elves and dwarves, we learned the elves had evacuated those planets. We sent a war party to El'daShar, but the elves had already abandoned it. They'd left us enough problems here that we didn't try to find them.

Nodding, Harry said, "We are here for a day. Is there anything useful we can do?"

Bluff looked at Grundle. "The big guy could help get to some caves that are still shut off."

I piped in. "It's been weeks. You still have people trapped underground after weeks?" Did they expect to find them alive after that time?

Bluff and Harry looked at me. "They're dwarves," Harry said. "That's hardly a death sentence."

Okay.

"Just point me in the right direction," Grundle said in his deep voice.

"Not afraid of the dark or confined spaces, are you?" Bluff asked.

"Sounds cozy," Grundle said with a grin.

"Melani, get him somewhere that he can do some lifting," Bluff said.

"You got it, boss," said the mage—bearded, but a female voice.

"Wait," Smith said. "I'm with him."

"I'll be blunt," Bluff said. "A human would only get in the way."

"Scan," Smith said, "can you give me a little boost? Something a little hardier?"

Scan put a hand on her exposed tricep. Her skin turned rocky and talons sprouted from her hands. Her eyes glowed with reflected light from the stars.

"Let's go," Smith said, looking at Grundle, who smiled and put a massive hand on her shoulder.

"What was *that*?" asked Melani, the mage. "Isn't that illegal, and how did you *do* it?"

"Galad warned you, you idiot," I told him.

"Aren't we talking to people who understand the necessity of occasionally bending the rules?" Scan said in explanation.

"You'll find dwarves are rule followers," Bluff said. "If you're deep in a dangerous mine, everyone's lives depend on those rules. Then there are the thieves." He waved his arms around at his comrades. "There are many things that get… stuck… when there are too many rules. Thieving, in dwarvish minds, is a profession that keeps the cogs from jamming. It is a rule that sits above the other rules."

"So it is an honored profession?" Scan asked.

"Not exactly," Bluff said, to the chuckling of the other dwarves. "Part of the job is to be excluded from proper society, but I assure you, we consider thieves to be rule followers."

"Just a higher rule," Scan said. "I can work with that. I'm following a higher rule—doing what is needed to help people survive."

Melani shrugged. "I still don't know what you did or how you did it. I'll be back. We should talk." She 'Ported Grundle and Smith away.

"Need the use of Healing?" Scan asked.

"Not so much," Bluff said. "The damage that could be Healed by the elven attack has already happened. Unless you can raise the dead?" His question sounded rhetorical.

"Can that be done?" Scan asked, genuinely curious.

"I've heard that some Healers can do it," Bluff answered. "If the death was recent. But not with the weeks that have already gone by."

Bluff looked at Scan strangely, like Scan's innocent question was more out of place than the transformations he'd performed.

"I think it is time to hear your tale, Harry." Bluff signaled to one of his fighters to follow. "Let's go in."

He marched off, one of his men following. Harry trailed after them, and Scan and I followed him.

I felt… thin. Exposed. Our party consisted of just Scan, Harry, and me. Rocks stayed back on Earth; Galad went searching for Cordoro with Mort; Grundle and Smith were doing rescue work. I wished we'd taken Lani along with us. Four was a more solid number. Incongruously, I remembered learning that a triangle, with its three sides, was architecturally stronger than a square. But four people on a team felt right to me. Three felt brittle.

Nevertheless, we three followed Bluff, traveling through a maze of rocky protuberances until we reached a cave entrance. Scan illuminated the interior, and revealed a nondescript cave. The cave turned about ten feet in, and Harry rounded that corner just as we entered the mouth. Scan and I shared a look, then trekked after. But we paused upon the view after the turn.

The cave opened up into something much more grandiose. From the entrance, the room expanded to something about thirty feet wide and twenty feet tall, with grand columns carved with the figures of dwarves in various acts of sneaking, climbing through openings, carting bags of gold, and other mischievous acts.

The exit was opposite the entrance, down a ten foot-wide walkway. Magelight illuminated the room dimly from above. Harry and Bluff moved down the ramp and into the deepening shadow.

Scan and I exchanged another look. I wondered if my face looked more skeptical, or his. He sent a magelight ahead, poking around the columns and down the ramp. Alcoves tucked neatly into the sides of the ramp, clearly meant to ambush intruders. It made sense, but it didn't make me feel any better about proceeding down the ramp.

Still, Harry had already passed through the room. Nothing to do but join him in the lion's gullet. We eased down. The alcoves held openings for crossbows, but we passed without incident. The ramp continued down, with more alcoves, plus grooves in the floors, walls, and ceiling that put me in mind of guillotine blades and Alfred Hitchcock movies.

We emerged into a larger room with several hallways leading off from it. Lit more brightly than the ramp had been, it welcomed guests. Unfamiliar stories of dwarves decorated the walls.

Many dwarves moved through or occupied the area, all of them casting glances our way. The men and women dressed differently, as did the spellcasters versus fighters, but they *all* had beards. Some women decorated their beards with beads or ribbons, but the men wore theirs plain. A few small children ran around, beardless, and their plain faces stood out, along with the young adults with short beards.

An ear-piercing whistle drew all eyes to Bluff. The room grew quiet and still.

"For anyone who has ears to hear," Bluff roared, "Harisidogle Darriunminer, uncle of Jordiafurd Dariunminer, will tell us the story of his journey to a world that is *fighting the Infected*. One hour. Here." Bluff waved his arms, and the room emptied out like a fire alarm had gone off.

Bluff disappeared, and Harry stared at nothing, a pensive look on his face. I approached him, wondering if he was nervous.

"He knows I was working to displace him," Harry mumbled, without my asking. "Or at least be his rival. He wants to discredit me, perhaps even pin this calamity on me."

"You wanted to be the head of the dwarven thieves?" I asked. In the time I'd known him, he'd gravitated toward the theatrical, but always to do good things—helping his friend have a fighting chance on a new world at the cost of his own future, sending his nephew away in order to spare him, battling the Infected to save a people not his own. If the dwarves thought of Thieves as those who stepped outside of rules to enable or achieve a greater good, then his goal made sense.

"Harisidogle Darriunminer," Harry mumbled to himself, "King of Thieves." He smiled, but it looked forced. "I know, Bessie, I know."

I still found his private conversations with his Hammer disconcerting.

"What's she saying?" I asked.

But Harry just shook his head. "I need a moment," he said, and moved away a small distance, drawing his hammer, and sitting down with it, staring off into the shadows.

Scan took off his backpack. "I've got the projector and footage that Rocks brought. I don't know what's on it, but it's got to be useful."

We set it up together. Dwarf-sized tables and chairs lay scattered about in the vast hall, and we purloined what we needed to set up the projector on a chair stacked atop a table.

We aimed the image to project on the wall above the ramp entrance. We watched the video once, not projecting it, and playing the sound low so as not to disturb Harry and Bessie. It was almost perfect, lacking only in that Harry wasn't in it. We had nothing else to do but wait. Before long, Melani came in, another mage in tow.

"My apologies," Melani said. "I didn't get your names before. I am Melani, and this is Shariela." They both had dark hair, dark eyes, and adult beards.

"I'm Red," I told her, "and this is Scan."

She looked at me, scrunching up her face in puzzlement, then shrugged her shoulders.

"Would you mind showing us what you did before?" she asked Scan.

Scan looked at me. "You mind?" he asked.

I shrugged, then nodded okay. He seemed to have worked out the magic—I'd seen him do it with Smith a couple of times.

Scan held out his hand, and I placed mine in his, trusting him.

I felt my skin harden, though not in a way that made it stiff. I started to tap my forearm with my free hand, and changed my mind when I saw the talons sprouting out from my fingertips. Those looked like they'd still puncture even my tougher skin.

Overall, kinda cool. I felt stronger, too, like he'd made the fibers of my muscles turn into sterner stuff. Hopefully, he'd strengthened the bones to take the increased pressure.

The mages, even Melani, who'd seen his spell before, stared wide-eyed.

"Can you cast a Healing?" Melani asked Scan.

I obligingly dragged a talon across my forearm—I'd already wondered whether the talon was sharper or the skin tougher. I was right—the talon won. Blood spurted out of my forearm like it was under pressure, then oozed out more slowly.

Scan followed up with a Heal, and my arm sealed itself back together.

"That..." Shariela said, "... was *not* a Heal."

Scan shrugged, responding, "Galad said that a Healing by a natural Healer works and looks different than a normal Heal, the way a natural Teleporter can Teleport differently."

"Whoever Galad is," Shariela answered, "he's right. Thing is, *I'm* a natural Healer. *You* are not."

It was Scan's turn to look... wait, he looked, if anything, relieved.

"So what am I?" he asked. "I'm a natural *something*, because this magic comes to me more simply than other spells."

"I don't know *what* that was," Shariela said.

Melani shook her head, indicating she didn't know either. "I'm not a Healer," she said, "but I'm better than average at a lot of magic, and I don't recognize what you're doing. That said, it *does* break the second Law of Magic."

"Good thing I'm in the right place for breaking rules?" Scan offered.

I winced.

The two dwarves looked at each other, measuring how Scan's transformations fit into the rules they were willing to break.

"He transformed a human into something much more useful," Melani said to Shariela.

"Hey!" I said. "I'm useful!"

The dwarves ignored me, but decided Scan's use of magic and his breaking of the second Law was acceptable. Desperate times call for desperate measures. They turned and walked away, looking back at us as they talked.

"Okay, Scan, change me back."

He took my hand and undid the transformations and returned me to my normal self. I wondered, what else could he do? It would be great not to have to shave my pits anymore.

Melani and Shariela didn't leave; they just sat at one of the remaining tables. Soon, others arrived. Ones, twos, sometimes families, and they sat down on the floor around us, forming a respectful circle. More and more came, filling the hall like they were preparing for Fourth of July fireworks. They talked excitedly to one another, and the noise level continued to rise as they filed in.

Soon, Bluff walked through the seated, noisy crowd, and Melani weaved her way to the front. She cast a spell, and the sound in the audience dimmed. She cast another, and Bluff's voice boomed.

"Fellow Thieves, you all know the story brought to us by Jordi." There were murmurs among the audience. "That Harisidogle Darriunminer, Jordi's uncle, did go unto the AllForest, *after* it had been overrun by the Infected, where he retrieved goods precious to the Warlord. He brought those to the Banishment chamber of the elves, sentencing himself to join the Warlord and the rebellious elf leader from the AllForest. We expected never to hear from him again." Bluff paused dramatically. "And yet here he is, and the Warlord, even now, is down in the depths of DwarkenHazen, clearing our passages collapsed by the elf attack. Let us hear his story!"

There was a *boom* as all the dwarves clapped their hands once.

Harry stood from where he had been sitting, still not facing the crowd, but looking off to the side. He slowly walked over to Bluff, securing his war hammer on his back as he went. Bluff cleared some space for him.

Harry looked over the crowd, still not speaking, as Melani cast a spell to boost his voice. And then he waited a moment more.

"Friends, dwarves, thieves… lend me your ears." I hadn't noticed Harry reading Shakespeare—he really was a thief. "I have dreamed of the day, longed for it—that you would hear my tale. Yet, I find, it is not my story that needs telling. It is the story of the people whose planet we were meant to die on. Not my story, but *hers*."

His hammer pointed at me, runes glowing alternating blue and yellow, and several hundred dwarven eyes reflected the light as they bore into me.

Chapter 52

Red

What the freaking hell!

"You sat there for an hour and this is what you came up with?" I whisper-yelled at him.

"Back off, Red," he whispered back. "This was hard for me. You try searching your soul and deciding what you really want in an hour."

"You could have given me a hint! I would have been at least *thinking* about what to say."

"You'll be fine," Harry said, waving me over with his hammer.

"Red," Scan said, and I looked back at him. "Let's start with the ending." He nodded his head at the projector.

Start with the ending. It would at least get their attention.

Melani cast her spell on me. Better than any mic I'd ever used.

And we did it. We started with the video. It ended with the heads of the Infected, making me almost wish I had Mort's gruesome trophy with me. But I told them the heads were on display on El'daShar, and they could go see for themselves.

I told the story from my perspective, growing up in a world without magic, starting a career in the military and guarding a grand building like the ones in the video. The audience liked that. I talked them through the attacks, and my fumbling attempts to understand what was going on. I explained discovering—and stopping—the attack on my building, and then finding Harry's camp. Then learning about the Infected, and how the buildings were like candy to a baby for the Infected.

"Like gems to a dwarf," Harry translated for my audience.

When I explained how we lost my building, and the Mana'thiandriel we needed to draw out the Infected, there was a collective gasp. So we needed to get more Mana'thiandriel, which meant getting our visitors back to El'daShar. I waved Scan up to explain how he constructed a machine to trace from where someone had Teleported. The mages all perked up at that. I'd come to understand that following a Teleport was one of the most advanced capabilities of even the best natural Teleporters.

I described our occupation of El'daShar—how we connected Earth and would connect Emerald Farms to El'daShar via Teleportation Rings. I talked them through how we wanted to take the fight to the Infected, and we thought the key hid on FreeWorld. We searched for the elves because we needed to find *someone* that knew how to get to FreeWorld. The audience groaned and growled.

I thought I was done. I was wrong.

They wanted to watch the video again. They asked questions about the vehicles from the video, about Earth's architecture, about the devices people stared at in the various scenes. Then they launched into questions about the projector and how we'd captured the images.

Scan flipped through the phone and found some of our old videos. He played back a couple, embarrassing me because I wore my mask.

Harry took the phone and recorded the audience, then played it back for them on the screen. The dwarves went wild with excitement.

Before I knew it, Mort joined us, coming down the ramp with a dwarf escort.

It couldn't have been a day already.

"Time table has moved up," he said in greeting.

"You didn't find Cordoro?" I asked.

"We did not," he answered. "Galad is in Emerald Farms. We expect, at some point, Cordoro will try to retrieve some of his things, and Galad hopes to recapture him."

Mort's jaw clenched as he chewed on Cordoro's whereabouts. Sighing, he continued, "He wasn't on any of the worlds I can get to, or he is hiding somehow. I expect he is in the Savage Lands, and I don't know how to get there."

A colony Mort didn't know how to reach?

"Wherever he is," Mort concluded, "we expect there will be an attack on El'daShar sooner rather than later."

"Why?" someone from the audience called out. "Why are humans fighting humans?"

"Greed and ignorance," Mort answered loudly. "There are many that would join us if they understood the stakes, but with communications broken, with so few Teleporters, people will see only that we have moved to take El'daShar."

"So we need to educate them," I said.

"Exactly," Mort answered. "You and I have some colonies to visit."

"The batteries on these are practically dead," Scan said, "and we've burned through the portable chargers. We'll have to get more."

Mort nodded. "Where's the Warlord?" he asked.

"I can get him," Melani said.

"We don't necessarily need him," Mort said. "Let him decide."

Melani nodded and blinked away.

The noise level rose as the dwarves broke into small groups and dissected the body of knowledge we'd just dumped in their underground plaza.

Bluff approached Harry, and I moved close enough to hear.

"Harry," Bluff said, "I just want to say that I'm encouraged by the dwarf you've become."

Harry didn't smile; he simply sighed.

"I'm not happy with the idea of finding the elves. But the idea of being free of the damned Infected—that's a goal worth fighting for."

Chapter 53

Cordoro

The people of the Savage Lands lived up to their name. Of all the allies I could have acquired, they would have landed dead last on the list. If their frightening visages had not been enough—with teeth filed sharp, piercings, tattoos, and various burns and scars—their wild screams and twitchy motions paralyzed me with fear.

The accommodations were horrid—tents with smelly furs. I longed for a chair or couch or bed. For food, they brought me undercooked pieces of meat, which I couldn't eat at all, or charred or dried meats coated in spices so strong as to be inedible. They never brought cheeses and, worse, no wine! They offered a heavily-scented alcohol, which they drank like water. Every breath from a Savage smelled of spices and strong drink.

I wondered how they fought so well with their stomachs in knots from the food and their heads spinning from the drink. I think it had to do with a fungus they ate that seemed to sharpen their reflexes, but, frankly, added to their drink-induced madness.

But they were the allies I had chosen. The only ones I could have chosen. I'd already thought through my options during my time imprisoned on Emerald Farms, and when the opportunity presented itself, I 'Ported to the Savage Lands. The dwarves would have been my allies of choice, but the only place I knew where Mort could not follow was the Savage Lands.

The pungent smell of a native of the colony interrupted my reverie. Many of them looked the same to me, and when he didn't continue on, but plopped near me by the fire, I let out the breath I held. He hissed a greeting. Was it the filed teeth that made them sound that way? Ridiculous.

"We have the firssst sssurprise for the Forsssaken ready." I recognized the voice as Blithe, a Second of the Savage. They weren't even sending in a First to consult with me.

I made him wait while I climbed to my feet, stiff from sitting on the ground. *Why am I living in this squalor?* But I had to. The only path to freedom was to take out the damnable Empath, and Mort as well. I needed to disrupt their plans, draw them out, and get rid of them. I would handle a miserable life on Savage for the duration.

Blithe rose with me and slapped me on the back, laughing at my stiffness, then escorted me to what he wanted me to send.

Oh. Those beasts would be an excellent distraction... but they were too big to 'Port.

"Is there some way we can work together to 'Port them?" I asked.

The Savage just shook his head no, still smiling that maniacal, dagger-toothed smile. He held up a slimy rainbow-colored leaf. He mimed taking it and eating it.

"I am *not* eating that."

His fingers flashed through some motions, then he stopped, sighing. He mimed a small ball, followed by a big one, then nodded his head, smiling.

"I don't know what you're doing. Why are you miming? You can talk." Imbecile.

"Yesss, I can. We find your language... ssslow. This ssslimeroot, it will magnify your power. Only when fresssh, and only for a ssshort time." He held it out to me again.

"You eat some first," I said. "For all I know, it's poisonous."

Blithe's eyes fluttered and his shoulders sagged. He cast a spell, showing a small magelight. Then he took a bite of the disgusting thing. He held up his finger, nodding his head as though counting out beats. Then he cast a magelight again, and it was the size of my body and as bright as the sun.

No actual proof. He could have just been holding back on the first spell. But it wasn't poison.

Harrumphing, I took the disgusting thing from him. I felt it move—the leaf was *alive!* Disgusted, I took a tentative bite of the "root." It was like eating rotten fruit. Which I think they had tried to serve me as well. But I swallowed the chunk I had taken out. Then I waited. After some time, Blithe nodded his head.

I cast a magelight, and it was like nothing I'd ever cast before. The spell burst forth with power and ferocity. I closed my eyes to the blinding light, and let the spell go. Then I looked at Blithe wide-eyed.

I felt a little silly… a little giddy. The feeling went beyond excitement about my amplified power; it felt something like the early stages of intoxication.

Blithe waved me toward the beasts. I proved to myself that the Savage had sedated the creatures, and I tried Teleportation. Giggling, I took them one at a time and left them in the forest near the Transport hub. I'd never moved anything so big.

I got back, and the giddiness transformed into a pounding headache. Blithe walked over to me, holding out a canister. That awful drink. I shook my head no.

He took a sip, and nodded his head yes. *See, safe.*

I still shook my head no.

Shrugging, he walked away, and the headache became excruciating. I curled up in a little ball, moaning, and Blithe turned and smiled. The last thing I remembered before passing out was those sharp teeth smiling at me, and wondering if the frightful man was going to eat me.

Chapter 54

Red

We began a tour of the colonies. Grundle did, in fact, decide to go with us, claiming he wanted to see the colonies. I'd known him long enough to suspect that he wanted to see the *people*. And to decide for himself how to move forward.

Our tour party comprised me, Mort, Grundle, Smith, and Scan—mostly people from Earth, there to convince people of *our reality*. We needed Mort for transport, but also for his status as a Regent of a colony. I tried to convince myself that Grundle added more than physical weight, that having a troll with us made our story more believable. I learned that the troll-elf narrative had only been a distant story for the struggling colonies, but Grundle's presence did, at least, get people's attention.

Galad stayed behind to monitor for the return of Cordoro, and so we wouldn't have a repeat of his warm welcome to DwarkenHazen. It surprised me how often I thought of him, wanting to share the little insights into the people and puzzles that presented themselves.

We'd started by restocking our supplies, including batteries, and Teleported to Galene, the other colony that primarily produced crops. They'd been able to take advantage of Hrushi's lack of Teleporters, securing more sales with the other colonies. So they weren't struggling as much as Emerald Farms, but they still felt the pinch of the vanished elven Teleporters.

Unlike Emerald Farms, Galene didn't have a room with a Dead Zone.

"The crystals," Mort whispered to me in an aside, "which created the Dead Zone are unique, but I don't know their history."

But the mages of Galene could tell our electronics had no "magical signature," and their astonishment convinced the non-mages. I ended up doing a modified form of the story I had presented to the dwarves, though to a much smaller crowd than on DwarkenHazen—just a couple of handfuls of leaders.

I could tell by the end that we had won no friends on Galene, but neither did I expect they would be a threat. They wanted to do what they'd always been doing—farming and selling their goods to the other colonies.

"What you're proposing," said a tall, thin man with reddish skin and kind, green eyes, "is too risky. We've lived for generations by laying low, hiding from the Infected. Seeking them out? That's a death sentence."

Mort had gently put a hand on my arm to halt my rebuttal. After leaving, he indicated we should be prepared for similar responses from the other colonies. "But pushing them would have driven them farther from us," he explained, "and getting their food still helps us."

"Mort," I said skeptically, "you know we don't really even need Emerald Farms for food, don't you? Earth can easily supply the amount of food for the growing population of El'daShar."

Mort chuckled. "If all we want is sustenance, then I agree. And I appreciate that Earth has allowed Emerald Farms to supply food and keep their economy going. But there's more to the food from the colonies." With a wink, he continued. "Much of the food from the colonies has magical properties. Healing, speed, faster mana recovery. The people of Galene are not fighters, but they may serve our cause better in their fears."

Well, that's interesting. I wanted to tell Galad, but I had to settle for Grundle's knowing nod of appreciation.

We 'Ported back to El'daShar and found ourselves amidst controlled chaos. Mort Blinked us to the command center near the Rings—just a large open air tent containing a table with papers, some of which were maps, and a pair of computers. There was a makeshift radio tower under construction visible over the tops of nearby tents. I heard generators running in the distance, though the command center nestled in the glow of magelight from arcane lamp-stands that, to my eye, clashed with the electronics and portable tables.

"What happened?" Mort asked one of his Firsts, a shaved-headed man with piercing, intelligent eyes.

"Savages 'Ported in a pair of those reptilian beasts that are all teeth, and three times the size of a man," he reported, with a twinkle in his eye.

"I take it we did well," Mort replied.

"Those guns from Earth tore them to pieces before they reached our lines," he answered. "Provided some much-needed meat, sir. They're roasting now." I pictured Tyrannosaurus on a BBQ spit, with a nice jalapeño sauce. Was it bad that my mouth watered?

A man in Marine fatigues nodded his head, not smiling, just noting the success.

"I'll restock our batteries," Scan said, satisfied that no immediate threat required attention, and set off toward a makeshift supply depot.

"So Cordoro went to the Savage Lands," Mort concluded. "He couldn't 'Port those great beasts into camp—nowhere to land them. But be ready; some of the smaller things he can bring right into camp. You can't use guns there without harming our own men."

"We've arranged the camp with that in mind, Regent," the former Marine piped in. Regent to the Twelve. I'd met three of them—Mort, Hirashi, and the tall Regent of Galene with the kind eyes, Anthos. "The Earthlings... Christ, that still sounds strange to say... the Earthlings are perimeter guards. The Forsaken hold the middle. We have mages placed everywhere, though they are thin." He pointed at a map he brought up on a computer screen. "Green is Earthlings, Blue is Forsaken, and the white dots are mages. This is currently just a guess, but we're getting RFIDs... identifiers... distributed, and we will be able to see the formations live."

"Have you considered," Grundle rumbled, "that our backbiting Teleporter might also send antagonistic fauna to your home world, Mort?"

Mort closed his eyes, weary and distraught. While his answer was clearly *no*, it was his First that spoke up. "We have. There are some troops from Earth that have moved in, with their long-range weapons." The First nodded at the former Marine, who nodded back.

Mort sagged with relief, putting a hand on each of their shoulders. "Thank you."

"Can I move the Ring from the Forsaken to Emerald Farms?" Mort asked his First.

"Yes, sir," the man answered.

Mort closed his eyes again for a moment, revealing to me his exhaustion.

"Why is it we can't go on the offensive?" I asked. "If we know the attacks are coming from the place you mentioned—the Savage Lands—why not take the fight there?"

"We don't know the way in, ma'am," the Marine answered. "The Savage are reclusive—the only colony that has kept their location secret. They use their own Teleporters to bring in goods, or to bring their people out to work."

"Then how did Cordoro get there?" I wondered.

"Based on the 'Port location he knew on DwarkenHazen, I suspect he ran illegal goods," Mort said, sighing heavily. "It is how he accumulated wealth."

"We've got the radio tower operational," reported a familiar voice. I turned to see Tali's flaming red hair. The young soldier, still garbed in her Israeli fatigues, nodded to me.

"Red," she said, not quite rolling her eyes, but I'd not forgotten that she didn't like my name—at least not for me.

"Hi, Tali. It's good to see a familiar face." She looked at Mort, her eyes pinching down in anger.

"You get the elf *and* the warrior mage." She cursed in Hebrew, and, unfortunately, my translation necklace did its job. It takes a lot to make me blush, but she managed.

Mort chuckled deeply, fatigue forgotten.

"We were about to travel to my world to move the Rings," he said. He locked eyes with Tali. "Would you like to see it?"

"Wait," she said. "Did you understand what I just said?"

Everyone nodded as her eyes darted to the necklaces we all wore. It was her turn to blush.

Scan came back in, quietly rejoining the group in the bemused silence.

"I would love to see your home," she choked out, despite her embarrassment. She looked into Mort's eyes, and whatever she saw made her grin mischievously. I had to admit, she managed a look I would never pull off: saucy and embarrassed all at the same time.

"Keep up the good work," Mort said to his First and the Marine. "Be prepared—they'll release something within the camp instead of outside of it, eventually." He turned back to me. "Let's get the other end of the Ring from Forsaken set up so we can transfer food from Emerald Farms, and take advantage of those supplies."

"Wait," I said, before Mort 'Ported us. Though he'd wrangled some energy when Tali arrived, I'd seen his weariness. "Maybe we should save a little effort here. We can use the existing Rings to get to Forsaken, instead of you having to do the work."

Mort sighed, "Thank you. Good thinking. I'll need the energy to move that Ring." Mort put his hand on Tali's shoulder, directing her back out toward the Rings, and double-checking with the Marine to be sure she had permission to go.

The Marine nodded, picking up a walkie-talkie. "Mayfield, the radio tower is up. Let's test RF."

We walked to the Rings, still bustling with activity, and more heavily guarded since our last visit. People and goods could pass through the Rings from either direction, and they'd set them up so that transport from Forsaken to El'daShar headed to the right of the command center, and transport from Earth to El'daShar headed to the left. It made sense; most of the travel came *to* El'daShar. Having the arrivals flow in opposite directions removed collisions. As Mort's First had indicated, only a trickle of exchange still traveled through the Ring to Forsaken.

Looking through an active Ring was much like looking through a doorway. Forsaken, presumably, lay on the other side—a cave lit by a red glow. The visual effect disturbed me—the elven towers of El'daShar stretched in the distance around the Ring, but a cave wall ended the view twenty feet into the circle of eldritch metal.

I stared into another world, only a dozen steps away, separated by a Ring of stone and metal, glyphs and runes. I glanced at the other Ring, saw the familiar tunnel under the Palace, and marveled—how far would I travel from home?

Chapter 55

Red

Mort led Tali through the Ring first, then Scan and I followed, Grundle and Smith last. Even as I neared the Ring, I felt the warmth from the other side, and passing through, I realized Mort's world rivaled Texas for heat.

Following Mort and Tali to the left, I found a line of troops guarding the Ring at the mouth of the cave, lit by a red glow behind them. Their visage caused my heart to skip a beat.

A group of men and women, some in various armed forces uniforms, cradling rifles, and some in leathers, with sword and spear and staves. Discordant, but so… right.

"Regent," one woman said in greeting, and no one tensed, no one shifted. Something about it struck me, but I couldn't say what. And it slipped from my mind as I looked past them to the world outside the cave.

Forsaken was volcanic. Night reigned, but the horizon glowed from several peaks bleeding molten lava. Rivers of it seeped across the landscape, like veins pulsing across some gargantuan beast, and one glooped by, popping and hissing, very near the cave.

"Holy crap," I said, almost speechless.

"You *live* here?" Tali voiced for me.

"Ahhh," Grundle said appreciatively.

"What do you drink, for God's sake?" Tali asked.

The heat, like an oven, began, unexpectedly, to diminish.

"There *is* water here," Mort replied. "The simplest source of water," he said, pointing at a distant peak that did *not* glow, "is when a volcano goes dormant. The top freezes over, at least temporarily. We farm our water from there."

They climb dormant volcanoes to get water?

"There are occasional geysers as well," he said. "Though

those are typically catastrophic. Sometimes we catch some water from them."

What makes a geyser catastrophic? Do I even want to know?

"We also get water, and meat, from those things." He pointed at a distant volcano. "We call them Death Wings." I peered more closely at the volcano and saw something—-some *things*—flying around it. I couldn't interpret the scale from where I stood. I doubted I wanted to meet something called a Death Wing.

Tali, Scan, and I looked at one another like we recognized a particular kind of insane that one would require to live there. Smith studied Grundle, who seemed pleased with the environment. She looked contemplative.

I thought the soldiers from Earth that ended up stationed on Forsaken must have been miserable, though it had cooled to a very manageable temperature. I touched a cave wall and jerked my hand away. *How could it be so hot, and I wasn't?*

"Dregor keeps us cool, ma'am," said a woman in fatigues with a rifle slung over her shoulder. She nodded to one of the Forsaken, a thin but toned young man with fire tattoos across his torso. He waved his fingers, imitating a spell casting, and winked.

Okay, so fire workers made the heat bearable, but I knew we were about to take away the Ring, the only exit for soldiers from Earth, and that gave me pause. "Can I see how you've stationed the people of Earth?" I asked Mort.

Mort nodded, but held up his hand to ask me to wait. He walked to one of his men and asked for some updates.

"How are you going to feel about us taking the Ring, leaving you here?" I asked the woman who had spoken to me.

"As I understand it," she answered, "we have little choice if we want to stay off the radar of the Infected. Frankly, I don't know that anywhere else is any safer." She had a point, but I knew most people on Earth wouldn't think that way. "What I really want is a chance to strike back. You're working on that?"

I sighed. Truthfully, we hadn't made progress on that front. With Galad cooped up on Emerald Farms, and my proselytizing for Earth to the colonies, the search for the vanished elves had stalled.

"We've got some roadblocks," I mumbled.

She gave me a wicked grin. "Move them or go around."

A small laugh escaped me—she wasn't wrong, and it sounded like something I would say. Mort had finished his conversation and raised an eyebrow. I nodded my readiness; then he 'Ported us elsewhere on Forsaken.

The temperature felt comfortable where we arrived, cold compared to the cave. We stood on a slope, a human encampment some distance below, with light from live volcanoes on the horizon, rivers of molten lava far below, and a glistening reflection of red up-slope. Magelight sprang to life, revealing a group of men—formerly Airborne Rangers—bearing the insignia of the Guardians, along with a couple of Forsaken women. Glancing up, I confirmed that the reflection above came from sheets of ice.

"Report," Mort said to a woman who looked to be in her forties, carrying a spear but also sporting a sword at her side.

"With their long-range weapons, we can hold this pass with fewer people," she said. She looked at Mort with grave seriousness. "We took down a Death Wing," she said, nodding downhill and to the right. I followed where she indicated—*holy crap on a cracker*. I'd never been much of a fantasy reader, but that was a dragon. A big-as-a-house dragon. "We will survive," she said.

Those in charge had stationed the people of Earth where they would preserve supply lines, using long-distance weapons to hold positions they'd stretched thin with all of the Forsaken who had departed.

Mort nodded. "What do you need?" he asked everyone.

"I'm concerned about our ammo," said one of the former Rangers.

Mort nodded again. "I'll be sure you get some. You know what they need?" he asked Tali.

"I do," she said, looking at their weapons, "but the issue is getting it here once we move the Ring."

"We will 'Port it," he answered.

Mort looked torn. "I'd like to pull you all out," he told the soldiers. "But, if I do, the population on El'daShar would climb too high, and we'd risk drawing the Infected. We need some people here, and to keep them alive, we need this pass to keep the water supply."

The Rangers looked at one another. "We'll keep the pass, sir."

Mort looked resigned.

"Let me take you to Emerald Farms," Mort said to us. "I don't want to carry you and the Ring at the same time."

Turning back to the soldiers, he said, simply, "Thank you."

***

Mort took us to the antechamber outside the Dead Zone. They'd converted it to a mini-library that had ambitions of becoming a wizard's lair. Smack in the middle of peering into a tome as ancient as the world itself was my elf.

I felt his presence in my mind like a balm on a sunburn I'd been trying to ignore. He was facing away from us, but I saw his shoulders relax.

"Honey, I'm home!" I called to him. I was so far from freakin' home…

He turned around and smiled, and I realized the joke was on me. I *was* home.

Damn.

He closed the distance between us, and I found myself lost in him, heat rising.

"I guess she picked the elf then." Tali's voice pulled me partly back to reality.

"She calls him Minty," Scan loud-whispered, completely killing the mood.

"Mmm," Galad purred/growled. I needed to come up with a name for that noise.

Mort opened the door that led outside the building and looked around. "I'll go get the Ring and bring it out here," he said, and disappeared in a big flash of light.

"I take it the stakeout isn't going well," I said, just to have something to say.

"It's been fine," Galad said, smirking. "I've caught him and let him go several times now. Just seems more sporting."

"Ha and ha," I said, jabbing him lightly in the ribs. Were elves ticklish? I rooted through the bits of memories I'd stolen from him. They were! And I knew just where.

Galad yelped and jumped awkwardly, causing Grundle and Harry to draw their weapons.

Oopsie.

I steered Galad toward the door. "What are you reading?" I asked, trying to recover.

"Some history and law, how the colonies organized themselves and why. I don't know what else I can do here, and it may prove useful."

"Have you found anything you can use?"

"Oh, yes. Did you know that, in the colonies, it is illegal to sell one's eye? And, in Emerald Farms specifically, it is illegal to carry wire cutters in one's pocket."

"Ah, yes, that should help. Great sleuthing, Minty."

"Indubitably."

Mort appeared on the lawn, Ring in tow, looking tired as hell.

Galad cast a spell, and Mort regained some color and vigor.

"Thank you," he said.

"It is no substitute for getting some actual rest," Galad told him.

"Noted," Mort responded, sighing. "Once our traveling roadshow is done. In retrospect, Galene was not the wisest choice to seek out first. We should go to the colonies most likely to swing one way or the other."

"And those would be...?" I asked.

"Wild Grove, Vibrant Woods, Bedrock, and Brickworks," Hirashi said, appearing from behind me where she had Blinked in to join us. "Allania let me know you were here," she explained.

I nodded to her, and she returned the gesture, then gave Mort a concerned look-over.

"I am very happy to see you," she continued. "Yet we walk a thin line, with one 'Porter for two colonies. We cannot afford to lose you. Please do find time to rest."

"I can move the Ring now that it's here," Galad said. "Hirashi has already shown me where it should go."

Mort nodded.

"Is there one of those colonies where you could rest while I do the dog and pony show?" I asked. At their puzzled looks, I amended, "It just means an elaborate performance."

"Vibrant Woods," he answered. "I've done many contracts with them over the years. They're a colony I expect might side with us."

"Vibrant Woods it is," I said.

"I'll sit this one out," Scan said. "I have an idea I want to explore here." That got an arched eyebrow from Hirashi. "With your permission, of course," he added. But the look she gave him as she granted him permission said more than their simple words. It said something like, *don't be a fool.*

Scan handed me the backpack with equipment. I gave Galad a kiss, a kiss packed with a promise to return. He made his noise—maybe I'd call it a *gnar*? It wasn't fair that we had to keep spending our time apart. Or constantly in a group.

"Be safe," he whispered, letting me go.

The familiar light picked me up and whisked me away.

Chapter 56

Red

Each of the worlds we visited displayed unique—sometimes bafflingly unique—landscapes. Vibrant Woods generated lumber; their community literally had carved their town into an enormous tree. They didn't cut down trees; they just carved limbs, the size of normal trees, off of the giant tree they inhabited. Over time, they'd learned to cultivate the tree, grafting and growing different types of wood which they farmed and harvested.

"Plant magic," Mort explained, as I gazed at the wonder of trees growing from trees, wondering what the base of the planet must look like when I couldn't even see an edge to the limb on which we stood. "All of the colonies that work with plants have more natural skills and more training with plants, just like the Forsaken mages manipulate heat."

"Heredity or environment?" I asked casually, distracted by a shadow of something big passing overhead, though I couldn't get a bead on it through the canopy of leaves.

Mort chuckled. "A long-debated question." His eyes sought the origin of the shadow as well. "I suspect a little of both. Lesser Bristler," he said as the airplane-sized shadow moved on. "They like the Ironwood grafted over there." He pointed at an army of trees, and I had no idea which one he meant. "When the Greater Bristlers move in, that's when they call the Forsaken. Of course, we can't use fire here."

"Mort." A middle-aged woman approached; garbed in dappled green, with brown skin and blond hair, she blended in even when moving.

"Regent Uwume," Mort answered. They shared friendly smiles, putting me at ease—the battle would not be uphill on that colony. Mort introduced us, explaining that I had an eye-opening tale, asked for their Cabinet to be called, and the Regent obliged. Mort excused himself to go rest, which gave me a moment of anxiety, despite it being my suggestion. But I did still have a nine-foot walking rock pile on my team. Tali left with Mort, to "make sure he was safe." I growled quietly—I could use a little time "ensuring Galad's safety."

I recognized a pattern in how the colonies organized themselves. Though they each called their governing boards something different, they all used the concept of Firsts and Seconds to establish hierarchy. Did the Forsaken struggle to understand the chain of command of the people from Earth back on El'daShar?

We gathered in a room that appeared to be partly grown and partly assembled. Boards stretched horizontally between trees which they had grafted to the greater tree beneath, and the roof swayed in the wind, tightly woven fronds, still green with life, whispering as they stirred. Grundle, Smith, and I—mostly I—delivered the presentation. And Mort was right—the wood-harvesters did not sit on the fence. Ha!

I let them talk themselves into helping. As a colony, they wanted to grow, but they couldn't. No one could grow, with the threat of Infected if populations climbed. Without the elves, they couldn't even find more planets to colonize. One town on Vibrant Woods would confine them for eternity, or until they made a mistake and had one too many children. It took only a modicum of ambition to want a brighter future. Oddly, I found myself wondering… many people on Earth would have considered Vibrant Woods a slice of heaven.

But I had a mission. I wondered, as the colonial leaders debated, whether Galad's world, the AllForest, had been like Vibrant Woods. Had Galad been born in a tree?

More importantly than their role as a colony, they offered a Teleporter, a Second named Arrillius, excited to help. Smith volunteered to 'Port with him, along with members of their Cabinet, back to El'daShar, where they intended to determine how Vibrant Woods could contribute to the effort. Interplanetary travel had proven to be one of our bottlenecks, and, in my book, recruiting a Teleporter made the journey to Vibrant Woods a win.

We visited Bedrock and Wild Grove next, and neither

encounter went well. The Council—or Board or whatever they called themselves—of Bedrock would not even listen. Mort said they had a long-standing relationship with Savage. And Wild Grove took offense that we had gone to Vibrant Woods first. *Bunch of dolts... someone had to go first.*

Already feeling painfully slow to me, our campaign deteriorated to the pace of a geriatric snail in a salt mine.

We learned from resupply visits that the Savage continued to Teleport nasties to El'daShar. Ferocious beasts most commonly, but also smaller poisonous critters, bugs that caused rashes, and a cute big-eyed furball that burst into flame when cuddled. I wondered if Cordoro made the attacks himself. If so, we should have moved Galad to El'daShar.

But the incidents occurred on other planets as well. The Cuddle Flamers caused some serious damage in the Vibrant Woods. The Forsaken and Earth military had to cover more ground, moving to Vibrant Woods, while some wood-crafters shifted to Earth.

Brickworks listened. They wanted in, but their reasoning surprised me. They wanted access to Earth, to the knowledge of Earth's metallurgical technology, while retaining rights to their own planetary resources. I loved that they bet on winning... and they bet big.

***

We sat in an open foyer that connected a suite of rooms Brickworks had provided; having already dissected the day's discussions, we'd moved on to our larger strategy.

"The Savage are playing things right for their success," Mort conceded. "I'd hoped they would do something stupid." He paced the room with his head down, voicing his fears. "They're taking advantage of our split forces and thinning us out even further. Everyone who sides with us knows they'll get a dose of the same medicine, which means we're going to have even more trouble convincing any other colonies to join us."

"Should we just stop?" Grundle asked. "Fortify what we have? Focus on finding the elves?"

Mort shook his head, not looking up. "It wouldn't be right. We should give every colony the information they need to make a choice. I don't even know if the Savage have heard anything but whatever lies Cordoro might feed them."

"Wait, you're not even pissed at the *Savage*?" Tali asked, incredulous. She had become a permanent part of our entourage. "They're killing your people and mine!"

"Imagine what they've been told," he said. "'*The Forsaken are making a power play, trying to take over El'daShar and double their numbers. If they succeed, will the other colonies still need you?*' It would be easy to portray our actions as completely selfish and hostile."

His words did not mollify Tali. "That's stupid. We're trying to save humanity."

"*You* know that, and *I* know that, but the Savage don't," he told her.

She grunted in irritation.

Smirking, he wrapped an arm around her and pulled her close. "Is it so hard to give people the benefit of the doubt?"

"Tch!" she snarled. "You know nothing!" She shoved him away and turned to storm out, but he Blinked in front of her, causing her to walk right into his arms, where he pulled her close and kissed her hard.

"It's a little warm in here," Smith said. "I think I'll step outside and cool off."

Grundle chuckled deeply and followed her out, ducking even in the large doorway.

Though embarrassed, I couldn't look away. After an eternity, Tali pulled her head back, breathing hard.

Without taking his eyes off Tali, Mort said, "We'll be back," and they disappeared in a bright flash of light. Great. They'd left the planet.

"There's a bedroom right here!" I called into the silence, not liking that our Teleporter was worlds away, but mostly just irritated at the state of my own love life.

Chapter 57

Rocks

I meandered toward the Teleportation Ring, stopping to chat or watch preparations along the way. "What would happen if we threw our Ring into the bottom of the ocean?" I asked Gil. "Would we flood El'daShar and drain the ocean?"

"No can do, sir," Gil said as he matched my pace. "Can't move the Rings once they're on."

Oh. Good to know. But then what if—

"And you couldn't activate it from the bottom of the ocean. Even if you could get there, the Rings won't activate if the differential between locations is too large." Gil smiled. "I asked something similar when Mort set it up."

I smiled back. Gil had been a first-rate find. Like Simmi, he had a knack for getting things done, though his skills were less about reading people and more about supply chain. His ability to keep things moving through the obvious bottleneck of the Rings astounded me. It reminded me of Red.

But, oddly, watching the transition in operation paled when compared to my idea of the Ring. It looked like a door or window had been left open, and I felt heat coming from the El'daShar side. *We're air-conditioning an entire world.* It was a silly thought, but ultimately the bills came to me.

Walking through the Ring, I moved out of the way and looked around. They'd established a command center, a tent with generators powering laptops atop foldable tables. I couldn't hear the generators over the din, but I saw their familiar shapes, gently vibrating as the motors drank liquid fuel and spat out electricity. Nearby, a makeshift tower held radio heads aloft. Metal poles dotted the horizon, giving me an idea of the perimeter. Men and women in garb similar to Mort's moved freely among men and women in uniform, some building stone perimeter walls on the forest side, others standing guard, and many bivouacking in small clusters. Plenty of GL carried guns or rifles—easy to spot despite the mixed fatigues from different former services.

"Oh," I said, startled to recognize one of the SmartGuard engineers. "You look better. What are you doing on El'daShar?" *Why would we have drones hunting Infected on El'daShar?*

The man squinted at me. He looked at Gil and said, "Didn't you want me to get the drones doing perimeter checks?"

"That's right," Gil said. He turned to me. "But not for Infected. Just any incoming."

Ahhh.

"Good thinking." I loved that Gil had kept the drones from Earth. "Nice field test. Thanks… I'm sorry, I can't recall your name." That used to be unusual for me, but I couldn't keep up.

"Carter. Carter Cooper." He held out his hand to be shook, looking at me like he couldn't place from where we knew one other.

"Penbrook," I said. "We sat next to each other at the SmartGuard introductory meeting."

His eyes got wide. Embarrassment? More like panic. I almost laughed. "Don't worry about it. I'm very forgettable." *Yes, wearing the same elven robe. Easily forgettable.* "We'd shared a joke. What do you prescribe to a man who orgasms when he sneezes?"

Carter, who'd frozen like a squirrel sensing a dog, visibly relaxed. "Oh, yes, I remember now. Pepper. Good one. Well, I'd better get back to it." He waved and started on his way to wherever he had been headed when I'd stopped him. So he'd heard that joke before, but it wasn't the joke we'd shared back on Earth.

"They'll be waiting for you, sir," Gil urged me as I watched the retreating back of Carter Cooper. A man who didn't recognize me or remember the joke we had shared. The hairs on the back of my neck stood at attention.

"Lead on," I said, losing Cooper in the crowd. That mystery would have to wait.

Gil led me out of the camp toward the elven city. The last time I'd been on El'daShar, wild creatures had poked about the city, but the people and noise had clearly made the area less appealing. A mix of Forsaken and Earth guards defended a building whose former function I could not guess. Elegant and aloof, the smooth stone with its arches and curves loomed as though sculpted from one massive rock. Elfin.

The guards let me through, and I found myself in a small but elegant room with a table that four humans stood around. Hrushi, Regent of Emerald Farms, with dark skin and hair and a bright intelligence. Mort, Regent of Forsaken, a light-skinned warrior and Teleporter with a shaven head and a difficult-to-ignore dancing flame tattoo on his arm. Konit, Regent of Brickworks, a solid man, like his world's namesake, brown of skin with short brown hair, looking stern. And Uwume, Regent of Vibrant Woods, brown-skinned like Konit, but with lighter hair, she wore green and brown leathers. Though it was my first meeting with the latter two, I'd had a quick briefing on who to expect.

Chairs nestled around the table, unused. A palpable tension thrummed through the room. I knew the background—as the leaders of their worlds, they'd had their disagreements, but there had never been a schism as large as the one created by the elves disappearing and the 13th colony arriving.

I'd also had partial explanations from Hrushi and Mort on the political landmines created by Mort having killed Crooney on Emerald Farms, and our use of the Teleportation Rings to connect Earth to El'daShar, where we'd pumped in troops to secure a foothold. Cordoro's escape and the attacks by Savage had skewed the game in Mort's favor, making Crooney's death a by-line of the greater story, though the order of events would have unleashed hell from conspiracy theorists on Twitter. The soldiers from Earth added a whole new player to the game board… heck, more like they created a whole different game. And I needed us all to play a game where humankind could win.

"Penbrook, acting Regent of Earth," Hrushi began. "Allow me to introduce Konit, Regent of Brickworks." Konit slapped an open hand into a fist, a traditional greeting of the colonies. Luckily, they'd coached me. I repeated the gesture. "And Uwume, Regent of Vibrant

Woods." We performed, again, their equivalent of a handshake. "We have much to discuss. Shall we sit?"

I had purposefully chosen a round table—no head of the table. I picked the seat closest to me, and the others did the same with the chairs nearest them. That left me with the unknown Uwume on one side, and the slightly better known Hrushi on the other. The table stretched before me, too large and empty for the number of occupants. "Let's hope we can fill out the rest of this table soon," I commented. "This is not a time for division."

Uwume cocked her head. "Division is how we survive."

Large populations drew the Infected. *How does that affect a culture? A people? How does that change the way you think day to day?*

"Not a time for division of spirit, division of intent," I corrected.

Uwume nodded. "Apart, we stand together."

"Apart, we stand together," the others echoed, spoken like a mantra.

"And yet we do not," Mort concluded. "There have always been problems. Fights, natural disasters, power plays, but our lives have hung by a thread for generations uncountable. Everyone knows there are limits to how much one can rock the boat."

"Records show that there used to be hundreds of colonies," Hrushi added perfunctorily.

Konit grunted and shifted uncomfortably. "There have been only twelve for as far back as anyone alive remembers."

I suspected Konit was not a big fan of history. Or reading.

"And the point is the same," Konit continued, "whether it's twelve or a hundred colonies. We've got a hole in the boat the size of…" He waved his massive arms looking for a word. "A boat!" he declared, slamming his arms on the table. The wood held, but Uwume petted the table like one might soothe a frightened pup.

"Indeed," Hrushi said, straight-faced and sincere. "And how would you like to… plug… said hole?"

"I work with *stone*. If you want the ship sunk faster, I'm your man. Maybe we should ask the woodworker?" He nodded to Uwume, passing the buck.

She pursed her lips. "I think you took your metaphor too far. I cannot keep my people fed. No one buys our goods... people are scared. And with good reason."

"With an even darker backdrop," Mort added, smiling. "The Infected are drawn to what remains of us, to our turmoil."

"Quicksand," I said. They all looked at me quizzically. Did their planets not have quicksand? "We have sand on Earth that pulls you down, and the more you struggle, the faster you get pulled down."

"Is there a way out?" Hrushi asked.

I wasn't sure what she meant, the quicksand or our situation. "You get rid of extra weight—it pulls you down faster. You move slowly," I said. "Deliberately." *Quicksand or our situation?* "Thrashing about pulls you under, but if you are mostly still, carefully extracting your legs, keeping your arms free, you can get out. Panic is your worst enemy."

"Don't panic," Mort chuckled.

"When you're stuck in this... sinking sand," Konit began, "and moving slowly is your only way out, what if you're also being chased?"

"Best to have a friend to cover your back and help pull you out," I said.

Chapter 58

Red

Enough was enough. I'd gone back and forth with my feelings—my duty versus my own interests. I lived a bizarre form of the career versus family problem that most women struggled with. I didn't exactly have a career goal, and saving the human race didn't map to a known professional path. But then I didn't exactly want to start a family either. I did spend more and more of my alone time picturing a life with Galad, and wasn't that a family? *Hadn't what's-her-name reconciled herself to a life with a vampire who would outlive her? Or was it a werewolf? No, she'd married the vampire and had a daughter that bonded with the werewolf... whom she'd also been interested in. Weird.*

Anyway, it wasn't right that Tali and Mort, who'd known each other much less time than Galad and I, found time to play hide-the-wand in the chamber of secrets. I didn't even have a book to keep me company. My frustration festered; I'd shot past my reservations and grew irritated that Galad hadn't taken another shot at intimacy.

When next we had to stop in El'daShar for batteries, I let Tali know I needed to check up on Galad.

"Give him a thorough exam on my behalf, too," she said with a laugh, earning a glare from me. *Surely she doesn't seriously want Galad, too?*

I stopped in surprise when I recognized a pair of dwarves who stood near the Rings. Melani and Shariela admired the decaying heads of the Infected on the spear where Mort had impaled them.

I purposely did not draw their attention.

Nerves spiking, I moved through the Ring to Emerald Farms, finding myself in an open commons area that had as much activity as did the other side in El'daShar. While more supply-oriented than the hub on El'daShar, the Emerald Farms side also held its share of soldiers, both from Earth and Forsaken.

Stairs led up to doors that I suspected held the council chamber. I had only been inside, never outside, having been 'Ported in by Mort in the past. I had paid little attention to the inside of the doors, but they looked maybe right.

When I started up the steps, I found that, with each one, my excitement waned and my anxiety increased. Step. What if I couldn't get past all my memories of Galad with other women? Step. Would *he* be comparing me to all his other… *liaisons*? Step. How could he *not*? And I didn't have the beauty and elegance of his past lovers. Step. What if his passions had cooled? Step. What if it was wrong to have sex outside of marriage? "Well, that cat was out of the bag," I said to myself, groaning miserably. Still, Mom would not be pleased.

My climb had faltered to a stop.

Shit.

That wasn't like me.

As I stood there, looking up the last few stairs before the stone landing, the doors opened, and out came the object of my deliberation. He smiled and came to me.

"To what do I owe this honor?" he said with a playful smirk.

"It was supposed to be a booty call," I said, flapping my arms in irritation.

"Well, it has certainly been to my benefit to have you travel with Tali!"

I made a noise of irritation deep in my throat.

Half sighing, half laughing, he said, "Do you trust me?"

I pinched my eyes at him. "What?"

"Do you trust me?"

"Well, let's see. You're a spy that trapped me in your head and clothed me as you pleased, and has repeatedly put me in harm's way."

"Exactly!" he proclaimed, earning himself the stink eye.

"Look, when you were in my head, did I ever clothe you in anything you disagreed with? And harm's way… that's your location of choice." He paused, struggling to find the right words. "I never forced my will on you. Or anyone, at least not consciously." He frowned, looking at something from his past. "I... gave them what they wanted."

"I'm not sure you're making the case you think you're making."

Galad sighed heavily. "I didn't force my will, and I could have. I *could* have for a long time. So... I'm asking you—do you trust me?"

He spoke the truth... I'd seen him do nothing but good things with his powers, even feeling bad about using his powers for the greater good over an individual's rights. And, well, I thought... maybe... shit, maybe I *loved* him. Didn't I have to give him at least *some* trust?

"I trust you," I told him, wanting it to be true.

"All right," he said, smiling. He took my hand, leading me back down the steps and across the busy courtyard. We walked through one of many doors that lined the quad, with a pretty little floral bed decorating the entrance.

Galad pulled me through the door, into a sitting room, and he closed the door behind me. "My rooms," he explained, letting me cast my gaze about. We stood in a quaint little wood-floored home, with a fireplace, a couch with a coffee table, and a magical lamp perched on a stand. Columns of books decorated the corners, and more tombs lay strewn across the coffee table, alongside arcane gadgets whose purposes eluded me. Only one other doorway left the room, and a bed lay on the other side.

My eyes narrowed, but before I could say anything, Galad wrapped me in his arms, his lips on mine. And after a knee-jerk reaction of pulling away, I just... let my worries go. Closing my eyes, I enjoyed the sensations, his minty fragrance, the taste of his lips, the feel of his hands roaming my body, finding their way under my shirt. He made that gnar sound, somewhere between the purring of a cat and the growling of a dog, and the vibrations added to the fire blooming within me.

He scooped me up and carried me to the bedroom, somehow navigating the doorway despite me obstructing his view. When he set me on the bed, I wrapped my legs around him and pulled him down to me, the movement jarring our bodies and giving me a small, sharp pain on my lip.

He stopped, checking if I was okay, and in that moment, my brain jumped to the myriad of Galad's past encounters, and the floodgates of memories unlocked.

I closed my eyes hard, and when I opened them, Galad's eyes were there, concerned.

"I'm sorry," I said.

He smiled wistfully. "That was my doing."

"What was 'your doing?'" I asked, confused. The cut lip? As much my fault as his. The passion? Perhaps I could blame him a little for that, but I hoped I brought out the same in him.

"You forgetting," he said.

And it all made sense.

"You blocked my memories."

"I did. For a time. I thought, perhaps if you had some of your own?"

My doubt flared. "But, it's not me then. It's like... I dunno, like being drunk I suppose. Except instead of general loss of inhibitions, it's loss of a specific one... or something."

"Sometimes we take medicine for a time, to get better." He offered a metaphor that felt like a rationalization.

But he had a point. I'd wanted that passion. The frustration had driven me to seek Galad out. Only the memories interfered. Made me feel smaller. If I'd never been stuck in his head, I wouldn't have had those memories to contend with. But I'd also not have come to know him so well, and would not have felt the way I felt.

Damn.

I nodded my head slightly. "Not today, but maybe." I *did* like the brief memory of what we had experienced. I lay down and he lay beside me. Rolling on my side, I gave him a kiss, sweet with a hint of passion, and I felt my lip heal... and smiled.

"Tell me about your childhood," I said. "The AllForest, your sister... tell me things I wouldn't have seen while stuck in your head." Teasingly, I prodded, "Things that weren't in the giant ball of electrified memories."

We lay in each other's arms, and he suggested, "Okay. How about the story of how I met Grundle?"

I smiled. I liked the idea. So he spoke, and as I learned more about the man I thought maybe I loved, I began nibbling on his ears.

Galad's story stumbled to a halt. "That's rather… distracting,"

"Ish it?" I whispered, mouth busy.

He answered with his gnarring purr.

"Keep talking," I breathed. "Your shishter… "

He groaned as my tongue slid across the point of his ear.

"C'mon, elf," I purred. "Keep talkin'. Rise to the occasion." All of the memories of his past loves—he was right, they were all about giving others what they wanted. They weren't about Galad and his wants.

"Already… risen."

"Well, sure enough."

We made memories of our own.

Chapter 59

Galad, two hundred years in the past

"Are you *insane*?" I hit my head with my hand, wishing to hit hers instead. She had openly insulted the High Lord. Even if no one else occupied the room, such talk could be dangerous. The walls had ears.

Lomamir glared, her green eyes reminding me of our father. She had his dark-brown hair and lighter skin, but it was her eyes that brought him to mind. Those eyes had burned into mine with the exact same disapproval when I'd Coerced Lomamir to bring me the Bow of Anerion from the trophy room. I'd paid dearly for crossing that line.

I wondered if my eyes, golden like my hair, reminded her of our mother. If so, it would have been the only similarity. Arafaela had been all love. Real love, full of care and character, not the brand of love I pandered.

"Undoubtedly," she said. "I'm talking to *you* after all. That goes against any *rational* behavior."

I scowled, irritated with her, and irritated with myself that she'd gotten under my skin so easily. I was an Empath, for tree's sake!

"Explain it to me then," I growled through clenched teeth. "Because I heard rumors of unrest in the AllForest all the way from El'daShar. It appears to me that you're going against the will of the High Lord, which is a death sentence. And those same actions might aid our oldest foe. The only *rational* conclusion is that you have a death wish."

"Oldest foe," she scoffed. "How long has it been since we've fought with the trolls?"

"I don't know!" I said, irritation ringing in my voice. "What difference does it make? They've been our foes throughout history."

Lomamir narrowed her eyes. "Whose history?"

"Mother and Father fought in the troll wars. That's *our* parents. It's *our* history."

"Galadrindor," she said softly, using my full name as one would with a child. "That was almost fifteen eons ago. Fifteen *thousand* years. Do you know how long a troll lives?"

"As long as they don't bother elves! That's how long!"

"They die from old age at around two hundred years," she replied calmly. "They start having children at around twenty, and stop having them at about one hundred. So a generation is thirty years, maybe forty. Let's say thirty-five. How many generations in fifteen thousand years?"

I scowled again. She knew I wasn't as good at math as she.

"That's 430 generations. You probably can't wrap your mind around that, since elves don't easily grasp the concept of generations. You and I, we don't even know who our grandparents were, they are so far back in time. And we are *old* elves, the two of us. Think how far back in our history 430 generations would be."

I paused. Yes, we were old, but older elves existed. When I was a child, there'd been stories of an elf named Elliahspane, once a hero to elves, who went insane and disappeared around the time I'd been born. Elves had talked about her like she was ancient. But realistically, she'd been about the age that Lomamir and I had achieved. She'd lived through a tougher time, the Troll Wars and whatever had come before. But wasn't that my sister's point? I didn't know *what* came before the Troll Wars, much less four hundred generations of elves.

"They're not the brightest creatures," she continued on. "They don't read, and they don't pass down stories. The trolls alive today... they literally have no idea they ever fought elves."

"What of *Warlords*?"

Lomamir's eye twitched.

"Warlords have always appeared, gathering trolls and inspiring them to fight." I enjoyed watching my sister squirm. "Besides, they don't have to remember their history. *We* do."

Lomamir had no rebuttal.

"Have the trolls birthed a Warlord, Lomamir?"

She remained quiet.

"Lomamir," I sighed. "A Warlord explains *everything*. They're known for their cleverness. Any unrest or attacks are explainable—we just need to take care of him."

"Take care of him," she said, voice deadpan. "Do you plan to make him dinner and scrub his ears then?"

After a second, I realized my mouth was hanging open. Lomamir had never been so filthy-mouthed. Scrub the ears of a troll?!?

"This unrest you mention," she said, before I could chastise her. "Where did you hear that?"

"On El'daShar, of course. I worried that the High Lord would hear the same rumors, so I came here to straighten out the *unrest* before there was any real trouble."

"You've been here an hour, and you have the situation worked out then. Aren't we so lucky to have you, *brother*?"

I rubbed my eyes in irritation. I'd traveled back to the AllForest in secret. While I'd dreaded the thought of having to discipline my sister, I'd mentally prepared myself for the necessity. It would not have surprised me if she had soured the AllForest to Slooti's rule. I let her nasty remark go, so pleased was I with the idea that any unrest the High Lord had heard about had come from a Warlord being born. Perhaps it was time to put an end to the trolls altogether.

"I'll tell you what," she said, her lip curling into a snarl, then relaxing. "I'll see what I can do to arrange a meeting with this Warlord." So there *was* a Warlord! "Meanwhile, why don't you take some time to talk with *your people*," she said, spitting out the last words. "Maybe you'll learn some more about the *unrest* your puppet master mentioned."

With that, she turned and strode from the room.

Chapter 60

Red

We didn't get the time together that new lovers hope for. I didn't have the convenient ability of a Teleporter to pop back and see Galad every night. While he guarded Emerald Farms, waiting for Cordoro to appear in his native land, I continued on my mission to explain to the human colonies the imminent threat of the Infected attacking Earth. The time and travel wore on me, but not in an "absence makes the heart grow fonder" way. It frustrated and agitated me.

After a slow failure to convince the artisans on Artifairium to join our cause, I returned to El'daShar deflated. Already irritable, my tension ratcheted up a notch when I found a dire message awaited me—I needed to report back to Earth. The message read simply, "Return to Earth for a family issue."

I tried not to worry, but the vagueness of the missive disturbed me. A part of me wanted to tell Galad, or drag Scan along with me. The idea of learning bad news all alone made me feel... isolated. On the other hand, I had never involved my friends in family matters since I'd gone into the military. As the only one of our old squad who had family that *cared*, I didn't want to flaunt my good fortune.

I let Mort know I needed to cross over to Earth to deal with a family matter, but I promised I would return quickly. I couldn't ignore my responsibilities to my world, no matter the dire circumstances of my family. Could I?

Alone with my worry, I traveled through the Ring that led me back to Earth. I noticed as I approached the Ring the noise coming from the other side—sound traveled through like an open window.

On the Earth side, they had activated the Ring in the transport tunnels under the remains of The Palace. Rej had designed those tunnels for moving supplies around The Palace, which would have housed thousands of people. I had no doubt they proved sufficient for the job of supplying the troops on El'daShar. It also bottled up any potential nasties that got through to the Rings from the El'daShar side, preventing them from running amok on Earth. Undoubtedly, housing the Ring in The Palace had its drawbacks in terms of flow of materials and people from the world outside that building. And the size of the Ring itself had surely presented a problem, being smaller than the tunnels, but I had to acknowledge that they had used the space well.

A desk waited on the Earth side of the Rings, with multiple people staffing it. It rested near a wall, allowing the tunnel to be used for moving goods. Down the tunnel on the receiving side of the Ring, where less traffic moved, a peculiar looking little tank underwent mechanical work. It looked old… a war machine heralding from around the two World Wars. Scan had asked for that—he knew a crazy amount of odd things. I would have to ask why.

I approached one of the personnel manning the desk, a young man in Army fatigues with the Guardian pin on his breast. It appeared they hadn't worked out uniforms yet.

"I'm Garnet Hernandez," I said. "There should be a message for me." The young man began clicking his keyboard.

"This says I'm supposed to call… erk… Penbrook *himself*?" He leaned over and tapped the woman next to him on the arm. "Kelly, am I reading that right?"

Kelly, for her part, stared at me, making me uncomfortable. At the young man's question, she just pointed at me. He looked at me more closely.

"Oh! Right then. Um, let me just get that call in."

Hell, what exactly had happened to my family?

"You're to go to his office." he said, after the call ended. "He's one floor up, sub level one, room SL143. It's just up those stairs." He pointed back to the main stairs for the building. "And then hang a sharp left."

"What time is it here?" I asked.

His eyes flicked to the screen. "8:32 pm, ma'am," he answered.

Working late, Rocks. I nodded my thanks and turned to walk down the hall, past the Ring, past the boxes of supplies lining the halls and the men working to organize them, to reach the stairs.

I felt a sudden peace, a cooling balm on the hot river of my worry and fear, and I stopped in my tracks. From where I stood, looking back the way I had come revealed only the people going from Earth to El'daShar, and a hint of the bustle on El'daShar through the Ring. I could not see past the Ring to the desk and tank that hid on the other side... but I *knew*. Striding from behind the Ring, looking my way, came Galad.

He smiled, and my heart warmed. We'd had only passing moments together in the past week. Even before receiving the message about my family, I'd longed to see him.

In my peripheral vision, I witnessed the work in the hallway come to a standstill.

Galad ignored them all, eyes on me. I waited the long seconds it took him to walk the length of the hall. Someone began clapping, and others saluted—whatever contempt of elves existed on the human colonies, Earth did not share the sentiment. "What are you doing here?" I asked. "Did you catch Cordoro?" I didn't speak loudly, but he heard me.

"No," he said. "But he's not popped his head out of his hidey hole since he fled. I can take a few hours off."

"Mort told you I got a message..."

He shook his head no. "Not Mort. Tali. She came through the Rings and told me I'd better come make sure you're okay."

"She told you that?" I said, slightly amazed.

"I think what she said was, 'Humans don't live very long. If you want to get your hands on that ass before it gets wrinkled and flabby, you better head to Earth... now.'"

I barked a laugh. "That's more believable." I embraced him and turned, with an arm around him, to lead him up the stairs. "So you want to get your hands on my ass?" I asked mischievously.

"Even wrinkled and flabby," he said. He lingered behind a moment, letting me go up the stairs to get a better look. "Did I wait too long?"

"Ass!" I said, swaying my hips to give him a better look.

"Seems okay, but could be anything going on under those fatigues," he said playfully.

I laughed inside, and immediately felt guilty. My family could be in danger, or even... I paused at the top and he caught up with me, sliding an arm around my waist but trying nothing more. I knew that *he* knew I was wrangling with internal worry. His presence and his distractions... they were perfect.

I spotted Rocks's office. He'd picked a room closest to the stairway and had it converted to his needs. Armed guards flanked it, and a mini-control center nestled in the hall. *Sec Ops Lite*, I thought with amusement.

We found Rocks discussing an image on one of the many monitors with several people in the room. He looked up and smiled. "See what you can do with that. We'll talk again later," he finished. Then he walked—walked!—around the desk and gave me a hug, patting Galad on the shoulder like an old friend.

"It's good to see you both. I'd ask how things are going, but I think I'm up to date." He grimaced. "Come back to my office, and we can talk in private."

We followed him, and he closed the door behind us.

"I got a call from your mom, Red," he said without preamble. "Your father has had a problem with his heart."

I felt like I had a problem with my own. "Heart attack?" I choked out.

"She didn't say," Rocks said. "She just said to let you know when I could."

I chuckled darkly, "That sounds like Mom." She'd never actually ask for support, but she knew how to guilt. I always found that funny, because Dad had been raised Catholic. But for Mom, it came naturally.

"Here," Rocks said, handing me his phone. "It's under 'Red's Mom.'"

My phone's battery had died—I hadn't found any charging stations on the colony worlds. I took the phone from him, dug up the number, and dialed, pacing the small room.

"Hello?" came the voice I'd known my whole life.

"Mom, it's me. Garnet."

The last time we'd talked, she'd chewed me out for putting my life at risk fighting monsters... and making videos out of it. Words like *reckless* and *foolish* echoed through my mind.

"Tibbies!"

Wonderful. Mom had reverted to my childhood nickname. Apparently that was the sound I'd made as a baby. *Tibby tibby tibby...*

"Mom, what happened to Dad?"

"Oh, don't worry about it, sweetie. Probably nothing. I just didn't want something to happen without giving you a chance to say goodbye."

"Say goodbye?!?" I ratcheted my volume back down a level. Maybe two. "Mom, where's Dad?"

"He's resting, sweetie. Like I said, I'm sure everything will be okay. Assuming we all live through this alien invasion you're a part of."

"I am *not* part of an alien invasion!" Oops. Ratcheted volume again. "Mom, are you home?"

"Yes, I'm home. Why?"

"Just stay home for five minutes. I'll talk to you in five, okay?"

"Well, my cell phone works whether or not I'm home," Mom said. "I don't really see..."

"Just stay there!" I practically shouted.

I hung up the phone and took a moment to fume. Mom was so *frustrating*. "Well," I said, "what are you waiting for? Figure out how to 'Port me home!"

"Welcome to Club Red," Rocks said to Galad.

Rocks opened the door and waved in a tech guy, closing the door behind him.

"Charlie, show me how to use someone's address and connect it to the global maps we use for Teleportation with Elliah, please."

"Any address in particular?"

"Just use the address of The Palace for now. I want to know *how* to do it," Rocks said.

Charlie walked us through how to punch in an address, how that connected to longitude and latitude, and brought it up on the global map. Rocks thanked him and showed him back out the door.

When he left, I punched in my parents' address and brought it up on the system. Galad cast his spell and worked out the right magical coordinates. We fumbled more than Scan would have, but we got it done.

"Now, I need an image of the destination," Galad said.

"Take it from my head," I told him.

"You sure?"

I gave him the stink eye. "Just do it."

I closed my eyes and pictured my parents' home as I remembered it last, looking at the front door.

"You want to arrive outside of it?" he asked.

"Yes, please."

"Then we should go outside for the spell," he told me. Oh yeah, he'd told me that before. Teleporting between similar locations made it easier to work the magic. I'd seen Mort and even Galad break those rules, or guidelines, but conceivably it required more skill or effort, or a Talent. "Can I still return by using the room on sublevel two?" he asked Rocks.

Rocks nodded. "Yes. Elliah uses that room. We've kept it clear for Teleporting."

"Okay. We won't be gone long, Rocks," I told him.

"Take whatever time you need," he said.

I knew he meant it, but I wasn't going to let the fate of the Universe ride on some drama created by my mother. *Please, let it be drama!*

Galad and I left the building. It was cold in New York at… what was it, the end of October? Halloween. Or I'd missed it possibly. I'd sold Lani on the idea of seeing the kids in costumes, but I'd completely forgotten. It was a silly thing to feel guilty about, but I felt a small pang anyway. Lani's cooing about the idea had been so sweet.

He walked over to a column of etched concrete that decorated the outside of The Palace, and marked it with some magical runes

that faded into transparency. He gave me a, "Ready?" look.
 I took one deep breath to steady myself and nodded.
 Galad's effort to cast the spell, complicated for a non-Teleporter, drew looks from New Yorkers walking past The Palace.
 Then, *bamf*.

Chapter 61

Galad, two hundred years in the past

What the rotting vines? Talk with my people?

I stared at the open door. I leaned against an ornate wooden table that stretched the length of the room. Open shutters allowed in light and a gentle breeze, along with birdsong and some noise from the courtyard below.

The AllForest housed a Transport Hub in the courtyard, though it couldn't have been even a tenth of the size of the one I'd left behind on El'daShar. But I hadn't 'Ported into the Hub. Technically, I was the Duke—a title inherited upon my father's demise hundreds of years before. And though I hadn't been back much since my parents' deaths, or even for a long time while they'd lived, I still had the right to Teleport within the castle. Lomamir had stalked out, leaving me within the same section of the Barrakrea where my 'Porter had deposited me .

Sighing, I stalked to the hall and looked around.

"Throra," I called with civility, despite my anger, to a raven-haired elf leaning against the wall and reading a book while she waited for me.

She put a finger in her book and raised an eyebrow in question.

"It seems I will stay a little longer after all. You need not wait. I'll find a way back."

Elves came and went from a stairway leading down, some passing through the hall we occupied to reach deeper into the castle. Their eyes flitted to me in curiosity. I didn't recognize any of them, and I let my Empathy run freely enough to tell they also did not recognize me.

Throra nodded and looked around, then gave me another raised eyebrow.

"Yes, I'm sure. I grew up here, you know."

She smiled playfully. "I'm sure you could find a way to make it worth my while to wait."

I peered into her mind—to my surprise, Throra, a younger elf born on El'daShar, had more than pleasure on her mind. She had never before traveled to AllForest, and she'd decided she liked it more than she'd expected. Her eyes saw not a backwater, but a castle nestled in a beautiful forest, and thoughts of a royal heir swirled through her mind.

Children were not part of my plan. And if she had any sense, she would not risk a child Empath.

"If you can wait," I said, "'til after the spell testing on the new wastewater and sewage treatment? I hope they've got the kinks worked out from last time—"

She disappeared in a bright light—she'd left the planet. And I felt a touch of sadness at how easy it had been to drive her away.

Sighing again, I turned and descended the stairs.

I'd commissioned a replica of the Barrakrea on El'daShar, including the statues in the gathering hall. Each gathering hall had something of an air of a social arena, but on El'daShar it embodied conversations in a relaxed getaway. On the AllForest, the discussions in the gathering hall were of a functional nature. Trade, family business, instruction. I found the timbre of discussion in the AllForest to be off-putting, slightly raucous compared to the more refined tones of my replica.

My eye lingered on the statue of Elvonduil, the mighty warrior who gave his life in the Second Troll Wars, his role in the defeat of the Nameless One being one of my favorite childhood stories. The replica did not do justice to the hammer he carried—something about the original remained timeless.

Perhaps I should have the original brought to El'daShar?

"Galadrindor?" My musings derailed, I turned to search for the voice that had called my name, the slight Empathic tug helping me home in on the caller.

I smiled when I found the owner of the voice. "Celymir!" Her roguish smile and attire reminded me to appreciate the lack of refinement of the AllForest. I descended the last stairs and wound my way toward her through the crowd, but I could tell Empathically that she headed to the main gates that led to the courtyard. I changed direction and nearly intercepted her just as she stepped from the relatively small crowds inside the gathering hall to the much louder and more crowded courtyard.

She teased me, swaying her hips as she walked away, playing an emotional catch-me-if-you-can. My kind of game. *Talk with my people. I'll do more than talk, dear sister.* I laughed appreciatively at my own humor.

It immediately became harder to pick her emotions out of the crowd. Maybe part of her game. I had to jump backwards when a cart passed through a crossway in the paths created by vendors, their booths establishing streets in the open yard. I stood on my toes to keep an eye on her attractive, retreating form, but lost her in the crowd. Silently swearing, I darted forward when the cart passed, finding her again only because my Empathic ability glimpsed her after I'd passed her by.

She'd stopped at a booth, and I spun about and walked into the sheathed sword she turned and pushed toward me.

"Oof!" I blurted, taking a scabbard in the gut.

"If you're going to be of any help, you'll need a sword," she said with a quirky smile. "You still remember how to use a sword, I hope."

On El'daShar, the aristocracy did not walk around displaying arms. The reports of unrest on AllForest must have been accurate. But the idea that it could be more—that the AllForest might prepare for war against the Crown—ridiculous.

I couldn't read Celymir accurately in the crowd. Still, I knew women. Time to plant the seed. I smirked as I delivered my joke. "I assure you, there are no complaints about my swordplay."

She laughed, but it wasn't the right kind of laugh. Not coquettish. Not playful.

I had known Celymir for—I realized I didn't know how long. She hadn't been a childhood friend of Lomamir's, but before our parents' deaths, they had become close. So several eons of friendship. I couldn't remember if we'd slept together, but we probably had at some point. So, I didn't let my chagrin at her laughter show. I'd find the right cues to trigger her interest as soon as we worked our way out of the crowd.

"Put on the sword," she said. "Seriously. We're going for a walk, and I'm not going to 'defend your honor' or similar nonsense."

We stood next to a weapons vendor, the ornate yet easily dismantled stand holding swords and daggers. The vendor produced a wan smile for me, the coins from his sale already tucked away.

Celymir wore dark brown leathers with boots to match. Her brown hair was much like my sister's, but cut shorter, and my target's eyes were a lighter green. She had freckles, which was unusual for an elf—it would be fun to find them all. As I fastened the sword belt, I noticed she carried a longbow and small quiver, with a sword at her waist, and daggers at belt and boots. I pursed my lips, slightly concerned, though not sure exactly why.

No matter, as soon as I get her alone on the walk, I shall know.

Celymir did not wait for me, but strode away, throwing a green cape about her shoulders and securing her hair with a talisman. Magical devices of some kind, no doubt, meant to boost her speed, her tracking—something. I had been acquiring exactly those types of items for Slooti over the millennia, secured by the Crown through a legal system I had proven to be very skilled at manipulating. Leaving AllForest with those items, and Celymir thanking me for taking them, would be the icing on the cake.

She left the courtyard through the east exit—that would lead to troll caves. The pieces were already sliding in place in my head: a Warlord had been born; the trolls were amassing; they had attacked travelers from El'daShar; and the AllForest had not yet put the Warlord down. All of that would have reached the ears of Slooti through aggrieved relatives, elves who saw the ruling powers of the AllForest as rebellious when the response to lost relatives was not swift and harsh.

If Lomamir could truly arrange for a meeting with the Warlord, then the problem would be taken care of swiftly, by me.

I hastened to catch up with Celymir, ready to get her away from others, where I would read her clearly, and learn what made her tick. I looked forward to making her tick. It made me feel good to make others—well, *female* others—feel good.

The road was not empty, but there were few enough people that I would be able to pick out her emotions. I leaned my emotions forward, and found only the slightest hints of her own—amusement, irritation, determination. I went from *leaning* to *pushing* on her emotions, with no better result.

A spredix bleated behind me, startling me into the realization that I had stopped in my tracks. I nodded an apology without thinking, and as I hurried forward, it struck me that I was the Duke, not some riffraff to be squawked at. But turning to rebuke the driver of the spredix-pulled cart would not help me catch up with Celymir.

Another cart rolled toward me on the wide road, again pulled by a spredix. It dawned on me as I jogged forward that spredix were not native to the AllForest. They had not been there when I had last visited. As I caught up with Celymir, I spotted another cart strapped to a spredix, driven by an elf, loaded with boxes.

"Your headband is illegal," I told Celymir.

"Headbands are illegal now? I've heard legends of your legal skills, but banning headbands—really impressive. Unless there's a wind, of course, and then your illegal headbands might be missed."

"Not just any headband," I said, irritably, "but your Empathy-blocking headband."

But Celymir ignored me and continued on. "The legends I've heard would suggest you'd perhaps banned clothing altogether, at least for women. Or perhaps all but suggestive clothing. Much to the delight of all women everywhere, of course."

What?!? All I'd ever done was help people find happiness.

I couldn't read Celymir. I didn't know what the cloak was doing, but her headband, with its light blue crystals at the ends, blocked my Talent. She marched on, ignoring my irritation, drawing us farther down the road.

The road widened enough for two carts to pass, plus foot traffic. We moved to the side so the spredix could accelerate. The forest walled us in on either side. Tall trees with long, overhanging limbs kept the road shaded, and kept the walk pleasant, though it stretched on without end.

We walked in silence for some time, my irritation at her words keeping me quiet. I did not know, *could* not know because of her illegal hairpiece, what kept her from speaking.

I used the time to listen in on the feelings of drivers going by. Drivers in both directions felt concern, not quite reaching worry. A tenseness or readiness. Perhaps troll attacks? I scoured the trees for any sign of danger. But trolls were gigantic creatures, and even those massive tree trunks would not have concealed them.

In fact—"Wasn't this path once wider?" I asked, breaking the silence.

"It was, I suppose, a long time ago," came the answer.

The road we traveled was the most direct route between troll territory and the Barrakrea. When the trolls marched, they destroyed the trees. But the trees nearest the road were large, hundreds of years old. Had it been so long since a troll uprising?

If so, what made the drivers tense?

"Where are you taking me?" I asked, curiosity finally getting the better of me.

Celymir didn't even look my way as she answered. "I'm not *taking* you anywhere. I'm going somewhere and you're following me."

First, I squinted in confusion, then I rolled my eyes, but she saw none of that.

"Okay," I drawled. "And where might you be going?"

With a dagger, she pointed straight ahead, down the road that tunneled through the forest.

I stopped myself from rolling my eyes again. *Fool woman.* I stayed quiet as another cart rolled by, not wanting to shout over the racket it made. When it had passed, I picked up my thread. "Would you not reach your destination faster on a spredix?"

"I would indeed," she answered, "but I would miss out on this scintillating conversation."

"Yes, that would be a pity," I said, giving up on trying to make sense of the situation.

And, to my surprise, she chuckled.

"What brings you to the AllForest... *Duke*?" I heard scorn behind it.

"The Crown hears rumors of unrest," I said, watching her out of the corner of my eye. I suspected already that the real problem was trolls and upset vacationers.

"And should you find *unrest*, what is your role, *Duke*? Report back to *The Crown*?" Even more disdain permeated her last words than when she uttered my title. "End the unrest yourself? Or perhaps understand and lead your people?"

Her response spoke much more than I expected. Was there unrest? Perhaps even preparation for rebellion? Something lurked behind her words, and she masked her thoughts for a reason.

"My people," I intoned, "are under the authority of the High Lord."

"And *your* authority as well. Were there unrest... were your people to rebel, you would be culpable in either The Crown's eyes, or your people's.'"

I stopped in my tracks. I hadn't said anything about rebellion, had I? What was going on? Would Slooti blame me if AllForest rebelled? Ridiculous!

Celymir did not stop, and squinting at her as I considered her words, I spied something in the distance down the road. I jogged to catch up.

"You talk of rebellion as though it is a real possibility," I accused. "Elves fighting elves is wrong!"

"There are worse things," she said calmly. "And we merely talk of what you would do should you *find* a rebellion. Whose side you would choose. I know nothing of a rebellion. Is it illegal now to *discuss* loyalties?"

"You are... very frustrating," I told her.

"You are not the first to have mentioned that," she said with a smile. "If it comforts you at all, your sister finds my discussions similarly frustrating."

"Does she? And do you talk with her of similar matters?"

"She does, and I do."

So there *was* talk of rebellion. Could I believe her when she said she knew nothing of a rebellion? I wanted to believe her. My loyalty would be to the High Lord, but I hated the thought of standing against the world where I was born and spent my early childhood, the world my sister called home. I wanted to believe Celymir, because that would be easier.

We walked on in silence for a long time. The sun moved lazily from behind us to the front. Celymir pulled a leather-bound skin from beneath her cloak, took a drink, and handed it to me. It contained only water, but it proved cool and refreshing, and as I handed it back, she gave me a bag of dried fruits and nuts.

We spoke no more, and I wrestled with the demon of not knowing how my sister had answered the same questions Celymir had put to me. I doubted our answers aligned.

The sun continued to pull ahead, but the shade of the trees blocked its direct blinding effects. I wondered if, when it reached the ground, it would shoot its rays directly into the tunnel. I watched with interest as it ducked under the canopy, only to find that it had distracted me—instead of peeking into the tunnel, something blocked it.

"What is that?" I asked, breaking our silence again.

"Galadrindor's Folly," she answered, a mixture of amusement and distaste clear in her tone.

Chapter 62

Cordoro

Savage would be the death of me.

Possibly, if one were born there, and knew nothing else, it could *somehow* be palatable, but anyone who'd seen *anything* else of the Universe would recognize it for the shithole that it was.

The entire colony smelled like sewage, and if you found a place to escape the stench, the stink of sweat replaced it. I'd been told that the nose adjusted to smells, no matter how bad, but either mine did not, or Savage exceeded any limit. The food tasted like some combination of sewage and sweat, with heavy, probably toxic, spices meant to disguise the festering grime. Swampy and hot… even the rain came down hot from the sky! And ignoring the smell, the tastes, and the heat, the noise was enough to drive one insane—chirps and squeaks I could live with, but so many of the animals screamed and roared, and the constant buzzing of the biting insects reminded me I had no escape.

"Why the hell do these things keep stinging me, and leave *you* alone?!?" I complained for the thousandth time to Blithe, the Teleporter for the Savages.

He reached his hand out and offered me his canteen of that foul, spicy alcohol they all imbibed. I closed my eyes and shook my head no. When I opened them, he offered me a meat-like glob with more spicy sauce. I couldn't stomach either. I was wasting away.

Blithe shrugged helplessly and had a bite and a sip. He was *feasting* while I ate nothing.

"How do you expect me to keep doing all the 'Ports if you starve me?"

"I don't know how elssse to offer you food," he said. "You eat nothing we provide. You don't drink our sssabli. If you did, you would not get ssstung. And you're hardly doing *all the 'Portsss.*"

Sssabli? Sabli—I corrected myself. The drink would keep the bugs away? Why hadn't he ever said that?

"Everything that we send against the Forsaken, *I* have to send." It wasn't fair. I held my hand out for his canister of sabli.

"Everything we sssend to *El'daSSSar*, you are sssending," he corrected. "I've handled the 'Portsss to the other coloniesss, plusss all my normal workload. You're getting off easssy," he said, waving away my indignation.

I took a sip of the proffered drink. It tasted like a spicy licorice, with a slimy texture that reminded me of mucus running down my throat.

How dare he! Getting off *easy*? I'd never done so much 'Porting on Emerald Farms. Oh, Emerald Farms. How I longed for my cabinet of wines, fine meats and cheeses, fruits from exotic lands.

"How much longer?" I asked.

"Until the drink worksss? The time it will take usss to eat. Until you can get back to your life of luxssury?" Blithe asked, shrugging, amused at my expense.

Luxury? Having drinkable wine was hardly the life of luxury.

He saw the look on my face, and shook his head, sighing. "I don't undersssstand you. We're winning—the Forsssaken are being ssslowly whittled away, and we've had no losssesss. They've ssstretched their line too thin, and they will sssoon hit a point where they collapssse."

"But those damn Earthlings!" I said in disgust. "They seem to be endless, and with those long-range weapons…"

"Doesssn't matter," Blithe said, waving away my concern. "Whittling away the Forsssaken isss what mattersss. If they have only their long-range weaponsss, we can ultimately 'Port within their linesss and desssimate them. It isss only a matter of time."

A matter of time. But I was sick of Savage, sick of the so-called life lived by its inhabitants. I craved *my* food, *my* drink, the comfort of *my* home. My heart longed for Emerald Farms, and I felt my anger and resentment grow. I replayed all the things they had denied me, again and again, like a clock spinning in circles. I grew tired of waiting.

"You *will* wait," Blithe said, not liking what he saw on my face. He sliced a piece of that disgusting meat with his dagger and slid it into his mouth, his calm movements belying the steel in his voice. He implied something dangerous, though I knew not what, which made it all the worse.

I let my face fall, defeated, but inside, I added it to my list of resentments.

Chapter 63

Galad, two hundred years in the past

"My *folly*?" I asked, scooping a healthy dollop of irritation into my words.

"To show the splendor of his home world, our Duke, in his great wisdom, created a replica of the Barrakrea on El'daShar." Celymir spoke of me in third person, as though I did not walk right by her side.

"Of this I am aware." *And in terms of inhabitants, the replica is proving superior.*

"One of the interesting and clever things our Duke did was convince the inhabitants of the AllForest that it was in their best interests to show the glory of the original home of the elves to their off-world descendants. It would spark interest, bring tourism, connect elves up with their heritage. And so he convinced them to fund the construction of that replica."

"And did it not do what he predicted? Do you not have a tourism trade? I am told you do."

"By whom, I wonder, are you told that?" She did not wait for an answer. "We surely do get visitors, but not from any elves of the aristocracy. Not from visitors with heavy coin purses. But maybe that's for the best. It has strengthened us."

We moved close enough that the obstruction became clear—a wall with a gate. The spredix drivers waited, a line on either side, before going through.

"That," Celymir said, "is a toll gate. There were several constructed along the main roads to raise funds for building the replica of the Barrakrea on El'daShar."

"But we completed the replica eons ago. I cannot even remember exactly when—"

"And yet the tolls continue," Celymir interrupted.

"But where do the funds go?"

"Where indeed?" she asked. "It would have been more aptly named 'The Folly of the Elves of AllForest,' but that's quite the mouthful. Ironically, the effort to show our history to elves that had left the AllForest *afflicted* our future, taxing us without end, without even representation in the High Council. I have been to the replica, you know. It is quite the relaxing getaway for young lovers." She was shaking her head, and I felt a twinge of shame. *I* was AllForest's representation at the High Council.

"I don't understand. Why did my sister not just send a message, asking for the tolls to be stopped, or at least asking where the money was going?"

Celymir finally stopped, for the first time since our walk began. I halted and turned to face her, finding her eyes glaring, full of suspicion, into mine. After several tense seconds, she looked away, and started walking again. "That does seem like the natural move, doesn't it?" But it wasn't a question. "I wish we would have thought to do so."

Had my sister sent me letters about tolls? Hundreds of years... no, it had been at least a couple of millennia since my parents' deaths. I wouldn't have forgotten a letter from my sister. There couldn't have been letters. Nor messengers. Could there have been?

Several carts started back to Barrakrea, loaded with wooden boxes, kicking up dust that danced in the brilliant glow of the sun. Celymir pulled her cloak up over her mouth and nose as they rolled past, so I followed suit. We passed dust-covered elves removing tack from their spredix, and empty carts resting off the side of the road. They had grown the trees with shelter for overnight stays in mind.

We approached the gate, and the sun ducked below the horizon, allowing me a glimpse of what lay beyond. Rocky red and brown peaks freckled with trees in an otherwise desolate landscape had hidden behind the stone wall and canopy of forest leaves. And I felt the vibrations underfoot that the lumbering carts had masked—I knew what I would see when I reached the gate.

Chapter 64

Red

Despite having been back many times as an adult, my childhood home always looked smaller than I remembered. Even with the hour change between Texas and New York, night had jostled its way in.

Time of year. Kids ran around in costumes with bags in hand, screaming with playful fright, joy, and sprinkles of sugar-induced hysteria. *Of all the days.*

"It's Halloween," I said aloud.

"That explains it then," Galad said, a good dollop of sarcasm coating his words.

"Um, I think I've mentioned this. Kids go door to door, dressed in costumes, asking for candy."

"Related to your egg-hiding rabbit?"

"Nope. Separate thing."

"Mmm-hmm."

I followed a troop of pre-teens to my parents' home. They rang the bell, and my dad answered in a pirate costume.

"Trick or treat!" the kids yelled.

"Arrrrgh," my father said, "you're after me pirate booty then," and he started dropping candy into open bags.

"Two elves, is it?" my father said, and I looked at the kids I had followed. One dressed like Galad. Ha!

Wait, was that girl wearing the mask from my videos? Dang, she had glowing plastic daggers.

"What the fudge?" I said, the proximity to my dad modifying my language.

"Garnet?" My dad, the pirate, reached beside the door and grabbed a pair of glasses, banging them on his eyepatch. "Frak," he mumbled, trying, without setting the candy bowl down, to get the eyepatch out of the way and right his glasses with his free hand. He popped the elastic of the eyepatch, snapping it onto his finger, which made him jerk his hand, flinging his glasses off. Trying to catch the glasses with his other hand, he dropped the plastic bucket of candy, sending Halloween treats sprawling out the door.

"I see from whence you inherit your coordination," Galad remarked.

I elbowed him in the ribs. "It's me, Dad."

Down on all fours, he found his glasses and put them on. I knelt and started chucking candy back into the bucket, Galad following my lead.

"Well, *this* is a surprise!" Turning, he yelled, "Hunny, you'll never guess who's here!"

"Did Garnet bring anyone?" Mom shouted from around the wall that separated the front room from the kitchen.

"What the jeebers?" Dad said to himself. Then, more loudly, "How on God's Green Earth did you know…" More softly, to himself again, "That's why she's making cookies."

Cookies? They better be dark chocolate chip.

"Dad, I'm glad to see you're up and about." I gave him a tight hug as we both stood, the candy returned to the bucket. He stood a head taller than I—I'd always loved the way I fit in his hugs.

"Up and about? Why wouldn't I be? Who's this then?"

"This is Galadrindor Arafaemiel Terebra'an." See, I did freakin' learn it. Take that, Smith. "He's an elf. Mom mentioned your heart issue over the phone, but she didn't give me any details."

"Nice to meet you…" Dad said, already struggling to remember the name I'd just said. Some people.

"Galad," Galad said helpfully, taking Dad's proffered hand.

"Galad!" my dad echoed. "I'm a human." Oh, brother. "A *Mexican* human."

"Geez, Dad."

"*Nombre*, mi muñeca…"

Whoaaa… the cookie smell wafted me back fifteen years.

"Hunny?" Dad boomed to the kitchen. "Did you tell me I have a heart condition?"

Wait, what?

Dad looked chagrined. "Dang," he said to himself. Was he having trouble remembering too?

"I *think* I told you," she yelled back. "In the shower?"

Gah!

He shouted back, "I've mentioned that our *showers* aren't the best time to bring up things you want me to *remember*!"

I felt thigh-high jostling behind me, and I turned to see a group of kids looking skeptically at the pirate in his glasses, pondering his declaration.

One brave girl declared, "Trick or treat?"

But I went from worried to fuming in a heartbeat. Pushing past my father, I yelled, "Mother! You can't *make up* a medical condition! I was on another damned *world* for Christ's sake!"

"Red," Galad whispered, but I heard him through all the noise in my head. I stopped before reaching the kitchen. I looked back at him, my breath coming hard.

"Daggers," he said, nodding down at my hands as he strolled into my house. My parents' house. I didn't have to look down—I felt myself clutching them tightly. I smoldered, and they had become an extension of my anger.

"Oooooh," came the chorus from the doorway, eyes on my glowing daggers.

I put them away.

Rounding the wall to the kitchen, the memory-laden smell of dark chocolate chip cookies overpowered me. Mom was *right there*, stuffing a cookie in my mouth. I could have avoided it, but... I didn't want to.

It tasted like childhood and the warm comfort of family. "Mom," I said, my tone calmer, but my anger still burning, "I was literally on another planet. Did you lie about Dad having a heart problem?"

"Of course not, Sweetie," she said. "I told you he'd be fine." She waved away my worry and gave me a hug, the top of her head reaching my nose. "It's good to see you."

"It's good to see you, too," I said. And I found I meant it. But... "I don't get it. What's the heart problem?"

"There's someone I'd like you to meet," Mom said, just as

Galad came around the corner. "Oh! You're that elf, from the videos... Galfry... Salad... ?"

"Galad, Mother. This is Galad."

Sighing, I looked more closely at everything. Even when I lived there, Mom liked to change a room every six months. The layout and essence of the floor plan were the same, but the colors differed from what I remembered; the fixtures had changed; and they had replaced the furniture and arranged it differently.

It still offered a big, open kitchen plus family room, with a dining room to the side, but the white kitchen cabinets had become stained light wood—that had to have been hard to do. I would have bet the colonists on Vibrant Woods had some spell for it, but on Earth... no simple answer. She'd replaced the reclining sectional that had been big enough for all five of us to watch a movie as kids with a smaller sofa and simple chairs angled toward the TV at its sides.

In one of those chairs slumped a young man of Indian descent, in blue jeans and a T-shirt, drinking a beer.

"Galad, so nice to meet you," my mom said. The man in the living room stood up, leaving his beer on the coffee table. Mom quickly tried again. "As I was saying, I have someone I want you to meet."

"Mother," I said in warning, but she plowed over me.

"This is Venki," she said. "Venki, this is my daughter, Garnet."

"A pleasure to meet you, Ms. Hernandez," Venki said politely, no hint of a foreign accent—unless you consider New Jersey foreign, which most Texans would.

Still, I didn't take the hand he offered. I didn't want to play Mother's games.

"I don't know what you're playing at, Mother, but you don't *trick* your daughter into coming home just to set her up with a man."

"Oh, that's not what this is," she said. "You need to talk. The three of you. Trust me."

I squinted at her. The doorbell rang.

"Let's get that, Hunny," Mom said to Dad, moving him toward the door.

I turned my gaze back to Venki, popping the remains of my

cookie in my mouth and lowering my hands to my daggers.

"Please, don't do anything rash," Venki said, watching my hands as he moved to put the kitchen island between us.

"Rash is my middle name." Yikes, that sounded stupid. Oh well. "Are you going to threaten my parents now?" I'd feared someone might use my family to get to me. It's why I'd worn the mask for so long.

"What? No. I just can't control what happens when I get anxious," he said, not making me any more comfortable. "Look," he said, "I came to you because you're not part of the government, and I don't want to hide forever. I want to help."

Great, a fugitive. So I had a criminal on my hands.

"I'm sorry," he continued. "I'm not saying this well. Your mother said to just be straight with you, but I'm scared, and if I get too scared, poof, I'm gone. So I'm…"

He stopped mid-sentence and turned back to the living room. He took the beer off the coffee table and downed the rest of the bottle, then stared at his feet for a few seconds.

"I can do magic," he said, not facing us. "I was in The Palace the day it blew, and I came out of there with powers." He spat the words out, then went silent. In the reflection from the windows of the living room, he had closed his eyes, tense, as though waiting for a blow. He thought what? That I wouldn't believe him? When proof of magic would be so easy?

"Why have you waited to come forward?" I asked.

He sagged. "The government. *My* government locked me up. They were experimenting on me. I got away. I've been hiding ever since. But I see you doing good, working with others like me. I joined the FBI to help people, and now I'm hunted by them, and I did nothing but follow orders."

Okay, he was babbling now, but I got the picture.

"Calm down," I said, as gently as I could, which probably wasn't that gentle. "I hear you. I think I understand. There is definitely a place for you with us if you're being honest with me. So, you find you can do *what* now? Move water with your mind? Start fires?"

"No… this," he said, followed by a *bamf* and a flash of light, and he was right in front of me. As I drew my daggers, there followed a second *bamf* and he was back across the room again.

"Holy Mother of Trees," I said.

Galad put a hand on my shoulder, saying, "Trick? Or treat?"

Chapter 65

Galad, two hundred years in the past

Celymir slipped the guard a coin as we walked through the gate. The light of the setting sun showed the retreating backs of trolls as they headed away from the gate and toward the mountains.

I looked to the side—the wall stretched for miles, but not indefinitely. Six guards controlled the gates. I spotted a guard post in the trees on the thickly wooded side of the wall, housing another ten or so elves. Totally inadequate to halt a troll attack.

I put my hand on the scabbard of the sword Celymir had gifted me, but she placed a hand on my arm, stopping me. Or at least letting me know we were in no immediate danger. She began walking again.

A trail, almost a road, rose into the foothills of the mountains. Spredix-pulled carts might have been able to navigate the uneven surfaces and rocky debris; trolls would have had no trouble lumbering about.

"Is this safe?" I asked, catching up again.

"It is not."

I put my hand on my sword again. "How unsafe?"

"Learning the balance of your sword might be wise," she suggested. "But let us get a little farther from Galadrindor's Folly first, so as not to frighten the guards."

I let my sword go. "The wall is not such a terrible thing if it keeps the trolls so far from Barrakrea," I suggested. Still, it nagged at me that the money from tolls had been going *somewhere* for ages.

"That wall would not keep out a troll for long," she answered. "And a group of them would demolish it in seconds. Or they could go around, and smash their way through the forest to get back on the road. Or just clear an entirely new path to The Barrakrea."

"Then what good is it?" I almost asked, but realized the folly of my question and halted. Galadrindor's Folly. It existed to funnel money somewhere. "Why have people not worked around it?" I asked instead.

"And betray the law of The Crown?" She raised an eyebrow in question. "Who would suggest such a thing? That sounds like the beginnings of a rebellion."

She teased me, but she had a point. Learning to work around the rulership, that would provide a taste of rebellion. "Why do any use it at all?" I asked.

"It is easy for the trolls to find," she said, as though that explained anything. She turned, and, drawing her sword, said, "Okay, we are far enough out." She cast a magelight and let it hover over us in the dying light. "No one will hear you scream."

She grinned wickedly and lunged, but my sword sprang into my hand, enabling me to keep my head. Literally. I backed up as I tried to wrap my mind around the situation. Was she actually trying to kill me? I couldn't read her mind, at all. But I could read *her*, at least in terms of swordwork. Double-entendres about swordplay had become a natural part of my vocabulary, but they rang true—I had mastered the sword. What I didn't know was whether or not I fought for my life.

I began counter-strikes meant to disarm her, hurt her, weary her, but not kill her. The sword she'd given me proved reliable. It surprised me she had picked up such a decent sword in a common marketplace sale. It spoke well of her eye for weapons. Would she have purchased a decent sword if her intent was to kill me? Why get me a sword at all? I didn't think her intent was to kill, despite the attempts with killing blows—she merely tested my swordwork.

So I fought back hard, but not hard enough to end her life. Several times I thought I had her, but each time, she escaped, once bloodying my leg in the process. I Healed it when I had a moment, without stopping the fight.

It made me nervous that we fought out in the middle of troll territory, magelight revealing us, sword clashes ringing out into the ever-darkening sky. It seemed... ill-advised. She'd picked a region with elf-sized boulders around—would we see a troll coming in time to avoid it? I tried to remember the 'Port locations I knew on the AllForest. There had been a time, in my young adulthood, when I knew several. The one back in the Barrakrea would be the most useful escape route. But it had been too long. I couldn't dig up the memory.

"Well?" a feminine voice asked out of the shadows of a boulder.

I moved away from the voice and cast a magelight, while Celymir stepped back and lowered her weapon. I sent my magelight darting around the rocks and found—my sister! My light danced between more boulders, convincing me she came alone.

"Your brother is a fool," Celymir said, shrugging.

I was a fool?

"But you let him live," Lomamir replied, her voice cold.

Celymir shrugged, not having sheathed her sword. "It is not my first time to meet a fool, nor my first time to be one. He has not yet made foolishness against the law." In the magelight, I felt sure she winked at me.

But I didn't find that comforting. "How have I been a fool?" I growled.

Celymir rolled her eyes. "So many, *many* ways. You wanted to meet the Warlord? We should do so."

She knew about the Warlord? And that Lomimar would set up a meeting with him? How? When had they talked? She'd called me a fool, and I felt foolish. She'd strung me along from the first seemingly random encounter in the gathering hall, all the way to a secluded area in troll territory. What game did they play?

I tried to read my sister and found I could not. I didn't know if she wore magical protection, or as my sister, she'd had enough practice at blocking me that I could not get through her mental barriers.

Still, I wouldn't go easily. I moved in, intending to disarm the unprepared Celymir.

The next thing I knew, I stared at the stars, flat on my back, her sword tip at my throat, my sword on the ground nearby.

"Fool," she said, shaking her head. "Get up, and try, for just a little while, to rein in your foolishness." She stepped over to my sword and picked it up. I whispered a spell and Healed the slight bruises just handed to me. To my surprise, she tossed my sword back to me. She sheathed her own.

Okay, she's not going to kill me. Not right now anyway. Saving me for the Warlord to kill?

I sheathed my sword, still wondering what gambit they played, frustrated with my inability to control my fate. Frustrated at my vanity that, as an Empath with millennia of experience, I towered at the top of the food chain. Convinced of my invulnerability, I'd succumbed to a hairband and nice hips. "So what now?" I asked.

"The Warlord awaits us," my sister said, striding closer. She looked at Celymir. "Along with another."

"Should we warn him?" Celymir asked.

"He won't believe," Lomamir answered. "Any of it. He's always had to make his own mistakes."

I will not make this day's mistakes again.

Then I wondered if she had even been referring to me.

She cast a spell, and my night vision sharpened. We would go someplace dark.

"Be silent when we arrive." Lomamir cautioned us.

Celymir nodded, and my sister, who like me had struggled to learn Teleportation, 'Ported us away in a small flash of light.

Chapter 66

Red

Mom and Dad came back and, between sugar-craving costumed visitors, we had a few brief conversations about nothing. Dad wanted to look at the daggers—I'd inherited my fascination with knives from him, much to Mom's chagrin. He oohed and ahhed with appreciation, then handed them back when another knock at the door interrupted us.

The trick-or-treaters reminded me again of my telling Lani about Halloween, and how she had wanted to see the kids in costumes. She displayed a rare balance of innocence and ruggedness, where the innocence shone through. It reminded me of a girl I once knew, before she learned her lover betrayed her, and then he died to make amends. I missed that girl, and maybe Lani helped me dig her out just a little.

Thinking of my past reminded me of Bear, who also maintained innocence despite a very difficult upbringing. I'd never gotten to see him spend Halloween with children, but I bet he would have enjoyed it immensely.

Finally, Mom pulled me out of my musings. "You might as well go, Sweety. Your mind is clearly elsewhere. What is it you used to say... 'subordinate everything else to the system's constraints.'"

I sipped at the coffee she'd handed me at some point. I'd missed the hot brew on my travels, but drinking it didn't create the euphoric peace it had used to grant.

"You remember that?" I said, mildly surprised. It had been the basis for how I'd attacked all problems since I'd learned it. How I'd reformed villages and towns overseas while in the military, how I'd improved security at The Palace, even how I attempted to convince the otherworldly human colonies to unite.

"There was a point when you said it so much, you must have

been chanting it in your sleep," she remarked, handing me another cookie, then doing the same with Galad and Venki. I absently enjoyed the dark chocolate encased in loving sugary dough, as my mind pondered how best to use a Teleporter that we didn't *really* know.

I leaned into Galad, putting my free hand around him. Warm cookie and hot elf, interesting problem to solve—mmmmmm.

Galad nudged me with *his* free hand. I nudged him back. He made a light cough and nudged me again. I looked up.

Mom was looking our way, observing our casual embrace and saying nothing. *Oops?*

"We should go," I said as I extracted myself from the embrace.

"Mmmhmmm," Mom hummed.

"So we'll be going outside to Teleport back to New York," I said, and Venki tensed. "From there, we'll travel to the elven home world."

Galad corrected me, "*Adopted* home world."

"On El'daShar," I told Venki, "we can get you to a Teleporter who can coach you. Train you in your abilities."

"I thought I'd be helping those other mages fight Infected," he offered.

"We've got a real logistics nightmare going in our attempt to fight the Infected. That's where you would do the most good right now."

He nodded to me. "If it helps. I don't mind getting involved in something more risky. I *was* an FBI agent." He didn't sound offended.

"These logistics," Galad chimed in, "involve an ambitious Teleporter sending random killing beasts into the midst of our allies. Lack of risk is not our dilemma."

"Oh!" Venki said. "Um… wonderful… I guess."

My mother put her hand on my arm as we walked out, pulling me behind the men for a moment.

"Is he Christian?" she asked me.

Oh, boy. "He's from another *planet*, Mother. What do you think?"

"Don't get smart with me," she said. "I just want what's best for you." She wrapped her arms around me.

She let go and my dad took her place.

Putting a hand on each of my shoulders, he just stared at me for a few seconds, then pulled me in for a hug, saying, "Be safe, mi muñeca."

He let me go, and after a long look at the two of them, I turned to catch up with Galad and Venki among the people out celebrating the holiday. I felt my parents' gaze on me even as Galad cast his spell and whisked us away—a fun treat the kids would remember long after they'd consumed their candy.

We popped into the old maintenance room, where guards radioed in our appearance. We briefed Rocks in his office, then took Venki back down to the tunnels and worked our way through the busyness to reach the Ring.

Details had changed even in the short time we'd hopped to Texas. Different boxes, different people—the only thing the same was the frenetic activity. Another desk sat near the people going *to* El'daShar—a final checkpoint. As we approached, they waved us through.

I looked behind the Ring, the visual effect still disturbing me. Open boxes, filled with big electronics, had replaced the little tank.

Venki walked between us as we walked up the tiny ramp and into the Ring. He took a deep breath like he was about to walk somewhere with no air. I got it—walking through a Ring felt a bit like diving underwater.

The cacophony on the other side differed from the din when last we'd been on El'daShar. It was the sound and movement of a people returning from a fight—there'd been another attack while we'd been on Earth.

From the backslapping and grim smiles, I sensed victory, but I knew from reports that the death toll of Forsaken battle-mages climbed. As cold as it sounded, we could not replace the mages and fighters from Forsaken as readily as infantry from Earth. Whatever battle we had won, we'd still lost more than the attackers, who stayed hidden on their home world.

Galad and I hastened to the command center, which wasn't far. When I realized Venki hadn't followed, I turned back to see him taking it all in. He took deep breaths, like a lumberjack enjoying fresh air after being too long indoors, and his eyes were closed, his face pointed up toward the sun.

Like a flower, he opened his arms to the sunlight.

"Venki! Over here, now!" I shouted. He opened his eyes, and *bamf*, he stood beside me. He looked around and spotted a high roof of one of the distant shops and *bamf*, he appeared there. Then he disappeared and I lost track of him.

"Well, shit!" I declared.

Then *bamf*, he appeared back at my side.

"Holy…" Venki began.

"… Mother of Trees?" I suggested.

"… crap on a cracker?" Galad offered as an alternative.

He sputtered, then said, "This is *incredible*!"

I smiled and turned back to the command center. Everyone huddled around the same table, looking at something.

"You had an attack?" I asked, to get their attention. "What was it this time?"

Mort turned, looking pleased. "Slitherati. They're semi-intelligent reptilian beings native to Wild Grove. I guess Wild Grove has chosen sides."

Well, hell, that wasn't good. We were splitting up the colonies instead of uniting them.

"Why do you look so happy to learn that our enemy has increased?" Galad asked.

"The fighting took us into the city a bit, past the edge of the Transport hub. We found this," he said dramatically, moving aside.

Before me lay a large gem, about the size of my head, glassy yellow, with spots of darkness inside. Were the spots moving? I had no idea what it was.

Galad froze. Luckily, Harry huddled among the people at the tent, and explained. "That's the Banishment Stone." He looked mildly perplexed. "That's what was down in the bore when the elves sent us to Earth to be trapped forever. I'm sure of it."

Grundle, stooping to get his head under the edge of the tent, grunted his agreement.

"I think he's right," Galad said like he'd seen a ghost.

"Don't know why it was there," Harry said, "right outside the hub like that."

"I think I get it." Galad mumbled, his face animating, lighting up in fact. "Holy crap on a cracker, I think I get it. Let's get Scan!"

"Go get him," I told Galad. "I'll introduce our new colleague to Mort."

Galad nodded his head and ran off to the Rings. I couldn't remember ever having seen him excited before. Well, *excited* I'd seen, but not the childlike excitement just displayed. Strange.

Mort waited expectantly.

"Mort," I said, "this is Venki. He has manifested powers—he's a natural Teleporter. Venki, this is Mort, leader of the colony called Forsaken, a military community. Mort is also a natural Teleporter."

Mort's eyes widened in surprise. "You're serious?" he asked me.

I squinted an eye at him. "Why would you ask that?"

"It's just unusual. You don't come into powers as an adult."

"He was in our building where the Mana'thiandriel exploded," I explained. "His powers manifested at the same time as the others on our planet that were in the explosion. He was just… delayed... in making contact." Held by our own government for their experimentation, then hiding at my Mother's house, to be specific.

Mort studied Venki for a few seconds, and Venki waited.

"If you're new to Teleportation, there are a few things you need to learn quickly. Follow me." Mort walked a few feet out of the command center, away from the noise, and Venki and I followed.

"The first thing you need to learn is how to figure out *where you are*. If you're new, you're likely finding yourself in… odd places... when startled."

"Yeah!" Venki said, "There's this abandoned amusement park from when I was a kid. Sometimes I'll wake up there."

"That will go away with experience. But, for now, you need to know how to change that location. I'll show you how to Rebind so that you end up here."

"Okay," Venki said, the excitement clear in his voice.

They didn't need me in that conversation, so I walked back to the tent to wait for Galad. The others had resumed their preparations for the next surprise attack.

I looked over some details they coordinated while I waited. It struck me as odd, to be "in" enough that no one tried to keep their plans concealed from me. No one stopped me from trying to look at *anything*. They even offered to explain details and listen to suggestions. Unfortunately, I had nothing helpful to suggest.

Within the hour, Galad returned, his enthusiasm dimmed, Scan in tow. I set down the paperwork I perused and joined them—Harry, Grundle, and Smith extracting themselves to do the same.

We converged upon the yellow gem, Grundle plopping to the ground with a small crash just outside the tent. Scan bent down to get a closer look at table height. Was he using his *vision* to look at threads of magic? "Tell them your theory," Scan said.

Galad nodded. "I think the elves used two of these gems in parallel. Well, technically, I think the egg-thingy on the tower is another of these artifacts, and they used it as well. So three… artifacts. But only two at a time."

"Aren't elves supposed to be eloquent?" I pondered aloud.

Galad grimaced as Grundle said, "Long-winded. Often confused with eloquence."

Galad plunged ahead. "They used the Amp with the glowy egg to Compel everyone to come here, maybe one world at a time. Then they used the Amp with the Banishment Stone to carry everyone away."

No one said a word, contemplating Galad's theory. I broke the silence. "You think they left from *right here*, in the transport hub."

He nodded yes.

"Why wouldn't they take the Banishment Stone?" I asked.

"It can't banish itself," Galad said. "It won't go into the field it creates, at least to my understanding."

"So," Grundle said, "we can get Scan's Teleport Tracker and follow them!"

"That's why I was excited when I left to get Scan," Galad responded, "but..."

Scan stood back up straight and waved his arms around. "Look at this camp. I have to track the bacteria. We've demolished the traces. Not to mention this was a transport hub even before we arrived. There will be bacteria going to every place anyone has ever Teleported to—or from—in this camp."

Everybody looked crestfallen as we absorbed the impact of Scan's statement.

"Worse than a needle in a haystack?" I asked.

"I would imagine," he replied. "Though I don't know how to do the math on that."

"What did you see?" Galad asked, opening his eyes wide to illustrate the kind of vision he meant.

"Ever heard of a black hole?" Scan asked.

"That's a *black hole*?" I asked, incredulous.

Scan shot me a look that said *don't be an idiot*. "I'm just trying to draw a metaphor. A black hole is a collapsed star with a gravitational pull so strong that even light cannot escape it. We call that distance from which light cannot get away an event horizon. That's similar to what I see when I look at that gem. The threads inside don't get out. I can't see in to get an idea of how it works."

"Should we at least try using Scan's invention?" I countered.

Scan sighed, nodding his head yes. "I'll go get the... what did you call it? Teleport Tracker. But I don't know how to get back to that cave."

"C'mon," Harry said, "I'll show you."

Nodding again, Scan followed Harry out of the command center. I put an arm around Galad, his troubled gaze locked on the gem. He'd been so excited; he thought he'd found a way back to his people. Then that hope had been dashed, destroyed by the efforts of humans, my people, to save themselves. He didn't look angry, just sad. Had he lost hope? Finding the gem was good. *Right?*

Chapter 67

Galad, two hundred years in the past

Lomamir 'Ported us into a cave, proving my hunch to be correct. Three exits led from the small, natural cavern. The floor shook, a thunderous crack of rock echoing through the chamber, then stilled again. We cast looks at all the exits, unsure from which direction the sound had come.

Wasn't this their cave?

The boom came again, and we all turned the same direction. Lomamir put her finger to her lips and crept quickly through the tunnel. Every few seconds the cave shook with a rumbling crack of noise. We turned a corner and a hint of light appeared, and turning the next, the light grew brighter. Soon the tunnel opened to a large, magelit cave. We stood at the top of a deep stone pit, and inside that pit?

An enormous troll. It had to be four times my height, the largest troll I'd ever seen. It rhythmically pounded the wall, knocking holes into it. But it did not look angry. It paused, grabbed a protruding rock, and ripped a stone twice my size out of the wall. I ducked, sure the cave would collapse from above, but it held.

"He's perfect," an elven voice said from below, the sound coming up the chamber and echoing off the walls. "For the job, I mean. He's a troll, so very far from perfection." The voice laughed. I knew that voice. It couldn't be.

I crept to the edge and looked down. The troll started pounding on the wall again.

"Well, get him out before he destroys the cave!" Slooti—the High Lord himself—shouted at another elf.

"I'll need the Amp, your High Lordliness." The second voice came from Gavrial, the High Lord's own Teleporter.

"I don't know why I suffer your continued flippancy," Slooti said. His tone dismissive, he carried on. "You brought him *here*. Take him."

"I barely managed to get him here, on the same planet," Gavrial explained. "I have no chance of 'Porting him to another world."

Slooti sighed and pulled from his robes a red gem the size of a finger, and even from my distant hiding place, I saw the faint lights in the crystal move, like a flame burned from inside it. He held it possessively as the troll continued to pound the wall. A rock the size of my chest tumbled down toward Slooti, and I caught my breath as it became clear it would hit him. But a few feet above, it bounced harmlessly to the side in a flash of red light—Slooti's Talent for shields.

The High Lord's Teleporter reached for the gem, and Slooti pulled it back. "Just a finger on it, mind you. Don't get grabby with my royal jewels." He chuckled at his own wit.

The Teleporter reached out and touched the crystal, and he and the troll disappeared in a blinding flash of light. I literally couldn't see for several seconds. When my vision cleared, Slooti stood alone, the crystal tucked away. He moved to one of the fallen rocks and leaned against it, waiting.

With another flash of light, bright but not like before, Gavrial returned. Slooti stood, dusting off his robes where they had leaned against the rock. "Back to El'daShar, 'Porter."

"High Lord, you do understand that if I brought the troll back in a few days, he could recover, and live a lot longer."

"But you'd have to take the Amp with you, and we can't have that. Besides, it's just a troll. We will find another. Now, I have dinner awaiting me. Let's get going."

Gavrial wasted no time, but took them away in a big flash of light—off planet.

"Disgusting," my sister muttered.

"Trolls are not the most attractive creatures," I quipped. Silence must have become unnecessary. "But that was not a Warlord."

"No," an unknown voice rumbled. I spun to see who snuck up

behind me, just in time to take a fist to the chest, knocking me well over the edge of the hole we stood next to. "But I am," I heard, as I plummeted to the bottom of the pit.

Chapter 68

Red

Mort, Harry, and I resumed our otherworldly tour. Mort brought Venki along, to take advantage of occasional opportunities for training.

Grundle decided to remain on El'daShar. "I think they need my combat skills here," he said, gnawing on a roasted leg of *something*, the bone as long as I was tall. It reminded me of our first meeting, in a tent in Central Park, when he'd pretended he ate humans.

Smith, unsurprisingly, made an excuse to stay with him. "I think perhaps I'm too old for all this Teleporting. It's making me a little seasick."

Scan had to abandon his project on Emerald Farms to work on using the Teleport Tracker, while Galad resumed his vigilant watch for Cordoro. Galad felt sure that Cordoro would show his head at some point, and Galad was the expert on knowing people's minds.

Like the combat lines of the Forsaken, I felt thin. Our group had stretched too thin. I'd felt a similar fragility on DwarkenHazen.

Nevertheless, we continued our mission. Two more worlds—Maikersburgh and Nautica. Maikersburgh, like Artifairium, was a world of artisans, taking goods from the other colonies and converting them into magical equipment. Like the Artifairium, they prized education more than most of the other worlds, as the crafting of magical items required a broader spectrum of knowledge than some of the more pure goods-creating worlds.

However, unlike the people of the Artifairium, who wanted to argue endlessly, the Maikersburghians were of a mind similar to Brickworks—the idea of technologies without magic intrigued them. They wanted in. It surprised me to find an ally so late in our efforts. It takes some guts to stick your neck out when you know you will take on the wrath of a people like the Savage.

Nautica reminded me of the movie *Water World*. The water that covered Nautica was not so salty as the oceans on Earth. The people of Nautica informed me I could drink it, though the water nearest to the floating city was always a bit risky. It was also much prettier than the post-apocalyptic scenes of *Water World*. Winds blew on sails of fishing vessels, magically-enhanced when needed. They exported fish, and their companion/rival colony was the meat-producing world of Drovers. Like Galene and Emerald Farms, they produced related, but different, types of food.

We talked late into a clear night, and I counted myself lucky to experience the flying starfish. Magical in their very nature, they danced in the skies, creating a kaleidoscope of moving stars among the distant fixed ones. I missed Galad.

Unfortunately, word had reached Nautica of the Savage attacks on colonies that aided the Forsaken and Earth. "I'm sorry," their Regent ultimately told me, "but our colony is *the most* vulnerable to attack from the Savage. Even if you reinforced us with warriors, we live on a floating city—it would not be hard to destroy us and take whatever reinforcements down to a watery grave. We are nothing but a liability in combat."

After saying our goodbyes, Mort ported us back to El'daShar, about as far from the command tents as one could get and still be in the makeshift colony, roughly a half hour's walk away. Mort liked to walk among the troops.

"What a waste of a day," I said, wrung out and weary.

Mort smiled. "I'm happy to tell you you're wrong."

"Is that just a general statement about your taking pleasure in my mistakes?" I asked, giving him a look that I hoped translated as "just kidding."

"Ha!" he barked. Then, still chuckling, he reached into a pocket on the backpack I carried and pulled out a glass of water with a lid. Inside swam a fish the size and shape of a silver dollar.

"Has Galad ever tested you to see if you were a mage?" Mort asked.

Um, nice segue, dude. What's with the fish? "No... " I started, "but I've never been able to see magical threads..."

"That's your Gifted friend. That's not normal."

"Okay, no, he's never tested me. Do you have reason to think I am?"

"None whatsoever," Mort answered.

"Nice talk, Mort," I said, rolling my eyes. Hmm, that felt good. I hadn't had much opportunity for eye-rolling of late.

Noticing that I walked alone, I stopped and looked back. Mort stood there expectantly, and, puzzled, I returned to him.

"What?" I said.

"Try to summon light," he said, casually.

I looked at him like he was nuts. "That's nuts," I said, in case the look wasn't enough.

"Why? Just try. Close your eyes."

I raised an eyebrow, but he didn't back down. He was serious.

Sighing, I closed my eyes, then opened one briefly to make sure he wasn't about to pull some silly prank. But he stayed where he was. I closed my eye again.

"Deep breaths. In," he said, taking a deep breath, "and out." He released the breath slowly. "In…. out…"

I did as he bid me. It reminded me of that Headspace app I had tried but couldn't afford to pay for, and stopped when the free trial ended. I did the steps, concentrating on my breathing and counting my breaths.

"Now, slowly hold out your hands, like you're going to hold water in them."

I followed his instructions, repeatedly focusing on my breathing as I became distracted.

"Now, think of your hands as filling with light, like you're catching all the energy from the sun and just keeping it there, pooling in your hands."

That was a pretty thought. Light pooling in your hands like water from a waterfall. I wished it worked that way.

Mort chuckled. I opened my eyes, moving quickly from peaceful tranquility to self-anger at letting myself be deceived. But when I opened my eyes, and my mouth, to chew Mort out, it shocked me to see a pool of light evaporating from my hands.

I stood there a moment as the light dissipated, my mouth working as I tried to form the words.

"You tricked me," I finally said. "You put light in my hands. Why?"

"I didn't," he said. "But it wasn't all you." He held out the glass with the fish. "It's called a magefish. Very, very rare. It helps you find people with nascent magical abilities. I did not know if it would work for you."

My mind spun. "It's just what we need," I said.

He nodded his head. "One of their Firsts handed it to me while the Regent was telling you she could not help us. They were clever. Any spies would see only compliance, but with this—"

"We can find more mages," I said. It would help us bolster our troops.

He nodded his agreement and smiled. He started on toward the command center. "It helps, but ultimately it won't be enough. We can't train new mages fast enough to be as useful as we need them to be. Still, we are better off than we were."

As we walked, my mind shifted from thinking about how the magefish affected our ability to hold our position, to the realization that *Holy Mother of Trees, I can use magic*!

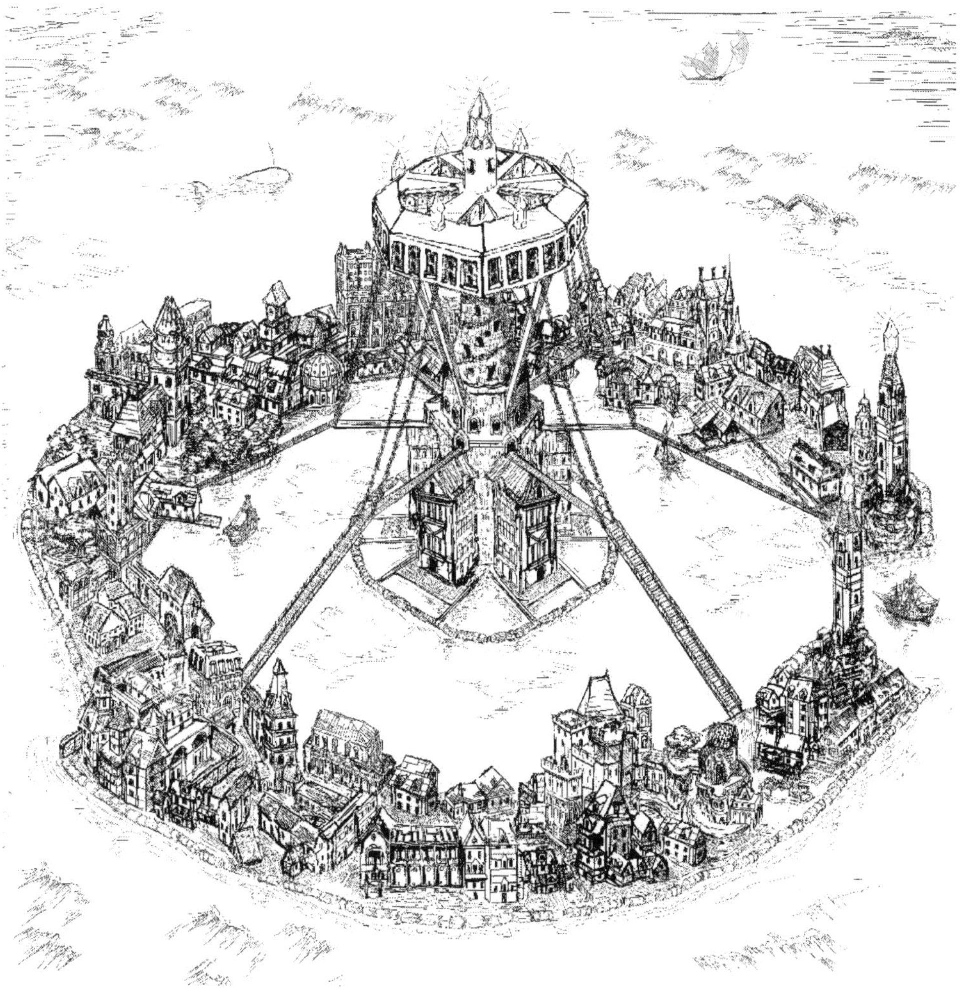

Chapter 69

Galad, two hundred years in the past

"You could have killed him," my sister chided, but not harshly, as I felt my bones knit back together.

"Elves are fragile," the unfamiliar voice said from far away. "Bird bones."

"Relatively speaking," Celymir answered.

I rose slowly to my feet, looking around. Celymir and Lomamir had joined me at the bottom of the pit. I thought my sister had Healed me, but both women looked irritated... with me! The monster that had hit me was nowhere to be seen.

With a ground-shaking thud, it joined us, having *jumped* from the top!

I drew my sword, but the beast before me, the monster that had hit me, stood no taller than I. It sauntered over, cocky, unafraid of my sword. Lanky, with thin arms and legs composed of rocks and stones, it rumbled at me from somewhere inside its rocky chest.

"You're just a boy," I said.

"A boy who just knocked you on your sorry ass," it said.

It dawned on me that the creature before me, the elf-sized troll, spoke to me in elvish. Who had taught him?

With a bright flash of light, Gavrial reappeared. I turned my sword to him, but he cared no more about my weapon than the Warlord boy.

"Are you ready?" he asked. Who was he asking?

"We are," my sister answered.

Whatever plot, whatever gambit they played at, it went all the way up to Gavrial, and I could not fathom that it did not, in some way, threaten The Crown.

"Prepare yourselves," Gavrial said. "This world will tear you apart." And, whether or not I wanted to be involved, he cast his spell.

Chapter 70

Staci

Life goes on.

It sucked, but I still had a job to do, and my self-loathing and buried anger made me a very effective Infected-killer.

I almost didn't need the others. Maybe I *didn't* need them. If Elliah would teach me to Teleport, I could do it on my own.

I'd even tried to get her to stop watching me at night. With attitude, I'd slammed the door on her before she could walk into my apartment.

She'd simply opened it anyway and walked in, like it was her own damned place!

"I don't need you here," I'd said with narrowed eyes and a quiet tone.

"Make me leave," she'd said, a sad smile on her face, but steel behind her words.

Angry, I growled and raised my hands. The water in the sink rose up and formed a spear, one she'd seen me use hundreds of times in practice and in actual fights.

She didn't flinch; she showed no fear.

I narrowed the spear, and she had the gall to roll her eyes. She was in my home and rolling her eyes at my attack?!? I wouldn't kill her, but I'd show her I could hurt her!

The water shot toward her, but splattered harmlessly off of her, like it had hit a wall. I gathered it up and shot it at her again, and it had the same result.

Frustrated, I reached for the blood in her body and found... nothing. It was like with the Infected—I couldn't feel it. Couldn't touch it. And I couldn't hit her with my spears. Lacking anything else, I tried to punch her in the gut, but I found my arm twisted around behind me painfully.

"You're not ready to be alone," she said, and released me, pushing me toward my bedroom. "Get some sleep."

I stomped away, got ready for bed, and lay down, feeling like a chastised child.

As I fought my demons, she sang, as she always did, her sad melodies. I felt hot tears run down my face.

When she stopped singing, I froze. In all the times she had been in my rooms, singing as I tried to nod off, I had never been awake when she had finished her song. A few moments later, she came into my bedroom doorway, texting into her phone. "Get up. We have another Bata."

"Where?" I said, getting up and throwing on clothes.

"Kolkata, West Bengal, India," she said, already heading to the door. "The others will meet us in the security operations room."

She left, but I wasn't far behind, and caught up with her at the elevators.

We rode down in heavy silence, and I finally offered, "I'm sorry."

"I know you are, MoonPetal," she said, not looking at me. "I know."

It was enough.

We talked with the military arm of the League, working out the coordinates for a Teleport. We learned we would not have military backup. The states in India had split in terms of support for the Guardian League. West Bengal was one location that had chosen not to cooperate.

So we were going in, without military backup, for a battle the scale of which had ended in a nuke when we'd fouled it up. I thought back to El Paso, and how the two mounted machine guns had kept the Infected from flanking us. Madness!

"I can bring another two people," Elliah said. "It is almost certainly a death sentence."

She still had volunteers. The man in charge picked two men, who ran off to arm themselves better, and would meet us in the stairway—Elliah said she needed a little more quiet in order to cast the spell to get us there.

"How do you manage nukes?" Alex asked while we waited.

"Matt's brothers and sisters," she answered. "They have subs."

"You have nuclear subs?" Alex looked incredulous.

"They can launch nuclear missiles," she said absently. "The subs are not nuclear powered."

The two men, ammo draped over themselves like metal shawls, joined us.

"Are we ready?" Elliah asked, short-tempered and impatient.

We all nodded, though I, for one, felt even less ready than the last time we had gone to fight.

She began her spell, the newness of the destination taking her longer to cast. And with a flash of light and a *bamf*, we 'Ported.

We stood in a clearing, trees within a stone's throw in each direction. The sun peeked above the trees, just beginning its work, but the warmth of the day was a surprising adjustment from the air-conditioned Palace. I felt a river very close by, not far beyond the trees to the south.

Elliah set up the Mana'thiandriel, activating them without preamble, to draw the Infected. And then we waited. I had carted jugs of water from The Palace, prepared for me ahead of time. I didn't need to open them, but I did, giving myself easy access. Alex lit up his flame, and I saw rocks wiggling their way to the surface all around the clearing.

I felt a pang of worry and guilt. What if we'd just sent the Infected through a throng of people and sentenced them to death?

But what else could we do?

When they came, they were thickest from the west. And they came like a tidal wave. Monsters beyond count, with their night skin and eyeless heads, their talons sharp as razors.

Our shooters did what they could—it would be hard to miss an Infected, firing into that mass, but with their sheer numbers and at the speed with which they moved, they might as well have fired into the ocean.

I cleaved a line of them apart with a blade of water, but I couldn't keep the water moving through the flood of bodies.

Stones ripped through them, shooting up from the ground, then did the same on the way back down. Small tornadoes ripped Infected apart and dispersed them to the winds.

Unfortunately, while the south remained pretty clear, there were some Infected from the north, and a few from the east.

My magical energy remained charged—the Gift that Elliah had explained she would use to fuel us.

It felt like we fought, worked our magic, for five minutes, then ten, and I silently thanked Elliah for all the training she had made us do. The military men had reloaded their rifles many times, and then had switched to handguns, holding their fire until they had a sure hit.

We'd had a couple of times when the line had reached us from one direction or another, but the waves of Infected had peaks and troughs. We never suffered from a sustained breach, and each time we dispatched the ones that had reached us.

The waves became smaller, and my hope stirred.

It so often feels like it is that moment of confidence that some Supreme Being is waiting for, in order to show me how wrong I can be.

Life goes on.

Something struck a soldier. A dismembered limb from a mini-tornado or water saw, or a falling rock perhaps. Whatever it was, it had caused his shot to go wrong. He had fired into our midst.

Phillip went down.

Life goes on... only, sometimes, it doesn't.

I'd seen Phillip die before, in simulation, many, many times. And I'd fought on. It honestly took a few seconds to register that we weren't in the Bubble. That Phillip would not get reset.

Then it struck me like a blow—the man I so wanted to let myself love, who I wanted to let love me, was down. Shot.

Still, my training held. I knew I had to fight. And I fought with a vengeance, stealing the blood from the corpses, switching from saws of water to saws of blood. I inched over to Phillip, tearing through the Infected all the way back to the trees. But I couldn't push farther, and they kept coming.

I worked my way over to his body. The wound was through his

chest, his breath came in shallow, raspy gasps. He neared the end. And I couldn't stop fighting. I would fight there, still waiting for Infected, while he gasped his last breath.

And I couldn't stand it.

Life goes on.

I knew what I had to do. I took my water, and the blood, and drew it back to me, spinning it into a blade that hovered over me, just like at El Paso. Elliah moved the rest away from us.

She knew. MoonPetal. The flower that only blooms when it pushes through a briar of deadly thorns.

I knelt down, closed my eyes, and I let myself remember. I thought of my childhood, of the betrayal, when it all had started, when my father had entered my bedroom, given me a kiss… and then hadn't stopped. A sob escaped me as I let it come flooding back, the first night I had dreamed of the Infected. Then I lowered the saw, and the real carnage began as the Infected Blinked in around me.

Chapter 71

Galad, two hundred years in the past

The High Lord's Teleporter had not lied. At least not about the world we entered.

Icy wind assailed me. Blinding flashes of light danced off the crystalline cliff before us. My magic felt… taut, worn. My mana whipped about like the physical wind drove it forth.

I struggled to even look around—the extreme conditions battered me so violently. But I saw the monster. The beast from the pit towered over us, hammering its fists into the crystalline wall, causing shards to litter the ground around us.

"For what?" the child Warlord asked. He reached down and scooped up a fallen crystal, not nearly so bothered by the harsh conditions as I and my fellow elves. Trolls had a natural resistance to magic, and were much heavier, with skin like stone. "These?" he asked.

But no one answered him. I didn't know how he did it—Gavrial's ability to focus was phenomenal—but he cast a spell that took us back.

I could not see the flash of light, but I leaned over, panting as though I had run a great distance, my relief at being off that world palpable. Getting my bearings, I recognized that Gavrial had not returned us to the cave. He had taken us back to the spot where I had practiced swordplay with Celymir. Stars winked from the night sky, with enough moonlight to see the small clearing among the rocks where she had bested me.

"Why did you not bring back Thudd?" the small Warlord demanded of Gavrial, fire in his eyes, but cautious with Gavrial in a way he had not been with me.

"Thudd is too big," the Teleporter said, with genuine sadness in his eyes and voice. "I cannot bring him home without magical aid."

"That crystal *he* held," the troll concluded. "Your *High Lord*," he said with intense scorn.

He paced in a small circle. Though still befuddled by the circumstances, I believed it to be the wrong crowd in which to declare the High Lord's sovereignty. I could not Empathically read the High Lord, with his being so much older, but he had been gracious to me my whole life. I did not understand how a little harshness toward a troll warranted rebellion.

"So Thudd will remain there until he perishes," the troll said, "collecting these!" He held up the crystal. "Why?"

"Not for what you grabbed, but the gem *he* held," Gavrial repeated, stopping the troll. Gavrial sighed. "There's another elf, one whom the High Lord keeps imprisoned, who has visions."

Imprisoned? Elves didn't have prisons!

"This visionary dreamed of a world composed of white crystal and cold, magic-stealing winds. I traveled there and found the colored crystal laying in a landscape of white. I brought it back, not knowing what it was, but Slooti determined that it amplified spells."

"And it is not enough for him that he has just one," the troll snarled.

Gavrial sighed again.

"So this?" the troll spat. "This is *nothing*? He takes trolls there, leaving them to *die*, hoping to stumble upon another colored crystal?" The troll slammed the clear crystal down, shattering it into a thousand pieces. A wave of magical power washed through me. Where the magical winds on that crystalline planet had ripped away my mana, the aftermath of the shattered crystal recharged it. Watching the other elves, their faces told me they had felt it, too. "Why do you not take his Amp then?"

"I could," Gavrial agreed. "But he would hunt me down."

"You would have the protection of the trolls," the Warlord said.

"Realistically," Gavrial said gently, "that's not enough. You know that. We would need more to stop Slooti and the forces he would bring." He looked at me. "But if we had the Amp *and* an Empath..."

They all looked at me. Lomamir's face held a grim neutrality.

Celymir looked hopeful. Gavrial—irritated.

I was appalled. "Fight the High Lord? Leader of the Elves? He practically raised me!"

The slap caught me off guard and rattled my head.

"Fool," Celymir muttered.

But it was Lomamir that stood, seething, hand bared and ready to slap me again. "You spoiled brat!"

"He was a child when Slooti took him," Gavrial said to my sister. "He grew up under Slooti's lies."

Was Gavrial *defending* me? By saying I was, what, *brainwashed*? I was an Empath! I couldn't be brainwashed!

Flabbergasted, I spoke the first thing that popped into my head. "Why in the world would you risk *anything* for a troll?"

"Because anyone worth his skin would do so," my sister said.

"We are not ready," Gavrial said, looking at the others in turn.

"What do we do with him?" the troll asked. "I vote we leave him with Thudd."

Monstrous troll.

"That seems fair," my sister said.

What?

"Agreed," Celymir chimed in.

Wait, they weren't serious, were they?

"You're sure?" Gavrial asked my sister.

She looked at me, and I felt sure she had been teasing. A cruel joke. But she nodded her head yes.

And, in a flash of light, against my will, I left the AllForest behind.

Chapter 72

Red

Scan worked with his Teleport Tracker, a new battery attached, near the command center. He had a little card table set up with his laptop, and he was taking notes, or solving the mysteries of the cosmos—hard for me to tell.

"How's the Elf Tracker 2000?" I asked, smiling.

"Operational," he said, grimacing. "But…"

"No luck finding the elves," I concluded.

He shrugged his shoulders. "I've found many bacteria that disappear, but they're all going to different places. We should have a little powwow," he suggested.

"I'll go get Galad," I said.

"I'll look for Grundle," Harry added.

Scan sighed, clearly bothered by our chances of using that crystal. "I'll go with you, Red. I have some work to check on in Emerald Farms. Mort, we'll need you—don't disappear." Mort winked, pulling Venki aside for some training.

We said our goodbyes and headed to the Rings, not far away. Light shone forth from the window to another world, through which they moved plastic bins of grain from Emerald Farms. A magical opening to another world, delivering plastic bins filled with magic-enhancing carrots or something, on a forklift—truly an odd sight. We entered the other side of the Ring, going from evening to early midday in moments.

They had set up the Ring on Emerald Farms in their commons, a place left flat and clear for events, market days, or transport of goods to other worlds. My eye sought Galad's lodgings, the little bed of flowers outside his door making me smile when I found it.

The tiny tank I had seen on Earth sat there, placed out of the way, partially deconstructed. Or partially constructed. A pair of Earthly-clothed mechanics prodded in it, along with a couple of... mages?

I felt Galad's presence as soon as we walked through the Ring. It was more than just the knowledge that he was there; I literally *felt* something Galad-y nearby. It didn't surprise me when he walked out as we approached the council hall.

"Time for some experiments?" he asked, smiling at Scan, then turning his gaze to me with a wild sparkle in his eyes. *Really? Now? You're hitting on me* now, *you pointy-eared—*

"Hirashi's inside," he told Scan as he stopped in front of me. Scan kept moving into the building. Why did Scan need to see Hirashi?

Galad's lips on mine interrupted my musing. He put one hand behind my head and the other behind my back, pulling me close.

Tired and confused, I resisted. I felt him rev back the heat a notch. Then two. The kiss went from hungry to cozy in the space of two heartbeats.

It became a kiss I could relax into.

We pulled apart. I felt a little silly about my reaction, but all he said was, "Did something go wrong on Nautica?"

"You know the human colonies now?" I asked, dodging his question.

"To a degree, yes. I've been reading about them when I'm not helping young Scan with his experiment."

Why was I avoiding telling Galad what troubled me? Was I worried about what would change between us? "They weren't willing to publicly help," I said, "but they secretly sent us back with a magefish. Do you know what those are?"

"Magefish? No, but perhaps I know them by another name? What do they do? What about them bothers you?"

"They help sniff out mages that didn't manifest," I told him.

He looked thoughtful. "So it will help you replenish the mages you're losing to Savage. I wonder if it would work on Earth."

I hadn't thought of that. If we had the same percentages of mages on Earth as they did on the colonies, we could bolster our lines, maybe indefinitely. If we could train them quickly enough.

"I doubt it would," he said. "Just not enough ambient magic. Still, we can test those on the El'daShar side of the Rings." He took a deep breath. "But that wouldn't upset you. You'd like that. So there's a fish... what else?"

"No, it's the fish." I squirmed, uncomfortable for reasons that eluded me. "Galad, I tested positive. I can use magic."

"That's wonderful," Galad said, not euphoric, not hiding concerns, just pleased.

"Why? Why is it wonderful?"

"You're a warrior. Warrior-ess? Being able to Heal gives you a much better chance at survival."

"Heal?" I was having trouble processing. I thought he might be overjoyed. Maybe he'd be upset. Pleased? No.

"Yeah, that stuff we do to put you back together after the bad guys cut you up. Heal."

"I know what Healing is, Minty." He grinned at my barb. "It just... I dunno, it's magic! I just found out I can do magic. And you're being so... *practical*."

Galad pulled me close. "I'm sorry. That was foolish of me. You take so many big things so matter-of-factly. I should not have let that fool me into thinking your own foundation could not be shaken."

Was that it? It felt like my foundation had cracked.

"It's not like it's been so long since I've had such turning points," he said, giving me space to be quiet with my thoughts. "Losing my parents, joining the resistance, losing my world and my sister. Those all changed who I was in some respect."

He's got it... I think.

"So who are you now, Garnet Hernandez?" he asked, not teasing. Just... allowing. Yeah, he got it.

"We'll see," I said, feeling some of the heat that had eluded me earlier. I leaned back in and planted a kiss that revved us back up a notch. Disengaging, but feeling more myself, I said, "That Healing thing seems like a good way to get started."

He barked a laugh.

Scan popped back out. "Okay, troops. Let's head back."

So much for the passionate interlude.

"Took care of business mighty quickly there, sport," I teased him.

My fishing paid off—he blushed. So there *was* something going on there. Cool. I couldn't remember Scan ever making an effort for an intimate relationship, so... good. *He just needed someone outta this world. Ha! Oh, wait, I better not go with that one considering my own guy.*

We headed back to the Rings, Galad sneaking in another kiss as we walked. *Dang!*

Dusk had settled in more soundly on the other side of the Rings. It took a minute for our eyes to adjust, then we moved over to the station Scan had set up for his tracking equipment. Mort must have spotted us, for he Blinked himself and our comrades over.

"Okay," Scan said, "brainstorming time. But I think, to get everyone on the same page, we need to follow one of these."

I guess that makes sense.

"Galad, how many of us can you connect at once?" Our group had grown. Besides Galad and me, we had Scan, Grundle and Smith, Mort and Tali, Venki, Harry... and Bessie. But I didn't think Bessie counted for the communal Vulcan mind meld. We'd gone from being too thin to a nice, fat team.

"Getting as specific as we need to, for this large a group, will push my limits," Galad answered.

Scan shrugged. "Do what you can. I think everyone needs to see this, so that we can figure out what to do."

"Okay," Galad said. "Everybody ready?"

Nods of readiness, some more hesitant than others, provided Galad with his answer.

Galad began casting his spell, and I tried to pay more attention. If I could use magic, I needed to learn. Right? Galad wiggled his fingers—I'd heard Scan say the finger-wiggles were just mnemonics. It meant nothing to me. All that time Galad had been teaching Scan, and I could have been listening. Why hadn't I tried? Why hadn't Galad asked me to listen?

Sorry... Hunny, Galad thought, and I heard.

You're going with "Hunny" then?

Your parents used it. I thought it would resonate with you. I could go with Inamorata? Ladylove?

Oh, Minty. Those are all crap-tabulous.

I felt his laughter. Then one by one, the rest of our crew popped in. Even though it was *all* in our heads, I felt in some way closer to Galad than the others.

Okay, Scan told us. *Let me just watch a few of these. I want you all to see what I'm seeing first. Then, we'll follow one. Okay?*

We all waited as Scan got to work on the tracker. Wait, were Grundle and Smith whispering to one another?

Got one! Scan thought. *Now, just watch.*

Like when watching a movie, I suddenly tuned into the image through someone else's eyes. Unlike a movie, I couldn't look away, couldn't see the edges of the screen.

A tiny bacteria crawled among others, and around it, some of its fellows would occasionally disappear in a firework of images. I could see the fireworks, but they were off to the side, partly out of screen. I waited, watching, knowing the jack-in-the-box would pop out eventually.

The thing glitched a few times, spasming, and then moving on.

Then *BAM!* It vanished, sound effects added by me, but it packed a brilliant light show! Firework companies would have to up their game.

Give the equipment a moment to find another, came Scan's thoughts into my head.

That's a Teleport location, Mort thought loudly, his astonishment clear.

Yessir, Scan responded. *These are tiny little cells, too small for the eye to see. My scope amplifies their images, and I can see where they go. They return to the other end of the Teleport.*

In the time it took to explain that thought, the equipment had latched onto another. We played the jack-in-the-box waiting game and got a similar prize at the end. To my mind, very pretty, and different from the first.

That was totally different, Mort thought.

Right, Scan thought. *That… is the problem. When we did this from Earth, they were all going to the same place. But this was a transport hub. It was used to go to countless places, and we've walked in residue from Forsaken and Earth and the other colonies. Finding the elves… I'm just not one to rely on luck.*

Let's follow one, Scan thought, *just so you'll understand. Mort, do you think you can copy the next one?*

With that much of an icon? Yes, I can follow it. Would that I had your eyes.

So we waited, knowing the next flash of color would result in our visiting another world. The tracker locked into its target and we waited again, like waiting for the clown that had disappeared in "Poltergeist" to suddenly pull the kid under the bed. Um, I hadn't seen that—did it come from Scan or Smith?

BAM, the fireworks sparked and **bamf*,* we followed it.

***

Like in any good horror movie, we arrived in the dark.

Who the hell has horror movies stuck in their head? I queried.

Me, Tali thought sheepishly.

Well, that came as a bit of a surprise.

A mage cast a light, and I pulled a flashlight from my pack. I'd have to learn that light spell. Very handy.

We huddled in a demolished city of elven architecture, the base of the curved tower nearest us leaning at an angle, it's top half snapped off and impaling the smaller building next door. Skeletal stone vertebrae protruded from each end. We stood atop a pile of debris at least a single story high. It smelled of decay.

Someone sent a light into the night sky, illuminating destruction as far as was visible amongst the debris toward the bottom. I saw all directions at once, the amalgamation of multiple pairs of eyes.

Anyone recognize this? I thought, but before anyone answered, I found myself alone in my head.

"Anyone recognize this?" I said aloud.

"I do," Galad said gravely.

Something lunged out of the rubble, and Grundle, ever vigilant, tore through the torso of the Infected with his war axe. Another dashed in, and we formed our line of defense, one getting sliced by my daggers and then smashed with Bessie.

"Time to go!" I shouted.

More appeared, creating their own line of attack. They didn't form any clever lines of attack—no organization—but so many appeared that it didn't matter. I stabbed another, as Galad sliced into one, while Tali fired loudly into their midst.

"Now!" I shouted. Mort's spell activated and *bamf*, we left that world behind.

***

My shout ended in a land I recognized from a brief but memorable visit—we had arrived in Forsaken. Flat dark rock held us at the bottom of a range of volcanoes. A dark and cloud sky floated above us, but several active volcanoes lit the night.

The hot air smelled of faint sulfur, a welcome exchange for the smell of decay we'd left behind.

"I've never been so scared in my life," Mort admitted, his breathing rough. "That was a full-on attack of the Infected. Do you realize how uncommon it is to escape, even for a Teleporter?"

"It wasn't full-on," Harry said. "Those were just the nearby ones."

"How do you know?" Mort asked.

Harry just shrugged. "Experience."

"So where *was* that?" I asked Galad.

"Garathal Vapil, the City on a Cloud. It was a floating city, an elven colony. It was still full of life when Slooti Banished me."

"They must have invaded after AllForest," I concluded. "That gives some truth to the rumor that the Infected targeted elves."

Galad just nodded, lost in some memory.

"This random following of bacteria isn't going to work," Scan said. "It was already a needle in a haystack. Now we know that the hay is out to kill us."

"Really?" Smith said irritably. "That's the metaphor you're going with? Imbecile."

At Scan's raised eyebrows, she mumbled, "Sorry," then turned and puked all over the black stone.

Chapter 73

Galad, two hundred years in the past

The icy wind burned through me again, ripping at not just my body warmth, but also my mana, tearing it away. I recognized what my body and mind told me on that second trip. The first time I hadn't realized until we'd left.

I turned to Gavrial, ready to beg. Ready to tell him I would throw my lot in with his. I didn't know if I would be lying or not. Didn't matter. I couldn't stay.

But Gavrial had left me.

I looked around quickly, thinking I had to be wrong. He had to be around somewhere. Light. Crystals. Wind ripping through me. Giant troll.

No elf.

I was doomed.

The troll continued to hammer at the crystals, knocking pieces loose to pile at his feet. What was he even thinking? But trolls were magic-resistant. Even if the wind hadn't drained me of my mana, I wouldn't have been able to read his mind without great effort.

They'd called me a fool. I felt foolish. I'd let them condemn me to death. Why? Because I knew too much? They wanted to overthrow Slooti. Why? Because he had condemned a troll to death? Trolls were evil, the enemy of elven-kind. There had to be more behind their rebellion. Slooti had taken me in and raised me, given me everything I needed and wanted. He'd given me a home, teachers, opportunities to refine the law—I'd made the Hall of Contested Gifts a success! And Slooti had encouraged and helped me make it so.

And the one time I stepped away from the home he'd created for me, and tried to help my actual blood sister, she'd sent me to die on a hellish planet with only a disgusting troll that enjoyed hitting rocks.

I sat down and huddled my legs close to my chest. The icy wind ripped at my body, tearing my mana away, leaving me empty. There was no point in looking for help—nothing could survive that brutal climate for long. Even the troll would die, though his resistance to magic and overall bulk would protect him for some time. But the planet had no food, no drink—he would starve or die of thirst.

Didn't matter. I wouldn't last an hour. Mother of Trees, how did that thing still stand there, pounding on the crystals, smashing them to bits?

Smashing the crystals. My freezing brain latched onto that. When the crystal had broken, it had filled me with mana. I looked up. Fist and head-sized crystals lay around the feet of the giant troll. Maybe if I smashed one of those?

All it would take is one stomp and I'd be a mushy puddle.

But I was going to die anyway.

Groaning, I realized I wasn't ready to freeze to death. With a little mana, I could create some heat.

Hunched over, I snuck up behind the troll. I grabbed a small, fist-sized crystal, and smashed it on the crystalline ground. It shattered, and I felt a wave of mana, but the wind ripped it away before I could do anything with it.

The troll remained focused on smashing the crystalline wall before it. Shivering, I dashed forward and grabbed a head-sized crystal, then dashed back.

The troll continued.

I threw my prize to the ground, ready to cast a Heat spell, but to my chagrin it didn't break.

I picked it up, raised it over my head, and hurled it to the ground. It shattered, and with the wave of mana, I managed a Heat spell. I sighed with relief, feeling warmer, but recognizing that my mana depleted rapidly, and so would my Heat.

I ran back to find another big crystal, not concerned with the ultimate futility of my endeavor, just wanting to live. Again, I picked one up and shattered it, and kept my Heat going.

Looking around, I grabbed another, but I stopped after lifting it high. Something had changed. The thrumming of the troll's fists had stopped. I looked up in time to see a giant palm close around me.

"Urk," I grunted, my breath squeezed from my lungs as he lifted me up and held me before a nose half the size of my body.

Mother of Trees, this thing is enormous!

We apparently both had the exact same next thought—that I could fit inside its mouth.

Chapter 74

Elliah

"Leah," Matt urged, coming into the control room of the bubble, "it is *time*."

I raised my eyebrows, but from his wide eyes, I quickly realized what he meant. Surely not. Had I gotten so busy?

Alex and Rej sat at the small table, helping me organize my crystals, the jigsaw puzzle that just kept giving. I held up a finger asking them to wait, and walked to the open hatch of one of the small rooms along the hall.

Staci relaxed in the crook of Phillip's reclining body, on a small couch I had set up, watching some show on a computer monitor affixed to the wall.

"Game of Thrones?" I asked.

Staci looked up at me. "No, *The Guild*." Phillip laughed at whatever he saw on screen, and Staci wrapped an arm around his neck and pulled his head down for a kiss.

"That will have to wait," I said.

They didn't listen, and I didn't mind. They deserved the moments they found. I was not great at Healing spells, and Phillip almost didn't make it. Staci had gone through her own hell, explaining to me and Phillip what she had done to summon the Infected. She hadn't had to tell Phillip, but telling Phillip was the only path to a genuine relationship, and I was proud of her for doing it.

There was no way I would have let her get away with not telling me, but she'd decided somewhere in her pain that she wanted to confide. Again, proud of her bravery, and I made sure she knew it.

Still, they had a long and careful road to tread if merely remembering the assaults from her childhood would summon the Infected. Achieving any physical intimacy would prove a serious challenge.

Matt popped his head around from behind me and said, again, "It's *time*," while dancing from foot to foot impatiently.

"Time?" Staci asked. "Time for what?" The urgency in Matt's voice had created a palpable tension in the small room.

I raised my hands placatingly, intending to calm the humans, but Matt's excitement was uncontainable, and I almost laughed.

"It's time for the eggs!" he said, bouncing back and forth. The humans looked puzzled, again bringing me close to laughter. "The women are ready to lay!" he said, explaining further.

"I understand your excitement," Phillip said, earning a back-of-the-hand smack from Staci.

"Ouch!" he yelped, smiling.

Matt's eyes pleaded with me. "You have to go help them."

"Have I ever *not* helped?"

"Well, actually, yes. You had years, when you were older, that you got confused." My heart felt suddenly heavy. That must have been a horrible time for them. I didn't remember.

"I think this year we do something different," I said, thinking about all the pain the goblins had gone through.

Matt didn't like the sound of that. "Leah. We can't do this without you."

I kept my eyes on his. "Technically you *can*, just not on this planet."

I didn't think Matt's eyes could get any rounder. The possibilities unfolded before him. "Where..." he began, but he couldn't get the words out.

"The elves abandoned El'daShar. That's where you were meant to be. I think it is time for the goblins to return to their home."

Matt looked ready to explode.

"Go tell the others," I told him. "I've got to go make the arrangements. Quickly." If the females were ready to lay, I had little time.

"Gather up," I told the humans. "Training is on hold." It pleased me to see at least some mild disappointment. I'd make a battle troop out of those civilians yet.

Then, I cast the spell that brought us back to the sublevels of

The Palace. When I walked out to the tunnels, the admin at the desk already had eyes on me.

"I need Penbrook," I said. I always said that.

"Mrs. Elliah," a man said behind me. "My name is Gil Rosenberg. I am one of Penbrook's Firsts."

"First?" I asked. "First what?"

"Just First, ma'am." He looked to be in his late forties, a light-skinned man of medium build who looked tired, almost bored, but his eyes shone with intelligence. "We've taken up the nomenclature of the human colonies," he said, nodding toward the ceiling and the heavens beyond. "We hope it will make communication simpler. So Firsts and Seconds, then more specific roles."

He let that sink in a moment. How the human colonies organized their leadership was news to me.

"I'm the only First on this side of the Ring at present. Maybe I can help?"

"In about fifteen minutes, I need direct access to the Rings from my side tunnel for about an hour. I'll be bringing through some beings not from Earth to return them to El'daShar, their home. What I need from you is this: keep people out of the way."

"I can do that. I'll inform Penbrook, but I don't need to run it by him. What else?"

"Who on the other side should I tell the same?"

"Any of the Firsts in the command center. It's near the Rings on the other side."

"Clear Elliah for travel!" First Rosenberg called in a raised voice, just to be heard over the din of machinery and people. He nodded for me to go through the Ring.

My team followed, and he added, "Clear Elliah's ducklings for travel!"

I'm sure that didn't make my team happy, but I didn't stop to do anything about it.

I walked toward the Ring, seeing, through the window of the Ring, a land I had fled thousands of years before. The camp on the other side prevented any clear view of the world. I wondered what it would feel like to return to El'daShar, a world soaked in magic and filled with pain.

Without adieu, I walked through the portal, seeing the distant treetops and the elven towers of the city, and I found the heartache to be only a distant memory, replaced with the single-minded desire to see the goblins returned to their home, where they had a chance not only to survive, but to thrive.

"You can wait here if you wish," I told the team. "I will be but a moment." The command tent stood open on all sides, with fabric that they could lower in inclement weather. The attacks must not have been very direct or well orchestrated, or *the enemy* would have targeted and destroyed that tent long ago. At least, that's what *I* would have done.

"There are Firsts here?" I asked, announcing my presence among the humans. The people from Earth looked up from their work, and a woman nodded and raised her hand briefly. The humans from the colonies had a different reaction, hands going to swords or daggers, not attacking, but ready should the need arise.

Was there anyone my species *hadn't* pissed off?

"May I have a moment?" I asked the woman, stopping with enough room that I could fight if need be, though I didn't expect there to be a fight.

The woman extracted herself from the group. "I saw you fight the Infected in Texas," she said. "It is a pleasure to meet you, though I don't know how to properly address you. I am Simmi Guruswamy, First to Regent Penbrook."

I'd had so many titles I just wanted to shrug, but I reigned that impulse in. "Just call me Elliah. In ten minutes I'm going to bring some creatures through the Ring that you may find alarming. Leave them be. It may take me an hour to move them all. Then we will be out of your way."

I wasn't sure where we would go, but we would have to figure it out quickly.

"Understood, Elliah; *we* will leave them alone. But this is a war zone. There is always a risk of external attack."

I looked around. I knew the situation there, but hadn't realized it was that bad.

"Okay, I'll amass them on the other side of the Ring, and bring them all in one group. In about an hour."

"Understood." She looked at me expectantly, and I nodded my head that I was done.

She walked back to her previous conversation, and I returned to my team. "Let's go," I said.

"Already?" Rej asked. "We haven't seen anything." He was eyeing the elven constructs.

"Rej, go find out where the nearest bore is. Giant holes in the ground. They'll be able to tell you." I pointed to the command tent I had just come from. "I'll need to know how to get to it. You've got about an hour."

Rej's face lit up, and he hurried over to the command tent while I led the rest of the team back through the Ring.

"Wrong direction," a man at the admin desk said as I came back through. I looked at the hallway, cleared for me like I'd asked it to be, not seeing the issue.

The man blushed. "I'm sorry. To avoid collisions, we have a policy of only going through the Ring from this direction, and coming back here you would exit on the other side. It's part of my job to enforce the policy so that everything runs smoothly."

I could appreciate that. "Noted. Do you need me to walk back through and come out the right way?" It wasn't just elves that could be sticklers about rules, and I didn't want his little head to explode from broken *policy*.

"Um, that won't be necessary, ma'am." He had the decency to turn a deeper shade of red.

"Wait here," I told the three of my trainees still with me. "I'll get the goblins. Keep them safe."

They nodded, clearly unsure what they should keep the goblins safe *from*. From monsters, obviously. Monsters took so many forms.

The goblins and I had a process worked out for egg-laying time. The females all produced eggs at the same time, and they had a rhythm to when that would happen. While a year on El'daShar spanned longer than a year on Earth, the length of the year also differed on FreeWorld, and their rhythm had adjusted over that time. Once a year, in Fall on Earth, the females—and the goblins that did not yet know if they were females—needed to be involved in their egg-creation magic. So we kept our equipment running—the submarines and information-gathering electro-magical devices—with just the males during that time. The females gathered at a location in the Rif mountains of northern Morocco. Even in our modern era, with eight billion people on the planet, there were stretches of that mountain range that remained unexplored… except by us of course.

I 'Ported from the small hallway between the tunnel and the room we had once used for training. Arriving in a cave in the Moroccan mountains, I took the short trek through the tunnels to our meeting point.

Only twelve females waited there—they had established some norms based on watching the human culture on television and the internet. They displayed their gender by wearing dresses, though the styles were distinctly goblin. Another six goblins, gender unknown, wore neutral shorts and T-shirts. For many years, I could tell the females by pierced ears, but following human trends, that indicator broke.

Eighteen goblins. I thought there would be more. Three trips of six I could handle. More in a pinch, but we weren't in a pinch. Still, it wouldn't take an hour. If the government of the USA had known how small my army was, they would never have buckled. Well… nukes helped.

"Hello, ladies and prospective ladies. Did you all hear the news?" There was enough fidgeting even on a normal egg-laying day that I couldn't tell if they knew.

They turned to one another, their mouths and shoulders tight in the goblin version of nervous smiles. They knew.

"Concerns?" I asked.

"Leah," one spoke up. Julia. In recent years, they'd taken to naming their children after movie stars, but I didn't keep up, so it wasn't helpful for me. "What if the elves come back?"

"Worst case, we leave again. But I have no reason to think they'll be back. I suspect they've fled the Infected with no intention to return." Okay, worst case, the elves fry the goblins before we could evacuate. But given the chance that any of us were going to survive in an unInfected form for the next year, I didn't think the elves frying the goblins was a high probability.

There was a murmur of quiet discussion among the goblins.

"We're ready for the next chapter of our story," Julia said.

I smiled.

***

We had them gathered in the tunnels before the Rings, getting wide-eyed looks from the humans. The GL kept the area clear for us though, which was all I had asked. I wished suddenly that *all* the goblins, females *and* males, could have gone at once. With a little more planning, I would have trained humans to take the place of the goblins. I'd stayed clear of using humans—the goblins needed me, and I needed them—and humans had gone well past needing my help eons ago.

Well, until recently, when they'd started drawing the Infected to them.

Ready to go through the Rings, I had my human team take the lead, just in case they needed to defend the goblins from any misunderstandings on the other side. I stayed at the caboose to make sure of the same on my end.

When about two-thirds of the goblins had gone through, I heard shouting at the other end. I abandoned my post and dashed through the portal, preparing for battle.

I found Alex had engulfed himself in flame, Staci had spears of water poised to strike, and a mini-tornado hovered over Philip. Simmi, the First I'd asked to have the area secured, stood with a rifle pointed at the enemy. Good. Our adversary was…

"Galad?" I uttered, surprised.

He stood, sword drawn, anger and fear burning in his eyes, trying to make sense of what lay before him. Others stood with him, ready for combat, but not sure of the situation themselves. Grundle clutched his war axe; Harry wielded Bessie; and Red clenched her daggers. A myriad of humans had guns pointed or swords drawn, some defending the goblins, some siding with Galad, all looking alarmed about the sudden snafu.

"Anyone seen *Captain America: Civil War*?" Phillip asked.

All of the goblins raised their hands. One of them quoted, "I don't know how many fights you've been in, but there's not usually this much talking."

Chapter 75

Galad, two hundred years in the past

The frigid, mana-stealing wind, nearly forgotten, tore into me once again. Dizzy, unsure of where I was, I felt as though I fell from a great height. I couldn't see, couldn't think. I vomited, nauseous from all the sensations bombarding me at once.

"Well," a familiar voice said. "Isn't this a surprise?"

The world slowed its spin. My eyes adjusted. I looked up into the face of Gavrial.

"It seems your role here is not yet done," he said.

"Gross," grumbled a second, also familiar, voice.

I felt the mana I had regained draining in the wind, and I quickly cast my Heat spell. A chomping noise made me look up. The troll had a spredix in one hand, a horned porcine native to AllForest in the other, though the spredix already had a chunk torn from it.

"You brought him food," I said, dumbly.

"I did," Gavrial answered. "I can't get him back, but I can keep him alive, for a time. Just as, apparently, he can keep *you* alive."

It was true. The troll's magical resistance protected whatever hid in its mouth. And it… Thudd… it had a name. And Thudd had kept me alive in his maw, protected from the mana-stealing winds.

I'd had time to think, squeezed inside the rocky teeth of a troll. Time to think about my life, and what I had done with it, and what I had not. Time to ponder the life-saving help of a creature I had written off. Elves were taught to value life, but I'd spent mine focused on base and trivial endeavors. I had to admit to myself that all the work I'd done regarding elvish law was meaningless, adding no real value. All of my exploits had, in a roundabout way, accumulated wealth and power for the Crown, and for myself. I'd even convinced myself that using my abilities to read women's desires to please them in bed was an act of charity. I had believed myself to be a giving person.

On the contrary—I had no values, and I added no value.

I shifted my gaze and found the small Warlord who stood with Gavrial, not shivering in the icy wind as I would be without my Heat spell.

"We must go soon," Gavrial said to the Warlord. "My mana drains quickly here."

The giant troll produced a deep grumble, words I could not understand without a Translation spell, and I did not have the mana to cast it.

"What did he say?" I asked the Warlord.

The troll, a boy my size, stared down at me with scorn. "He asked if he could go home."

I understood the feeling. Thudd didn't deserve the fate that befell him. A home—I had a sickening feeling I didn't *have* a home. That I longed for a gilded cage I'd been pretending was a home for a very long time.

"Does he have family?" I asked.

"Parents," the Warlord said. "Brothers. Sisters. Nieces. A nephew."

"I'm sorry," I said. And I meant it.

The diminutive Warlord said something in trollish to the giant, who kept at his meal.

My mana almost empty, I took a crystal and smashed it, refilling a little. Gavrial inhaled deeply, as though the mana came in through our lungs.

"We have to go," Gavrial said again.

The Warlord nodded, patted Thudd on the leg, and Gavrial disappeared with the Warlord in a bright flash of light.

Sighing, I picked up another crystal and smashed it, prolonging my life a little longer. I looked up at Thudd, who had finished his meal, bones and all, and returned to smashing the crystalline cliffs. Gavrial would continue to bring him meals, but there was no path that returned Thudd to his family. Not without an Amp.

Not without an Amp.

They had found the first Amp on the very same world on

which they'd trapped us. What if there was another? I smashed a crystal and cast a bolt of fire at the wall. It splattered harmlessly to the sides.

Smashing another crystal, I tried a focused beam of Heat. That worked. It cut into the crystal wall, a hole a few inches deep. I needed more mana. A lot more mana.

Looking around, I found a crystal the size of my body. "Thudd!" I yelled. He couldn't hear me. I took a crystal and smashed it on his foot—I needed the mana anyway.

Thudd looked down. I waved to him to get his attention, pointed to the elf-sized crystal, then picked up one I could lift and smashed it on the ground.

Thudd cocked his head in question. I took another crystal and walked over to the crystalline boulder. I smashed the one I had, pointed at the bigger one, then Thudd, and I mimicked picking the boulder up and smashing it.

Thudd laughed. He reached the boulder in two mammoth steps and wrapped his enormous hands around it. He growled as he picked it up over his head.

I excitedly mimicked throwing it to the ground one more time. "Yes! Yes!"

When it hit the ground and shattered, my mana filled up, and kept going. I blasted a beam of molten fire into the crystalline cliff, starting at my height and then aiming up, closer to where Thudd's fists would land.

Thudd took the two steps back to the crystal cliff and pounded his fists into it, and I jumped behind his leg as the cliff exploded into shards, some of which fell to the ground and shattered, refilling my mana faster than the wind stripped it. I stepped from behind the protection of Thudd's legs and blasted the cliff with molten rays.

Thudd stepped forward, and laughing thunderously, like he'd found the best game ever, he pounded deeper into the cliff wall. We moved together, Thudd stomping down on crystalline debris joyfully, bashing into rubble whatever I weakened with my magic.

Chapter 76

Elliah

Hearing a goblin quote from a Marvel movie took the wind out of the sails of the combatants from Earth—*I don't know how many fights you've been in, but there's not usually this much talking.*

"Hear, hear!" Harry riposted, not registering the confused fidgeting of those around him.

"Elliah? What is this?" Galad said.

"I'm returning these beings to their home," I said, exuding calm. "Put your sword away."

"These *beings* are assassins!" Galad said. "When I was a child, one attacked a friend. They're not *from* here—they wanted to take our home. Slooti told me…" he paused then. "Oh, shit, Slooti told me that." The same elf that had Banished him.

"Still," he persisted, "they attacked my friend, a child… would have killed her if the Guardian had not intervened." A Guardian. Created not directly by Slooti, but he drove their creation. How could one elf, one person, cause so much trouble?

"Do you know why elves are vegetarian?" I asked him.

That startled him, as I meant it to. "We just are. We don't eat meat."

"Are you an idiot?" I asked, startling him more. "Have you never looked at your own teeth? What do you think the pointy ones are for, nibbling on ears?"

Red snickered.

"We're vegetarians," I said, pausing for dramatic effect—*see, Matt, I can still learn*—"because once, long ago, I took part in a feast for a peace treaty we had signed with a Warlord." I pointed at Grundle, who cocked his head curiously. He hadn't heard this. "I found out after the feast that the meat he served came from my own children, captured, killed, and baked into little pies."

Grundle blanched—a strange sight on a troll.

"Many of us could not stomach meat after that. It became a habit, then a norm, and eventually the tale was lost in time, and you think now that elves don't eat meat."

Galad's mouth worked noiselessly, while others shifted uncomfortably.

"Here's the point—I don't blame *Grundle* for what *that Warlord* did. Intelligence and kindness are independent."

A bit of Grundle's color returned.

"Put away your sword, Galad," I said. "I will acknowledge that it was a bad chapter in goblin history, and the goblins would admit it as well. But you also don't understand everything that was behind that. Someday I hope you hear the tale." I hoped we would all *live* long enough for him to hear the tale. "Put your sword away."

Galad put his sword away. Both forces stood down, the goblins' eyes big and frightened and excited all at once.

I walked to the Ring and ushered the rest of the goblins through, and pointed them toward the town, intending to get us all out of the human camp. First Guruswamy stood by the Rings, and I gave her the thumbs up that we were done. She nodded and traveled through the Ring back to Earth.

"Can I walk with you?" Galad asked.

"You may. But no funny business with the goblins."

"On my word," he said. Elves and their *word*.

As we left the camp, Rej returned from the elven ghost town, a warrior garbed in alien clothes by his side.

"You found a bore?" I called out.

"Yes! It would be hard to miss."

That's what I thought. We followed Rej, and the warrior that accompanied him joined our retinue.

"We think we've worked out how the elves vanished," Galad said, "but not where they've gone yet."

That was interesting. "I thought you had become entangled in capturing a mad Teleporter."

"Still am," he said, "but we've worked out the pieces of the elven disappearance… we think."

"Go on."

His discomfort with some aspect of his speculation showed on his face. "There was a stone—a gemstone—mined by enslaved trolls from the 4D Realms. It had the power to amplify magic."

Like Jeb. My too powerful son, Jeb. I had resisted that truth for a long time. It was his Gift.

"We'd secured it with the dwarves before our Banishment." He took a deep breath, and cringing, continued on. "The elves attacked the dwarves after our Banishment and recovered it."

"The elves *attacked* the dwarves for this artifact?" That wasn't right. That couldn't be right. Elves *valued* life.

Galad didn't answer the question. "That tower over there with the glowing egg atop it," he said, pointing. "It's another artifact used to duplicate magic over distances. We think they used that to Compel all the elves to come here."

How would that work logistically? All at once, or a world at a time? How did the artifact work?

"Once here, they combined the magical amplifier—we called it the Amp—with the Banishment Stone, and sent the entire population of elves away."

Wow. Okay. But... "If you can figure out where the elves performed your proposed evacuation, you can use the machine that the Gifted human created, follow the bacteria to find where they went?"

"In theory," Galad answered. "Unfortunately, they left from the transport hub, so there are too many false paths, some leading to worlds already lost to the Infected."

The Banishment Stone... that was how Slooti had sent Galad to Earth. The same stone that had sent me to Earth. What had I called it those millennia ago? I could not remember. "You sound confident that the elves left from right here. Why?" My nerves tingled.

"We found the Banishment Stone near the hub," he explained.

Mother of Trees. My priority was the goblins. The elves had fled. They would wait. But if we'd found the crystal for crossing worlds—Crossing Crystal, that's what I'd called it—then we had a way to follow the elves. I had a sudden fear in the pit of my stomach.

After thousands of years, the goblins returned to their world. *The same day, I learn how I can find the elves.* Slooti would exterminate the goblins. Slooti attacked the dwarves. I should have listened to Gavrial all those lifetimes ago. Overwhelmed, I turned my thoughts elsewhere, and found another grim topic to discuss.

"I have news for you as well," I said. "I understand better what draws the Infected." Something related to abuse. Maybe any form, but clearly sexual abuse—or fear of it—triggered a connection. I suspected Staci was a Talented mage, on a world with a dead sun. She would have been powerful if born on any of the worlds I had lived on prior to Earth. I couldn't prove it—didn't *want* to prove it—but I believed some nascent magic shined through, even on Earth. It was why she had made the connection at such a young age, seeing them in her dreams and drawing them nearer.

Each of the big attacks on Earth—Bata, El Paso, Kolkata—I had a hunch that Talented mages, caught in unspeakable circumstances, summoned the Infected, and the conditions of the trigger revolved around abuse.

I'd seen natural mages on Earth before, and had even trained them to get past the planet's lack of magic. Always in heavy population centers, and in retrospect, I think humans had gotten better at using the collective magic emitted by their own clusters of people. Evolved. Quite possibly we would have eventually seen mages on Earth, if the Infected had not shown up.

But we didn't have time to go into it—we had reached the bore. Elves had constructed a bridge atop it. Was it Dhura? I couldn't remember. Couldn't tell.

The goblins huddled around me, peering into the darkness below. I heard "Wows" and "Look how deep!" and "Can you imagine what that must have been like as a city?"

But I heard Julia the clearest. "That doesn't look safe at all."

I found her in the crowd. "I understand," she said, "that our people living above the eggs somehow amplified our magic, allowing more eggs to be created and to survive." She waved at the bore. "But that wouldn't be the case now. No goblins above us. No added magic. Just a big, scary hole in the ground. Probably *things* running around in there as well."

Okay, the tide had turned from wonder to fear pretty quickly. And rightly so.

"I may know a place," Galad offered.

"Oh, goblin friend now, are we?" I asked sweetly.

"It was a long time ago," Galad said. "I was a child. Things were simple. Now, I've fought alongside trolls. I've had about every trust I believed in betrayed. It can be eye-opening."

"Ha!" I barked. "We're two of a kind. In another ten thousand years, you may sound wise."

"I guess it must go downhill after that," he said, smirking.

Did he just make fun of me? When was the last time anyone made a joke at my expense? That was... off-putting.

"Where's this place of yours?" I asked.

"A forest retreat," he said. "I used to go there when I was young, and then... well, you'll see. It should look familiar."

"Philip!" I shouted.

"Yes, ma'am!"

"You're in charge. Julia, you're with me. Galad is going to show us another location. Philip, get the rest of the goblins back to the outskirts of the camp—we will 'Port back there. Keep them safe." I looked at Galad, nodding at him to carry on.

He cast his spell and 'Ported us away.

***

"We called it Daria'matia Forest," Galad said. "It looked very different when I was a child, but we had eons to groom it."

It looked like the AllForest—even the trees hailed from the AllForest. My children had brought the memory of our home world with them. Complete with a palace nestled in the woods. Nostalgia with the weight of a mountain crushed me, squeezing tears from my eyes. By modern standards, it was a modest construct, but when I was young, elves had built something like that for me, and it had been a wonder.

"Just like the building my parents occupied in the AllForest," Galad said, enjoying his own memories.

He didn't know the history. He didn't know elves built the

original when the trolls destroyed our forest homes—that the enchanted rock shelter gave us a fighting chance. He didn't know that the home from his childhood was not the original, but a rebuild after the fighting had diminished.

So much memory. So much time.

"The quarry from whence they pulled the rock is this way," he said, drawing himself and me away from our past.

Once we crested a hill, I spotted it in the distance, the clear day presenting a view that would allow us to Blink over there. A river ran between us and the quarry, passing out of sight to the... wait, the contours of the land looked hauntingly familiar.

Something I'd seen on Earth?

No.

The vegetation had changed completely; the river had moved a little; but I'd been on the same hill before. My mind drifted from memories of Earth, to early life in the AllForest, to my relatively brief time on El'daShar. It tried to make sense of the nagging sense of familiarity, and then all at once...

"My cave..." I mumbled.

Galad waited, puzzled.

Where was it? There had been no quarry. Put a small expanse of stone there. My cave would have been...

"Come on," I said, dashing down toward the river.

As I ran, all I could think was that it felt amazing. Back on El'daShar, where the magic poured down gloriously. But also back in the forest from my youth, where life was full of promise. Back in my own skin, in a way I hadn't been in eons. The wind stirred the leaves above me, and though it was impossible, for a moment I thought I heard the joyful laughter of the Mother of Trees.

The distance was long, but it was too short by far.

I reached the river, and the semblance to AllForest ended. Only El'daShar remained, and the cave where I'd hidden the goblins lay nestled somewhere across the river. I found a ford in the river and crossed it, starting up the other side—the cave was near.

"Wait!" Galad called, far behind me.

I stopped and turned to look at him. He was walking downhill, carrying Julia in his arms. Of course she couldn't move as swiftly—I was so caught up in my own feelings, so lost in my past, that I hadn't thought about my speed.

"No one comes here," he said. "There's an evil, dark and malevolent." He didn't look nervous. He questioned his own memory. As he should have.

I pursed my lips, turned, and started forward, slightly uphill, looking for any sign I could remember.

I tried not to see the trees. Just the landscape. Hadn't there been a shallow dip outside of the cave? Gah! It all looked so similar, and the trees hid everything. I remembered several caves, but the goblin I had traveled with rejected them before choosing the right one.

Wait, hadn't I left a mark? Would it hold for fifteen millennia? If I was right about the "dark and malevolent" evil, then conceivably the mark held as well. I cast my spell to recall my marks and saw a glow to my left. I had passed it.

Retracing my path, I cast my spell again to draw out my mark. Clever trees concealed the entrance. My cave.

It had changed but a little. Most notably, the ward, on this planet overflowing with magic, was still intact. I'd never removed it. Haunted? I'd haunted it. It was my ghost that scared elves away. Even Galad, who *knew* wards, held back, cradling Julia, frightened for reasons she did not know, in his arms.

I removed my ward.

Galad and Julia visibly relaxed, and he set her gently down. She came over and took my hand, careful with those sharp talons—they were always careful around me with their talons.

We walked into the cave and looked around. Other occupants had come and gone, beasts not frightened by the haunting ward, but nothing large called the cave home. We explored the cave together—a nook for eggs, a pool of water, clearly fed from the pressure of some springs—and Julia pronounced it acceptable.

"I'll go get the goblins," I told Galad. "Keep Julia safe."

***

It took a little time to get the goblins moved, and more time to convince them they did not need my magic for them to produce eggs. They logically knew it—they knew their own stories, but they didn't trust it.

    I stayed with them, having sent my troop of humans back to Earth to continue their fight against pockets of the Infected. But I kept Galad—he needed to see. I stayed with the goblins to reassure them they could do it without me. We stayed through the Song, the Choosing, wonder in the eyes of the goblins who had come of age and learned their gender, as they sang their first eggs into existence.

    I pulled Galad out when the goblins finally admitted to themselves they didn't need us.

    "I've seen some amazing magic in my life," Galad began, "but that was…"

    He couldn't find the word.

    "It is how they fertilize the eggs as well," I told him.

    "I've never seen anything like that. How did they ever figure that out in the first place?"

    "That's a great question, but a story for another day."

Chapter 77

Galad, two hundred years in the past

"I found him!" someone shouted. "Over here!"

I was cold, so cold and empty.

"How in the world?" It was the Warlord's voice.

"I don't know," came Gavrial's voice from a distance. Then, much closer. "Does he live?"

The world shook a little. Then it shook a lot, and I grew much colder still as the wind whipped around and through me.

I climbed weakly to my feet as the rock wall around me moved. Thudd and I had eventually stopped. He had lain down to rest, and I nestled in the rock wall he created, knowing a single untoward movement would flatten me, but knowing I would not last a minute without him. And I needed to last.

Thudd pushed himself up to a sitting position, saying something in trollish.

The Warlord answered and Thudd groaned.

"His food is over where we 'Ported in," Gavrial said. "I'll go get it."

"Wait," I said, barely able to talk. "No. Take him home."

"I appreciate that you may have had a change of heart," Gavrial said, "but we cannot. We need that which we do not have. Either magic from a race that elves have already eradicated—"

Wait? What?

"Or the magic of The Amp, which we cannot take without declaring all-out war that would take us down the same path as the last race that threatened the elves."

I shook with cold. Fumbling, it took me a minute to find what I sought with numb fingers, while Gavrial Blinked away and returned with food for Thudd. But I finally pulled out a red crystal with tiny lights dancing inside. Bigger than the one the High Lord had held, mine was the size of a fist. An elven fist, not Thudd's. "Will this get him home?" I asked.

Gavrial hurried over, while the child Warlord studied me. Gavrial held out his hand, and I provided the Amp, relinquishing the treasure we had found from smashing a swath of crystalline cliff that was deep enough that we could not see back to the 'Port location.

He clutched it tightly and turned to Thudd, casting his spell. Gavrial tensed, but nothing happened. "Rotting vines!" he shouted. "My mana drains too quickly."

"Thudd!" I yelled, and he looked down, eyes sad.

I mimed picking up a crystal and smashing it, and pointed to a large one. "Be ready," I said.

Gavrial tensed as Thudd picked up the crystalline boulder and smashed it to the ground. I felt the mana recharge me, and I cast a Heat spell. Gavrial and Thudd both vanished in a flash of light.

"Father of Stones," the Warlord breathed. We stood there a moment, staring at the spot that moments before had held Thudd.

The Warlord turned and looked at me. "It will be good to have Uncle Thudd home." He got very close. Though we were of the same height, his stony form intimidated me—he could easily crush me. Then his face split in a grin. "Hello. My name is Grundle."

Chapter 78

Elliah

"I should get back to Earth," I said, missing El'daShar without yet having left it, but knowing my duty.

Galad nodded and 'Ported us back to camp, close to the command center. I followed him into the tent, the constant hustle and bustle of new information and logistics keeping everyone busy. I'd done the same enough times to recognize it.

In the middle of the open tent, atop a table and covered with a glass dome, lay a large gem, yellow with specks of moving darkness inside. The absurdity of seeing the glass cover struck me—like an enormous cake dome, but clearly it had been some audacious light fixture in its past life. They had glass protecting *that*, the artifact that Hughelas had pulled from the 4D planes so many eons ago.

I stopped Galad, my hand on his arm.

"Galad, please tell me *that* is your Banishment Stone."

He followed my gaze to the gem, saying curiously, "It is. Why?"

"If that's what the elves used to flee this world, then we can follow them."

"What? You know what this is?" he asked.

"I do. We called it the Crossing Crystal. And, unless someone has messed with it, it will lead us right to whoever used it last."

Galad stood, flabbergasted, wheels spinning in his mind. "Stay here," he commanded, dashing off. He paused in his run and turned back to shout, "Please!"

Gazes kept flitting over to me. I wondered what people saw. A vibrant young adult female, tanned skin and dark hair—I had enjoyed the red, but lost it when magic had restored my youth, returning my hair to its natural black. Or did they see my eyes, that had witnessed the rise and fall of whole worlds, seen every form of pain and joy that sentient beings could produce? *Never true*, I corrected myself.

They did not leave me waiting long. Galad came trotting back, the Gifted wizard close behind, and others trailing. Mort appeared beside me with Tali, facing the returning people like he'd been waiting with me the whole time.

Mother of Trees, staring down a charging Warlord, even knowing he was an ally, brought back disturbing memories. So many battles. Such long waits in between.

The time had come to stick my head into the mouth of the lion once more. To do what I didn't want to do. Said I wouldn't do. Deep inside, I felt an anger at fate, at the universe, at whoever ran the show and decided on my role in it.

The Gifted wizard spoke first. "Galad said you know how to work the Banishment Stone."

I waited for the others to reach us. Whatever Grundle saw in my eyes, it made him break eye contact. Red, the woman with the daggers—I liked her—had no trouble making and breaking eye contact, at *her* will. She was the glue, and I liked her all the more for not knowing it. Or perhaps I was just being nostalgic—she reminded me of a youthful version of myself, or how I *pictured* my younger self.

What a day for nostalgia! Fitting, given that, after millennia, it would be the day I would see my children again.

"Banishment Stone must be a name it acquired after I left. It uses dreams to seek out new worlds. Crossing Crystal. I used it to get to Earth when I fled to save the goblins eons ago."

Galad pinched his eyes. "You left El'daShar to *save* the goblins?"

"I told you their story is not what you think," I scolded him.

He held up his hands placatingly. "It's not that," he said. "It's just the story we were told is so different. You're Elliahspane Baelsbreath, the bogeyman... bogey*woman*... the evil behind the goblin assassins, the evil that created the Infected." He shook his head like he was trying to clear it of cobwebs. "You left to *save* the goblins."

I dismissed his disbelief with a wave of my hand. "Were there Banishments before you?" I asked.

"Yes, every few hundred years, some rebellious elf..." he stopped, blushing as he realized he fit that characterization.

"They didn't go to Earth. I would have seen at least one of them. So how did the artifact get calibrated to Earth?"

"Someone fiddled with it the night before the ceremony," Harry reported.

"You're suggesting that?" Red asked.

"I saw it," Harry said. "Elf crept in, fiddled with it, crept back out."

"What did he look like?" Elliah asked.

"A sneaky elf," Harry said, shrugging. "It was dark."

"Okay," I said. "Someone rigged it. You," I said, waving to encompass multiple people, "came to Earth. While you were there, someone changed the destination, and it seems likely the elves have gone there. Shall we go see if my theory is correct?"

Silence.

"Let's saddle up," Red said. I knew I liked her.

Chapter 79

Cordoro

It was time to take matters into my own hands.

Hungry, thirsty, itchy, and gross. Hungry, thirsty, itchy, and gross.

My mantra.

I couldn't do it anymore.

And, that very day, the Savage had presented a golden opportunity. The beasts Blithe had brought me to send to El'daShar, they would mask my presence. I hoped.

I had never heard of them before—small creatures, four-legged scavengers with white fur, about the size of a human skull. They exhibited a most unusual defense mechanism—they made noise in your head. A cacophony of your own thoughts that made it hard to focus, most notably interrupting any ability to cast spells.

They weren't vicious creatures—the mind-noise kept predators at bay while they had their fill of someone else's kill. They had to be paired with something else to do significant damage. The kicker was when I pointed out that I also could not perform the magic to Teleport the creatures to my enemies, because by their nature, they interrupted my magic as well.

Blithe handed me a flea-ridden hide cap with tufts of white fur on the outside. A winter hat for certain, and not something one would wear in the miserable heat of Savage, but Blithe had one on.

He sighed. He looked at me like I was a child and created a magelight.

Understanding dawning on me, I took the hat and reluctantly pulled it on. The noise in my head quieted down.

"We call them White Noisssemakersss," Blithe explained. "Their own ssskinsss and fur provide partial protection, but only when fairly fresssh."

Revulsed, I ripped the cap off, and the din in my head rose back to a clangor that made even thinking difficult.

Miserable, I put the disgusting thing back on my head, quieting the clamor once again.

Blithe nodded. "Thessse ssshould disssable their cassstersss. Ssso we pair it with sssomething that one needsss magic to combat, yesss?. A ssstone golem?"

"Do you still have any of those wind elementals?" I asked.

"Not at the moment."

"Hmmm..." I didn't like using the golems. They were easier to stop with magic than without, but surely there was a better choice. I thought but for a moment, then all of the pieces clicked into place. "I have an idea," I told him, and I proceeded to explain, leaving out a minor detail.

Chapter 80

Galad, two hundred years in the past

"I suspect this is a terrible decision on my part," Gavrial muttered.

I awoke under blankets in a cozy bed—warm, comfortable, and utterly spent. With no recollection of how I'd come to be in the small room, I nevertheless appreciated the world's unfamiliar magic over the bitter, mana-sucking wind.

"Grundle convinced me to give you a second chance. But I think you are weak, and you will return to your old ways. Genuine change is hard."

I sighed. "I will not," I said. Knowing, deep down, that I couldn't. That didn't mean I was Gavrial's ally either. Or that I intended to be a pawn in his game.

"You're in the cloud city of Garathal Vapil. I would ask that you stay here for a time. There's someone I trust here. I think, if you helped her, you might understand better what is worth fighting for. But she's younger than you. She won't have my ability to guard her mind, and she won't have any magical protection. So my ask is this—don't Read her. Stay out of her head, help her, and learn."

"For how long?" I had some of my own plans. My own desires for information about what Slooti contrived.

"I don't know," he said.

Stay on a world I didn't know, helping someone I didn't know, for an indefinite amount of time.

"But I think you need to do this," he continued. "I think you need to prove to yourself that you *can* do this. And I know I won't let you help me until you prove it."

I wasn't sure I *wanted* to help him. I wasn't sure what I wanted, except to be something better than what I had been. And that I needed to prove to myself I could be better.

"Okay," I said. "I'll stay. And I'll stay out of your friend's head."

He squinted at me, trying to decide whether he trusted me. I didn't need him to. "But I won't wait forever. I need to know what's really going on."

Gavrial smiled at that answer. He disappeared, then reappeared a few seconds later. With him was an elf woman who looked as smug and determined as Gavrial himself.

"I'm Ara'andiel," she said. "and we have some work to do. Get some rest. We start your training tomorrow."

Chapter 81

Elliah

"Who's going to go with me through the artifact, the Banishment Stone?" I asked, raising my hand.

Galad was the first to raise his.

"How good of an Empath are you?" I asked him.

"Very," he responded.

"You couldn't get in *my* head," I reminded him.

He blushed. "Actually, I did." He didn't like what he saw in my eyes. "I had to know if you were sane and if your intentions were good. I thought you might be *the* Elliah. It turns out you are… but you aren't what I thought."

I continued to glare, but inside, I felt embarrassed. I hadn't practiced empathic defenses for thousands of years. Foolish. With my age advantage, I should have been able to keep him out.

"I stuck to the surface," he squeaked out.

I nodded. "Okay, I don't know what to expect, but I think we'll need you."

"We'll need a Teleporter to get back," Red said.

Mort looked at a human I hadn't met before.

"I don't think I'm ready," the new human said.

Mort nodded agreement. "It's good that you can tell. Keep practicing what we've worked on while I'm gone. There is still much you can do."

Grundle silently raised his hand, and Harry his hammer. Red drew one of her daggers and tapped Harry's hammer, like a weaponized high five. The one they called Smith looked queasy.

"You're not going," I said to her. "Nor are you," I said to the Gifted wizard.

Tali raised her hand.

"You can go," I told her.

"Why aren't I going?" asked Smith at the same time the wizard said, "I *am* going."

"You're not going," I told the wizard, "because we can't risk losing you. You're our best shot at figuring out what makes the Infected work and stopping them."

He pursed his lips, irritated but reluctantly accepting.

"You're not going," I told Smith, "because you're carrying a baby."

"That's impossible," Smith said, nausea belying her words, while Galad and the Gifted wizard emitted odd echoes of her protests.

Smith blushed and muttered uncomfortably, "I had to have a hysterectomy when I was in my thirties... cancer. I can't have children."

I'd seen a lot of pregnant women, including *many* humans. "You don't look well. Reason enough not to go. You should see a Healer if your nausea has been persistent."

"I think I get sick when we Teleport," she posited. "Is that a thing?"

Yes, for women who were pregnant, that happened. I looked at Galad, but he didn't have a clue. *Men.*

"There's a Healer on Emerald Farms," the Gifted wizard suggested. "Come back with me. I can look too—if your body is fighting something, I might be able to help."

Ah, they think the cancer might be back. Well, at least that got them both out of harm's way. The particular harm which awaited me anyway.

"You can bring seven of us back?" I asked Mort. Just to make sure. From the corner of my eye, I watched Grundle pull the sick woman aside.

"Yes," Mort answered. "I can manage seven."

"Okay, let's clear out of camp and activate this," I said, nodding at the artifact.

The gem was the size of my head, but I could have awkwardly carried it. I had done it before, ages ago. But the troll gently removed the glass and picked up the artifact with ease. I had a vision rise up of a Warlord crushing the head of my ally in its rocky hands. It tore at my very core to see similar hands work so gently.

"Come," Mort told the other Teleporter. "Bring the gem back after we use it."

"No," I said. "I need him back on Earth, supporting the team that is fighting the Infected. I don't know how long this might take."

"Umm," the new Teleporter began.

"You can do it," I said. "You have to." I saw the woman in the command tent who had helped me before. "Guruswamy!" I called. She came over while the young man stammered.

"Your name?" I asked him.

"Venki," he said, clearly uncomfortable.

"Venki," I repeated.

"He has some... concerns... with how he was treated on Earth," Red offered, stumbling over her choice of words.

I squinted at her. He was a criminal? Believed himself to be undervalued? I tried to read her body language, but I didn't know how to interpret her fidgeting.

"He was captured and subjected to experiments," Red blurted, blushing.

Guruswamy had reached us at that point.

"I need Venki," I said to Simmi, putting my hand on his shoulder, "to go back and help my team get to the Infected. Tell Rocks that, if anything happens to *my trainee*, Rocks won't have to worry about his child having siblings, because I will feed his rocks to him personally, in a way that the Gifted wizard won't be able to grow back."

The quiet of the crowd spoke volumes.

I squinted at Guruswamy, awaiting her response.

"Yes, ma'am," she said, escorting Venki away to the Rings.

Several of the humans in the command tent noted our activity and sent warriors to escort us, some from Earth and others not. Among them was a giant.

"*He* can carry the Crossing Crystal back," I said, nodding at the giant.

"Bellows," Red said in greeting.

The large man laughed and walked over to Grundle, touching the top of his own head and then estimating the top of Grundle's with his other hand. Grundle stood about a head taller. For whatever reason, the giant found that amusing as well, laughing softly to himself.

As a group, we migrated outside of the camp. Red and Galad walked in front of me, but with my keen ears, I still heard them clearly when Red asked Galad, "What about your vigil? What if Cordoro comes back while we're gone?"

"He hasn't yet," Galad answered. "I can't stay there forever, waiting." She wrapped an arm around his and pulled herself over to him, comforting him with their brief contact. She didn't believe that he believed his own words. But she stood by him.

"Before we get there..." Red began, hesitantly, "...just how many of your children am I likely to encounter?"

"Children?" he barked a little laugh. To my surprise, Red didn't take offense. She just waited.

"None, Red. No one wants to have children with an Empath. Almost no one. Child Empaths are very difficult, and the chance of having one is high."

"But your family was royalty. Doesn't everyone want royal children?"

"Do *you*?" he asked, but didn't wait for an answer. "My family chose what people considered a backwater planet. It may have been the world of our origin, but the magic there was not as bright as on El'daShar. It is like being the royals of a desert... without the oil like in your world. You have to *like* the desert."

"Bottom line," Red replied, "no kids, just a race of nearly-immortal beings that don't want to be found. Piece of cake."

"You've been thinking I had tons of children this whole time?" he asked. "I thought you knew from the time you were stuck in my head..."

Stuck in his head? Empathic breakdown?

"I..." she began, then started over. "You lost someone close when the Infected overran the AllForest—a woman. I thought she might be your daughter. I guess she was..."

A lover? Probably. Empaths were known to be either very good or very bad at lovemaking. They knew what the other person wanted. But some Empaths cared more about getting what they wanted, and they easily bent their partner's will.

"My *sister*," he said. I didn't see that coming. "It's ironic. I spent my youth embittered toward her. You see, I thought my parents had her because it disappointed them to have an Empath for a child. It's unheard of for elves to have two children at once."

Not unheard of, but rare. Still, *rare* described Arafaela in a nutshell. "It wouldn't have been the first time for your mother," I inserted.

Galad knew all along that I listened. Red most likely thought they were out of earshot. She shot me a look to let me know the conversation was private. *Tough.*

"She'd had multiple children before," I continued. "She tried to convince me there were advantages. I'm not shocked she would have multiples again."

Galad nodded his acceptance of that. He probably knew the info I'd shared already, but we all needed reminders sometimes. And perhaps he hadn't known; the other children had perished long before Galad had been born.

"In the end," he said, "it was my sister who drew me back to the AllForest, to fighting *for* the trolls. After we lost our parents… it hurt when I lost her."

Red pulled herself closer to him again, and I let them walk in silent connection. The troll also marched in silence, pensive, and the dwarf enjoyed a conversation with no one, nodding his head occasionally and grinning. *Bessie.*

We didn't need to go far out of camp, just far enough to reserve some space without interference. Grundle turned and raised an eyebrow at me questioningly. Were we removed enough? I nodded and he set the stone down.

"Go to the bathroom now," Red said, "because I'm not pulling this thing over until we get there." Tali laughed, and on another day, I would have grinned. No one else got the joke.

"Give me some space," I said, waving everyone back. "I'm not sure in which direction the field will incarnate."

They cleared out, and I activated the stone. It wasn't hard, just a simple spell to call out the elements—slightly more complicated than a magelight. A yellow field appeared next to me, a half-sphere about ten feet across.

"We should have brought someone with us that knows magic well enough to learn how to activate it," Red said, "in case we need a rescue party."

Grundle chuckled. "There's no such person here on purpose." He stepped into the field, getting in the middle where he could stand without hitting his head, and readying his war axe. He was right, the clever troll.

"If we can't manage this," I said, "I don't want any more lives spent trying to get us out. We're on our own." I stepped in, pulling out a single dagger much like the ones Red wielded. Me and the Warlord. How fitting.

"Mother of Trees," the Warlord said. He didn't fidget—as clever as he was, I suspected he remarked upon the same irony that ran through my head. He probably didn't know there was more to the phrase than just an epithet.

"Father of Stones," I replied.

He grunted, grinning. He'd at least heard the phrase. I wondered if he knew how his god-like progenitor had perished. Galad came in next, and the others flowed in after that. Red was the one who reached out and tapped the field from the inside. Someone always did. I remember when I had—it felt like glass, but impenetrable.

"So what now?" she asked.

"We just wait," I said. "This isn't like a normal Teleport. It's going to feel something like you're turned inside out and then righted again. Your clearly-not-pregnant friend," and I rolled my eyes, "would not have fared well."

We stood there as seconds ticked away.

"Why didn't the skeleton go to the party?" Red asked.

"What?" Galad said.

"Why didn't the skeleton go to the party?" she insisted,

playfulness in her eyes.

"What are you talking about?" Galad asked, clearly confused.

I couldn't help but let a small corner of my lip rise in a smile. He truly was keeping himself out of people's heads.

"Because he had *no body* to go with," Red finished.

"Ugh," said Tali. "That's terrible. What's the chance that translated?"

"None," I said. Unlike the rest of the non-Earthlings, I actually knew English.

"Be thankful," Tali said. "Sounds like a joke my father would tell."

"I've got more," Red said. "How long will we be waiting?"

And then, *thankfully*, the Universe turned inside out.

Chapter 82

Cordoro

For the first time in long weeks, I 'Ported to my home, fearful that the damned elf would be waiting, but fairly confident that the little creatures I'd carted along would keep my presence masked.

Nothing bad happened. No elf appeared. My mind remained my own... minus the light noise that made it through my fresh hide hat. I shook my head in disgust at the thought of what sat atop my skull.

The house lay empty, lights out, but the sun brightened the furniture through my curtained windows. It had remained vacant for weeks. But had they truly left it alone, or would I find my wine cellar empty?

I dropped the caged NoiseMakers in my living area and made haste to the cellar, not concerned about being seen through the windows, with my residence so far removed from any other.

The closed cellar door boosted my spirits. Flinging it open, I cast a magelight and scurried down, laughing aloud when I found my shelves still stocked. Wasting no time, I grabbed my corkscrew from the nail on the wall and opened the nearest bottle. Dark and red. I held my nose over the bottle and swirled the liquid around, stirring up the aroma. Nothing had ever smelled better.

I wasn't a drunkard. But I had missed the feeling promised by wine. I had little time, but I savored the sweet agony of almost-drinking. Then I slipped wine onto my tongue. Pure bliss. I had a few small swallows. No harm in that. Just a taste, a reminder of what I would get back to when I completed my unpleasant business.

I craved some proper food, but the foodstuffs there, in my house, would have spoiled. Still, rotten, it would be better than the food on Savage. I would have given up my wine for a loaf of bread.

Soon I will be done with this and have my fill. Better get to it.

I grabbed a couple of bottles and stuffed them in a rucksack from the cellar, then climbed back up the stairs and gathered the cages of the NoiseMakers.

I 'Ported to a place in the forest outside the walled enclave of Emerald Farms. On occasion, discretion required a private setting. It wasn't *safe*, at least not if you weren't a Teleporter—indigenous species wandered through. Visitors needed the ability to 'Port back out again in an instant. And not being safe was one of its advantages.

That wretched elf had yanked two of my secret 'Port locations from my brain, and Mort had traveled to my secluded forest clearing. Looking around quickly, I found no immediate threats.

My luck held. I spied just what I needed—at least *one* thing I needed. A group of Electrolights floated within sight. You couldn't fight them with anything *but* magic. Weapons simply passed through them. They stunned their victims, and given enough time, would drain the life force from their paralyzed meal.

I spied a Flor'maton in the distance, but that wouldn't be helpful. Without trees, it couldn't do much damage. But often, where you found a Flor'maton… I Blinked closer. Yes! A WallBanger. As good as a golem, but if I used them in conjunction with the irresistible stuns from Electrolights, the damage would be devastating.

I set one of my cages down, leaving a NoiseMaker. My plan would not take long—the NoiseMaker would be safe enough. I Blinked to the Electrolights with my remaining NoiseMaker, getting them in roughly the same place, then 'Ported to El'daShar.

I'd established many points outside of their land-grabbing perimeter I could use as drop-off points. The one I chose for that day's assault gave me visibility into the camp while keeping me hidden in trees. Knowing the glow of the Electrolights would give me away, I opened the cage, quickly Blinked into the enemy camp with the Electrolights and the NoiseMaker, then Blinked back alone. Since I wanted them thinking the attacks were entirely from the Savage, I'd avoided showing myself. I fervently hoped that anyone who spotted me would fall victim to the creatures I'd left behind.

I quickly 'Ported back to Emerald Farms and Blinked closer to the WallBanger. The next step was going to be the hard part. I took out my slimeroot and had a bite. I waited for the required seconds to tick by, then I gathered everything I had and tried to 'Port the massive creature to El'daShar.

Nothing happened. I was too weak.

But I had to do it. I had to get that beast to El'daShar, or the Electrolights and NoiseMakers would be ineffective. I could taste the prize of my return from the Savage Lands.

Resolute, I ate more of the nasty slimeroot, knowing it would give me a little more boost to my spellcasting, but also that too much would kill me. I pulled the open wine bottle from the rucksack and had a couple of swallows. Liquid bravery.

I sat down, eyeing my target, and I Blinked. To my surprise, the beast didn't notice or didn't care that I sat atop it.

My lucky day all around. I began my casting again, trying with all I had to move the monster beneath me. I almost laughed at the idea. But either I had to accomplish the herculean 'Port or continue my slow death in exile, and I didn't want to die.

Sweat pouring forth and teeth gritted, I pushed a 'Port on the behemoth beneath me.

Bamf

The stony behemoth may not have noticed me sitting atop it, but it sure didn't like being 'Ported. The commotion in the camp riled it up further. It gathered speed as it charged the camp, and I let the magic of the El'daShar sun bathe me and recharge my magical energy as I rode atop, leaning forward to keep my balance.

The WallBanger would do some serious damage, especially to the people already paralyzed from the Electrolights. I cackled maniacally as I gathered the energy to 'Port back. The 'Port was going to be tricky. I would go flying forward at the other end. I would have to give myself some room, and even so I might get hurt. Still safer than remaining atop the beast as it charged amongst my enemies.

I thought the El'daShar sun had charged me enough, so I concentrated, weary and exultant all at once. *Bamf*. I flew into the clearing on Emerald Farms and panicked, despite knowing what to expect. I crashed onto the flat rocks, gracelessly flipping end over end until I came to a rolling stop.

I ached, but nothing seemed broken. Skinned, yes; bruised, certainly; but not broken. I checked my wine. No, nothing broken. My luck held out. I took Blithe's canister from my pack and had a drink. I had finally understood that the spicy, slimy drink helped counteract the side effects of the slimeroot.

Looking around, I laughed. The cage with the remaining Noisemaker rested right next to me, like I'd planned my rolling stop, and I reached up to confirm what I already knew—the cap still sat atop my head.

The Flor'maton still lingered at the edge of the clearing. Wait, did my eyes deceive me? Another gift for me? A second WallBanger had appeared near the Flor'maton. I didn't have the strength to 'Port another one of those massive beasts across worlds… but a vengeful thought popped in my head. What about a 'Port within Emerald Farms?

I took a moment to celebrate with another pull of wine. The world spun for a moment, probably the effects of being thrown about from my crash landing. But it steadied out again, so I had another delicious drink and put the bottle back. It clanked strangely, and I pulled it back out and peered at it menacingly.

Someone had finished my bottle! And I'd had it with me the whole time. Some sneaky elven trick! Elfin? Elvish? "Elf… ven Bassstardsss!" Oooo, I liked the sound of that 's.' "Ssssssss," I hissed, then laughed.

Okay, one last trick for the day, and my mouth watered at the thought that I might get some food out of it. Hit the market with the WallBanger, nab some food, and get back to one of my old tents in the Savage Lands. I'd stash my stolen food away from the active camp, and I'd have some *proper food* I could eat.

Time to do some damage and, *for once*, do something to take care of myself.

Chapter 83

Galad

The Banishment Stone turned us inside out, tearing us apart in the process of moving us, or possibly tearing the Universe apart and reforming it around us. It felt the same as when I'd been Banished, with at least one difference—Red's consciousness parked right there with me.

So this Ara'andiel, Red thought to me. *You loved her?* Her mind clicked through puzzle pieces, always assembling and reassembling as she learned. She thought her knives were her superpower; she underestimated her sharp mind and determination. I hadn't finished the story of meeting Grundle, having left off with my time in the floating cities on Orbanos.

I did, eventually, I thought to her. *The first woman I loved.*

Ironic that I felt the slight concern from Red. I'd never shared an Empathic connection with Ara'andiel, kept my promise for more than a hundred years. And yet I *could not stop* my connection with Red.

But we never pursued romance, I explained. *I truly cared for her.*

Red processed that, a strange mix of warmth and worry. *When I spent time in your head, I saw her, I think. You were fighting a multi-headed dragon.*

I mentally sighed. *That was the last time I fought on Orbanos. We lost Jolor'ithnial. It convinced me I was ready to go back and fight for the elves. Fight for more.*

So, you went back to the AllForest?

There's a little more to it than that…

***

"You talked of rebellion. Did you not mean it?" I had finally cornered Gavrial on a visit.

Gavrial looked weary. "I did. But—"

"But what? I'm ready. I understand how corrupt the High Lord has become, or perhaps always has been. Truly, I'm ready."

Gavrial twitched. "You may be, but the chances of success are much smaller than they were when last we met."

"Has the AllForest fallen?" I asked. Surely not. Wouldn't I have felt... something?

"No," he said. "The AllForest stands, and there is no open rebellion. But Slooti continues to use the trolls inhumanely to mine gems, and the citizens of the AllForest strike back as they can. Neither side speaks of the conflict. Slooti must keep his efforts secret, and the AllForest can't risk being caught and called out for rebellion."

"What if the AllForest openly rebelled?" asked Ara'andiel.

"Slooti's forces would decimate them. His power has grown. He's found more Artifacts. He controls Empathy now, and he's also got these." Gavrial pulled a vial out of his pack, then twisted the lid. Mana spewed forth, reminding me of... I shot Gavrial a look. He nodded. "Yes, they're from *that* world. People are calling them Mana'thiandriel. Vessels of magic. The crystals from that world sit inside, and fire magic activates them, creating a controlled release of mana."

On the world where he'd left me, smashing those crystals had refilled my mana. Some clever elf had productized it, creating something much more useful.

"I thought to use these to distract Slooti from his quest to acquire more artifacts," Gavrial said. "But it just added to his arsenal. And I don't know what else he's found."

"If the fight must remain secret for now, maybe there is still something I can offer," I said, thinking back through my old life. "The AllForest fought with weapons forged of metal. What if they had magical armaments?"

Gavrial squinted. "What do you have in mind?"

"The House of Contested Gifts. I spent hundreds of years collecting items for the House. Creating laws that, even now, I struggle to pull myself away from, they were so pleasing to our nature as elves."

Gavrial groaned. "The House is an abomination. It has been since the day it was envisioned, playing on our love for rules to both distract and disarm the populace."

"An abomination I helped build," I told him. "But I also know where it hides its treasures. Some are not well guarded."

"A few weapons would do us little good," he said, shaking his head. "And we could not teleport in and out so many times as to get a lot. There are Wards and alarms—"

"What if it were quite a lot of weapons, and we could do it all at once?"

"I'd say 'what do you need me to do?'" Ara'andiel answered.

"I need you to stay and keep doing what you're doing here," I told her.

"There's a chance to fight back and you want me to stay out of it?" She looked indignant.

"This world needs you. Orbanos's threats are largely physical. My Talent has done little to help. Your skills, however, keep the people safe."

"You've been a big part of protecting Orbanos for a long time now, and with Jolor'ithnial gone, Orbanos will suffer from your departure even more."

I nodded my head, giving thanks to her for her words. "Others will step up. Orbanos forges people."

"And yet I am meant to stay behind?" she prodded.

"What good is a forge without a blacksmith?" I answered.

"Ha!" she barked.

"How?" Gavrial asked, interrupting our banter. "How could you get many weapons in one trip?"

"There is a magical trunk, a chest, that can hold many more items than its apparent volume, and it never gets heavier."

Gavrial grunted. "I know of what you speak. At least in nature. I've seen such things, on a smaller scale. I've long suspected that Celymir's cloak has a pocket like that—she carries more than seems possible. The means of their making is lost, but they came from the AllForest."

"I know where one sits in the House," I said. "At least where it sat, and most things in the House just… stay." I felt a moment of regret for all I had done to rob families of their heirlooms, thinking I had done good for the Crown. "Along with a cache of magic weapons and armor."

"That could tip the scales in a fight," Gavrial said. "But even so, the House is heavily guarded and has Wards. We cannot 'Port in without setting them off. We would not have time to load up very much—"

"Leave that to me," I said. "They built the House over a bore. The Wards cannot reach all the way down. And I am an Empath. I can walk among the House and none shall see me." Not strictly true—some Wards would trigger. "Here's what I need you to do…"

Chapter 84

Elliah

I had used the artifact several times in long-gone history. I didn't understand how it worked, but I knew how it felt. A normal Teleport had a moment of disorientation, but that was the mind trying to catch up with what was, in actuality, a very smooth transition. Teleportation came with a flash of light, brighter if it took you across worlds. Hughelas had long ago explained that light to be a burning off of the differential between the energy states of the two positions. However it worked, Teleportation moved you with a silky touch. Using the artifact was *not* a smooth transition.

I thought about how I would explain the Crossing Crystal if asked. "When you drop a boulder into a deep lake, it creates ripples on the water at a certain wavelength. Here's the thing about those waves… those are just the ones you notice. When that rock hits the water, many waves go much faster than what is visible." I'd learned a lot in the last two hundred years on Earth, as my aging reversed and my mental facilities improved. "The transition caused by the artifact is much like dropping a stone into a lake. Only we are the stone, being plopped into a new world. Ripples moving faster than us rip through us. Those going slower, we have to crest and then descend. The net result is like riding a tilt-o-whirl while strapped into a medieval torture rack."

My added knowledge from my years on Earth only made the ride more wild. Nevertheless, I anticipated guards waiting at the other end, and I couldn't afford to let the journey unravel me. Knowing what was coming, I looked ahead as we raced toward our destination, watching the reflected waves as they hit the termination point and bounced back. Something waited there. Likely elves, though it was difficult to tell—might have been Infected, or a group of Ravenous Bugbladder Beasts of Traal… Matt had twisted my arm about reading *Hitchhiker's Guide to the Galaxy*. Didn't matter.

Our rock came to a lurching stop at the bottom of the lake, but I had jumped forward the moment before the field dropped, my dagger an extension of my arm. The closest being hadn't moved, and my blade charged toward its target. I could always Heal if my victim turned out to be an innocent greeter.

My dagger plunged into an aged and withered form, and my victim didn't move to stop me, the body turning instantly to grey ashes and falling to the ground or floating away.

I scanned the area as my allies gathered behind me. Two more wraiths lurked in the gloom, neither doing much in the way of guarding. I paused my attack. Their haunting forms stood, frozen in the grey dusk, and moving closer to one, I recognized features that might once have been elfin.

"What in the freakin' hells!" Red exclaimed.

Red still looked like Red, full of color and life. Everyone that had come through the artifact beamed with life in the otherwise decaying realm. But the elf guards held on to life by a thread, and not by their choice. Blanched and skeletal, their eyes stared into nothing, their mouths hung open, like they were too weary to close them. How they stood I did not know, their withered forms so ephemeral that a mild wind should have torn them away. But not even a breeze stirred in that dismal place.

"That was *awesome*!" Harry yelled, prodding an elf-wraith with his hammer. It fell to the ground and crumbled to ashes, some floating away, just like what had happened with the one I'd attacked.

Grundle reached out to poke the last elf-wraith, but Red shouted, "Wait!"

Grundle stopped and looked at her. She waved her hands like she was trying to think it through. "Don't… vaporize… that one. I mean, what if it isn't a bad guy?"

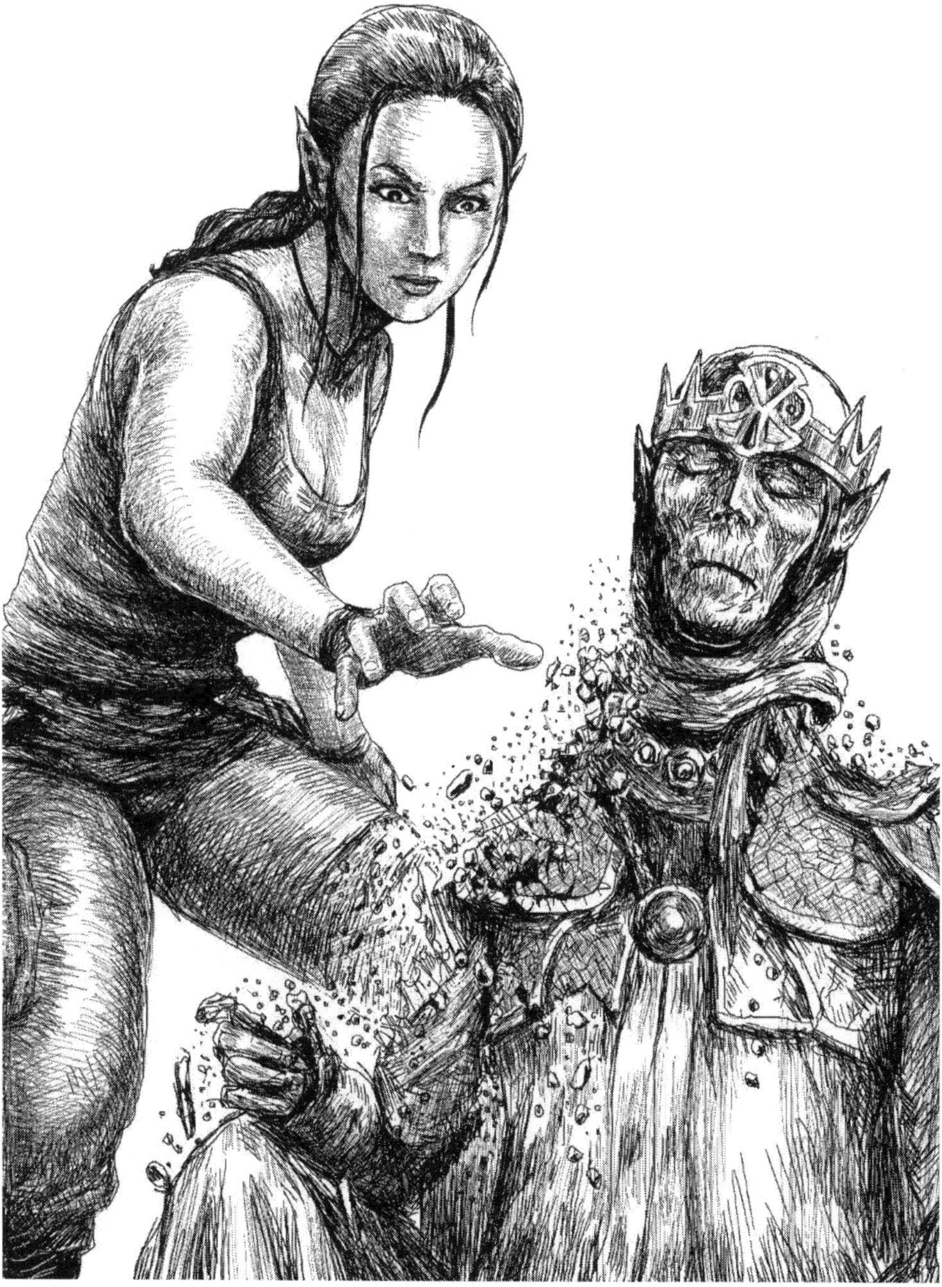

That got a lot of skeptical looks. But not from me. I walked over to the last remaining elf-wraith. We stood on a flat plane of ground, but a grey fog clouded the area, so I couldn't see far. Grey everywhere—dirt, sky, people—everywhere but on us.

I got close. I couldn't tell with certainty that it lived.

"Don't try any magic," I said. "I think someone will notice it. But do you sense anything, Galad?"

"Other than the supreme lack of magic, just like on Earth?"

I nodded at the elf-wraith, and he focused on it.

"Just a noise, like a moan, and that's it. This world's emotions are as grey as its appearance."

"Leave it be," I decided.

"So we think that is an elf?" Tali asked, looking between me and the grey, skeletal form transfixed before us.

"Yes," I said. "I've had the luxury of seeing elves age. This is an elf. A very, very old one, held together by a whisper of magic."

"Elliah," Galad said, "if this has happened since their arrival, which was only months ago at most, it won't take long before this world ages us."

I nodded my agreement. The clock was ticking. Again.

I looked around in the eerie fog to spot any direction of interest. The fog constrained visibility to about thirty feet—I couldn't see anything distant. Sound wasn't bouncing back, so I believed we arrived in an open area. The land smelled dead, the ground underfoot stirring like soot as we moved, and the very air tasted wrong, dirty with light ash.

Mort called out, "Over here! Footprints lead this way."

"Remember—no magic," I said, and started off at a light jog.

What the hell have you done, Slooti? Elves consumed ambient magic—the process somehow kept us young. I survived on Earth because humans emitted magic. Slooti took the elves and fled, because the Infected had targeted elves? He, what, followed my lead?

Was it the only choice? The humans had survived by reducing their population at any one place. Could we not have done the same?

Was it my imagination, or was the fog getting thinner? We moved onto slightly rolling hills. As the hills grew, and the valleys deepened, the fog settled more into the valleys. The view became clearer, and as I topped a hill I stopped.

"Oh, shit," was all I thought to say.

The others came to a staggering stop behind me.

"That looks totally fucked up," Tali said. "Why are we doing this again?"

Below us sat a city, nestled in the valley. The architecture declared itself elven, hints of arches, just like those on El'daShar, peeked from the fog. Pockets of fog stirred, as bodies moved haltingly through it, and I expected, if I looked closely enough, I would see arms occasionally falling off and getting left behind. Damn Netflix and *The Walking Dead*... why had I let Matt waste my time on that? I could have used a good Rick Grimes quote right then, but I was too appalled to dig one up.

Rising out of the city climbed a handful of towers, one mightier than the others. It reflected the tower on El'daShar, the one recreated by Slooti after our son's death, recreated yet again on a dead planet. It stretched taller than the one on El'daShar, reaching to crazy heights. Stupid men and their need for size.

The higher any of the towers rose from the floor of the valley, the more color returned to them, the main tower moving from dead at the base, to a normal tower somewhere in the middle, to glowing resplendence at the top. Glowing resplendence. There was magic at the top. On a dead planet, with its dead sun, Slooti somehow had magic.

"This is mind-staggeringly bad," I said.

"We're doing this because we need to find out more about the Infected in order to fight them," Mort reminded Tali.

"What are we *looking* at?" Red asked.

"You said Slooti had an Amp," I reasoned aloud. "Maybe he found something, an artifact, that produces magic. Do you have any idea if he found other artifacts in the 4D Planes?"

Grundle and Galad exchanged a look, and Grundle answered. "I know he did." Galad's cheeks reddened.

"Why the embarrassment?" Red said, more quietly.

"I know he groomed me for this role," Galad said. "I'm just embarrassed by the thought—I would have been the one enabling this." He gestured toward the undead theme park below. "But we *know* he found an Artifact that grants him Empathy."

Red put a reassuring hand on his arm.

"How did they build this so quickly?" Harry asked.

"Good question," I said. "I find it hard to believe the universe would provide a Build-A-City artifact."

"The same universe that provided a race that sings its children into existence?" Galad quipped.

"Fair point," I admitted, grinning despite the dire situation. "But now that you point it out, this entire city looks… wrong."

"Beyond being fucking Zombieland?" Tali asked.

"Yes, beyond that. Doesn't that look familiar?" I asked, pointing at a squat building enshrouded in fog.

"The House of Contested Gifts!" Galad exclaimed.

I shook my head sadly—that stupid, foolish idea of Slooti's had never been undone.

"And no plants," Red said. "An elven city without plants."

What the hell had Slooti done? The only source of light and life was at the top of that over-tall tower.

"He's in the tower," I reasoned.

"*He* being *Slooti*?" Grundle asked.

I rolled my eyes. A human reaction I'd adopted. "Yes."

"So we have to go through the ZombieLand Fun Park?" Tali asked.

"Not *have* to," Harry said. "*Get* to."

I sighed. "Stealth isn't going to work here," I said, letting go of the path I'd hoped to take. I looked at Grundle. "You look moderately strong. Do you think you could throw a stone into the city?"

Grundle chuckled. "What am I trying to do?"

"Hit a building," I said. "Just get some attention. I think if we get *his* attention, we can skip the zombie gauntlet."

"Aww," Harry moaned.

"Hmph," Grundle grunted. He found a stone the size of my

head, and picked the House of Contested Gifts as his target. We had height, but the distance was considerable. Still, I'd seen what trolls could do.

He took a running start and heaved the rock, firing it up and away like a catapult.

"Holy hell!" Tali said, astounded.

"Be glad you're not seeing that as the recipient," I said, remembering what it was like to be dodging even bigger stones—normal trolls were twice the size of a Warlord.

The stone continued its flight, beginning its descent. On and on it traveled, closing in on its target and then…

"Where'd it go?" Tali asked.

"Through the wall," Galad said.

"But nothing broke…" she insisted.

"It didn't *hit* the wall," Galad said. "It passed through it."

"Illusion," I said.

"Why? For whom?" Galad asked. He looked around like we might get ambushed, but nothing happened.

"Are the zombies *illusions*?" Tali asked.

"They're not zombies!" I snapped. "If they were, you'd be safe. And no, they're not illusions."

"I got that!" she said resentfully. "I do have brains." She looked down at her own body. "Not my best feature perhaps."

"I don't think we caught anyone's attention," Red interrupted, to stave off any argument.

"Mort," I said, "can you Blink us to that tower?"

"Maybe in two steps, if I had any magic." He held his arms up as if that would increase the amount of magic that hit him—like I'd seen countless Earthlings do with their phones to get a better signal. "This is worse than Earth. I'm not sure I can even get *myself* across this hill."

"Wait a minute," Red said. "There's not enough magic to get us out of here?"

Mort looked uncomfortable, but I answered for him. "There's enough magic." I pointed at the glowing top of the tower.

"The only way out is through the rabbit hole," Red concluded.

Galad looked confusedly around the ground.

"It's a book," I said at the same time as the Warlord. He'd found time to read *Alice in Wonderland*?

Red soothingly patted the arm of the man who could fry all our brains if he chose to do so.

"And realistically, *who knows*?" I said. "There might be other ways out. But *that's* the way that's going to get us more information."

"So we're back to fighting our way there!" Harry happily concluded and started down the hill.

"Hold up," I told him, rolling my eyes. *Men and their fighting.* "I promise I'll get you a fight."

"Yak yak yak. Too much talking." Then he paused as though listening, and chuckled.

"What did Baessandra say?" I asked him, glaring.

He went tight-lipped, piping out, "Nothing."

Baessandra and I had never gotten along, even before she'd gotten stuck in that hammer. For just a moment, I appreciated the irony of how our roles had reversed.

"I can get you magic," I said. "Just be ready to use it. Two hops and get us in that tower, at the top."

He looked down at the city, and like a pool shark, he pointed at the smaller tower he would take us to first, then pointed at the destination at the top of the larger tower.

"What if those towers are illusions?" Mort asked. "Blinking to them would be our last mistake."

I took a deep breath, closed my eyes, and concentrated. To my despair, I sensed the elves as a whole, a drain on the magic coming forth from the tower, barely maintaining a stasis that kept them alive.

"The main tower is real," I said. "At least in some form. I can sense the power emanating from the top. Grundle, can you check on the reality of the smaller tower?"

He obligingly took a smaller stone and launched it at the tower, where it hit the wall and bounced away, still drawing no attention from any of the elf-wraiths.

I closed my eyes again and fished for a magical power

source. My Gift. I couldn't use the humans—there were too few. I already knew that though I could sense the elves, I could not draw magic from them—they would turn to ash and float away. So, I reached out to other sources.

The sun there, as Mort said, emitted even less magic than Earth's. I inched toward the magical source in the tower. It emitted radiant magic. Good to know, but I couldn't draw on it without risking the zombie elves crumbling to dust—it might have been all that held them together.

I let my consciousness seep down into the ground. Crawly things moved through the dirt if I reached far enough, but they had the sense to stay away from the nastiness of Slooti's creation. There must have been plants somewhere, making the air breathable, but none lived within my range—whatever Slooti had done must have pulled the life from them.

Well, hell. This world sucks. And what I had to do sucked even more. I'd just gotten whole again.

"Ready?" I asked Mort.

"Ready," he answered.

And I gave him some magic.

Bamf

We appeared at the top of the first tower Mort had pointed to, looking up toward the central tower and the beaming light. A moment, and then *bamf*, we arrived on a balcony of the main tower, looking in.

I didn't know who looked more startled—Slooti or me.

Chapter 85

Cordoro

I thought my good luck had broken, but my gambit had worked out splendidly! When I'd Blinked atop the second WallBanger, I thought the caged NoiseMaker must have startled the behemoth. It began spinning, and my equilibrium struggled to keep up.

But I was very familiar with the 'Port to the market square on Emerald Farms—the most common 'Port I'd had to do while I still slaved to the demands of that world.

Despite the size of the thrashing creature, and its attempts to throw me off, I 'Ported us to the market. I didn't know they used the market for a staging ground, but introducing an angry WallBanger to the soldiers and food transport was a *riot*.

The beast threw me from its back, but the Universe owed me for my weeks of misery and pain, and I landed in a bin of grain that cushioned my fall. The noise in my head grew loud, and I snatched up my cap and replaced it on my head.

I stood and watched people run in all directions. Some ran from the carnage, but others ran *to* it. I joined those running away, partly because they had more sense, but for other reasons as well. One, it took me away from the council hall, where I would more likely be recognized, and two, my disheveled look fit the group of injured people. Looking back, I giggled as the WallBanger raised hell behind me. What I assumed was one of the Teleportation Rings sat near the stairs to the Council Hall. Had I known its location, I would have 'Ported the beast closer—destroying that Ring would have advanced my cause.

The smell of fresh bread assaulted my nose, and my body jerked to a stop without me telling it to do so. After getting bumped a couple of times, I got out of the way of the people fleeing past. I closed my eyes and breathed it in.

There! I opened my eyes and spotted the overturned table and bread on the ground. Darting through the evacuees, I ducked behind the table and grabbed a roll. I stuffed it in my mouth and had it swallowed faster than I'd eaten anything in my life. The second roll took more time, as I split my attention between the roll and stuffing more bread in my rucksack.

Oh, the day was turning out to be glorious!

My third roll I actually savored. I didn't think I'd ever realized just how good ordinary bread could be. I sipped some sabli between bites. Relaxing in my shelter behind the table, I looked out at the fleeing people, listening to those powerful long-distance weapons with their explosive *pops*. I peeked over the table in time to see a really large version of one of the noisy weapons cause a massive fireball that left the WallBanger collapsed with a smoking hole in its side. The creature hadn't made it to the Ring—if only my luck had held.

It was time to go. I looked for anything else within distance to safely grab, when I spied something that caused *me* to freeze. Oh, what a day! My luck *had* held. I saw what I really, *really* wanted.

Chapter 86

Galad, near-present time

Gavrial brought me to El'daShar, but only I knew the 'Port location of the bottom of the bore. Since I couldn't be seen in public, he 'Ported me into a cave. I didn't expect to encounter an occupant. Gavrial lit a dim magelight, revealing a thin elf waking up on a cot. The stranger squinted at the light, and attempted to talk, but nothing came out.

Gavrial shook his head, saying, "Not now. I'll come back and explain." The room had metal bars on one side and rock walls on the others. A small table and two chairs almost cluttered the room. The table held a pitcher and a single book.

The man grimaced and raised an eyebrow, then smiled. He reached for the water and drank straight from the pitcher.

"What?" Gavrial said, flustered for the first time since I'd ever met him.

The elf coughed lightly, then said, "I'm just glad that, one way or another, I will soon be done."

Gavrial made a noise of disgust, then turned to me. "We are in the dungeons under the Tower." The dungeons. The very prisons I had sworn to my sister did not exist. *Unbelievable.* I didn't know if I meant that about Slooti's lies or my gullibility. "You should be able to reach the bore from here. Let's go."

I looked at the other occupant, then back at Gavrial. Neither provided an explanation, so, shrugging, I cast the spell to take us to the bottom of the bore.

I showed Gavrial the location so he could 'Port back later, and he provided me with a phone. "Call me when everything is ready," he said. "I'll be here." If he didn't show up, trusting him would be the last mistake I ever made. I started to explain again how critical the timing would be, but he rolled his eyes and 'Ported away before I finished.

Sighing, I took a moment. I could give it all up, 'Port to any of the public locations I knew on El'daShar and Slooti would welcome me back. Why did I trust Gavrial with my life? But, I didn't. I just knew I couldn't go back to what I had been. I couldn't unsee what I'd seen, couldn't unlearn the knowledge I'd gained, even though it killed me to admit my role in Slooti's rule.

Determined to move forward, no matter the cost to myself, I cast a spell to see in the darkness, and then a spell to manipulate wind, and started up the bore. The incredible width of the bore allowed that. It took a considerable time to reach the landing, and once I saw light, I Blinked my way to the cave I knew existed. It sat just under the Wards. I used my considerable experience on Orbanos with grappling hooks to latch onto the stairway above the cave and pull myself up through the Ward, not able to use any magic. Crawling up the wall of the bore like a bug exposed me more than any other part of the whole endeavor. I hoped.

Once through the Ward, I reached out with my mind. I'd told Gavrial we needed to infiltrate at night, when very few people roamed the Hall. Still, I found a pair of guards, several floors up, coming to investigate the noise I'd made.

All it took was a little mental *bump*. "Look," one said. "Dusk flyer. Must be injured, separated from its flock." With a scrape, I had the "injured" dusk flyer take off from the landing and sail down the bore. The two guards, curiosity satisfied, wandered off.

Thank the trees that I hadn't set off the Wards.

I climbed up the stairs that wound around the inside of the bore, looking for the side passage I remembered. My job had sent me there many times, depositing collected possessions over the eons of work for the Hall. I erred on the side of caution, renewing my night vision while I still climbed the stairs—I did not want to use a magelight, nor did I want to cast *anything* after entering the room.

Thinking I'd found the room I sought, I carefully entered, and discovered it to be more or less as I remembered—the room contained some ancient artifacts, guarded well from above, and protected via the unfathomable abyss below. The details seemed wrong, but I suspected my memories to be at fault.

After searching the room, I felt a creeping dread that I had been wrong about the trunk. But shifting a giant mirror aside, I found it. I quickly but quietly shifted more items around so I could open it. I wished I'd brought some oil or something, in case the hinges squeaked. But, tucked in a cave, many, many floors down from the main level of the Hall, the chance someone would hear a squeaky hinge and investigate should not have bothered me… yet it did.

I slowly lifted the lid of the ancient trunk, and it slid open like the metal had been well oiled for the centuries it had sat, gathering dust. The inside was empty, but I did not intend for that to remain true for long.

I grabbed a nearby sword and placed it inside the chest, then closed the lid. Then I opened it again, and the sword had vanished. I closed and opened the lid, and the sword reappeared. Smiling, I shut and reopened it again, and the trunk, again, lay empty.

I began placing items in, as much as I could with nothing crashing around and making noise, and then shutting and reopening the lid, and starting anew. I put in weapons first—axes, hammers, swords. Then armor—breastplates, shields, belts, leggings. Then I started throwing in miscellaneous items, often empowered with magics—rings, amulets, an entire box of necklaces.

Satisfied that I had captured everything reasonable, I moved on to the next, crazy part of the plan. If Gavrial failed me, my end would be abrupt. I closed my eyes and took a deep breath. I was on El'daShar—I had plenty of mana. Letting out my calming breath, I pulled out the phone and readied it. Then put it back in a pocket and, with great effort, I took several tries to shift one end of the trunk to face it toward the open cave entrance, and get it far enough from the wall that I could worm my way between the trunk and the wall. The contents did not make the chest heavier, but it was heavy in its own right.

I checked the phone again. It was still ready.

One more deep breath.

Exhaling, I cast a spell, and a gust of wind pushed the chest out the door amidst the glaring of multiple alarms. I charged after it, and Blinked myself atop it as it broke through the railing and soared out into the middle of the bore. As though I rode trunks down bottomless pits all the time, I pulled out the phone and sent Gavrial the signal, and then tucked the phone away. I cast a magelight, sending it ahead as I rode the trunk down the enormous bore hole. If only the pit *were* bottomless.

Any day, Gavrial.

I knew, by the time I could see the bottom, it would be too late, but the magelight would help Gavrial.

As calm as I tried to appear, I didn't think my heart beat even once as I plummeted to my death. I did not know how close I came to the bottom, no idea if Gavrial performed a last second rescue, but I disappeared with the trunk in a flash of light.

I arrived where I expected in Orbanos, falling into a kind of magical net that had become a necessity on a world where the cities floated hundreds of feet above the ground. My fall, and that of the chest, slowed. When I stopped, Gavrial appeared beside me and Teleported us away. I could have 'Ported myself, but I didn't know if I could manage the trunk. Maybe. Maybe not. It wasn't the best time to find out.

But 'Porting it to two worlds, in as many minutes—Gavrial was an impressive Teleporter.

I found myself back in a cave, but the magic of the world tasted of the planet where I was born—AllForest. It startled me, but did not shock me, to see trolls roaming about the vast cave.

"Why here and not the Barrakrea?" I asked Gavrial, trying to sound calm despite the racing heart that had refused to beat as I'd plummeted down the bore. A troll spotted our sudden appearance and stomped a mighty foot on the ground three times.

"Too many eyes in the Barrakrea," he answered. "Besides, the people who need these are all here."

And sure enough, a group of people ran out of a side tunnel too small to fit a normal-sized troll. They spotted us immediately and calmed, sheathing weapons and calling a greeting to Gavrial. The group comprised several elves, Celymir and Lomamir among them, a mighty troll Warlord, heavily muscled and wearing leather and scale armor with a worn war axe strapped to his back. And a dwarf.

"Gavrial," the Warlord rumbled. "What ill news do you carry

today?"

"For once, Grundle, perhaps I bear fair tidings." The group surrounded us. Finding myself tired from the day's adventures, I leaned against the trunk. "You recall Galad?" Gavrial asked.

"I believe I once punched you off a cliff and sentenced you to death," the Warlord said to me. He turned back to Gavrial. "We are old friends."

I chuckled. He'd been no bigger than me at the time, but he'd grown. The tallest elves would not reach his shoulders. "How is Uncle Thudd?" I asked.

"Dead. He was too obvious a target for the dark elves. They picked him up again and took him somewhere we could not find him. But I thank you for the time he had."

Dark elves. The term described those willing to get paid to do Slooti's dirty work, seeking power or wealth in return for their foul deeds. The moniker befitted me, a hundred years before, and I felt sure many dark elves were convinced, as I had been, that they did the right thing.

"I am sorry for your loss," I said. I looked at Gavrial. If dark elves had taken Thudd again, and Gavrial did not know where, then Slooti had other Teleporters working for him. Or he'd found an artifact that granted Teleportation.

"This is a day I will remember," Celymir said. "Gavrial bringing good news. Or did you just bring us a pretty toy to warm our beds at night? Has your swordplay improved, Galad?" she asked with a smirk.

It stung, but not too badly. I had been all the things she mocked. Elves had long lives and long memories. I had reconciled myself to dealing with ridicule for many, many years. Ironically, neither my sister nor Celymir wore magic that protected them from my Empathy. And while I stayed out of Celymir's head, Lomamir dropped her guard and shot a question to my mind.

I hear you have been fighting on Orbanos, she thought to me. When she wasn't outright blocking me, our connection was quite good. Perhaps because I had first connected with her before she'd cut her first teeth. Regardless, I sensed her sadness at her last words to me, her sentencing me to die alongside Thudd.

You were right in what you did, I reassured her. *Or at least not wrong. I needed my eyes opened.* The depth of love and sadness I felt through the connection surprised me. Ara'andiel had been like a sister to me. How ironic that I could use that relationship to understand what it meant to have my actual sister be like a sister to me.

"I'm here to help," I said simply.

"And he's brought weapons," Gavrial said.

The dwarf squinted. "A single trunk of weapons," he said. "They'd better be something special."

"Relax," Grundle said, resting a hand on the dwarf's shoulder. "I am confident we will need your dwarven weapons as well."

So the dwarf smuggled goods. And I'd interfered with his business by doing some smuggling of my own. That didn't bode well for our relationship.

"Let's get this somewhere more protected and take a look," the Warlord said. He picked up one side, and said, "Harisidogle, would you do the honors?"

The dwarf picked up the other side, and the troll led us back up the hallway from which they had all come—a passage too small for the bigger trolls. We passed rooms, mostly without doors, though a few doors decorated the walls. I followed beside my sister, who watched me peer curiously into the chambers.

He is not the first Warlord, you know, she thought to me, smiling. *There were many trolls not hellbent on destroying the elves. There was Chisel, who first carved out this warren that only Warlords and troll children could fit in. Carve, who created some of the more intricate architecture of the rooms.* We passed, of all things, a library. I had a quick glimpse of intricate stone columns and shelves lined with books. *Smolder amassed the books in the library. He was alive when we were children.*

Smolder? I questioned. It was nice, very nice, conversing in my head again. And with Lomamir, it reminded me of our childhood.

Trolls don't generally get the concept of reading, she sent me. *They didn't know why he stared so long and hard at paper.*

They don't understand reading, but they know the word smolder? I threw in a hint of laughter.

Shows what you know, she jibed. *If you're around them long enough, you'll see a smolder.*

The connection felt so comfortable, so old, so familiar. Crazy that I had ever given that up for the life Slooti had presented me.

We stopped in a room that held maps and lists, and not just of the AllForest. The walls held maps of Orbanos, El'daShar, and many others, even a place labeled DwarkenHazen. I bet if I'd cast a spell to bring forth magical markers, I would have seen Teleport markers everywhere. They had been planning and preparing for war.

They set the chest down, and the troll opened it. It was empty. Of course! I had last filled it, so now it waited for more.

The troll merely raised an eyebrow. I held up a placating hand and walked over. I closed the lid and opened it again.

"Nice trick," Grundle chuckled. The last load had been odds and ends, the box of necklaces, some amulets and rings. The troll picked up a bracelet and held it to a magelight that hovered in the room. Shrugging, he slid it on a massive finger. He looked at it oddly and shrugged again. "I can't tell that it does *anything*."

"It may not. The last load was all sundry knickknacks. If we take them out, close and open the lid, we will get to the next load. There are hundreds of magical weapons and armor in there. We will need a bigger room to unload them."

"Nice trick," the dwarf echoed. "*That* could be an enormous benefit to my job."

The troll laughed, but stopped abruptly, slamming the trunk closed. I knew why—I felt two things at the same time. One was the thudding foot-stomp warnings of the trolls. The other was a very powerful Coercion.

I threw an Empathic shield around the occupants of the room, keeping them hidden and protected.

"Go!" I shouted to Gavrial. My gut told me we dealt with an attack from Slooti. Maybe a counterattack from my raid on the Hall? Gavrial's presence would put the spy network of the resistance in jeopardy.

"Wait!" Grundle urged. "Take him," he said, pointing at the dwarf. "You know what we need. That," he said, pointing at the chest, "changes nothing."

"Fool," the dwarf said amiably, hurrying over to Gavrial. "That changes *everything*."

Gavrial and the dwarf disappeared.

"There is a strong Empath in the caves!" I shouted. "You should all wait until I neutralize him."

The troll chuckled and tapped his head, his magically resistant head. It wasn't foolproof, but it was something.

"Go," he told everyone else, sliding something into the trunk. "You know the plans if this goes wrong."

Brother, Lomamir sent me. *Keep him safe. I know I told you that many Warlords were not hellbent on war. Grundle is. We need him. Even knowing his plans, I can't pull this off without him.*

I felt a moment of pride. Lomamir was the second in command. If the Warlord died, the resistance fell to her.

I'll do the best I can, I reassured her. *I'm proud of you, Lomamir. And I love you.*

And I, you, brother! she shot back.

I felt a hint of Mom and Dad in the bond, the shared memories making them almost real, and smiling over us.

Grundle and I charged down the corridor. I had my sword out, and he held a war axe. I wished we'd had just a few more minutes—enough time to go through the chest and pick some magical weapons. But we had what we had.

As we got closer to the enormous cavern, the Compulsion grew stronger, beckoning us to come out and surrender. No Empath had shown such power when I had left El'daShar. Where had the new Empath come from?

We charged out of the corridor into the chamber where Gavrial had originally 'Ported us in. It surprised me to see Slooti there himself, along with a small cadre of elves surrounding him. Which was the Empath?

I charged in with a roaring Warlord by my side. Other trolls remained in the cave, and with the Warlord's yell, they charged in as well. One threw a boulder as it attacked.

A translucent red shield shot up around Slooti and his team, and the boulder bounced harmlessly to the side. We hadn't reached it yet, but I suspected it would fail before a continued battering from the trolls. Whichever elf could Teleport would whisk them away when the shield failed.

I just had to keep the Empath at bay until then. As long as no one surrendered, Slooti and his crew would leave empty-handed.

"Galad!" Slooti said, not loud, but I heard it over the roaring of the trolls. "I thought you dead. This all makes sense now. I can't believe I didn't see it. I knew there were spies in my court, but I thought you were mine."

He wasn't shouting. How did I hear him so well?

"I was," I answered. "But I learned you were using me." I continued charging forward.

"Everyone uses everyone," he said. "You know that. But I am glad to know I've found the leader of the rebellion and his battle planner."

Leader of the rebellion? Well, if it kept him distracted from Lomamir, that was all for the better. And the troll Warlord my battle planner. Ha!

An odd thought skittered across my mind—I should have reached Slooti's shield. I charged on, looking at the shield and Slooti inside, the trolls closing in. One threw a boulder and charged.

Wait! That image nagged at my brain, somehow familiar.

I did a double take. The troll still charged. The boulder bounced harmlessly off the shield. I watched the troll, focusing.

"You *are* strong," Slooti said. The scene shifted. Slooti stood before me. I looked around, confused. The Warlord crouched on his knees beside me, arms pinned behind him by something. The ground appeared to be too close—because I knelt. When did that happen?

"Up," he said, and I rose to my feet, powerless to do otherwise, as did the Warlord. "Take me to what you stole from me."

I started walking back up the corridor.

"Ghhhhhh," Grundle growled next to me. He seemed no more

418

able to resist than I.

I'd been an Empath a long time and had some tricks up my sleeve. I split my mind, letting a piece continue to be controlled. But with the other piece, I watched, and I poked and prodded.

An elf Compelled me. But which one? Though I watched carefully, none seemed to do anything I recognized as my own spells. I'd heard Slooti above the shouting. I'd heard *Slooti*.

Slooti had the Amp, albeit the finger-sized one, and he had another crystal. *Mother of Trees.* He'd found a way to Compel. We marched into the war room.

"You've been busy," Slooti said. "Show me what you took."

I walked over to the trunk.

He approached the trunk, Grundle following in his wake. The others had fled the room—good.

He flipped the lid open and glanced in. "Empty," he stated. "What a stupid way to lose," he said to me. "But I'm happy with how this new crystal has turned out."

He closed the trunk, and turned to his small cadre. "Faraviel, take us back to El'daShar—I need to get the leader of the rebellion on a very public trial. A lesson must be taught. Adridd, hunt down any remaining rebels and destroy them."

Locked in Slooti's spell, I could witness, but I could not break free from the Compulsion. He could have been combining his finger-sized Amp and a new crystal. Regardless, once he took me away, I would get locked in chains that sapped my magic. I felt my last chance evaporating. I *pushed*. I *fought*. And I *cringed* as the Teleport picked me up and took me away.

Chapter 87

Elliah

I didn't know who looked more startled—Slooti or me. Slooti, seeing the woman he believed to be stranded on an entirely different world, accompanied by humans, a dwarf, and a troll, standing on his balcony. Or me, looking into a resplendent and luxurious feast, hosted by Slooti, accompanied by the spitting image of *myself*, giggling next to him with a glass of wine, all while the world below had the life sucked out of it.

The room bubbled with people, but at a wave of Slooti's hand, they all froze. Not the *uh-oh there's danger and I'm a squirrel* kind of frozen… but rather the *someone has control of my mind* kind of frozen.

"Ahhhgh," Galad moaned, clutching his head. "If you have a plan, now's the time."

I noticed the crown on Slooti's head, embedded gems glowing. He'd somehow crafted a magical device that enabled Empathy.

I didn't have a plan. It didn't seem the time to point that out.

"Why, Slooti?" I asked the crown-wearing megalomaniac. "The man I once loved would not condemn his own race to this living death."

"Zombies," Tali muttered.

"It's temporary," he said, his demeanor moving past the initial surprise, his emotions hidden. "The MultiGel will grow, and more magic will come through." He waved at the marble-sized ball of light over the his-and-hers throne which rested behind him. He looked at my twin, frozen next to him, younger than me by ten or twenty human years, dressed in beautiful robes, hair coiffed, bejeweled and beautiful. "I captured the best of you, don't you think?"

I'd realized long ago that he didn't like the real me, but it surprised me to learn how much he had obsessed about my looks. "You should see me with red hair in my Vera Wang," I tossed his way, hoping to derail his monologue.

"She isn't as nasty as you, of course," he said, smiling at me. He casually ran a hand down her cheek.

While he ogled his trophy, I scanned the room for other elves I knew, and found none I recognized.

"It might be fun, having the *actual* Elliahspane back," he said, making his younger copy twirl around like a dancer, with a wave of his hand, then freezing her in place again.

Mother of Trees, Slooti has lost his mind!

"Galad," he said, turning his attention to the struggling Empath. "So good to see you again. I hated having to Banish you, but I did have to set an example. You'd been like a son to me. I was *so* disappointed when you started that silly rebellion. You almost kept *this* from me." He held up a scepter that brandished a yellow gem at its head.

Harry, Grundle, and Red all moved to attack, and Tali took aim with her handgun. A field popped up between Slooti and the rest of us, the images on the other side tinted slightly red, and the dwarf, troll, and human all came crashing to a halt when they hit it. Tali fired again and again, but the bullets' momentum dissipated when they hit the field, and they clattered to the floor, the tinny dings quiet after the noisy blasts.

"Interesting," Slooti said, looking at Tali's weapon. He took stock of his attackers, as I squinted at his crown. Another artifact—it housed multiple gems that enabled Talents and transferred those powers to Slooti. His accumulated power unnerved me.

"The pesky dwarf!" Slooti declared happily. "I never thought I'd get the chance to rip your organs from you one by one, yet here you are! Oh, thank you, Elliah, for this *little* gift."

"Too... much... talk!" Harry declared, whacking the semi-transparent field with Baessandra between his words.

"Oh," Slooti carried on, "and the last living troll. I get to kill the last troll! That is *sooooo* fitting." He practically crooned.

"You can't hold me out forever, you know," Slooti told Galad conversationally. "You may be good, maybe the best! But I have the Amp," he said, rapping the butt of his scepter on the ground. The fist-sized red crystal danced with light at the top, promising power and pain, but reminding me, incongruously, of the promise of laughter that died with Jeb.

"I can't let you do this," I told Slooti. "You're killing the elves, my children."

"Oh, dear, despised Elliah, *you* are the one, *once again*, killing *your children*!"

His slam, targeting my beloved Jeb, riled me.

"Even for this little bit of fighting, I've had to redirect power from the Amp, which was boosting the radiant magic from the MultiGel, in order to fight *you*! It is *your* actions that kill the elves."

I did my thing, letting my consciousness drift to the ambient magic, and confirmed his statement. The magic from the tower had diminished, and elves below died. I felt their tiny magical presences, the pinpricks of energy-absorption that marked an elf, snuffing out. I felt the diameter of the circle of life closing in on the tower.

"Please, stop," I pleaded.

"You first," he said, nodding at Galad.

Shit. If Galad stopped, all our minds would fall under Slooti's control. I could cut off the magic from the thing he called the MultiGel—that was my Gift—but I would sentence all the other elves to death. What if Slooti spoke the truth? That the MultiGel would grow, and more magic would emanate from the other worlds? If they lived through the day, the elves might return to their youthful state, as I had on Earth.

But if his artifact drew that much magic, wouldn't he draw the Infected to his new world as well? Had he really solved anything? More likely he would live the illusionary life of his dreams, with little care how others suffered, keeping just enough Elves alive to serve him without drawing the Infected.

Slooti's words from millennia before echoed through my mind. "We cannot respect life that does not respect us! They killed my son!" *You never respected the goblins, Slooti. You never thought of our son as more than a means to an end. You never respected any of them.* I should have listened to Gav and taken on this fight... long ago.

I couldn't pull the plug on the magic that kept the elves alive. But I also couldn't let Slooti take us over. He continued to draw magic away from the elves through the Amp, fighting Galad in an Empathic battle, keeping up the shield that blocked us from him, and holding the other elves in stasis. I looked at him, the man I had once, long ago, loved. The man I had spent years trying not to fight—a choice that led to thousands of years trapped on a desert island of a world. I locked eyes with Slooti, and watched as I clipped the magic that flowed *from* him to form his spells.

The entire room jerked into motion as the magic Slooti channeled lost its outlet, and the man I had sworn never to fight... burst in an explosion of light.

Chapter 88

Hughelas, about 15 Earth millennia in the past

The darkness suited me. Grim. Quiet. Empty of purpose. I shivered, and a passing thought made me chuckle soundlessly—El'daShar was not naturally cold and damp; Slooti must have assigned mages to purposefully keep his dungeon in that condition. What an amusing waste. Still, the damp chill as I hung by my wrists, chained in the dark, suited me well.

A light ambled closer. Magelight.

Clang! I'd expected the noise, but jumped all the same. Better if they thought me cowed. "No sleeping, ear sucker!" Kamilia barked. My jailer. She did try—she went a little over the top, but she tried. She'd get better at it, undoubtedly.

"Please," I pleaded. "I'm so tired." Which was true. They'd shackled my arms above me, but not so high that my feet left the ground. I just couldn't sit or lie down. But my plea was just an act, probably no better than Kamilia's. I'd lost too much. Given up too much. But I played along. Gav needed me to.

"You'll get sleep when you tell me where *she* is."

I groaned. "Can't tell what I don't know."

"You know," she accused.

I didn't. At least not specifically. And I'd already told them what I knew. Because—why not? "She fled to another world. She's gone. I don't know where."

"We've been over this," she said. "When you're ready to talk, ready to tell me, let me know." She tried to look scornful, but she couldn't really pull it off. Her face was made for joy. How had she ever landed the role of jailer?

She banged the bars again for emphasis and stalked down the hall, continuing her route, though I didn't think they caged anyone else down there. Though possibly, in a distant cell. Sometimes I imagined I heard someone else.

The ironic part—*one* ironic part—was that I probably *could* use my Gift to see where Elliah had gone. But I couldn't do that without sleep. My jailer, and the High Lord, did not know how my Gift worked. They, inadvertently, prevented me from helping them.

The light eventually faded to nothing, and I hung there, in the dark damp chill, and let the bleakness creep over me again. As an elf, I literally could not die of old age in the damp cell, but I'd also lived long enough to know better than to worry about forever—things always changed. Eventually. The bleakness would fade. One day there would be light, beauty, and joy. Being chained up in a melodramatically damp and bleak cave reflected my inner landscape, suiting me just fine.

Bamf. There was a flash of light and then an even deeper darkness as my eyes bleached from the flash. Kelivine must have been far enough on her route that she hadn't seen—I heard no rush of footfalls in the hallway.

"Gav," I said in greeting, still unable to see him.

"Hugh," he said, as tired as I'd ever heard him.

"Your plans didn't work out the way you hoped?" I asked.

"Hugh," he said again.

"Please tell me you got back in Slooti's good graces. That I'm not here for nothing."

"Hugh!" he whisper-shouted.

I shut up.

He sighed. "FreeWorld is gone," he informed me.

Gone? "Gav, what does *gone* mean?"

"Destroyed," he said. "Something new. Something horrible. Everyone's dead."

"Gav, it's not *your* job to break my spirits. Besides, they're already pretty broken." But I didn't think he was joking. Or lying. It wasn't Gavrial's style of lies. I didn't think my heart could sink any further. But once again, I found myself wrong.

"This creature—" I began.

"Creatures," he said. "Millions. Maybe billions. They took over. I can't even get close to any cities."

"What do they want?"

"I can't tell." My night vision had returned—the grey outline of Gav's lips pursed as he thought. "Nothing. They seem to be waiting."

"For what?"

"I don't know."

We stood in silence for a time. He cast a spell and freed my arms. They fell to my sides, useless. I lowered myself to the ground using just my legs and the wall behind me.

A small, dim magelight appeared, but the pain of blood returning to my arms consumed me. He must have done some summoning, because the next thing I knew, he poured two drinks from a bottle, and set them down on a small table that hadn't been in my cell minutes before. Two chairs appeared, and he helped me into one of them.

"So what's your plan?" I asked. Gavrial always had a plan. I took a sip from my cup. It burned pleasantly. "This is from FreeWorld?" I asked, holding up the glass.

"Yes, from your warehouse. I can still get there. Two of those creatures sit in the field outside. Waiting. And I don't have a plan. I'm out of ideas. FreeWorld is lost, so the goblins are again decimated."

Ah. The goblins. Always the goblins with Gavrial. "Well, I suppose without the goblins, you won't have to obsess over removing Slooti from power." It was an ill-considered statement. But I'd been through a lot too.

Gavrial just grunted, then took a drink from his own cup. "My problem with Slooti predates my knowledge of the goblins. But what he did to the goblins was *bad*."

I took another drink. "He didn't know what he was doing. No one knew we were killing them. When they attacked, Slooti's response was that of a grieving father. A grieving father who had too much power, but a grieving father."

Gavrial tapped his glass repeatedly on the table, like a clock ticking. "He knew," Gavrial choked out.

And just when I thought I had nothing left to lose, another piece of my world fell apart.

"He knew he was killing the goblins. The day the goblins killed their son, I was there. Jeb was telling his father about the goblins, about their cities, about their shows, about their eggs and their magic." He took another drink. "About their population declining since the elves had shown up. But Slooti already knew."

"That," I said slowly, taking another drink, "is so much worse."

We sat in silence for a time, each in our own hell, until I broke it. "Why did you never tell Elliah? You wanted her to fight Slooti. That would have done it."

Gav grunted. He took another drink and then refilled his glass. "For such a smart elf, you have a gift for ignoring reality."

I knew that to be a fairly accurate statement. Perhaps it was because of my Gift—I spent too much time in other realities. I liked believing that was the reason. Alternatively, I was self-involved, which I'd been told by people close to me. Either way, what was he specifically getting at?

"Maybe," Gav said, and I thought he meant Elliah might have fought Slooti. "You didn't know Slooti well back then. But you've not ignored him entirely. He's manipulative. He's greedy. He's self-serving. Do you really think Slooti would have been content to let Elliah go? Just go?"

I chewed on that for a minute. There had been a time, when Elliah first arrived on FreeWorld, that I believed Slooti would hunt her down. After all, Slooti had sent Gav to find me. So I assumed he would send someone to find Elliah. When the realization struck me, I gasped. "You were reporting back to Slooti!" I couldn't believe it. "The whole time we were on FreeWorld, you were reporting back to Slooti." It was unfathomable. We had shared a table, shared drinks… over hundreds of years. He had bed Elliah and had a child. My mind spun. "I thought you were my friend," I choked out.

"I was not." His speech slurred with drink. "Would a friend have landed you here?" he asked, gesturing grandly in my tiny cell. He took another drink.

So, what then? He was there to kill me? To end it? Why else tell me? But what could I do about it? I had no significant magic. I had no clever ruse. He was a Teleporter—I didn't stand a chance. But those thoughts passed quickly. I found I didn't really care—I had lost too much. Dying in a cell where a self-serving leader had imprisoned me, betrayed by someone I thought to be my friend—it fit my mood.

"So why are you telling me now?" I asked, pushing the issue into action. May as well be done with it.

But it didn't work.

"I may not be your friend," he said. "But you are mine." He took a drink. "My only friend, I think. And today, when the entire world went to *shit*, I wanted to drink with my friend."

His words appalled me. "Our friendship was a lie!"

"It began that way. At some point, I began protecting you."

"Protecting me? Why would I believe that?"

He drank again. "Don't care if you believe it. You have nothing I need." He shrugged. Then he held his glass up, waiting for me to take mine.

I glared. The seconds ticked by. He shrugged again and downed his glass.

My anger flared. I mean, in the scheme of things, I'd been more angry. My anguish muted any emotions. But I *knew* that, if I wasn't so depressed, I'd have been *really* pissed.

"You're just like Slooti," I accused.

He froze. That was more like it. He didn't deserve to sit and drink with anyone, finding comfort in a false friendship.

"You manipulate," I said. "You deceive. You use people to achieve your own ends." He nodded along, then started chuckling to himself. That wouldn't do. "You even *look* like him." He stopped laughing. "Blond hair. Blue eyes." He slammed his glass down. Wait, why had *that* hit a chord?

"So, you've figured it out then," he said, voice slurred.

"That's right," I told him, with no idea what we spoke about. I held my silence. He held his.

Finally he sighed and poured another drink. I kept quiet. "Slooti cheated on Elliah," he said, then gestured grandly, like he had just earned a standing ovation. "The iron nut seed doesn't fall far from the tree."

Mother of Trees.

I was so confused.

"Why did you try to convince Elliah to fight him?" He had done so. Many times.

"I had to know she wouldn't."

"So you were protecting him."

"For a time. And then I was protecting her."

"Why the goblins then? Why did you incite them?"

"That was after I changed my mind. My heart." He stared into a dark corner. "Slooti is a monster. My father is a monster." He tried to stand but hit his leg on the table and sat back down clumsily. "I'm a monster."

He was. A monster. He'd cost so many lives. Whether in the name of Slooti, or in order to overthrow him, Gav had cost many lives.

And yet… "You *know* where Elliah is," I reminded him. If he came clean, she would fight. Yes, she might fight *Gav* as well, but she would fight Slooti.

"I'm not bringing Elliah into this," he said, drunkenly. "She's earned her peace."

Well, I'll be a troll's uncle.

We sat in silence for a time. It was my turn to sip and think. Gav may have even dozed off.

"She should have the choice," I finally said.

Gav snorted. I couldn't tell if I'd just woken him up, or he was mocking the idea.

"We need to give Elliah the choice of whether or not to fight," I explained. "You may think you're protecting her by keeping her remote. But you may be killing her. And the elves. It isn't your call, Gav. Yes, she might die. She might lose. She might choose not to fight. But it isn't fair for you to make the choice for her."

I wasn't sure if he was even awake. He just sat there. I thought of what to say to convince him.

"I'm out of moves, Hugh. What do you propose we do?"

And we spent hours coming up with a basic plan. The first steps of which would get me officially out of my shackles and granted a limited freedom—by giving up the secret of the Scrying Stone. The plan would give the goblins a chance, no matter Elliah's decision. Either she would fight for them, or she would run away with them. But I felt sure she'd stay and fight Slooti.

We would pull Elliah in; Elliah would change things.

Chapter 89

Slooti, near-present time

"She's down the hall," Adridd informed me, immediately after Faraviel 'Ported me to a cave on AllForest in a bright flash of light. "The map room—third door on the left. We caught her sneaking into their war room. Norielia zapped her from behind." Norielia had a Talent for electricity; a crude, dim-witted woman, but good in a fight. "We wrapped her up in numb-metal. We hoped to force her to reveal where the other rebels hide." His instant awareness of my arrival spoke volumes about his state of mind. I still considered Coercion something of a last resort—it meant I hadn't created the right framework. I had no need of Coercion nor Compulsion with Adridd.

Illusion, on the other hand, I used with no qualms. After all, creating a perception that people bought into—I'd mastered that aspect of illusion ages before. Gaining the power of Illusion through a TalentStone had been the most natural extension of my mind that I had encountered. I should have been born an Illusionist. Sadly, I still had to be discreet in the Council. Several Illusionists sat on the council, and I couldn't risk any of them seeing through my spells. But I had no such limitation in my secret war on the AllForest.

"Come," I told Faraviel. It saddened me that I resorted to using Coercion on her. My own wife! But I had no time to help her see reason. I'd built up Galad for thousands of years, and something or someone on the AllForest broke him. He'd disappeared, and an Empath can be almost as hard to find as an Illusionist. I suffered for lack of an Empath of Galad's caliber. He never understood how well he kept the population distracted—probably my best illusion. I sighed as we walked down the hall. He'd turned out to be helping the rebels. I'd needed to make a public display in order to rebuild my foundation. And then Faraviel had taken his side! I'm sure she'd felt that, as my wife, as High Lady, she could speak up. But I'd only married her because I needed a 'Porter—we hadn't yet found a world with Teleportation TalentStones—and I couldn't manipulate Gav. I sighed again. At least it wasn't a complete waste; Faraviel had sympathized with the rebels, and I could use that.

A guard stood outside the door, tall and proud, doing his duty. "Good job," I told him. "Thank you for your work. Go see Adridd about your next tasks." The guard nodded and strode away down the hall. I could have kept him under Illusion, but having him gone simplified things.

My enchanted crown helped me use multiple TalentStones at once, but it took concentration. And I didn't enjoy Coercing the way I enjoyed Illusion, where the game of making people believe through magic, instead of just using words, still intrigued me. But the situation before me required both Talents. So I kept Faraviel under Coercion, and cast an Illusion on myself. Let the game begin!

"Galad!" Lomamir shouted as I banged the door open, charging in with Faraviel on my heels. The room threw me off—I'd been there before. The maps littered the floor instead of the table, but the walls still held glyphs of Teleport destinations. A massive treasure chest sat in the room; I remembered finding it empty.

"Lomamir!" I rushed to her side of the room, my Illusion of Galad illustrating my grief about the blood and bruises that marred her face and arms.

"Faraviel," Lomamir said, closing her eyes. "By all that's green, you got him out."

"Lomamir," I panted. "We have to get you out of here." Though chains held her imprisoned, Galad would have said something similarly heartfelt and stupid.

The shackles sucked her mana dry—a general spell that burned off the mana of anything it touched. They wouldn't stop a Talent, or even an old enough mage, like Lomamir. We must have been drugging or beating her, or both. I fumbled with the chains for a moment, then feigned frustration and created a beam of heat that carefully melted through one shackle, and then the other.

"We have to get you out of here!" I made Faraviel exclaim. She looked around desperately at the markings on the wall—my skills at using two Talents at once continued to improve! "Where? Where is safe? Hurry, Galad!" She looked back at the door as the chains pulled apart with a racket of metal against metal and stone.

"Quickly," Lomamir said, desperate, "take us to…"

The world spun. I opened my eyes to see Lomamir reaching for my crown of TalentStones, laying on the ground a body length away. Growling, I ignored the pain in my head and covered the crown with a shield. A blast of wind shoved me against the wall. I created another shield to stop the wind. Fire flew from Lomamir's hands, stopping midway between us with a third shield.

Enough! I clamped her hands with shields, preventing mnemonics. Vines crawled up my legs anyway. Her skill was phenomenal. But unlike the culture I'd encouraged for eons, I had not been idle. I severed the vines with a scythe-like swipe while pushing the crown my way with a shield. Lomamir tried to fling the crown back with more vines, but I had her beat. She looked away and I followed her eyes. Blood dripped in front of my left eye, but I still spotted what had caught Lomamir's attention.

Faraviel's mad dash for the crown came to a crashing halt on a translucent red wall.

I reached down and retrieved my trophy, scowling as blood dropped on it. My blood. Lomamir had slugged me with her chains. I coerced Faraviel, and she climbed to her feet, mesmerized. But I left Lomamir free to think. Locked in even tighter shields with the boost from the crown, but free to think.

"How did you know?" I asked. I walked to the table and found a cloth map on the floor.

"Does it matter? I could tell you weren't my brother."

After Healing the wound on my forehead, I wiped the blood off. "I suppose not, though I'm disappointed. I'd had such a clever ruse. You would have been so happy to help me. And now I'm just going to resort to brute force."

I felt something hit the shield I'd constructed behind me. I turned to see a simple stone, albeit one that would have knocked off my crown.

"Your control is outstanding," I said. "In retrospect, I chose the wrong sibling to make mine."

The first stone turned out to be a distraction, but none of the others reached me, glancing off impromptu shields. I grew increasingly frustrated by Lomamir's impertinence.

Coercion it was.

I'd hoped to do this the easy way, I spoke into her mind. *Now, where is the Amp?* The Amp was the key. Other pieces of the puzzle still needed to slide into place, but I needed that Amp. The small one I'd found helped, but I needed the one I'd learned about from my spies. I showed a picture of the Warlord, holding the Amp.

I felt her mental gasp.

Yes, you are not the only one capable of enticing betrayals. Let it eat at her, not knowing who had betrayed her rebellion. In reality, Lomamir had used the Amp to stop a raid where I'd sent loyalists to conscript more trolls. When they didn't return, Adridd's investigation discovered a loyalist survivor. A clumsy mistake on the part of the rebels.

I'd been content to let them pick at my forces, knowing that the power I amassed with a single TalentStone far outweighed the losses I incurred. Until I'd plucked the memory of that Amp from the survivor's mind. That had changed my plans, instigating the attack that had netted me the Warlord and Galad.

You'll tell me where you've hidden that GiftStone. Your brother, the strongest Empath to live, couldn't resist my Coercion. I tapped at the small Amp in my crown, showing her what I'd used to defeat her brother.

"The thing is…" She spoke aloud, not deigning to share the mental connection with me. "My brother never had to hold back an Empath. Whereas I spent my entire *life…* practicing against the *strongest Empath to live!*" And with those words, my Coercion slipped away.

Her defiance put me in mind of Elliah. Mother of Trees how I'd loved and despised her. She'd constantly thwarted my plans, never caring that she'd done so. She'd been so unaware of people's sentiment, and yet led them so powerfully. It had taken a child to distract her enough that I could make any genuine progress on capturing people's hearts and minds.

On the bright side, keeping me out of her head prevented her from assailing me with stones, vines, and fire. "I almost hate breaking you," I said. "You would have made a fantastic High Lady."

Lomamir's eyes darted over to Faraviel, who still stood, trance-like, and slightly bruised and disheveled from her headlong plunge into my shield.

"You have such power and control," I said. "It is truly sad that you cannot see what we could accomplish together."

"You... *disgust*... me!"

Unfortunate.

I stalked toward her, holding her imprisoned in shields, wrapped in a bubble of Coercion. I smiled, inches from her face, then leaned in and slid my tongue slowly up her neck to the base of her ear.

"You... sick... *bastard!* Your... wife... *watches!*"

I bade Faraviel come closer.

Pulling away, I teased the lobe of Lomimar's ear with my teeth. I wanted her to see the Illusion I'd crafted. "Ahh, my sweet sister," I crooned in Galad's birdsong voice, as I leaned back in to lead my tongue up to her other ear.

I followed her anger and loathing deeper into her mind, using it to set hooks.

She growled and jerked free, both of my tongue and my mental barbs.

"You... will... not... *break me!*"

"Maybe not," I said. But I'd seen a spike of interest in Faraviel's mind. She'd desired Galad! And I needed the Amp. I stared into Lomamir's eyes. "But perhaps breaking *her* will break you."

Faraviel screamed as she dropped to the ground in pain and fear induced by my Illusions and Coersions, and Lomamir gasped.

It wasn't the right kind of gasp. I threw a shield behind myself and dodged to the side.

Mother of Trees!

It stood tall, skin black as night, mouth and eyes covered with skin, clawing at my red, translucent shield. An Infected. The things that had obliterated the humans. And it clawed through my shield, shredding it.

Screams echoed from the halls. Lomamir still snarled—if she feared her fate, I could not see it. Tears ran down Faraviel's cheeks—I'd broken her. Something one of them did had been a trigger. Another monster appeared in the room, and I threw up new shields, which it also tore into.

Rotting vines!

On the bright side, Lomamir had new motivation.

"The Amp, Lomamir! I can stop them, but I need the Amp!"

"I… won't… fall… for… your… Illusions."

She thought I tricked her. It infuriated me to be blocked when so close. I sent a scythe-blade of a shield through the Infected, but it didn't decapitate them the way I'd intended, the magic fading before it did more than cut them. And more creatures appeared. The screams in the hallway had stopped.

I needed to go.

I looked around the room, desperate for some sign of the Amp. But the room offered too many possibilities. Glyphs on the walls marked Teleportation spots. Maps on the floor hinted that the Amp could be anywhere. No maps sat on the trunk, but…

The empty trunk. I peered through the shields and the monsters trying to get past them. That trunk had elven engravings on it. Why did a chest of elvish design sit in the caves of a troll Warlord? I pushed on my shields, trying to carve a path.

Lomamir laughed, dark and low. "How… ironic." Her belief in the reality of the Infected came too late to benefit me. She couldn't help me.

The monsters tore my shields faster than I could create new ones.

I Compelled Faraviel to take us back to El'daShar. The chest wasn't going anywhere. I would send someone to pick it up later. Did the Infected appear because of Faraviel? Perhaps it was time for a new High Lady.

On the bright side, I thought, as Faraviel and I vanished, *the*

Infected decimated the rebels, and the threat of the Infected will motivate the remaining elves to follow me.

Chapter 90

Hughelas, about 15 Earth millennia in the past

Despite myself, I felt a glimmer of excitement. Yes, my insides felt hollowed out from loss, my future held together by a slim thread of trickery that I couldn't even convince myself to be worth it, but a better life for elves hinged on the next hour. That warranted a little excitement, didn't it? She would have appreciated the endeavor, which made me smile, then cry. *Mother of Trees, why do we have to lose the ones we love?*

Bamf

With a flash of light and a quiet *bamf*, my prison cell no longer contained just me. I couldn't breathe, and I couldn't see. The air literally withheld from my lungs, kept back by magic, yet the thought running through my head was irritation that they'd arrived while tears ran down my face. Slooti didn't deserve that satisfaction. The flash of the Teleportation, and the summoned Magelight, had overwhelmed my eyes, but dark blobs in the light coalesced.

"Where is she?" Slooti demanded. *She's dead. But you didn't even know about her.* "And if you say 'who,' it will be the last word you speak."

Air returned to my lungs and I sucked it in. I took a couple of breaths, realizing that my tear-stained face worked in my favor.

"I don't know," I groaned. "*She* came to *me*. You know I cannot Teleport." Hopefully he would not push on how Elliah would know where to find me. Bit of a weak point in our story, but ascribing mysterious powers and knowledge to Elliah would have to do if he pushed me.

"You lie!" Slooti accused. My eyesight had adjusted sufficiently that I could make out other visitors. I knew Gav would be there, but it surprised me to see a third visitor. *Who?*

"I've never been able to Teleport," I said matter-of-factly. "Life would have been much simpler, though likely much shorter, if I could." A Teleporter with my Gift? I would have traveled to a world of my dreams and been incinerated, electrocuted, drowned... dead is dead.

"You lie about not knowing Elliah's whereabouts," Slooti spat in frustration. "Tell me where she is!"

"Why would I tell anything to the man who locked me up just for existing?" I countered.

Smack

The world spun dizzyingly. Who had hit me? The third elf stood before me, clad in shining silver-colored armor, wiping blood off his gauntlet. Not silver, but an enchanted metal, untarnished and not soft at all. The passing thought of whether the metal came from FreeWorld made me think of *her*, and I had a moment of disorienting anger before the hollowness returned. I spat more on his boots, and he raised a hand to strike me again, but a red translucent shield appeared before my face, and the warrior withheld his blow.

"I need answers, Hughelas Do'wood," Slooti said more calmly. "Why did she come to your cell?"

"She was looking for something," I said. I looked away, like it pained me to tell him. "An artifact I discovered long ago. A crystal."

"Why?" Slooti asked.

"Why should I tell *you*?" I asked in return, returning my gaze to his, showing how little I had to lose.

The warrior struck me again. I spat blood awkwardly while the stars danced around my head.

"If you help me find her," Slooti said, "I will free you from your shackles."

I couldn't speak—my jaw sat askew, dislocated or broken. I tried anyway. "Uh wa oo ee ee."

"Fix him," Slooti said, irritated.

A wave of Healing washed through me, coming from Gav, not the warrior with the malicious grin.

"I want to be free... free of the dungeon," I said. "I want to walk among my fellow elves, feel the sunlight on my skin, watch the trees grow." A touch melodramatic, perhaps, but once I spoke the words, I recognized that somewhere beyond the hollowness that engulfed me, they rang true.

"If wishes were dragons, then elflings would ride," Slooti said.

"Wouldn't that be something?" I said, letting some wonder creep into my eyes. Again, a touch over the top.

"Idiot," the warrior said. Not a word from Gav. We had to be careful not to reveal any connection.

"Eternity is a long time to be shackled," Slooti reminded me.

Truth be told, getting out of the shackles had been all I'd hoped for. I had little mana, but the damn shackles stole even that. At least, unshackled, I would have the freedom to end my misery if I chose—not part of what I'd advertised to Gav. The quiet stretched on. If I waited, would he offer me more, or would he give the degenerate warrior free rein to convince me to talk?

"She wanted the *Banishment Stone*," I said. Gav and I had come up with that name. I thought it sounded sufficiently menacing.

Slooti squinted skeptically and the sadist readied his gauntletted fist.

"It sends people away to worlds with no magic," I said. "One-way trip."

"If the trip is one-way," Slooti questioned, "how do you know where they go?"

"My visions," I said. Fortunately, his question didn't surprise me. "I've seen the other end."

Slooti remained skeptical. "Let's say I believed you. Why does Elliah want it? *Where is she?*"

"A way to be rid of your enemies?" I asked, leading him with my voice.

Slooti paused. His eyebrows knit in concentration. Not a good look on Slooti; I understood why he spent so much time smiling.

The Magelight turned on in his head. "She's here! She means to send me away." Slooti grabbed my bloody, ragged shirt and lifted me, which relieved some of the long-endured pressure on my shoulders. "Tell me where she is!" he demanded.

"Like I said," I groaned, "I don't know. She told me she'd free me if I told her the location of the Stone, but she left me here." I tried to sound bitter as I enjoyed the sensation of not hanging by my arms.

The warrior reached out to strike, the logistics confusing me. With Slooti holding me up, the angle for a good smacking looked wrong.

"But I've heard her!" I shouted, cringing.

"What?" Slooti said quietly, throwing a shield up to catch the warrior's blow. I tried not to laugh as he pulled his fist back in pain.

"Noises," I said. "Down the hall. I'm sure of it. If you all weren't so busy questioning me, you'd have heard—"

"Quiet!" Slooti shouted, dropping me.

I couldn't help but gasp when my body's weight attempted to pull my shoulders from their sockets. But I quieted myself as quickly as possible. I needed them to hear.

Slooti Blinked himself into the hall, turning each way, then stalking to the right.

"Whether or not he frees you from your shackles," the warrior whispered to me, "I will enjoy causing you a great deal of pain for all eternity."

Gav raised an eyebrow out of the line of sight of the warrior.

"Gavrial!" Slooti shouted. "Bring me Bomar!"

Gav disappeared, taking the dark-hearted warrior with him. They flashed into existence outside my cell but immediately vanished again. "The StoneWorker?" I heard Gav ask from down the hall.

"Bring my whole menagerie, plus Bomar. He will carve me a path to Elliah."

Chapter 91

Galad, near-present time

Distant shuffling broke the near-silence of our breathing. Grundle and I waited in the pitch black cell, and even our breathing became more quiet as the shuffling approached.

I winced as I thought of my declaration, long ago, that elves had no prisons. I'd been so naive. We hung by our arms in just such a prison, waiting for Slooti to create the proper spectacle of our Banishment.

The shuffling stopped outside our cell door. I dared to hope for some kind of rescue. Why else approach so secretively?

A Magelight flared, revealing a disheveled and gaunt elf. He sent his light into our cell, illuminating us all.

"Gentlemen," he said, polite for a man in rags.

Neither Grundle nor I said a word.

"So what brings you to my little hole in the ground?" he asked.

He didn't know? My hopes of rescue shattered.

"*Your* hole?" Grundle asked, speaking Elvish.

"Not *mine* perhaps," the gaunt elf answered thoughtfully. "Except in the sense anyone creates of a place they have lived for sufficient time." He pointed down the hall from which he came. "My room is down there if you'd care to join me some time. It gets terribly lonely. You'll see."

Grundle balled himself up, pulling at the manacles that held him aloft. But they did not give. "Would that I were free to join you," he said.

"Indeed," the elf said. "You speak Elvish. I've never had the opportunity to chat with a Warlord before. I mean, not a pleasant one. Grchuck Rugh."

Grundle raised an eyebrow at that. As did I. "I've never met an elf that spoke Trollish," Grundle said. By implication, our fellow prisoner had met Warlords before. "Unpleasant chats" suggested he'd fought trolls, making the elf before us very old indeed.

"I've been down here a long time," the elf said. "So what news have you? You've clearly run afoul of our High Lord." He looked at me. "He's got you in mana-stealing manacles, so you're some kind of magical threat. Teleporter?" He didn't wait for an answer, but turned his gaze to the Warlord. "And your manacles steal strength. Your capacity for threat is apparent. But your presence on El'daShar intrigues me. Why bring a Warlord here?"

I had nothing left to lose. "Empath," I said. "I'm an Empath. And we won't trouble you for long. We are to be Banished." Only then did it occur to me that the elf before me might be a trick—someone, or even an Empathic fake, sent to get information from me. And yet, I could not think of anything I knew worth such trickery.

"Banished!" the elf exclaimed. "Oh my. It's been hundreds of years." He fiddled with the cell door, then swung it open. He shambled in and closed the door behind him with a click, then moved closer to Grundle. A StoneWorker had reshaped the prison cell, moving stone to create a pit, enabling them to hang Grundle by his arms so that he dangled at eye level. "Why did they not just kill you?"

Grundle nodded back at me. "He convinced them it punished him further to Banish him with a troll. It is a far better fate than what Slooti had planned for me."

"Gavrial might have saved you," I said.

The elf whipped around to look at me.

"I think Slooti had grown suspicious of Gav," replied Grundle, shaking his head. "And it no longer matters…"

"… the AllForest is gone." I finished Grundle's thought.

No one remained to fight.

"What?" the emaciated elf asked. "Slooti attacked the AllForest?"

"Not Slooti," Grundle said. "Well, yes, he *did*, but then…"

"… the Infected," I concluded. "They overran AllForest. Elves, trolls, all gone. I felt it from here." My sister, gone.

"The Infected?" the curious elf asked. "What are the Infected?"

He had never heard of the Infected? The Infected had

plagued human worlds my entire adult life. Only my childhood memories remained free of them. How long had the poor elf been locked away? Or quasi-locked away, given his apparent ability to enter and leave cells at will.

"Creatures whose very skin absorbs light," I said.

"With talons sharp enough to cut through stone," Grundle added. "They overrun entire worlds in hours."

"Leaving no survivors," I concluded, my gut sour at the thought of FreeWorld.

"How do you know what they look like?" the elf asked with his head cocked. "If there are no survivors, I mean."

Despite our situation, Grundle chuckled.

"But I know of what you speak," the feeble elf continued. "FreeWorld's Blight."

FreeWorld? Blight? Doubts about the elf's sanity crept into my mind.

"Well," he said, "You've come to the right person."

Yup. Definite sanity problems.

"I can get you to a world without the Infected. I just need a little nap first."

Mother of Trees.

He lay down on the floor.

"Oh," he said, popping back up. "You'll need this spell to find your way." He cast a spell and little pinpricks of light darted off in opposite directions, then he let the spell fade. "Did you catch that?"

Right. "No," I sighed. "How is *that* going to help me find my way?" I regretted the words as soon as they spilled from my mouth. Would I have to listen to a tale of elves chasing fairy lights?

"I once told El… I once told a friend it was impossible to map out the Teleportation coordinates of a world. Turns out, it's not that hard. You just need this spell and a map, and a good idea of where you're going." He cast the spell again, letting the lights dart off then fade. I paid as little attention as the first time the mad elf had tried to show me. "Got it?"

"Of course," I said, with a roll of my eyes.

"Galad," Grundle rumbled. I looked into his serious face. "I think you should learn the spell."

"What? How? They've got me in these mana-stealing shackles." I felt dead inside. "I can't learn a spell just from watching!" I felt helpless and stupid. After all, Slooti had caught me; my sister had died; and the elves had convicted me and sentenced me to Banishment!

"Galad," Grundle said calmly. The mad elf looked appraisingly at Grundle. "When you're trapped in a dungeon, facing certain doom, and the only lifeline before you comes from an ancient prisoner of questionable sanity, take it."

"Grundle's words of wisdom?" I couldn't believe, with all that I'd lost, I still had any capacity for humor, even the grim, sarcastic words I'd eked out.

The mad elf smiled. "Now watch." He moved his fingers slowly. "A little fire… bound by water to read the signal… with lightning connecting to earth." All four elements. I only caught pieces, and couldn't feel the effects of the spell, but whatever he wove, it would prove interesting.

"Again," I said.

The water bound the spell back to the caster. The lightning connected the earth with the water. It fed something back to the caster. And the fire led it, like a dart, into the world.

"Once more," I asked. I thought I had it, though I didn't understand what the result would be. I wished I could try it.

"Trust me," the smiling elf said, "it's a powerful spell. Don't let it get into the wrong hands. You know, like an imprisoned Empath sentenced to Banishment."

He curled up on the ground and cast a spell putting himself to sleep.

"Really?" I voiced.

"For what it's worth," Grundle said, "I do appreciate what you tried to do for the trolls. And for me. I'd rather be Banished with you than finishing my days with Slooti."

"Glad I beat out a short life of slavery to Slooti," I said, grimacing.

Grundle chuckled. "It's been an easy year to beat."

"Okay," the mad elf said, popping up. "I've got it. Gentlemen," he said, nodding to each of us. "I wish you luck on your adventure. A world without magic. A part of me wishes I were going with you. Maybe I should." He cast a spell and disappeared with a *bamf* and a flash of light, leaving us in sudden darkness.

After a minute I said, "Did he say a world without magic?"

"He did."

"Assuming he could actually make that happen, what good was the spell he just taught me?"

Grundle's chuckle echoed through the prison.

Chapter 92

Elliah

The illusions dropped immediately as the artifacts clattered to the floor. Elves tumbled around the room, the magic that kept them Compelled suddenly gone. The room itself lost its luster, revealing a poorly-built table and makeshift chairs within a stone—stone?—floor and walls. Light still beamed forth from the marble Slooti had called a MultiGel, the only truth in the room until we had arrived.

I looked where the fake *me* had been, and found a dark-haired elf maiden that looked nothing like me. Glancing over to where Jeb had been sitting, I discovered a boy, frightened, and not my son.

"Does anyone know how to work the Amp?" I shouted into the din, quieting everyone.

In the quiet, frightened whispers spread around the room like wildfire... "Elliahspane" ... "Baelsbreath."

"Elliah!"

I searched for the source of that shout. An old elf at the end of the room waved madly and hobbled toward me. "Elliah, I can't believe you're alive! It's me, Hughelas! I sent Galad to get you, but it was a long shot."

"You *sent* me?" Galad asked. "Do I know you?" Galad squinted at the ancient ruin of an elf, then his eyes widened, and he exchanged a look with Grundle.

Whispers of "Galadrindor" circled the room on the tail of my name.

"Hughelas," I said, waving away Galad's questions. "Do you know how to work the Amp? We need to get that magic," I said, pointing at the marble of light, "amplified now! Or more elves will die."

Hughelas rushed as fast as his aged body could carry him toward the scepter lying on the floor. Harry and Grundle had already moved to that spot, where the artifacts lay, looking at the burn marks on the floor from Slooti's explosion.

"Pardon me, gentlemen," Hughelas said politely, as he creaked to pick up the scepter.

Hughelas was not a powerful mage. His Gift had been the walking of worlds in his dreams. I had just offered him the means to power—he had the Amp in his possession.

I felt the magic emanating from the MultiGel grow stronger. He had done what I'd asked.

He handed the scepter to Grundle, smiling, and walked over to me, giving me a big, unexpected hug. "I hoped you would come to your senses," he breathed. He patted me on the back. "Stubborn woman. Go tell Gavrial you were wrong."

"Gavrial is here?" I asked, suddenly uncomfortable.

Hughelas turned me around, and nodded to the end of the room. An old elf helped some other old elves rise from where they'd fallen, recovering from the mess created by the blast. The old elf who Hughelas pointed out cast a look my way and then looked down again.

"Gavrial," I said quietly, speaking to Hughelas, but also to myself. "He always knew it would come to this."

Hughelas patted my back again and moved off to help others right themselves.

Harry had picked up the crown. It hovered over his head, but he stopped himself.

"Really?" he said into the air, then paused.

He shrugged and dropped the crown to the floor, drawing attention from the room. He ignored them, took his hammer, and smashed the crown, then repeated the maneuver. No blinding light or explosion occurred, but the gems crumbled, and the metal snapped, creating a broken mess. He picked it up, touched it to his head, then tossed it into the debris.

Good call, Baessandra.

"Start getting elves out of here," I told Mort. "Off this planet, I mean. Scatter them as best you can. Assume they are human in terms of drawing the Infected. If you can find some willing humans, move them here. It should be able to take a large human population, like on Earth."

"Pair of Rings between here and Earth?" Mort suggested.

"Yes!" I said, getting excited. "Getting a large group of humans here would help the elves recover *and* decrease the chance of an attack on Earth." I thought for a moment. "Okay, not the latter. We can't reasonably move enough people to help Earth. But if you can get some humans here, it would help."

Mort nodded. "You!" He barked at a small group, four aged elves and the boy, looking withered but not old. "You're coming with me."

They stood as Mort began his spell, and in a bright flash of light, they vanished.

I turned my attention back to the other end of the room. Gavrial, aged and creaky, pulled a man from a tangle of broken wood. I crossed the room to help.

"Gavrial," I said, establishing the disentangled man on his feet and sending him away.

"Elliah," he responded, looking, for a moment, right into my eyes, showing me a wall of pain. Then he turned and began walking toward the balcony.

"We need your help, Gavrial," I said, but he ignored me and kept moving. I stopped and let him continue on his way. Rubbing my eyes, I sighed.

"I'm sorry, Gav. You have no idea how sorry. But I need your help now, to right the wrongs you always wanted to right."

He moved onto the balcony, looking out over the edge.

"All this pain," he said, gesturing below him. "You could have stopped this *eons* ago." Angry and weary, he dropped his head and closed his eyes.

I moved to the balcony. It surprised me to discover that we stood on a rocky bluff, not in a tower at all. No city lay below us, just a canyon, though it did contain people. Starving, dying, dead. Very few moved.

It was worse than I thought. The Illusion had made it seem better. The Empathic control that had made them move about had given the elves at least a semblance of life.

"I can't change the past," I said. "You think you know, Gav, but you don't."

"We've had this argument before," Gavrial said. "I don't understand what it was like when elves turned against elves? Look around and tell me I don't understand. Look!"

I turned my gaze back to the grey death below. He was right—Slooti had turned against everyone. He'd been clever and manipulative, and he'd nearly destroyed us—conceivably still would. But Gavrial was also wrong. Slooti had become a madman, but that differed from a war among our people, from brother killing brother and parent killing child.

Perhaps it didn't matter—death, in the end, was death. But a part of me screamed that it mattered. Civil war left a scar on a people. Not just a scar, but a festering wound for a race with such long lifespans. If nothing else, it would have torn me apart to cause such a war. The mad reign of Slooti, we could recover from as a people. As long as Slooti's legacy of the Infected didn't destroy us all.

Long seconds ticked past, and Gav's anger burned down. I hadn't tried to correct him. I hadn't continued the argument. But I hadn't left.

"I need you to take us back to FreeWorld," I said into the weighty silence.

He barked a single laugh.

"We have a shot at stopping the Infected," I said gently, slowly, not wanting to rekindle his anger. "But we need to know more about their origin."

Just then Harry joined us on the balcony, tapping his hammer against the stone ledge, which I thought to be an incredibly stupid movement, but as a dwarf he probably had a sense of what the stone could take.

"You owe me a fight," he said.

I turned and raised an eyebrow.

"No zombie slaying, no fight at the top of the tower. You exploded the crazy elf before I repaid him for Jordi."

Jordi? He turned and marched away again, saying once more, "You owe me a fight."

"Can you get us to FreeWorld?" I asked.

He sighed. "Ellah, that's insane. It's a death sentence."

In a bright flash, Mort appeared behind us. I turned to see him walking away from a Ring. He'd brought the best chance I had to save my people.

"Gather up!" he shouted. "There's been an attack! We need to go back!"

Grundle was already near him. The rest of the crew that had accompanied me to Slooti's dead world moved quickly to Mort, except for me. Mort looked at me in question.

"I need to stay," I said simply.

He nodded, and they walked through the Ring.

Chapter 93

Red

On the other side of the Ring, El'daShar boiled with the pandemonium I expected from an attack. Smoke rose at a point along a far perimeter of the camp, near the woods, and I turned to Mort to see if he would Blink us there.

Could *I* Blink us there? I knew I didn't know how, but I wondered all the same whether I had it in me.

Mort shook his head. "They've got that under control. We're needed elsewhere. I just need a moment. Those Rings require a lot of energy to move."

"Where are we going?" I asked. Did the Savage attack multiple colonies?

"Emerald Farms." Mort wasn't kidding when he said he just needed a moment. He nodded once and then *bamf*, we appeared in the aftermath of a war zone.

The smoking carcass of a WallBanger lay in the middle of the courtyard, and destruction encircled it like a bombshell had been dropped from above. The beast had toppled tables, knocked over bins of grain, and stomped their contents flat. Some of that debris had once been people.

Healers worked on those with non-fatal injuries, a makeshift hospital operating out of the council chamber's anteroom, whose doors stood open.

I didn't see Scan among the Healers, and my heart skipped a beat. "Where's Scan?"

Mort nodded to a place far down the commons, and I spotted someone working behind a makeshift barrier. It might have been Scan.

"You may come with me to help the Healers if you wish," Mort told Galad and Harry. "I'll fill you in." Mort told me, "Go help your friend. Come get us when he's ready."

He turned and walked into the council chamber, Tali on his coattails. Galad looked at me and shrugged, then followed Mort, and Harry joined them.

Grundle started righting equipment that would have been too heavy for humans, doing what he could.

I headed across the commons, seeing as I got closer that it *was* Scan, with Hirashi standing over him asking questions and looking anxious. Scan calmly went about his business, something I could not see until I got close—he was setting up his Teleport Tracker.

"What's going on?" I shouted, when close enough to be heard.

"He took her!" Hirashi blurted out, then slapped her hand over her mouth like she'd said something terrible.

"Cordoro showed up. He caused this," she said, waving at the destruction of the commons, "and he took Allania!"

Oh, shit.

Hirashi started pacing in the small space, and Scan gave me a look doused with irritation.

I scooped an arm behind the Regent as she got close, and she jumped like I'd snuck up on her. Nevertheless, I steered her away from Scan and his machine—beyond being annoyed by having to answer her questions, her movement would disturb the samples he needed to follow Cordoro.

"We *will* find Cordoro now. In fact, this will likely end the slow defeat on El'daShar as well—if Cordoro is hiding in the Savage Lands."

"None of that matters!" she hissed.

I steered her away from people, a quiet corner where she could have some privacy.

She closed her eyes and pinched the bridge of her nose. "Of course it matters," she amended. She flailed her arms and spun away from me, and as I followed, she spun back around. "Allania is my responsibility!" she said, forcing me to halt.

I tried to speak, tried to put my hands on her arms, hoping to calm her, but she jerked away and plowed over my voice.

"Cordoro already stabbed her once! Tried to kill her," Hirashi told me. "I'm the reason she's in peril. She's such a bright girl, and I wanted her near. I'd hoped to groom her to become a First. I kept her close since Cordoro fled—he'd already tried to kill her once." She paced in a short line, back and forth. "Now he *has* her, and it's all *my fault*!"

I wished I could give her a hug, tell her that everything would be okay. But we weren't close enough friends, and I didn't actually know if it *would* be okay.

Well, shit.

I grabbed Hirashi by the shoulders. "It is great that you care this much about the people you feel responsible for," I told her. "And I'm sure that is why Allania *chose* to follow you. *Chose* it, Hirashi. You didn't force her into this life; you presented her with a vision and an opportunity."

Oh, what the hell...

I pulled her in for a hug.

"She has to be okay, Red."

"Red!" Scan shouted. He circled his finger in the air then pointed outward.

Galad! I shouted in my head, running to the town hall.

Seconds later, Galad strode out, looking right at me. I stopped running and he nodded. Mort and Harry came out as Galad headed toward Grundle. I shifted gears and headed back to Scan.

I reached the makeshift enclosure where Scan worked while Hirashi hesitantly edged her way closer to the Earth-born construct that must have looked so alien to her eyes.

"You've got it?" Hirashi asked. "You can really track where he went?"

"I got something. Do people often 'Port from here?"

"From the commons? We sometimes transport goods. From this specific corner? Not likely, but possible."

"Then it's possible we follow a false trail, but let's see."

Our team gathered. I signaled them to flank me.

"I'm going, too," Hirashi said.

"Your people need you," Mort said.

Hirashi scowled. "As do yours need you, Regent."

"Can you handle another person, Mort?" I asked.

He nodded.

"Me too," Scan said, not looking up. "This isn't an elf-hunt, just a rescue mission. I'm going."

"Link us up," Mort said to Galad.

The seconds ticked by—Galad didn't pull me into the link, and yet I felt it when he created the link, and knew when he broke it. I drew my daggers and found that Grundle and Harry stood armed and ready as well.

Chapter 94

Cordoro

What a day! I'd accomplished all I'd hoped for and more. Damage to the usurpers in El'daShar. Destruction to the fools in Emerald Farms. I'd nabbed some real bread and wine, and then *she'd* passed by.

While helping that archaic bag of bones, Elder Greenly, get away from the destruction in the commons, she hadn't even seen me. She'd tucked him in a corner of the commons, where I Blinked and grabbed her, 'Porting her back to the Savage Lands. She slept in a tent, one not in the current rotation of the Savage camps. I'd intended to simply stash my plunder there, and technically, she qualified. I laughed to myself, then hushed, then laughed again. That camp sat a great distance from the nearest occupied tents. No one would hear us.

I'd had to cast a sleep spell to get her properly ready, and I sat, sipping wine, overly-stuffed with bread, as I waited for her to wake. I was practically giddy with anticipation.

Allania... beautiful Allania, who had scorned me since we began school together. Scorned *me*! She was nothing—no Talent, no magical skills at all. All she had was her beauty, and yet she had rejected me and belittled me, no matter how much wealth and power I had accumulated.

I loathed her. I despised her.

And, yet, I wanted her.

She's lucky I'm the forgiving type.

I prodded her feet with my own. From atop the stump I had pulled in for a makeshift chair, I gazed down at her slumbering form, and my hunger grew. Hair, lips, face... every inch of her form was perfection. Including those feet I had prodded. To my delight, she stirred.

Her eyes fluttered open, kicking off the effects of the spell.

Lying on her side, her eyes found me, sitting on my stump-stool, watching her. She tried to move her arms and found her hands tied behind her back.

She groaned when I smiled.

I had hoped for a scream. I'd hoped to tell her, "There's no one to hear you scream."

A groan was just... unsatisfactory.

"Kidnapping. What do you hope to gain by this, Cordoro?" she said, maneuvering so that she sat, legs in front of her, hands tied behind her back, facing me. Even with her hair mussed, she stole my breath away. Her eyes locked onto mine, not afraid, just irritated. "Or are you planning to stab me to death... again?"

I scowled. The conversation wasn't going as I'd hoped. Fear, compliance...

"Quiet, or I'll cut out your tongue," I said, pulling out my curved dagger.

"That's the only way my tongue will touch you," she said, shaking her head with her lip curled.

In a flash of anger, I popped out of my seat and moved toward her.

Intense pain took my breath away when her foot connected with my groin. Then, I lay on my side, as she popped to her feet, even with her hands still tied behind her. She moved to kick my gut again, but I turned enough that she kicked my side... painful, but bearable.

I cast my spell as she tried to kick my head.

The blow didn't land, and she toppled back to the ground.

I lay there for a few minutes, letting the pain recede. The sleep spell would keep her down for a while.

I crawled over and cut a piece out of the hem of her dress, then used it to tie her feet together. I double-checked her hands as well.

Breathing hard, I sat back on my stump, appreciating that my wine bottle had not toppled from its seat beside the stump. I drank my wine and waited, growing angrier, but waiting, holding it in, because I wanted her to know it.

She was not out as long that time... she grunted, and tested her bonds, then inch-wormed her way back to a sitting position.

"You are such a coward," she said, her tone irritated again. *This just won't do.*

I approached her, knife in hand, careful that time. I knelt by her side and held the dagger under her chin, forcing her to hold her head back in order to avoid being stabbed.

Turning the blade around, I slid it down her neck slowly, not breaking the skin, but letting her feel the sharp, cold metal. I sliced into the dress between her breasts, dragging the blade more quickly, tearing the material. I ripped it all the way down, the dress falling to each side, but catching on her tied hands. A small trickle of blood ran between her breasts where the knife had nicked the skin.

She was exquisite. Like elven wine and fine cheese, I appreciated her beauty like no other on Emerald Farms. Why, on Emerald Farms, had I stabbed such beauty? *Because she hurt you.* She had caused me pain. She had chosen another. My lust and anger burned in equal measure. I stepped back to appreciate the scene. The only thing that detracted from my lust was the look of utter scorn on her face. But that look fueled my anger.

I slowly took off my own robes, keeping my knife in hand, revealing my proud manhood, being sure she understood all that was about to be hers.

"Well, at least it's not going to hurt," she scoffed.

Angry, but careful of a trick, I moved to stand over her, straddling her body to be sure she had a good look at my two weapons before I used them.

Finally, *finally*, her eyes grew wide with fear.

Chapter 95

Red

We 'Ported into a jungle clearing, a ring of tents surrounding us. A spike of pride shot forth at how quickly our group created a circle, facing outward toward the tents, ready for attack. Reminiscent of pictures I'd seen of teepees, the tents looked to be leathery skins, stretched out to create areas larger than I would have expected from pictures of American Indians.

But the night held calm and still... relatively speaking. Chirps and stuttering noises resounded from the woods behind the tents, but no human noises churned through the camp. The camp lay abandoned—at best, it was Cordoro's 'Port point; at worst, the wrong planet.

A woman's scream ripped through the night from my left. As I spun, Harry ran to the tent in front of him. I charged in the same direction, but seeing Mort walk backwards in case someone or some*thing* hid in the other tents, I slowed and entered more cautiously.

I walked in to find Harry battling an *Infected*, blood sprayed across the tent walls. Lani lay on the fur-covered floor, coiled in a ball, with Harry standing between her and the Infected. The lower body of a man rested on one side of her, and the upper torso on the other—his abdomen painted the tent wall behind her.

I sliced at the calf of the Infected as I passed, moving to stand over Lani's body.

She swatted at me when I touched her, but my enhanced speed while I held the daggers made that easily avoidable.

Changing tactics, I sliced a hole through the tent side and pushed her out with my legs, while Harry battled the Infected in the confined space. I jumped through the hole behind her, and found that Lani had enough sense to realize she still lived. She wriggled onto her knees with her back to me, holding her hands behind her, dress bunched around her hands... oh, shit, Cordoro had tied her up.

Moving with enhanced haste, I sliced through the ropes binding her hands. She winced when her hands came free.

I reached to cut the ropes around her feet and something coming from the tent bowled me over. *God, please not an Infected!*

I rolled with the hit, seeing Harry tumble past me. Not Infected.

Then an Infected jumped out of the tent, chose me as its target, and lunged.

I fought off the obsidian, eyeless creature, listening for more. I thought I heard far off shouting, but couldn't be sure. Galad exited the hole I'd carved in the tent, putting the Infected between us, and pulled the attention of the Infected with a sword swipe that tore off an arm at the elbow. Grundle charged around the tent, axe raised.

The boys had it under control—I turned to finish freeing Lani, only to find she had shaken off the remains of her dress and was pulling off the cloth that tied her legs. Grundle's axe tore through the Infected, separating its upper and lower body in a gruesome copycat slaying, the same as what the Infected had done to what I presumed had once been Cordoro.

Galad meanwhile took the head off of another Infected; I knew there would be more than one! We had to get out of there. As the headless body slumped to the ground, I pulled Lani up and looked for Harry so we could go.

I found, where Harry should have been, an obsidian body on the ground, its eyeless face staring up... *oh, Harry.*

My heart wept as Grundle's axe swept down.

The blade never reached its target—a blast of force knocked Grundle back before his swing completed.

Galad stood on the other side of the prone Infected. Remains of a spell sparkled from his hands, like the glow of a gun barrel after firing at night.

Grundle growled with the noise of a rockslide, but Galad merely held his hand out for Grundle to stop.

The Infected on the ground did not rise. Galad waved me

over, shouting, "Behind the tent! Now!"

I heard shouts in the distance more clearly. Far away, others fought for their lives.

The Infected twitched. It lived. Why didn't it attack? Why hadn't Galad let Grundle kill it?

My eyes ran over its horrible body, feet with long talons, legs too long and thin, emaciated body with long, thin arms and legs, and hands…

One hand looked like what I expected—long fingers ending in sharp talons. The other arm ended in the tanned, hairy skin of a dwarf, Bessie clutched in his still-dwarven fist.

The others found us, Hirashi providing Lani with a jacket to cover herself.

"What do we do?" Galad asked.

What do we do? He looked to me for an answer.

The clamoring in the distance rose, and an Infected appeared by Lani. Mort Blinked in behind the creature and disposed of it, but another had already appeared near Grundle.

Our time had run out. Did we take Harry, and risk losing another planet to the Infected should his transformation complete, or leave him there, where he would assuredly die?

"Earth," I said, an idea forming in my head. More Infected appeared around us. Then, a better option popped in my head.

"That hell the elves were on!" I shouted to Mort. "Nowhere else, Mort! And bring him!" I said, pointing to the almost-Infected-Harry on the ground.

Mort Blinked closer to us, bringing Hirashi and Lani with him. I pointed down to Harry's hand, still holding the hammer, still dwarven.

"Take us back to the world the elves fled to," I said more quietly. Infected surrounded us, and I imagined more appeared behind them. Just like our brief experience in Orbanos, which we'd fled almost as soon as we'd arrived. The Infected had overrun Savage.

And, with a bright flash of light, we left them behind.

Epilogue

Rocks

We needed more Teleporters, more Rings, and more Mana'thiandriel.

Ironically, the Earth could have supplied the food needed by the colonies that had sided with us. Fifty thousand people per colony, and they weren't completely without food of their own—the disaster relief from just my nation could have handled that. But Mort and Hirashi advised me to trade for food. If I simply gave it away, the colonies, whose existence depended on trade, would think food from Earth a trap or a trick.

I waited patiently in the tunnels while a forklift-pulled train of grain and foodstuffs moved through the Rings. We had a way to kill two birds with one stone. We took mages from the colonies and gave them work on Earth. The government required lumber companies to reforest. The mages from Vibrant Woods accelerated that process ten-fold. That became money saved by the lumber industry—money they passed on to Vibrant Woods to use for food to be shipped back through the Ring, then Teleported to Vibrant Woods. And that hadn't been the only industry interested in the magic of Vibrant Woods.

And Brickworks—I learned that elves had not crafted the building where I met with the Regents on El'daShar. Humans had crafted it, labor the elves had hired from Brickworks. Construction companies on Earth hired mages from Brickworks to speed up projects and make more money which, again, supplied food back to Brickworks.

Even mages from Emerald Farms, though they didn't need food, had found a place on Earth. The wine industry paid handsomely for magic that enabled them to sample wine early, and adjust the taste of the remaining crop.

But magic did not come easily on Earth. Our dead sun

handicapped the mages. We needed Mana'thiandriel. The Rings constrained the amount of food they bought—we needed more Rings. And once on the El'daShar side, the goods had to be Teleported back to other worlds, and we had overloaded and exhausted the Teleporters.

A different kind of train marched... no, hobbled... down the hall in the opposite direction. Humans escorted archaic elves, grey as ash and held together by God-only-knew-what, to the elevator, to be housed on the upper floors of The Palace. I welcomed the news that we had found the elves, until I understood their state. I felt bad for my pragmatism, but we housed on El'daShar only the handful of elves who could Teleport across worlds, where the high level of magic reversed their aging. The other elves traveled to Earth in large numbers, Earth being better for their health than Morrow, the name we'd given the dead-sun planet of the elves. But they didn't grow younger quickly on Earth.

Still, they couldn't all go to El'daShar. The elves had worked their way onto the Infected hit list—too many on El'daShar would be a death sentence. That decision created tension, even with Elliah's backing. Many elves complained that the Infected did not hunt them, that the Infected had attacked other elven planets for reasons unknown. And maybe they were right. The Infected had not, after all, attacked El'daShar. Still, Elliah, *their erstwhile Queen*, had stomped on those complaints. They would do as she declared and hide on Earth, no matter the grumbling. At least until they decided they knew better.

The grain-train finally finished its trip through the Ring, and I nodded to Gil as I passed through to El'daShar. Simmi awaited me on the other side. She used her head to indicate I should follow, rather than shouting over the din of the forklift. Cooing elves basked in the sun of El'daShar while they waited in line to pass to their perceived imprisonment on Earth.

When we'd gotten far enough that a raised voice would suffice, I could wait no longer to ask. "So you've found our mole?" She'd bid me come to El'daShar, no explanation given, and since the sole reason I'd sent her to the El'daShar side, swapping her with Gil, had been her keen sense of people, I hoped she'd solved the puzzle.

She shook her head no. "You said Carter Cooper was sick the day of the first meeting with SmartGuard." What had happened that she would ask me that? She was marching me toward one of the makeshift medical tents, the emblem of a red cross on a white background making it obvious, at least to someone from Earth.

"That's right. Sick, allergies… something. And he didn't remember me, or our previous conversation, when I ran into him on El'daShar." I didn't know what would make him forget, and while I didn't suspect Galad, Empathic magic *was* on my list of possibilities.

She pushed through the tent flap and I followed her in. She led me past beds of wounded, being treated with both modern medicine and magic, some beds lowered so that dwarven medics could reach, some beds occupied by dwarves.

My gut tightened when she led me on, moving a curtain to reveal a room at the back. Electrical lights illuminated at least twenty bodies, completely covered in white sheets, red stains peeking through some. A shorter body caught my attention. A dwarf or a child? The Forsaken had brought their children to El'daShar. We'd tried to convince them to tuck their children safely on Earth, but they'd refused. I found myself drawn toward it, some twisted part of me hellbent on knowing, when Simmi coughed politely.

She squatted by a body, sheet pulled back to reveal the burned body of Carter Cooper.

"I guess his drones were no help after all," I said, letting my grim mood leak forth.

"No, they were helpful. The last attack was something like a triceratops, with a body of stone, accompanied by some creatures that neutralized our mages." I liked that she said *our* mages. Hopefully it reflected the thinking of our mixed-world crew as a united body. But I'd already heard the report about the attack. "It caused several fires as it charged through equipment."

"How many died?"

"Twenty-one so far. We expect the rest to make it. But Cooper was the only one to die by fire."

"Bad luck, that."

"Extremely. It made me curious." She raised her eyebrows, and I drew closer, curious myself by her declaration. But I also felt a moment of hesitation. I was in a tent, alone with Simmi, surrounded by dead bodies. If she wanted to harm me, she'd brought me to the right place.

Simmi reached down and pulled back on his burnt skin at his neck.

"His throat's been cut," I pronounced like an idiot.

"Bad luck, that," she replied.

She covered him back up with the sheet, and we stood.

"What in the hells?" I proclaimed. "You don't kill someone unless—"

"They know something," Simmi finished.

"Something about the drones," I said.

Simmi was quiet.

"What?" I pushed.

"I think the drones are a distraction," she stated.

No way are the drones a distraction. My brother had pushed for the drones. Hubbard had pushed for the drones. They'd absolutely had something to gain, and I was going to figure it out if it was the last... thing...

Shit. I recognized that my thinking wasn't sound. Calloway had even suggested a diversionary tactic might be at play. I hadn't ignored her, but I'd remained focused on the drones. They'd handed me an opportunity to see evil in a conspiracy between my brother and Hubbard, so that all my attention went to uncovering their plot. Hubbard had played me masterfully.

Shit.

"Distracting me from what?" My voice came out quiet, the fight gone out of me.

"I..." she began hesitantly. "I have a guess." Hesitancy from Simmi was a new experience.

I waited and stared at her expectantly.

"An idea popped into my head after I heard what happened on Morrow. With the elven king." Her slight blush communicated to me how shaky was the foundation of her idea. "I talked to the Forsaken about a type of magic." That gave me pause. What had she told the Forsaken? "With discretion," she added, and moved on hastily. "I think our spy is an Illusionist, taking other people's forms." She let that sink in and then moved forward. "Cooper didn't forget your first meeting."

"It hadn't been Cooper in the meeting," I concluded.

"And Cooper knew that someone had replaced him in the meeting," she continued.

"And I got too close to that truth, so he had to be removed," I concluded, following her logic. "So someone overheard when I'd met Cooper that second time, on El'daShar." I tried to bring up my memory of that conversation, but many people had been around. Not a chance I'd pull a suspect out of that. Could Galad?

"Don't forget the technician," Simmi continued, seeing that I didn't argue. "The one who installed monitors—poorly—in your office… whose body turned up dead."

"And the time of death looked earlier than when he'd been in my office." I nodded my head, the pieces clicking. "So there are two minor little pieces we still have to figure out."

"Who is the culprit?" Simmi said.

"And what does he—"

"—or *she*—" Simmi added.

"—want?"

Acknowledgments

As they say, the third time's the charm... I still need to thank my mother for her continued cheerleading, and thanks to Marla Taviano (http://instagram.com/marlataviano) for her editing, advice, and friendship. Also thanks to my wifey and my kids, who cheer me on when I get the blues. I really appreciated my wife's best friend reading through book two and providing probing feedback. "Such as?" you ask. Such as, "I want to know what goes on in Steve's brain that he came up with a blood spear and blood saw in book 2." Trust me, you really don't want to know.

  Shout out to Edith Pawlicki (https://edithpawlicki.com), who has been my partner in forging a way through the forests of self-publishing. I recommend her books, and I truly appreciate finding someone who shares the same struggles, at least in terms of writing and publishing. I've never raised twins, so not exactly the same struggles.

  Thanks to early readers for their feedback, and ByTheBook VBP (https://bythebookvbp.com/) for gathering readers willing to review my writing. Also Sacha Black (https://sachablack.co.uk/) for The Rebel Author Podcast (https://sachablack.co.uk/the-rebel-author-podcast/), which has been a source of learning and growth, and Nat from Kindletrends (https://kindletrends.com/), who does gobs of work to help authors see which way the wind is blowing so that we can hoist our sails and get moving. And thanks to folks who left reviews on GoodReads and Amazon–I'm learning that's the lifeblood of the indie author's writing existence, with a special thanks to Brey War (https://www.instagram.com/breysreviews/), who does an awful lot to help the indie community, creating groups and connecting writers to people they need in order to succeed as authors.

  I'm excited for the Audiobook of Book 1, The Guardian of The Palace, to be coming out in November/December of 2021. Thanks, Jillian Yetter (https://www.jillianyetternarrator.com/), for walking me through the process, and for transforming your sweet voice into the fearsome Grundle.

Finally, thanks to readers and the folks willing to follow me to see more of the worlds I'm crafting.

Author's Note

If you enjoyed We're Going on an Elf Hunt, please leave a review on GoodReads (https://www.goodreads.com/book/show/56811451-the-guardian-of-the-palace).

Follow links on my website to sign up for my newsletter, where you'll receive updates on my writing, as well as early views of artwork and exclusive side-character stories.

http://sjmorriswrites.com

Thanks,
Steve

Made in the USA
Middletown, DE
30 December 2021